MEDICINE WOMAN'S REVENGE

MEDICINE WOMAN'S REVENGE

The Life and Times
of an Apache Woman

A NOVEL

BUD SHAPARD

SUNSTONE
PRESS

SANTA FE

This book is a work of historical fiction. Although portions of this novel are derived from real historical events and many of the characters are historically legendary personages, the events and character traits have been tailored to suit the story. Other characters are entirely drawn from my imagination and no resemblance to actual people, living or dead, is intended or should be inferred.

Sunstone books may be purchased for educational, business, or sales promotional use. For information please write: Special Markets Department, Sunstone Press, P.O. Box 2321, Santa Fe, New Mexico 87504-2321.

Book and cover design › Vicki Ahl
Body typeface › Californian FB
Printed on acid-free paper
∞
eBook 978-1-61139-441-2

Library of Congress Cataloging-in-Publication Data

Names: Shapard, Bud, 1937-
Title: Medicine woman's revenge : the life and times of an Apache woman : a novel / by Bud Shapard.
Description: Santa Fe : Sunstone Press, 2016. | "2015
Identifiers: LCCN 2015036234 | ISBN 9781632930972 (softcover : acid-free paper)
Subjects: LCSH: Indian women--Fiction. | Apache Indians--History--Fiction. | Revenge--Fiction. | GSAFD: Historical fiction.
Classification: LCC PS3619.H3557 M43 2016 | DDC 813/.6--dc23
LC record available at http://lccn.loc.gov/2015036234

SUNSTONE PRESS IS COMMITTED TO MINIMIZING OUR ENVIRONMENTAL IMPACT ON THE PLANET. THE PAPER USED IN THIS BOOK IS FROM RESPONSIBLY MANAGED FORESTS. OUR PRINTER HAS RECEIVED CHAIN OF CUSTODY (COC) CERTIFICATION FROM: THE FOREST STEWARDSHIP COUNCIL™ (FSC®), PROGRAMME FOR THE ENDORSEMENT OF FOREST CERTIFICATION™ (PEFC™), AND THE SUSTAINABLE FORESTRY INITIATIVE® (SFI®). THE FSC® COUNCIL IS A NON-PROFIT ORGANIZATION, PROMOTING THE ENVIRONMENTALLY APPROPRIATE, SOCIALLY BENEFICIAL AND ECONOMICALLY VIABLE MANAGEMENT OF THE WORLD'S FORESTS. FSC® CERTIFICATION IS RECOGNIZED INTERNATIONALLY AS A RIGOROUS ENVIRONMENTAL AND SOCIAL STANDARD FOR RESPONSIBLE FOREST MANAGEMENT.

WWW.SUNSTONEPRESS.COM
SUNSTONE PRESS / POST OFFICE BOX 2321 / SANTA FE, NM 87504-2321 /USA
(505) 988-4418 / ORDERS ONLY (800) 243-5644 / FAX (505) 988-1025

For Charlie

Acknowledgments

IT IS MY PLEASURE to acknowledge and express my appreciation to Nancy Purcell and Rich Schram, who freely gave detailed editorial advice, constructive criticism, and encouragement throughout the writing of this story. Also special thanks to my niece, Karla King, for her excellent proofreading of my final draft. Further, I would be remiss not to recognize other friends for their comments and support along the way; Aleen Steinberg, Attracta Hutchinson, Ann Ives, Susan Gabriel, Ann Finnen and Ann Evans.

1

Massacre

IN THE PREDAWN HOURS of a warm June morning in 1866, eleven-year-old Dah-zhonne was startled awake when a bullet crashed through her family's brush shelter. The gunshot sent her mother, Alope, and father, Nitis, scrambling to make yet another getaway from their ever-present enemies. Dah-zhonne's band, along with other Apache groups, had been pursued for years by hostile American and Mexican forces. Bloody ambushes of their camps were common occurrences.

"Get up, baby girl, hurry!" shouted Nitis. She sat up and snatched on her moccasins.

The three bolted from their wickiup into a maelstrom of fifty panic-stricken men, women, and children scurrying to escape the attack. With Alope pulling her along by the hand, the child shouted over the turmoil, "Mother, father! It was only one shot." Almost before the words left her mouth a bugle blared, followed by the deafening roar of a hundred Mexican rifles firing from the surrounding ridges into the pandemonium. In the blink of an eye, the placid flower-strewn valley had turned into a hellhole of horror. Clouds of dust and black powder smoke filled the air. The ground around the terrified girl bubbled like a pot of boiling gravy as bullets burrowed into the sand around her.

Old Chief Colleto, leader of the little tribe of Chiricahua Apaches, hobbled from his wickiup waving a white rag in an effort to show the band was peaceful. Dah-zhonne saw his head explode in a spray of blood, brains and bone. Seconds later, she glanced around just as her father threw his arms out and crumpled forward into the dirt with a bullet through his back. She whirled to go to him, but Alope jerked her forward. "Don't stop, child. Run for your life."

When she turned to check him for a second time, she stumbled over her Aunt Chloe, dead and still clutching a tiny squalling baby. Alope tried to scoop up the infant, but before she could, a Mexican bullet killed the child. She spun around to help Dah-zhonne stand. "Get up girl, get up! Run! They'll kill..." Three bullets hit Alope in the neck and chest just as she reached for her daughter. She tumbled dead atop Dah-zhonne, her body pinning the girl to the ground and shielding her from the shower of Mexican lead.

The mayhem seemed to last forever. Gunshots, shouts of the fleeing Indians, and moans of the dying ones filled the air. Dah-zhonne sobbed, too frightened to struggle free from her mother's weight. "No, no," she wailed, "Mother, say something!" Alope didn't answer. A death-borne silence had suddenly replaced the turmoil. The only sound was her own panicked breathing. The serene little valley, carpeted with colorful desert flowers the day before, was now littered with dead or wounded relatives and friends.

The bugle sounded again, followed by loud shouts as dozens of Mexican soldiers charged down the ridge with fixed bayonets. Those who showed any sign of life were bayoneted or shot. Dah-zhonne looked on, afraid to move. Her mother's blood covered her head, flowed over her face, and trickled from her chin dotting the purple flowers beneath her with red spatters.

One of the soldiers checking the bodies poked Chloe and her baby with his bayonet. He stepped over to the motionless Alope and half-heartedly nudged her with the toe of his boot. Terrified, Dah-zhonne held her breath. The sweating trooper moved on, satisfied the woman and the blood-soaked girl lying under her were dead.

The bugle sounded again. The soldiers and their Indian scouts rushed to gather before a short, heavy set man with a walrus mustache. Colonel Lorenzo Garcia, commanding a contingent of the Sixth Mexican Infantry, had been searching the desert along the international boundary line for signs of Apaches. He was unaware that his force was only seven miles from an Apache camp when his Tarahumare scouts brought word they found the Indians. The temptation was too much for the colonel. He illegally took his troops across the border and slipped onto the ridges overlooking the little Apache village.

After the men assembled, Garcia stared at his troops and blew clouds of smoke from an oversized cigar sending a blue haze over Dah-zhonne. I won't forget you, mister, she thought. I promise to get even for this some day. She never forgot her vow.

Arrogantly puffing his stogie, Garcia ranted, "Who the hell fired that first shot?" he demanded. "There wasn't enough light to tell the squaws from the warriors—pesos from my pocket." He kicked the dirt. No one dared to answer.

He stabbed the air with his cigar. "Since we couldn't make out our targets, at least twenty women and children are dead. A stupid blunder! I can't sell dead Indians in the slave market. That shot cost me four thousand pesos. We might have taken all of them."

The colonel's hatred of Apaches and his ability to turn his loathing into a profit were legendary. He would kill captured warriors and exchange their scalps for bounties paid by the states of Chihuahua and Sonora. The children and less appealing women were sold as domestics and field hands, but he kept the most attractive girls as "personal servants" or hawked them to brothels as sex slaves.

His voice rose even higher, "So men, if I have to settle for the damned bounty, I want a topknot from every one of these dead bastards including the babies. Kids' hair is only worth twenty-five pesos, but that's at least something. Start over there and work this way." He pointed toward the edge of the meadow. "Don't miss a single one."

On Garcia's order, the soldiers and scouts moved to the far end of the killing field and set about their grizzly work with methodical efficiency. Swallowing her sobs so she wouldn't be heard, Dah-zhonne stared, horrified, as the mob butchered their way toward her. Escape looked impossible.

She stifled a scream when the ugliest Indian she had ever seen ripped her father's scalp from his head. A skin condition covered the scout's face with discolored scales giving him a lizard-like appearance. A hooked nose over a lipless mouth emphasized his reptilian countenance. The soldiers called him "Lizard."

After the scout mutilated her father's body only yards behind her, Dah-zhonne decided to push Alope's corpse away and make a run for safety. But before she could move, two Tarahumare scouts who had been on the lookout for approaching Americans came running down the mountainside, hallooing, and waving their arms. The scalpers stopped their work and waited for the two runners to reach the colonel.

She remained unmoving under her mother as the Tarahumares frantically pointed north and gibbered to the officer. He blew another cloud, waved his sword, and yelled, "Bring the scalps you have. We need to get out of here! The Gringo cavalry is coming. There'll be hell to pay if they find us on this side of the border. Private Ramos, you wait. After we're out of sight, burn the wickiups."

Her face pressed to the ground, Dah-zhonne watched as Garcia's men marched off double-time. That's strange, they're running away. What could have scared them? she thought as she lay deathlike beneath her bleeding mother's body as a young Mexican soldier wrapped Colleto's white rag around a long stick for a torch.

When that soldier leaves, I'll make a run for it.

2

Found Alive

AT DAYBREAK on the morning of the massacre, Captain Nelson Davis observed several plumes of smoke billowing into the gray sky. Davis was a tall lean career officer commanding seventy troopers and Navajo scouts from Fort Craig, New Mexico. Three days earlier, they had rushed from the post after Colleto's Apaches who had abandoned their government-approved campground.

Before Davis could order his troops to head for the rising black columns, two scouts galloped in from the direction of the fires and pulled their ponies to a stop beside the captain. One blurted out, "Paches are all dead."

The other Navajo pointed to the smoke. "Every one of 'em is done for! Mexicans did it. We killed the one burning their wickiups." He handed Davis a unit insignia cut from the dead Mexican's uniform. "Here's the patch off his shoulder."

"Sixth Mexican Infantry," Davis said. "It's bound to be Garcia's bunch. That son-of-a-bitch hates Apaches. He'd rather kill 'em than drink whiskey." He turned to Sergeant Dale Tinker, "Sergeant, take the scouts and catch those damned Mexicans before they cross the border." Twenty Navajo mercenaries gave war-whoops as they galloped southward behind Tinker.

Davis nodded toward Surgeon-Major Jack Morgan, the unit's physician, then spoke to the nearest soldier. "Private Potts, give Doctor Morgan your horse and you bring the ambulance. Morgan, get a medical pack and keep up. There may be some live ones for you to look after. Bugler, blow forward-in-echelon." The troop moved into a side-by-side formation and galloped toward the ascending black spires.

Once they neared the burning wickiups, Davis discovered the troops had to dismount and climb a steep crest on foot for a clear view of the basin below. Davis shouted to one of the horse-holders, "Corporal, tell Potts to wait here when he arrives with the meat wagon."

Sweat soaked every uniform as the troopers clawed their way over the rocks to the ridge-top. From their perch 400 feet above, the valley floor seemed to be littered with rag dolls lying in contorted poses. The ruins of the wickiups set ablaze before their arrival still smoldered.

Davis studied the scene with his binoculars then ordered, "Up and at 'em men. Get down there, check for live ones, and bury the dead. Start at the far end and work back here to the ridge."

Later, Davis, Morgan, and Charlie Talker, the troop's interpreter, supervised from the foot of the mountain as the soldiers moved among the cadavers. The troopers checked each body for a pulse and shook their heads before they dug a shallow grave.

As the men finished their grim task, a shout came from the field. "I found a live one. I'm bringing her over." Corporal Warren Dockum walked to the officers, hefting Dah-zhonne under one arm. The child shrieked in Chiricahua at the top of her lungs as she flailed her arms and legs in a desperate effort to squirm free. Her head, face, and upper half of her dress were covered in blood.

Davis shouted, "Damn it, Dockum, be easy with her. The kid looks wounded."

"Hell captain, she don't act hurt. She's been fighting like a banshee since I found her, and she's plum mean too." He gave a loud yelp, "Ow! Dammit, the little she-devil just bit the shit outa my arm."

When Dockum reached the officers, he unceremoniously dropped the girl into the dirt. Dah-zhonne leaped to her feet and at the same time drew a small knife from her leggings. She screamed in Chiricahua, "Stay away—I'll cut you," and slashed the blade in wide sweeps to keep the men at bay. Her dark eyes flicked back and forth in search of an escape. As she spun in circles, her long black hair, still drenched with blood, flung sticky drops in all directions.

Charlie kneeled down and talked to the child in a calm voice. He was a good-natured Mescalero Apache who also spoke English and Spanish. "Easy girl," he said in Apache. "Nobody here wants to hurt you. We came to take you back. The Mexicans attacked you." He paused and asked, "Where are you injured? This fellow is a doctor, a white medicine man." He pointed to Morgan.

Still holding her knife at the ready, Dah-zhonne relaxed enough to take a breath. "I know the Mexicans did this but my father told me the Americans were after us too."

"That's right but they only want to return you to your camp at the hot springs. They think everyone would be safer there. Are you hurt? All that blood."

"That is my mother's blood. She's dead. My father's dead too. Everybody I know is dead. Mother fell on top of me when they shot her. She saved me." Her voice trembled and tears welled, but she quickly wiped them away with the back of her hand, leaving smears of blood under each eye. After Charlie translated the child's tale, the three white men relaxed, sympathetic to her circumstance. Dah-zhonne seized the opportunity and dived to escape. As she made her move, two shots rang out from a distant hill. One bullet passed through Dockum's bicep with a loud thwack. The second shattered his knee and knocked his leg out from under him. He fell in the girl's path and blocked her sprint for freedom. When she tripped over the fallen trooper,

Morgan seized her ankle and dragged her behind a large rock. "Some of the Indians must have escaped," he said as he put his body between the child and the snipers.

Dah-zhonne's mind was in turmoil. Nothing makes any sense, she thought. These white men were after us. Now he wants to protect me? Are these good people or bad people?

3

Saving Corporal Dockum

WHEN THE SHOOTING STOPPED, Morgan rushed to tend Dockum. "I need six men over here with a blanket, now!" he shouted.

"Charlie, keep an eye on the girl." Morgan opened his medical kit. "Find out what you can from her." He turned his attention to Dockum.

After he stopped the bleeding Morgan left the wounds uncovered and told Charlie, "There's not much blood. The bullets missed all the big vessels." He motioned to the litter bearers. "You men take him down to the medical wagon, but take it easy until I can get a better look."

Meanwhile, Charlie learned the girl's name was Dah-zhonne and she knew it was Mexicans who attacked her village. In shock, she repeated over and over, "I don't understand. We didn't bother anybody." She wasn't sure where those who survived had gone.

Based on Dah-zhonne's information, Captain Davis decided it was useless to pursue the escapees. Further, Sergeant Tinker reported by the time his scouts reached the border, the dust cloud from Garcia's infantry was visible in Mexico so he discontinued the chase. Satisfied his men could do no more, Davis ordered the troops to prepare for a return to Fort Craig.

While the squad made ready to leave, Morgan said to the interpreter, "Charlie, let's get this girl cleaned up. All that blood is attracting a swarm of flies."

Morgan filled a metal bowl with water from a five-gallon tank in the ambulance. He then used wads of gauze to sponge her mother's blood from Dah-zhonne's face, neck, and arms. To finish her bath, Charlie had the girl bend over and dumped the remaining water in the bowl over her head.

As the troops headed back to Fort Craig, Morgan followed the troop in a lightweight Rosecrans' ambulance. It was designed for off-road travel, but jarred the occupants with every turn of the wheels. Once underway, Dockum moaned with each jolt until Morgan obliged him with a large dose of opium.

Before he fell into a drugged slumber, Morgan told him, "You're lucky, Corporal. You haven't lost a lot of blood. The shot through your bicep just missed the big artery and the bone." He comforted Dockum with a gentle pat.

"My knee hurts the most, doc," Dockum groaned.

Morgan shook his head. "The second bullet destroyed your kneecap. Opium will numb the pain and knock you out pretty quick. While you're unconscious, I'll put it together the best I can, but you're going to be on crutches for a while and have a limp from now on."

The rough ride was too turbulent for Morgan's delicate work. After traveling less than a half mile, he jumped from the ambulance and flagged down Captain Davis.

"The Rosecrans needs to be still for me to put Dockum back together," he told Davis. "I should be finished in a couple of hours."

"Okay. We'll stop here 'til you are done, but hurry. We have to find some water soon."

"He's already out cold. I'll be quick," Morgan hollered and rushed back to the ambulance.

"Shit, Charlie," Morgan exclaimed as he climbed into the wagon. "She's cutting his throat!" Dah-zhonne was facing away from the two men. It was unclear what she was doing. She had one arm under Dockum's head and her other hand was near his neck. The soldier's blood streamed down the girl's arm and dripped from her elbow.

Without looking around, the interpreter backhanded the child, slamming her against the wagon's sideboard. She was followed by a stream of gore from Dockum's wound that spewed across the ambulance and sprayed her dirty dress. As Morgan rushed to compress the spurting artery, Charlie and the youngster had a rapid exchange in Chiricahua.

Charlie interpreted, "Hell Major, she weren't gonna kill him. She says he started to squirt blood. She was squeezing his arm to stop the bleeding."

Thinking fast, Morgan told Charlie, "Get her over here quick. Say I need some help." Dah-zhonne was wary and kept a close eye on the two men as she inched over next to Dockum. Morgan placed her fingers on Dockum's artery and pressed down until the flow of blood stopped. "Tell her to hold her hand there until I return. You keep an eye on her. Don't let her run again. I'll be right back."

Morgan hurried from the wagon and ran over to Captain Davis. "Dockum's had a setback. Concussion from the bullet weakened an artery in his arm. It took a while but his blood pressure finally caused a rupture. I saw that sort of thing in the war. I'll need more time."

Davis looked frustrated and spit into the dust. "How much longer? We're about out of water."

"I'm afraid it'll take the rest of today. Probably be at least two days before we can transport him safely."

"We either move him now, or I can leave a small escort with you," Davis said. He let Morgan make the difficult decision. "Your choice, Major."

"I'll stay here with Charlie and the girl. I suspect the Indians are gone, but it would be good if a few troops could keep us company. We'll be all right."

"Hell, you never know, Morgan." Davis scanned the area with his binoculars. "Damned bad country to stop. You can have eight men and our extra grub but I need to get this bunch on their way now." Davis saluted Morgan and waved as the column of cavalry and scouts rode off.

Billy Tinker, sergeant for the volunteers, hurried over as soon as Davis was gone and spoke quietly to Morgan. "Glad Captain Davis left the rations, but food ain't the problem. We're 'bout out of water. We'll need to be moving pretty quick."

Morgan said, "Dockum will bleed to death if we move him too soon. He needs some time."

"Hell Major," Tinker replied, "We'll stay as long as we can. He's got the medal you know." Dockum had received the Medal of Honor two years earlier for heroic actions in the Civil War.

The sergeant added, "Hero or not, we'll all be dead if we stay past tomorrow evening without water. Heck sir, the horses will die too."

"Then let's pray he improves before then," Morgan was already jogging toward the ambulance.

As he cleaned Dockum's wounds, Morgan asked Charlie, "How did a kid that young know how to stop the bleeding? She saved Dockum's life."

More Chiricahua chatter rattled between the two Apaches. "Her mother was a medicine woman," Charlie translated. "Says she helped treat wounded warriors."

The troopers set up dry camp and pulled out field rations for supper; hardtack, salt pork and beans. Morgan noticed Charlie Talker had cooked a double serving of beans for himself and Dah-zhonne. "Charlie, get some meat for yourself and the girl."

"Paches seen wild pigs eat snakes, doc. Anything that eats snakes ain't never gonna see the inside of an Apache." The child ate with gusto, scooping up dollops of beans with her small hand. Afterwards she cleaned her fingers by rubbing them in the sand.

Sitting by the campfire later that evening, Morgan and Dah-zhonne stared silently at each other. Both wondered what the other was thinking.

4

The Waterhole

TWO TROOPERS STAYED AWAKE that night to guard against an attack from any surviving Indians. Charlie Talker rolled up in a blanket under the wagon. Morgan put Dah-zhonne on the padded bench across from Dockum and was soon snoring on the floor of the ambulance between the two.

In the morning, when Morgan sat up and stretched the stiffness from his body, he was surprised to find Dah-zhonne gone. After he checked Dockum and found his patient still asleep, he jumped from the Rosecrans and called to Charlie. The interpreter was making coffee for breakfast.

"Charlie, where's the girl?" He looked worried.

"Thought she was in the wagon with you and Dockum. If she's gone, I 'spect she's run off huntin' for the folks who got away."

"How in hell did she get out of the wagon, past me, you, and two guards?"

Charlie smiled. "She's Chiricahua. They can vanish with you lookin' straight at 'em. No use trying to track her. She'll be okay in the desert. Tend to Dockum and forget about her."

Morgan returned to Dockum's side. "How're you doing today, soldier?" he asked.

"Like I've been beat with a stick. My knee's still hurting bad."

"I'll give you something for the pain. The big problem is we'll have to leave this afternoon. I don't want to move you so soon, but we're almost out of water."

Five miles away, Dah-zhonne slid under a low rock overhang, and slipped to a small dark hole concealed at the rear of the cave. She dropped into the semi-darkness below, landed on a rocky ledge, and waited for her eyes to adjust. She had been here before. She left her leather moccasins and knife on the stone shelf, but wore her blood-stained dress as she eased into a cold underground pool. A half hour later, she wiggled from the cavern and found a spot to dry in the sun. Despair consumed her as she stared through the heat waves shimmering across the desert. She agonized in silence over her loss: Mother and Father are dead. All my friends and relatives have been killed. No horses. Nothing's left. What can I do?

Sitting alone in the warm sun, she cried aloud with body-shaking sobs until she had no tears. After her weeping subsided, with her eyes still closed, her mother's image emerged in her mind.

Now baby girl, you're old enough to care for yourself. Enjoy your life but be careful.

I will. I promise, she said to herself.

She hugged her knees and thought, If I stay with the soldiers, I'll be able to eat on the way back to the hot springs and then I'll find another Apache family there to live with.

Late in the morning after Dah-zhonne was first missed, Morgan spotted her silhouette on the horizon. "I believe our little girl has decided to come back," he told Charlie.

Dah-zhonne walked slowly toward the encampment. She was scrubbed clean and her dress was spotless. The child's golden complexion radiated. Her blood-matted hair, now shiny black, hung straight down to below her shoulders. She carried a dead jackrabbit in each hand.

When she entered the camp, she refused to talk, threw the rabbits to Charlie, and moved away from the group. "Leave me alone," she mumbled in Apache as she sat stoically in the shadow of the ambulance and continued to struggle with the loss of her parents in silence. Apaches never revealed their emotions around outsiders.

"What's going on Charlie?" asked Morgan.

"Darn if I know. I 'spect she's grieving over her folks."

Dah-zhonne remained withdrawn, but after a while, Charlie managed to coax her into a conversation.

"You okay?" asked the interpreter. Dah-zhonne looked at the ground but didn't respond.

Morgan spoke up, "Charlie, ask if she'll tell us how she caught the rabbits and where she found the water to bathe."

A brief discussion in Apache followed. Charlie interpreted, "Well, she says after she took a bath and washed her dress, she fished the rabbits out of their holes, and killed them with a rock. Chiricahuas poke a forked stick like this down the rabbit-burrow, and twist." To demonstrate he held up a foot-long sprig. "The end catches the rabbit's hair so they can pull it out and hit it in the head with a stone. She told me rabbit's better than eating salty pig."

"Where'd she find the water?"

More chatter in Apache, and Charlie nodded. "She says its the tribe's secret water hole. Only her band knows about the place. The water's in a cave."

"Well, will she show us?" blurted out Private Puller.

The surgeon major threw Puller a shut-up look and held up his hand to indicate that he wanted the other men to remain quiet.

Charlie interpreted her response, "Says she'll lead us, but she hankers to ride a horse. It's a ways and she's walked there once today."

Dah-zhonne hesitated before she spoke again. Charlie translated, "She also says she would like to stay with us 'til we get back."

"Tell her she can hang around as long as she likes if she shows us where she got the water," Morgan said. "And she can ride Dockum's horse."

After they collected the ambulance's water tank and all of the canteens in the camp, the soldiers saddled up. Morgan left two troopers to keep Dockum company. "Help the girl mount up." he ordered.

Charlie Talker pointed to the horse and told Dah-zhonne it was her's to ride. She asked Charlie to unsaddle the pony, then put her forehead against the horse's muzzle, and spoke softly in Apache, "Let's be friends. I'll take this. You'll feel better." The girl removed the bridle, took the bit from the steed's mouth, and waved away the soldier who started to help her mount. Stepping on the saddle laying beside the pony, she grasped the mane in her left hand and vaulted onto the horse, straddling it bareback.

At Morgan's signal, Dah-zhonne walked her horse towards the waterhole, guiding the stallion with its mane and her knees. After she and the horse felt comfortable with each other, she urged it to a trot, and then a gallop, followed by Morgan and his troop.

As Charlie loped along with Morgan he yelled, "I 'spect that kid's been ridin' like that since she was four or five."

It was good to be astride a horse again, but memories of pleasant jaunts with her family sent tears streaking down her cheeks, unseen by the men who followed.

She halted and pointed at a nondescript boulder-covered hill. "Too many rocks. Better walk from here," she told Charlie.

Several soldiers peered back under the ledge and watched Dah-zhonne wiggle toward the cave's entrance. One fretted, "That hole's gonna be full of rattlers."

The youngster saw the soldiers hesitate, rolled her eyes, and squeezed into the crevice. She stopped waist deep in the opening, motioned impatiently for someone to follow, and vanished.

When the troopers heard no screams or snake rattles, they decided it might be safe. Elipahlet Smith, the smallest man in the outfit, volunteered to go. Once in the cave, he shouted, "There's a big pool down here. Hand us the canteens."

Canteens and the ambulance's water tank were handed down to Smith and Dah-zhonne who filled and returned them to the surface. The men emptied the water into their hats for the horses before they drank. The canteens were passed back for a refill before the trooper and the girl emerged from the cave.

With the water problem solved, the squad relaxed and resolved to remain with Dockum until he healed enough for the trip back to Fort Craig. While they waited, Dah-zhonne proved to be a first-rate nurse and helper for Morgan. She also showed a brilliant flair for language, prodding Charlie, Morgan, and the soldiers to say English words for things at which she pointed. She would sidle up to Morgan and say in English, "Teach me talk." By the end of the third day, she could name many items and form short sentences. Much to Morgan's dismay the troopers also taught Dah-zhonne several choice expressions. Morgan learned of the girl's vulgar language lessons one morning when she greeted him. "Sick soldier look pretty damn good today." He ended her profanity education with threats to put any trooper on report who taught her a curse word or swore in her presence.

Around the campfire after supper that night, Morgan and Charlie fell into a conversation about their new ward. "I'm surprised she didn't go off with the survivors when she had a chance."

Charlie picked up a small stick and stirred the fire. "She's figurin' she'll stay with the Apaches around the warm springs and wants to be a medicine woman after she's growed up." He threw the twig into the coals. "And she thinks if she stays with us a while, she'll learn some good doctoring from you."

On the fourth morning after Dockum was wounded, Morgan approached Sergeant Tinker. "I think we can move the corporal now, but we need to take it slow."

Tinker barked to the men, "Let's get this show on the road." Within an hour the caravan inched northward with Dah-zhonne sitting between Morgan and Charlie on the front seat of the ambulance.

5

Adopted

I'VE MADE UP MY MIND, Mary Morgan thought. Her decision was irrevocable and its consequences gnawed at her as she watched her husband's ambulance enter Fort Craig's main gate. It creaked past her window and went straight to the post hospital to deliver a wounded soldier. Jack will be upset but I need to get away from this place, she thought.

Seven years earlier, Mary Gwinnet was the belle of Savannah and living in luxury. Scores of men sought her attention. Today, as she surveyed the barren army post, she longed to see her family and old friends and she yearned for the civilized world back East.

Mary met Jack Morgan in 1859 when he and his cousin, J.P. Morgan, visited Savannah on financial business. Both came from wealthy families. After a whirlwind courtship, Mary married Jack in the Episcopal Church on Johnson Square and moved to Pennsylvania. They bought a large manor in posh North Philadelphia where Jack established his medical practice. Mary was 20, her new husband 24. It was January 12, 1861.

Three months to the day, on April 12, the newlyweds' idyllic life was shattered when the first shots of the Civil War were fired in Charleston harbor. The next week, Jack enlisted in the Union army's medical corps. He returned to Mary after the war in late 1864, and announced his plans to remain in the army. She didn't protest, but when he was ordered to New Mexico, she demanded to go along. They left for Fort Craig in early 1865.

One year later, she was living in the desert, somewhere west of nowhere, half sick, and bored with military life. At length, she finally made her decision; I'll go to my parents' place in Savannah until Jack can arrange a duty station on the East Coast. I'll tell him at supper tonight.

Minutes after the ambulance delivered Dockum to the hospital, a medical orderly knocked on Mary's door. "Ma'am, Major Morgan sends his regards. He instructs me to advise you he'll be home as soon as possible and requests you prepare supper for two guests."

Anxious to inform Jack of her decision to return to Savannah, she felt annoyed when she learned of visitors.

Nevertheless, the meal was almost ready by the time she caught sight of Jack with Charlie Talker and a young girl as they walked toward the Morgan quarters.

Mary gave Jack a long kiss and shook the interpreter's hand. "Oh, you have a good-looking daughter, Charlie," she exclaimed as she greeted the child standing between the two men.

"Ain't mine." Charlie raised his hands in denial. "Don't know where she'll end up."

Mary cast an inquisitive look at Jack who answered her unspoken question. "The Mexicans found Colleto's bunch before we did. She's the only survivor we found. I hope we can place her with an Indian family. Her name is Dah-zhonne—means Beautiful."

"That definitely suits her. She's lovely. You mean they killed every one except her?"

"Well, a few got away," volunteered Charlie, "but her parents are dead."

"You poor child." Mary's eyes moistened as she kneeled and hugged the little girl. Dah-zhonne cast a puzzled look at Charlie who nodded approval.

Mary took the child's hand as she stood. "Come in and enjoy some decent food. At least, better than what you've been eating."

Charlie chuckled. "The gal and me been doin' good. The soldier boys had to suffer with hardtack, beans and salt pork."

Morgan added, "These two dined mostly on rabbit."

Mary smiled as she headed for the kitchen. After several minutes she announced, "Supper's ready. While we're at the table, you can tell me what your plans are for the child."

As Dah-zhonne struggled with the unfamiliar flatware, Mary quizzed the men about the girl's fate. "What will happen to her?"

"We'll keep her here for the time being," Jack said. "It'll give her a chance to learn a little more English. In the meantime, Charlie will try to find a family to take her."

"I'll ride down to the warm springs tomorrow and talk to Chief Loco. He likes children a heap."

Mary thought of the thirty mile ride from the fort to the springs. "Shouldn't she go with you, Charlie? That might save a trip."

"She doesn't want to leave you and the major," he replied. "Maybe Loco'll come back with me."

After supper, Morgan directed an orderly to bring a bed from the hospital and set it up outside, next to his and Mary's. Everyone on the post slept outdoors protected by mosquito nets throughout the hot summer weather. Dah-zhonne remained dressed as she bounced on a mattress for the first time, but soon settled and fell asleep.

It was late when Charlie thanked Mary for the meal and headed for his bed in the rear of the sutler's store. He left before dawn, riding south toward Loco's village.

With Charlie gone and the child asleep, Jack and Mary at last had time to talk. Mary had mustered enough courage to tell him her plans but he spoke first, "Mary, I've decided to resign from the army. I'm sick of this incessant war on hungry Indians." He shook his head, "The massacre was terrible, and I never want to see an affair like that again. The Indians were unarmed. It was murder plain and simple. The Mexicans were responsible, but had we found Colleto first, it could have been our troops. I plan to talk with Colonel Grover tomorrow and resign. He sighed and added, "It'll take a while for the paperwork to clear."

"Thank God. I wanted to tell you tonight I was going home to Savannah and wait there until you could transfer back East."

The big event after Charlie left to meet Loco was a visit to the sutler's store where Mary encouraged Dah-zhonne to select several patterns of cloth. "No need to order shoes for her," Mary told the sutler, "Her moccasins will do for now."

To the girl's delight, Mary sewed their purchases into three dresses. "So pretty. I like," she exclaimed as she tried on each outfit.

In the days that followed, Dah-zhonne shadowed Mary for hours on end. Everything was new to the little ingénue but she was clever and adjusted faster than Mary expected. She began to make her own bed and help with housework and cooking. Although she struggled with English, she developed a sizable vocabulary which made communication with her easier. But to Mary's dismay, she continued to punctuate her simple sentences with curse words she learned from the troopers. She called the soldiers "goddammies" because she had heard them use the expression so often.

"Those are bad words. Ladies never say such things," Mary chided.

Dah-zhonne replied, "I didn't know. Apaches don't have good talk or bad talk." Afterwards, the profanity vanished gradually, but her speech remained spicier than Mary preferred.

In addition to learning a different culture and language, as well as how to read, Dah-zhonne often followed Morgan as he attended patients in the hospital. She studied every procedure and peppered the doctor with dozens of questions. As the days passed, the Morgans became increasingly attached to the inquisitive urchin.

Two weeks later, Charlie returned to Fort Craig accompanied by a short, middle-aged Apache. Charlie made the introductions, "This is Chief Loco. He heads up the Chiricahuas around the warm springs."

When the Indian shook hands with Jack and Mary, Charlie added, "Loco keeps two orphans already, but says he'll take the girl. He wants to talk with her first."

Loco turned and limped toward Dah-zhonne who stood a few yards away. When she recognized the chief, she scampered to him. He knelt down and hugged her. He then took her by the hands and the two talked. After a lengthy discussion, he went to Charlie Talker, angry over her account of the massacre.

Charlie interpreted, "He says the Mexicans had no cause to kill them. Colleto's folks just wanted to go where they could find food."

"What did he say about the girl?" Mary was anxious to learn Dah-zhonne's fate.

"Like I told you, he'll take her, but she don't want to go—says she would like to stay with you."

"Are you sure?"

"Ask him yourself. He talks a little Mexican."

Mary had spent a year in Spain before she met Jack and was fluent. "Español?" she asked Loco. He nodded and she spoke in Spanish, "You think she wants to stay here and refuses to return with you?"

Loco replied in of pidgin Spanish, "She'll go back if you insist but she says she wants to stay if you'll take her."

Mary told Jack, "His Spanish is terrible, but I believe he says Dah-zhonne prefers to live with us."

Morgan's eyes went back and forth from the girl to Mary. "Well, what do you think we should do?"

Mary didn't answer but spoke to Charlie, "Tell her we'll leave here soon and there aren't any Apaches where we're going."

Charlie translated Mary's concern into Chiricahua for the youngster while Chief Loco listened with intense interest.

Dah-zhonne puffed her cheeks and asked. "No Apaches. What kind of place is that?"

"All white people, I guess." Charlie answered.

Her expression clouded. "If I go, can I stay with them?"

"Yes, you'll be our daughter and we'll love you," Mary said in English. Charlie interpreted for Loco and the girl. The old chief smiled and nodded.

"Then I go," she said in English.

Charlie translated again for Loco who shook Jack's hand, and patted Dah-zhonne's shoulder. The chief left the fort later that day.

Jack and Mary always wanted children but they never had time, and when they did, it didn't happened. This girl would fill a void in their lives. Back in their quarters, Jack hugged Mary and motioned Dah-zhonne over to them.

6

The Prostitute and the Bum

JACK RESIGNED THE NEXT DAY. When he returned from the commanding officer's headquarters, he announced to Mary, "It'll be a month before the paperwork clears and I can call myself a civilian." Delighted, she spent the evening preparing a grand meal of smoked venison purchased from the sutler.

While the couple waited for Jack's retirement papers, Mary occupied her time teaching Dah-zhonne. The girl worked enthusiastically on her lessons, prompting Mary to tell Jack, "Dah-zhonne's studies are difficult for her, but she's already into McGuffey's First Reader and her English is getting better every day."

"I know. She chatters constantly to almost everyone at the infirmary, and she spends a lot of time talking with Corporal Dockum. He loves the attention."

One evening at supper, Mary looked at the child beside her and said, "We need to give Dah-zhonne an American name before we go back East."

The three agreed. Jack and Mary began pronouncing different names for the new family member. After dozens of suggestions, Dah-zhonne settled on Jada Phoebe. Mary smiled with satisfaction. "From now on we'll call you Jada,"

The child was delighted with her new name and kept repeating, "Jada, Jada, Jada."

"Cousin Pierpont will be pleased," said Jack. "They'll both have the same name—J.P. Morgan." Jada didn't understand, but one day the other J.P. Morgan would play an important part in her life.

Five weeks after Jack resigned, Colonel Grover ordered two schooners to Albuquerque to pick up supplies and arranged for the Morgan family to ride in one of the wagons.

Jack with Mary and Jada boarded an army dray for the first leg of the long journey. A small group of friends came to see them off and the hospital staff gathered in front of the clinic with a half dozen patients to wave their goodbyes. Warren Dockum stood at the forefront. Some thought they spotted a tear on the old corporal's cheek as Dah-zhonne rode away.

The next stagecoach was due to arrive within the hour after their army escorts delivered the travelers to the Albuquerque station. Sergeant Tinker told Jack, "The boys and I are going to wet our whistles before we load up and return to Craig."

While Jack was in the depot buying their tickets, a beautiful, young woman dressed in a stylish ensemble introduced herself to Mary in a lilting Irish accent. "H'lo, I'm Mollie Shepard. I'm going ta St. Louis for me work."

Mary smiled and answered, "Hello, we're the Morgan family. I'm Mary, and this is our adopted daughter, Jada. My husband, Jack, is in the station buying the tickets. We're traveling through there, then all the way to Philadelphia. What sort of business do you have in St. Louis?"

"I hope to hire a couple of associates to help me in Prescott, Arizona. That's where I'm established. I own the Prescott Social Club, Saloon, and Café."

Mary turned pale at the words social club. This elegant woman is a whorehouse madam, bar owner, and no doubt a prostitute. Mary's southern manners prevailed, but not without a struggle.

Mollie noticed. In her trade, it was important to be sensitive to other's reactions. "Mrs. Morgan, I can see you're uneasy in the company of a lady in my business. I just thought the time would pass faster if we could talk along the way. If you prefer, I'll bother ye nah more." Mollie smiled a sad smile and added, "But t'would be a bore to avoid one another's glances for a week while we're trapped in a stage. It's a long trip and t'would be nice ta have another lady ta talk to. I'll bugger off if ye want."

The plain-spoken woman's logic made sense. So with all the nonchalance Mary could muster, she said, "You're right. It'll be a dull trip if we can't talk while we travel. I don't think there's any harm in it."

Without thinking, Mary asked, "How long have you been a business woman?" She laughed at her own question. "I'm sorry; I guess I'm just flustered."

"I know we'll have a bonnie trip—but ta answer..."

"You don't have to," Mary interrupted. "I was just babbling."

"I s'pose we can talk 'bout most anything ye want—if it don't fluster yer husband. Oh, what of Jada?"

"We just adopted her recently. She's only been away from her tribe for a month. Her vocabulary is still quite limited."

"Well then I've been in the business about seven years. I'm just twenty now, and I'm making a dandy living."

"This is a rough trip for such a young woman to take alone," said Mary.

"Oh, I always travel with a friend."

Mary looked around. She saw no other passengers, but before she could ask about Mollie's companion, Jack came out of the depot with tickets in hand. Mary hurried to him and whispered, "Jack, the woman by Jada is a prostitute. Be kind to her. She's delightful—so congenial. I like her. She'll be pleasant company on the trip."

Jack cast a glance across the dusty lot where an attractive woman was playing a game of patty-cake with Jada. "I'm surprised it's all right with you, but she'll definitely add some pleasant scenery to the desolate landscape. I imagine we'll have some interesting talks." They walked over together to meet Mollie.

Jada giggled as the two played patty-cake. "Lady good friend. She knows games."

After the stagecoach arrived, the Morgans and Mollie boarded. They no sooner settled in for the long trip when a gigantic man lumbered from the shadows of the station, and bellowed, "Hold up, som-bitch. I'm a rider."

"Watch your lingo, mister," admonished the driver. "We got ladies and a kid inside."

"Don't tell me how to talk, peckerhead," growled the huge intruder, "I gotta ticket."

The passengers felt the stage tilt to one side as the three hundred pound man climbed aboard, crashed down beside Mollie, and drove her into the far wall of the coach. Without thinking, Mollie blurted out, "Ow's about a bit 'o room over here, ye feckin eejit." She covered her mouth, "Oops, sorry there, Mrs. Morgan. When I'm upset, I sometimes forget me manners."

Mollie tried to scoot away from the brute but with little success. As Jack, Mary, and Jada sat facing Mollie and the oversized wretch, Mary thought, He's obviously not Miss Shepard's traveling companion.

The rogue was not only grossly obese; he was filthy, and smelled like a sewer. His putrid breath flamed out over yellow-stained teeth. His shaggy hair was greasy and matted. Bits of stale food from past meals befouled an unkempt black beard. A wad of chewing tobacco bulging in one cheek required him to spit from the window every few minutes. The obtruder was incapable of uttering a sentence without an obscenity.

Jack wanted to make the best of a bad situation. "We're the Morgans, and this is Miss Shepard. What might your name be?"

"Rufus Rawls. Why the hell do you care," he snapped, followed by "Is that kid an Injun? Ain't right for a redskin to be riding in a stage with decent white folks."

"Mr. Rawls," Jack's immediately responded. "I would thank you to not refer to our daughter like that and hold up on that cussing too."

Rawls quieted down, but continued to mutter to himself, taking repeated swigs from a bottle he stashed in his side pocket. An hour out of Albuquerque, the stage hit a large bump, jarring all the passengers. The oversized ogre fired off another string of blasphemes.

Jack again objected, "Rawls, I've asked you to hold up on your cussing. There are ladies and a child present."

The giant barked in a loud angry voice, "The hell you say. Peers like I'm sittin' here with a whore, two Indian lovers, and a redskin nigger kid!"

Jack leaned forward to punch Rawls in the face, but the giant was faster. His huge hand shot out, caught Jack by his neck in a vice-tight grip, slammed him against the stage wall, and pinned him there unable to breathe. Jack gurgled and struggled to strike back but the man's arm was too long. Rawls gave a growl as he increased the pressure on Jack's throat, "How you like this, Injun lover?"

Mary screamed, "Let him go, he can't breathe." She began to pull on the brute's enormous arm. To stop Mary, Rawls reached across with his other fist and delivered a vicious clout to her face. She collapsed back in her seat, almost unconscious as blood flowed from her nose. Jack's eyes rolled up. He was turning blue. Mary kept repeating, "No, Please no."

Jada was already moving before Rawls punched Mary and drew her dagger from the folds of her moccasin. In one stroke, she jammed the dirk deep into Rawls's armpit, twisted the blade, and pushed it further up in his shoulder. He immediately released Jack as his huge arm dropped useless to his side. Rawls roared in pain and launched a string of curses. The profanity stopped when Jada leaped into his lap, straddled him like a horse, and slipped her knife under the skin below his left eye. She shouted into the Rawls' face, "Jada kill."

She intended to stab Rawls in the brain through his eye, but before she could move, Rawls struggled and bounced her away from him as he continued to shout curses. In the midst of the struggle, a loud explosion went off behind Jada. The coach filled with acrid smoke from a gunshot; Mollie had blown Rawls's knee apart with a small derringer.

Jada flinched at the unexpected blast behind her and instead of driving the dagger into Rawls' brain, the blade went up through the villain's eye. She recouped and was pressing her knife to his neck when Mollie stopped her, derringer jammed against Rawls's temple.

Riled by the scuffle, Mollie reverted to her Irish brogue, "Begorra, Mr. Rawls, 'peers like I've done yer knee. I truly be sorry 'bout dat. Dis thing hay such 'o hair trigger. T'went off 'fore I could shoot ye in yer head."

Rawls sat stunned and catatonic. He mumbled, "Can't move my damned arm." In an instant, he turned gravestone white. The trauma of being stabbed in the armpit and eye, and shot in the knee at the same time sent him into shock. Rawls fell into a stupor, his good eye fixed in a vacuous stare.

Mollie, still agitated, shouted, "Get dis eejit outta here!"

The stagecoach door opened as if on demand, and the shotgun rider peered in. "We heard a shot. What the heck is going on?" Jack had recovered enough to explain while the guard dragged Rawls from the coach into the dusty road.

Jack hurried to attend Mary. Two black eyes appeared as if by magic. "My nose, it's broken!" she cried.

Rawls' punch flattened Mary's nose and sent it to one side. Jack made an effort to comfort her. "Easy sweetheart, I believe I can straighten it." He slid a small glass rod from his medical bag into her nostril, and started to push the nose back into place a fraction at a time. Mary yelped with pain at every tiny movement.

At last Jada told Jack, "Nose broke. Better way—not hurt so much. Dead mother showed me."

Jack was dubious but asked, "Okay, show me how she did it."

With the rod in one hand, she gently pinched the bridge of Mary's nose with the other, inserted the glass dowel into her nostril, and pressed hard with one swift motion. Mary shrieked and pulled away. Jack jumped to stop Jada, but the girl pointed and exclaimed, "See! Jada fix."

Jack was amazed as he examined Jada's reconstruction, "You know, Mary, she did. You'll have a swollen beezer for a week and two shiners, but you'll heal up almost like new." Jack hugged Jada who smiled with satisfaction.

The three Morgans turned their attention to Mollie who was reloading her diminutive pistol. She grinned at Mary and held her Sharps derringer between her thumb and forefinger. "Like I told ye, I always travel wid a friend."

The guard interrupted and pointed at Rawls lying in the dust. "Doctor Morgan, ain't you gonna do something for him?"

Morgan looked disgusted. "He almost killed me, busted my wife's face, tried to humiliate my child, and insulted Miss Shepard. I wouldn't piss on him if he was on fire."

As the driver and the guard discussed how to get the three-hundred-pound Rawls on top of the stage until they reached their next stop, Sergeant Tinker raced up in a cloud of dust with his men and the supply wagons. "Are you folks okay?" he yelled.

Jack responded, "We're fine now. I thought you were enjoying the pleasures of Albuquerque."

"We were at the Red Dog Saloon when Private Smith found this wanted poster for Rufus Rawls." Tinker held up the flyer. "We spotted him at the station with a ticket."

Smith stepped forward, "The flyer says he killed two Mexican families and raped a woman. We figured he might give you some trouble."

"He did, but Mollie here and Jada fixed the problem," said Jack.

Tinker said, "There's a sizable reward for him, dead or alive—a thousand dollars."

"Well, I'll tell you what. If you men haul him away, you can have the money if that's all right with Miss Shepard."

Calmer now, Mollie lost her heavy Irish accent. "Give it to the soldier boys if they'll take this gobdaw off our hands. Troopers are a big part of me business."

Tinker thanked Jack and Mollie, and ordered his men to load the weighty Rawls into a supply wagon.

Jack waved 'so long' to their rescuers as they turned their freight-drays back toward Albuquerque.

Mollie's eyes followed the wagons for a short distance, then she crossed her arms and gave an old Irish curse, "May he keep to his bed 'til the hour he's dead."

Jack approved. "Amen."

7

First Train Ride

DARK SHADOWS STRETCHED across the road by the time their stagecoach was underway. It would be late night when the travelers reached Santa Fe. Inside the stage under the light of a kerosene lantern, Jada's eyes began to droop and at last she said, "Jada sleep now." To the surprise of the adults, the girl curled up on the seat and put her head in Mollie's lap. She nodded off in seconds.

"How can she do that?" whispered Mary. "I'm so wrought up after that ruckus, I won't sleep for a week."

Mollie studied the child's angelic face for a moment, then observed, "Peers to me our little girl knew what she was adoin' with her wee blade."

"I think she did," said Jack. He had quizzed Jada after the struggle, and learned some extraordinary facts about his new daughter.

"She doesn't speak enough English for me to catch all she told me, but I believe she's seen several men dissected alive. She obviously knows how to disable and kill a man." He went on to explain why Jada's knife attack worked, "She cut the nerves and ligaments controlling Rawls' entire arm. After Jada finished with him, he couldn't unbutton his pants with that hand if he wanted to."

"So that's what made him drop his choke. Why didn't she just stab him in the chest?" Mollie asked, her eyes wide with fascination. This was information she might need in her business.

Jack answered, "She said she needed to make him release his choke-hold quickly, and she didn't think her little knife would go through all his fat. She was probably right."

"Jack, Jada's roughly eleven years old. How could she react so rapidly with such a sophisticated attack?" Mary asked.

"The Apaches have been at war for a long time. The children learn fighting skills early."

"And might there be something positive in all this?" Mollie inquired.

"Good question, Mollie." Morgan smiled. "Jada helped her mother treat the sick and injured. She says her people believe she has strong powers to heal, and she'll be a medicine woman after she's older. If Jada's English was better, I think she could teach most medical students a bit about anatomy."

The following morning in Santa Fe, the travelers learned there would be several hours before the next stage left for St. Louis. They took the opportunity to replace the outfits Mary made at Fort Craig for Jada with a small wardrobe of off-the-rack wear. As they returned to the depot, Jada smiled and admired her reflection in each store window they passed.

Jack, Jada and the two women boarded a larger, more comfortable Concord stagecoach. The driver reminded the group, "We'll be travelin' fer a week and a day—no stops 'cept for meals and overnights." Thus for the next eight days, Jada was immersed in English and the strange ways of white people.

At the St. Louis stage depot, Jack and Jada went to arrange for carriages to deliver the family to the railroad station and Mollie to the red light district. As they waited, the prostitute and the doctor's wife embraced and kissed each other's cheeks.

"We'll never forget you, Mollie. If you're ever in Philadelphia, promise you will stay with us." Mary was emotional.

"Becheezus, your neighbors would love dat!"

"Don't be silly. You have our address. Come anytime." Mary watched as the coach left the station with thoughts of the hard life Mollie faced back in Arizona.

The Morgans arrived at the rail depot minutes before the train to Philadelphia pulled into the terminal. Morgan told Jada a railroad train would take them to their new home.

"I've never seen a railro..."

Before Jada finished, a blast from the train's whistle sent her leaping behind Jack and covering her ears. She peeked around him as the locomotive puffed into the depot. Smoke billowed from the stack; steam spewed from the underbelly; and hot cinders dropped on the tracks. For a child who just left an aboriginal life, the sight was terrifying.

"It's our railroad train, Jada," explained Jack.

"Railroad train," she repeated the words, committing them to her memory as she cautiously watched the huge iron monster snort steam.

"Where are the people? How do you ride it?"

"Those big boxes with windows." Jack pointed to the passenger coaches. "They're called railroad cars, and we go inside them to travel."

Anxiety showed on Jada's face. "Maybe we take another stagecoach?" Mary laughed and reassured her.

When the family boarded and took their places, they gave Jada the window seat. As the train began to roll she yelped, "Ee-yi, everything outside is moving!"

She started to crawl across Mary's lap toward Jack but Mary held her close, "We're okay, Jada. It's safe."

Jada soon settled down and watched the scenery flash past. The girl from the brown New Mexico countryside was amazed at the lush vegetation. "Everything is so green."

Jack's cousin, J. Pierpont Morgan, stood on the Philadelphia platform as his relatives arrived. He leaned on a silver-capped mahogany cane and puffed an enormous cigar. Pierpont's huge stogie and large mustache reminded Jada of Lorenzo Garcia, the killer of her family. At first sight, hatred roiled through her, but she relaxed when Jack smiled and gave his cousin a warm handshake.

Jada's newfound family member seemed gigantic. Pierpont's stylish clothes were exquisitely tailored to accommodate a massive potbelly. He elevated his six foot stature with a beaver skin top hat, but nothing about Pierpont impressed Jada as much as his nose. She pulled Mary aside and whispered, "His nose is too big and it's blue." Pierpont was afflicted with rhinophyma.

Mary replied softly, "Pierpont has a sickness. It causes his nose to swell up and turn blue. Don't say anything."

"I hope I never get that!"

Pierpont exhaled a cloud of smoke. "Welcome home, folks! I received your telegram from Santa Fe and took the train down to check the house before you arrived. Old Simon and Rebecca have the place in shipshape order." Simon and Rebecca were family servants and caretakers for the Philadelphia mansion—emancipated black Freedmen.

"Sounds great. We're ready to be home," Jack said.

"When the neighbors heard you were returning, they planned a welcome-home potluck. Everyone's anxious to see you again and meet your daughter."

Pierpont turned his attention to Jada and gave a big smile. "So this is the new family member. You must be Jada?" He put his hands on his hips, arched back, and smiled with admiration. "Oh, what a beauty. She'll be a popular girl." He leaned over and shook Jada's hand.

"Hello, how are you, Uncle Pierpont?" She had just learned the phrase.

"Uncle Pierpont? I've been promoted from cousin to uncle."

"Apaches refer to the elders in their tribe as 'Aunt' or 'Uncle'," explained Jack.

Pierpont patted Jada on the head. "Well, we should move along. It's getting late. I know you folks want to go home, and my train to New York will arrive shortly. I need to get back for a conference in the morning."

Darkness set in by the time the carriage hire stopped in front of the Morgan's three story mansion. A dense fog had floated in from the nearby Delaware River creating an eerie welcome for the near-stone age eleven-year-old. Jada clutched Mary's hand. Every window glowed with the mansion's gas lights. This looks like the mountain where the Big Owl Witch lives, she thought. In Apache lore, Big Owl Witch was a giant ogre that fed on humans. The monster lived on a mountain covered with caves.

"What is this place?" Jada asked as she stared at the fog-shrouded manor.

Mary smiled. "It's our home, Jada. That's where you will live."

"Does a really big person or animal live in there too?" The witch had the power to change shapes to be anything it wanted, human or beast.

"No it's just us. Simon and Rebecca live in the little house in the back, and they come every day to help."

Suddenly, Jada wished she was back in the safety of her family's dome-shaped brush wickiup and could smell the sweetgrass Alope piled under animal robes for bedding. The only buildings she had been in before were the one level adobe structures at Fort Craig and stage depots on their trip. Still squeezing Mary's hand, Jada reluctantly walked into the huge house and entered the world of upper class luxury. After the sparse army quarters, her new home was enormous; high ceilings, oil paintings on the walls, and luxurious carpets on every floor. She was intrigued with it all; bounced on the cushioned easy chairs, ran her fingers across the shiny mahogany furniture, and carefully studied the gas lights. It was all new for her.

That night Jada dreamed she watched her birth mother and a few other Apache women construct a small wickiup. The scene changed and the dream ended when Alope stood with her in front of the Morgan mansion. She told Jada in Apache, "This is a good place to live. The Big Owl Witch doesn't come here."

Jada woke the next morning in a soft, clean bed. She looked around the large room with high ceilings, lace curtains, and polished oak floors, then added a word to her mother's observation, "This is a very good place to live."

8

The Apprentice

ON THE SATURDAY following their arrival in Philadelphia, a dozen neighbors gathered for a potluck to welcome home the Morgans and to meet their new daughter. Susan Gatewood, who would become Jada's best friend, attended with her family and a gaggle of girlfriends.

After the party assembled, Jada soon found herself surrounded by a swarm of chattering and giggling white girls her age. Although the crowd seemed to like her, she felt confused and troubled. For her entire life she had been warned to be cautious of white people; to watch someone carefully for a time before you trusted them. Nothing was familiar and she didn't understand most of their babbling.

These girls act friendly but they talk so fast, I can't figure out what they're saying, she thought. Everybody is white. Can I trust them? What's right and what's wrong? I wouldn't be here if my Apache friends were still alive. Maybe coming here was a mistake.

Jada remained quiet but answered the crowd's questions with her limited vocabulary, if she understood them. Contrary to her natural tendency to be outspoken, she appeared painfully shy.

Across the lawn, Judy Lawson's mother, Deliliah, told Mary, "I hope you'll consider sending Jada to Miss Mather's school for Young Ladies. It's the best institution in Philadelphia for instructing young women in proper etiquette and preparing them for college. It's walking distance, only three blocks from here. Sadly, the only college in the area that admits females is the Women's Medical College of Pennsylvania."

Mary replied, "That sounds perfect for Jada. She's fascinated by the idea of a medical career. Her Indian mother was a tribal medicine woman and she told Jack she wanted to be a doctor. The medical college may be in her future."

"Well, Jada would be a natural for the Mather Academy," said Priscilla Gatewood, Susan's mother.

Mary glanced over at Jada. "I'm not sure. She looks quite intimidated by all those girls around her. She's just learning English and I worry how our little Pocahontas will be accepted. Let's wait and find out how she gets along."

That sparked a quick response from Amanda Armstrong's mother, Donna Lou. "Mary, you aren't in Georgia now. This is Pennsylvania. We abolished slavery in 1780, and now Philadelphia is the center of racial tolerance on the East Coast." She waved a hand for emphasis. "The mother of every girl in Miss Mather's school is a member of the Ladies Society to Fight Racial Prejudice and Promote Women's Rights. If anybody gives Jada any trouble, you let us know!"

Jada eventually eased away from her new acquaintances to tell Mary about her discomfort. Mary hugged her and reassured her. "All those girls just want to be your friends."

Susan Gatewood and Judy Lawson later found Mary and Jack standing with adults around a table, heavy with potluck offerings. Susan said, "Jada is so shy but we think she'll fit right in if she goes to school with us. We'll be able to walk to classes together."

Judy added, "If Jada comes with us, we could help her with her English, and I think she will be more relaxed when she gets to know us. She is very interesting."

Between the parents' recommendations and the girls' appeals, Jack and Mary decided Jada would attend the Mather Academy for Young Ladies. They learned most of the school's students intended to go to college. Sara Jane Mather, owner and sole instructor, held classes in her huge home. After interviewing Jada and her adopted parents, she told the Morgans, "We'll need to focus on Jada's English for a while, but I feel she'll do well here."

In school Jada was immersed in academic and etiquette courses, along with dancing and gymnastic classes. After six weeks, Mather reported to Mary, "Jada is struggling with her academics but her English is improving every day." Mather leaned back in her chair. "Living in the wild like she did, Jada has a natural bent for physical activity. She excels in my dance curriculum."

Jada received further instruction on her walks to and from school where her schoolmates provided daily lessons in the culture of wealthy Philadelphia teenagers. Jada took it all in.

When Jada reached age thirteen, two years after the Morgans adopted her, Jack called her into his office. "You've said you would like to be a physician. Are you still of that mind?"

"Father you know I am. I want to be a doctor more than anything."

"Well then, you can start helping in the clinic right away. You were very helpful in the hospital at Fort Craig. We'll begin slowly and you must keep up your studies with Miss Mather. It will be difficult for you to do both." He looked for any hesitation on her part and continued, "Some doctors—not the good ones—complete their training in two years, but others remain apprentices for as many as seven. I plan to keep you in training until you are eighteen, five years from now. Think you can hang in that long?"

"I'm sure I can, but why wait until I'm eighteen?"

"The Women's Medical College won't take students until they reach that age. The best physicians have an M.D. after their name." He looked thoughtful for a moment. "If we do this, I want you to go all the way—earn an M.D. degree."

"I hope to go medical school anyhow. Doing an apprenticeship with you will give me a head start."

Afterwards, Jada went to school in the mornings, worked in the Morgan clinic during the afternoons, and studied in the evenings. Initially, her medical studies consisted of reading medical books and observing as Jack treated his patients, but soon she began to serve as his nurse.

A year later Morgan told her, "Jada, all our patients are telling me good things about you. Some of the older women want you to examine them instead of me."

Several months after that, she began delivering babies with Morgan attending. "I've done this before," she told Jack, "I helped my first mother bring babies lots of times."

Jada was soon suturing surgeries and other wounds. Jack's confidence in her care of patients grew daily.

9

Consumption Strikes

JACK AND JADA HAD WATCHED Mary's health decline slowly after the family returned to Philadelphia. Except for some weight loss, she seemed well and fit for the first two years. During the third year, she lost ground rapidly. An annoying cough developed into spells of hacking and spitting. Then came specks of blood in the sputum and night sweats. Recently she spat bright blood.

Jack knew the symptoms—consumption. It was killing more people in the Northeast than all other diseases. He had seen several of his own patients cough and gasp their way into eternity. There was no known cause or any cure.

In mid-November of her sixteenth year, Jack sat with Jada in his office and discussed Mary's condition. "This is difficult to hear but I believe your mother is dying, Jada. She has end-stage consumption. I didn't want to tell you until I was sure. You should prepare yourself."

Jada started crying. "I knew something was wrong but I didn't realize it was so bad."

Tears continued to stream down her face as Jack went over the symptoms with her and told her what to expect.

"I saw all that with the Apaches. When they started coughing blood, they almost always died. Mother seemed so healthy until recently. Isn't there anything you can do?"

Jack's brow furrowed and he chewed his lip. "Unfortunately, not yet. I've written every doctor I know and tried everything they suggested; tannin, iodine, creosote, arsenic and tar inhalants. Nothing works."

"It's a terrible scourge among the Apaches. They treated it with a potion made from a root. That didn't work either."

"I've discovered one more thing to try. A pamphlet just arrived about a doctor who suggests a cold mountain climate as a possible cure." His heart was in his throat at the thought of losing Mary.

He pulled a bottle from a drawer, filled a glass with scotch, took a large swallow, and held up a small brochure. "The man is Edward Thudeau, a doctor in the New York mountains. He's doing research on the disease. His treatment involves recuperating in high mountain air. He's planning to build a sanitarium for consumptives if he gets some financial backing. He's already treating a few sufferers up there."

Jack took another sip of scotch and continued, "Thudeau claims the Adirondacks have the perfect climate for a cure. I'll wire him first thing tomorrow and find out if he'll take Mary as a patient. That is if she'll agree." He tossed down another swallow of whiskey. It might be Mary's only chance. I pray Thudeau can do something. Jack wanted to keep a professional attitude about Mary, but this was all too personal.

After discussing her condition with Mary, Jack suggested convalescing in New York. Mary began crying. "I don't want to leave you and Jada."

When he pleaded and reaffirmed his love, she at last changed her mind. "I'll go if you believe there is any chance. Let's find out what this Doctor Thudeau says."

In answer to Morgan's telegraphic inquiry, Thudeau replied:

Dr. Morgan: Consumption treatments experimental at this time. Treating a few afflicted here at present. Your wife welcome as patient. Treatment based on Hermann Berhmer's high-mountain outdoor living. Some success in Europe. Involves patients residing in open cabins under all conditions. Recommend she bring heavy clothing, several quilts and blankets. Cold weather approaching fast. Come at once. No guarantees. Dr. Edward Thudeau.

Jack purchased train tickets to New York and wired Pierpont:

Mary ill. Please make rail arrangements for me, Mary, and Jada, from the city to destination nearest Saranac Lake. From there, arrange carriage to Dr. Thudeau's Adirondack wilderness retreat. Will be in NY tomorrow and explain. Jack.

Pierpont greeted Jack and his family when they arrived at his house. "Hello Jack, ladies. Jada, you're more beautiful every time I see you. Greetings Mary, you seem a bit wan. Was the trip a rough one?" Mary didn't answer.

"Let's go into the parlor, Pierpont." Jack gestured toward the next room. "Jada, take care of your mother."

As soon as they were alone, Pierpont asked, "What the hell is going on, Jack? Nobody goes to that part of the state this time of year. The weather is already brass-monkey-cold up there."

Jack's voice cracked. "Pierpont, there's no good way to talk about this. Mary has a serious case of consumption. It may already be too late to do much for her."

"Damn Jack, why the Adirondacks?"

"A Doctor Thudeau up there is working on an advanced treatment. He claims the high-altitude and cold mountain air are the perfect cures for consumption. Says his therapy has worked with some cases. The regimen sounds brutal, but he's the only one claiming a remedy." Jack shivered as he thought of the icy weather Mary would be facing. "Anything's worth a try to save her."

Pierpont tugged at his mustache as he recalled recent correspondence with Thudeau. "That doctor has written me and requested financial help to start a hospital in the mountains. Since he's taking on Mary, I'll send him a check. You must think his treatments are worthwhile."

"Thudeau seems confident, but who knows. Every case is different." Jack could barely control his emotions. "This is a last chance for Mary."

"Well, I've made the arrangements. You leave this evening. Snow is already falling around Saranac. You better not waste any time."

What a bleak place, thought Jada when their carriage pulled into Thudeau's compound the next day. "I've never been so cold," she whispered to Jack, "How can this be good for anybody?"

A medical assistant came to welcome the Morgans and directed them to a small structure which served as the doctor's workplace. He took Mary's baggage to a larger building about 20 yards away while the three Morgan's went into the office to meet with Thudeau.

The doctor examined and questioned Mary for almost an hour. When he finished, the assistant appeared and led Mary to the second building.

Thudeau sat down, read over his notes and sighed. "She's kept the problem under wraps for a long time. She didn't want to bother you or upset your daughter." He nodded toward Jada.

Dread consumed Jack. "So what's your prognosis?"

"I just don't know, Doctor Morgan. Mary is very far along. One lung is virtually gone and the other is badly infected. Her prospects are not good but we'll try our best."

"Please, let me know if there is anything I can do. Here, I've written down what I've tried." Jack gave the list to Thudeau and shook his hand. "We'll stay around for a day or two to help her adjust."

Thudeau pointed at the clouds gathering in the north. "You better re-think that. An early storm is on the way. The roads in this area will be blocked for weeks."

"I'll miss you, mother," said a tearful Jada. "I'll write often and please, you do the same when you feel like it."

Mary smiled and hugged Jada. "You take care of yourself, young lady, and your father."

Jack kissed Mary. "We'll visit often." Don't worry about anything, just get well. I love you so much."

Mary's face clouded. "I love you too, my dearest man."

Jada looked skyward and raised her palms upward as if to catch the large snowflakes that had started to swirl around them. Please, Please Ussen, help her! She prayed silently to the Apache god.

Jack and Jada left Thudeau's Adirondack retreat and after a brief stop in New York to tell Pierpont of Mary's poor prospects, they returned to Philadelphia.

LETTERS

December 15, 1871
> My dearest daughter,
I hope you and Jack are well. I miss you both...
Dr. Thudeau is concerned. He says I'm not progressing as well as he hoped. The symptoms remain and I'm a bit weaker...
> Give my love to your father.
> My deepest affection, Mother

December 25, 1871
> Dear Mother,
> We hope you enjoyed a good Christmas and that you are doing better. It was a very sad holiday here without all the brightness you usually add to the occasion. Father and I put up a small tree and a few decorations...
> Judy Lawson's family is planning a New Year's Eve party at their home. They even hired a string ensemble to play. At last I will be able to use the dance skills I've learned from Miss Mather. I'll write and tell you about it.
> Both Daddy and I are well. We pray for you daily and think of you all the time. Try hard to get better.
> Much affection,
> Jada

10

The Big Dance

ON NEW YEAR'S EVE, 1871, festive partygoers were already crowded in the ballroom when Jada entered the Lawson's mansion. Gas lights and candles provided a subdued glow. Her attention was immediately drawn to a young woman holding court at the edge of the dance floor. A crowd of admirers brandished their dance cards for a chance to hoof it with the apparent belle of the ball.

"Ooh, who is she?" Jada was fascinated by the activity around the woman. "She's beautiful, such long golden hair."

Jada's best friend, Susan Greenwood made a face and said, "That's Patsy Fike. Stay away from that one."

"Why's that?" Jada looked quizzical.

Susan saw Jada didn't understand. "She'll try to embarrass you in front of everybody if she thinks you are prettier than she. You're a prime candidate for her sarcasm."

Jada had reached her full height, a petite five feet one inch. Unlike most of the women at the dance who wore their hair in ringlets, knotted buns, or chignons, Jada's straight black hair cascaded to the middle of her back. She held it away from her face by silver barrettes. A golden complexion emphasized her brilliant white smile. Her dark eyes added an air of intrigue. Harry Trenchcott soon spotted her and left the crowd around Patsy to see if she had room for him on her dance card. "Remember me? I met you at Amanda Armstrong's ice cream social last summer. I cranked the churn for most of the day. I was wondering if I could have the honor to be listed on your card?"

"Why, Harry Trenchcott, of course I remember you. I'll put you first in line. No one else has asked." Harry was a handsome giant, built like a Greek god, and very tall. He was also grievously shy.

Patsy missed none of it, and casually slithered her way across the room to Jada and Harry and interrupted their conversation. "I'm Patsy Louise Fike of the Philadelphia Fikes and who might you be? I've never met you before."

"Nice to meet you, Patsy. I'm Jada Phoebe Morgan of the Warm Springs Apache tribe of New Mexico. I'm adopted by Doctor and Mrs. Morgan of the Philadelphia Morgans."

Taken aback by Jada's forthright reply, Patsy was not deterred. She launched into a lengthy speech in French after which she put her hand to her cheek and looked contrite. "I'm sorry, Miss Morgan. I doubt an untutored savage from the West knows any French."

Jada's response was immediate. She began a soliloquy in Chiricahua, then said in English, "Oh, I apologize, Patsy. I suspect a sophisticate such as you wouldn't understand a word of Apache."

Jada turned back to Harry as Patsy's face flushed red and she retreated into the crowd. When the band struck up a smooth foxtrot, Jada asked, "Want to give it a try?

"You appear to stay in good condition," she said as they moved onto the floor.

"I exercise a little on most days." His answer was almost inaudible.

"I understand you are putting yourself through the university with your athletic skills."

"Yeah, I spend the summers boxing in the St. Louis professional boxer's club. I've done pretty well. At least it pays for college." An offset nose suggested Harry had a few setbacks in the ring. "I also wrestle professionally in New York in the off-season. Doesn't pay as much, but I can compete during the school year and not miss any classes."

As they danced, Jada noticed several couples stopped to stare at the huge athlete and his petite partner navigating the floor. She asked, "How tall are you?" She gazed up at him and smiled.

"A little better than six feet three inches." He stood more than a foot taller than Jada. When he realized why she inquired about his height, he froze in place and scanned the room. "Everybody's staring at us. We should stop." He started to pull away.

Jada tightened her hold and squeezed his hand. "You stay right here Mister Trenchcott and finish this dance!"

Much to Harry's relief, the orchestra ended the tune at last. He thanked Jada and turned to leave but she caught his sleeve and pulled him back. "Bend over here, Harry, I want to ask you something." He did as instructed and Jada whispered in his ear, "When you get a break from your schoolwork and fighting, would you come to visit me at Doctor Morgan's home?"

"Uh, maybe, sometime," Harry mumbled. He blushed, backed away, and stumbled into a cluster of amused partygoers.

"What in the world did you say to him?" Susan asked.

"I asked him to call on me at home."

"You didn't!" Susan appeared shocked.

"Did too. He's a mighty attractive fellow but he's so bashful, I doubt he'll take me up on it. I'd love to get to know him better. He's very nice."

11

Mary Morgan Dies

THE TELEGRAM ARRIVED at the Morgan residence on a cheerless, cold day in late January 1872.

Dr. Morgan:

Regret to inform you Mrs. Morgan died last night in sleep. Send instructions regarding remains. Can bury here or transport body to you via rail. Assume you prefer funeral in Philadelphia. If so, contact your cousin in NYC to make arrangements. Deepest regrets. Edward L. Thudeau

Jack read the wire, crumpled the paper, cursed, and tossed it on the table in the foyer. He went into his office and poured himself a scotch. He sat unmoving, his chin down, and his eyes moist.

When Jada came home from school the telegram still lay crumpled in plain view. She studied the message in stunned silence. Without warning, she gave a mournful wail and ran up the stairs clutching the yellow paper and bawling.

Rebecca Stokes heard Jada's cry and hurried after her. She found the door locked. "Miss Jada, honey, what happened? Can I come in?"

"Go away, I'm fine." Rebecca could hear Jada's sobs as she stood in the hallway.

She started downstairs to fetch Jack when Jada burst from the room in hysterics and dashed to the bathroom screaming, "Mother's gone, Rebecca. Mary's dead—both my mothers are dead."

As Rebecca followed, she peeked into the bedroom. Jada's knife was jammed into the floor through the telegram and a mound of her long black hair. Blood puddled by the pile and drops led down the hall to the lavatory.

She rushed downstairs to Morgan's office. "Doctor Morgan, I think Jada's trying to kill herself. There's blood everywhere! She's yelling something about Miz Mary dying."

Jack raced to the second floor bathroom calling, "Jada, Jada, open up!" Rebecca was two steps behind.

When there was no response, he broke the lock and found Jada sitting on the tile floor, weeping, legs crossed, and clutching herself with both arms. "Not again. Not again," she repeated. She had cut her long hair straight across below her ears with her knife.

Concern rushed through Jack. "Oh, sweetheart, how badly are you injured." Jada sobbed so hard her words were unintelligible.

He kneeled beside her to examine her wound. Blood oozed from a thin cut across the back of her neck, and soaked the top of her dress.

"Thank god it isn't deep. Hand me a towel, Rebecca," he ordered.

Rebecca sat beside Jada and cradled her. "Shhhh, hush your crying child. How'd you hurt yourself?"

Jada gasped between sobs, "Accident when I cut my hair." Even after years in Philadelphia, Jada clung to the demands of her Apache culture to cut her long tresses after a family member died.

Morgan cleaned and bandaged the wound, then took her hand. "I'm so sorry, sweetheart. I should have never left that telegram in the foyer. It was a terrible way to learn about our loss." He hugged her and helped her stand.

With their arms around Jada, Jack and Rebecca walked her back to her bedroom. Jada curled into a fetal position on her bed and continued to weep.

Once outside Jada's room, Rebecca grabbed Morgan's arm. "I've never seen a child cry like that. Can you do something?" she asked.

"I'll get her a dose of laudanum. It'll calm her and put her sleep. Stay with her and I'll be right back."

Rebecca sat by Jada's bedside and tried to comfort her until Jack returned with the medicine. As the laudanum took effect, Jada's body relaxed and she drifted into a drugged slumber.

Two days later, another telegram arrived, this one from Pierpont in New York.

Jack:

Expect Mary's remains in NYC tomorrow afternoon. Body has been in temperatures below zero. Brown and Alexander, Embalming Surgeons here are to prepare corpse for shipment. Arrive Philadelphia in late morning of 31st. Fanny in Europe. Will attend funeral alone. Pierpont.

Morgan went to Jada's room and found her awake, sitting in bed subdued from the laudanum. He read Pierpont's telegram aloud and asked if she was better. Jada nodded her head but didn't speak.

Later that afternoon, Rebecca said she wanted to repair Jada's ragged, self-administered haircut. "I think we need to trim your hair. You did a pretty rough job with that knife." Jada agreed quietly.

When Rebecca finished clipping, she gave Jada a smile of approval. "We've made you like one of those feminist women. You look real cute with this hair bob, and it's mighty fashionable these days. I know you prefer a straight hairdo, but I think a loose curl on both sides of your face will be nice. You'll be right in style. If you want, we could make a bun with the hair you cut off and pin it on."

Jada offered a tranquilized smile. "Thank you, Rebecca. My people out west cut their hair when they mourn. I'll do without the hairpiece. Both my mothers are dead. Fashion doesn't matter." She returned to her bed and closed her eyes.

Pierpont arrived at the Morgan home bringing Mary's body in a lavish black hearse with silver trim and large glass windows. Jada had regained her composure but was still morose. Sometime after Pierpont's appearance, Rebecca came into Jada's room carrying a black dress folded over one arm. "Time to be ready for the funeral."

Jada took the dress into the bathroom but returned wearing her oldest skirt and blouse. Rebecca covered her mouth, appalled. "Honey, you can't go to the service in those things. That's what you have on when you're helping Simon in the garden."

"You aren't supposed to dress in a nice outfit when someone dies." She handed the garment back to Rebecca. "I can't wear that to bury mother," Jada said. "My Indian parents told me good clothes mean you're happy."

"Miss Jada, these folk you living with now think a black getup shows you're sad. They believe a dark dress like this is respectful." Rebecca held out the mourning wear again. Jada was not convinced, but reluctantly changed.

Jack circulated with the mourners until Jada entered the doorway of the parlor where the service would take place. Those assembled fell silent as they turned to catch a glimpse of her. She stood grim and erect. With her short black hair, dark dress, and circles under her redden eyes, she was the epitome of utter grief.

Pierpont's jaw dropped when he saw her. "Jack, she looks terrible."

Jada walked into the room with tears flowing down her cheeks. After a few steps, she spotted Harry Trenchcott seated in the far corner wearing a brown wool suit with a black armband. He held a bowler in his lap. She hadn't spoken with him since the New Year's Eve dance, and a smile flickered across her lips. Without thinking, she moved toward her new friend, but when she saw Mary's body in the coffin, her knees buckled. Harry leaped from his chair and caught her before she crashed to the floor. Jack rushed to her, pulled a small bottle of smelling salts from his pocket, and wafted it under Jada's nose.

After she regained consciousness, Jack, Harry and Rebecca attempted to take her to her room but she refused. "I want to be here."

She remained silent throughout the service. She was horrified when the minister mentioned Mary several times, and afterwards was further shocked as some mourners eulogized her mother. She thought of her Apache upbringing. *This isn't right. You are never supposed to mention the departed's name. Talking about the dead disturbs their spirit and causes it to stay here on earth.*

At the cemetery, Jada sat in silence as she watched her adopted mother lowered into the grave and wept all the way back to the mansion.

She went straight to her room where she changed into her ragged work clothes, pulled an upholstered chair to the window overlooking the garden, and sat staring out.

I hope mother's spirit is not angry with all the people who mentioned her name after she had passed. She prayed for the Apache god, Ussen, to let Mary's ghost leave earth so it wouldn't haunt those who spoke of her at the funeral.

Later, Jack came to check on her. "Jada, are you okay? You were so brave today. I'm proud of you." He hugged her and held her close for a long minute. "Do you want any more medicine?"

"No, I don't think so." She continued to stare out the window.

Satisfied she was better, Jack left to search for Harry Trenchcott. "Where is that young fellow?" he asked Simon at the bottom of the stairs.

"He's in the parlor, Doctor Morgan. I think he means to talk with you."

On meeting Harry, Jack offered his hand. "Hello, young man. I want to thank you for saving Jada from a nasty fall. What's your name?"

"Glad I could help. I'm P. Harriman Trenchcott. Everybody calls me Harry."

"Oh, are you the boxer who's paying his way through school?"

"Yes sir, but the reason I'm here is to ask your permission to visit Jada every so often. You know, after she's feeling better. We met at the Armstrong's ice cream party and again at the Lawson's New Year's Eve dance."

Jack studied Harry carefully. "Well Mr. Trenchcott, frankly I was looking for you to ask you to do just that. When she saw you today, she smiled for the first time since her mother died. You might be exactly what she needs to help her recover from this. Visit as often as you want. In fact, why don't you go up and see her now?"

"I'll be glad to, sir, and I'll try to be here whenever I can, at least for a while. I need to start training for the summer fights in St. Louis."

Jack reached for the door. "You are welcome anytime, son. Now, let me find Rebecca to sit with you two."

12

Carriage Wreck

FOLLOWING THE MORGAN FAMILY TRADITION, relatives gathered after the funeral to lighten the day's melancholy. In Mary's case, it was only Jack and Pierpont. Mary's kin from Savannah couldn't make the trip for the services, and Jada refused to leave her room.

Pierpont returned from the burial shortly after Harry and Rebecca went to sit with Jada. "Jack, I've never seen anyone so upset. I thought Indians were supposed to be stoic—unemotional sorts."

"This is something different for her, Pierpont. I'm sure she cried, but I haven't seen Jada spill a tear over the deaths of her parents and friends since that massacre in New Mexico." Jack poured three fingers of scotch into a crystal glass. "The interpreter out West told me she was following the tribal custom of concealing emotions from outsiders. Apaches stay in mourning for quite a while but they don't speak of the death afterwards and never mention the deceased's name."

"Well she certainly wasn't holding back this time. If that's the Apache custom, why so many tears now?"

Jack drained his glass and poured himself another. "I believe Mary's death brought out all her losses. After she lost both her Indian family and Mary, she simply fell apart."

Jack's cousin, fascinated with Indian culture, leaned forward to inquire further, "So what's going on with her now?"

"Just today, she tried to get Rebecca to burn Mary's pictures. She said it too painful to see photographs of her mother, and I think all the talk at the funeral about Mary's life disturbed her greatly. I wasn't sure what to do at first, but I've found the perfect prescription for her depression. Jada will be fine in a week or two."

Pierpont gave a laugh. "I could use a bottle of that."

"Doesn't come in a bottle, old boy. It's in the form of Mr. P. Harriman Trench-cott. He's upstairs with her right now—Rebecca's chaperoning."

Surprise showed on Pierpont's face. "P. Harriman Trenchcott? Harry Trench-cott? Trenchcott the Terrible? He's a professional wrestler up in New York and he also boxes with the pros in St. Louis. He must be good. I read somewhere he's paying his way through the local university with his winnings." Pierpont lit a cigar and thought for a moment. "I've heard he's quite a paradox. Some say he's painfully shy, yet he's vicious in the ring. He trains with some mighty tough rowdies but he avoids the raucous behavior that sort seems to fancy—drinking, gambling, and tawdry women."

Jack finished the last of his scotch and shrugged. "All I know is when she spotted him at the funeral today, Jada smiled for the first time in six days."

About an hour later, Harry appeared from upstairs. "Thank you Doctor Morgan. I think I better leave now. I stayed too long, but Jada kept asking me to stick around."

"Harry, step in here. I'd like to introduce you to someone. Harry Trenchcott meet J.P. Morgan from New York. Mr. Morgan is my cousin and a fan of yours."

Harry politely shook Pierpont's hand. "A pleasure, sir."

"I've read great things about your fight career, Harry. I understand you are putting yourself through school with your pugilism."

Embarrassed, Harry edged toward the door to escape the attention. "Yes sir. I'm doing okay. Sorry, I have to go now—tough test in school tomorrow."

After Harry left, Jack called Rebecca in. "How's Jada?"

"She's better with Mr. Harry there. They don't do much talking though. He sits by her and holds that hat. Jada just stares out the window with tears flowing, then she looks at him and smiles a bit—after that she goes back to staring and crying."

"Did they say anything?"

Rebecca chuckled. "Well, not much and not so as I could hear. He's the most bashful boy I've ever known. Jada reached over and held his hand for a few minutes. I've never seen anybody turn so red. I thought he's gonna run right out the room. Jada got tickled too."

Jack frowned. "Is that all there was to it?"

"Weren't no fooling around if that's what you're asking. I tell you true, if there's gonna be any messing about, Miss Jada will start it. Folks say Mr. Harry is a fright in the ring, but he's a fraidy-cat with Jada."

Pierpont laughed. "I guess we better not let that secret out. Trenchcott the Terrible's reputation would be ruined."

Four nights after Mary's funeral, Jada slept without drugs for the first time since Mary died. She dreamed she had returned to a mountain hideaway with her tribe. Her older brother lay dead in his mother's arms. Her mother was crying and had cut her hair in mourning. Responding to Jada's anguish, she spoke to her in Chiricahua. "Dah-zhonne, Everybody dies. Continue your life. If you don't, you're insulting the dead."

As Jada's dream ended, Mary stood with Jada's deceased Indian family. Her two mothers hugged. Then they all waved, smiled, and walked off together. Jada woke feeling relieved because she knew Mary's spirit was safe in the afterworld with Nitis and Alope.

On the following day, a frigid Friday, Morgan sat in his office with a tumbler of scotch reflecting on the recent events. I need to slow down with this stuff, he thought. Mary's gone and becoming a drunk won't bring her back. As he pondered his personal loss and Jada's depression, Jada appeared at the door holding the doctor's record book. "I should update this. I haven't added any entries for over a week."

Jack scribbled observations concerning his patients on scraps of paper which Jada transcribed into a daybook: details about the patient, the medical problem, and the treatment. The journal provided a record for Jack and was a training tool for Jada. "Are you sure you're ready?" he asked.

"I'm positive." She walked a few steps, and then turned around. "I'll be attending school Monday morning."

Jack thought Jada was cutting the mourning period much too short and started to protest, but her tone made it clear the matter was not up for discussion.

The following Monday, Jada and her friends, downcast over the past week's events, walked to school slower than usual. Puffy black clouds in the distance underscored the group's gloomy disposition.

Susan Gatewood tried to lighten the mood. "Oh, I hope we don't get too much snow. Father's taking us to the Walnut Street Theater tonight to attend a play—The Black Crook,"

The group agreed attending a stage production would be exciting, but Jada raised a concern, "You might have a problem." She pointed skyward. "Look at those snow clouds. It's cold enough to make the roads icy this evening."

Susan held up both hands with her fingers crossed as they entered the school. "I feel lucky. It'll be a great evening."

By the time Jada and her friends walked from their classroom at noon an inch of ice and snow covered the ground. Simon Stokes waited in the Morgans' enclosed coach to take the girls to their homes. The gang of hoydens joked and laughed as they piled into the carriage. Jada shouted "Speed it up, Simon. We're freezing."

Simon popped the reins, the horse snorted clouds of frost, and began a slow walk. "I can't go too fast with these slick streets, Miss Jada."

Over the next hour he delivered his cargo of shivering students and returned to the Morgan mansion with Jada. "Whew, that was one scary ride," he said as he pulled into the carriage house. She laughed and dashed for the warmth of the mansion.

Rebecca had hot tea and an apple waiting for Jada on the table in the kitchen. She finished her snack and went straight to the clinic in the basement to check for any patients.

Several inches of snow had accumulated and was still falling at sunset. She looked out the window. I guess the Gatewoods won't be attending the play tonight.

After putting the day's entries into the doctor's log, she pushed the ledger aside, and opened a text book. She had missed almost two weeks of school and was anxious to catch up. If she wasn't seeing patients, Jada liked to study in her office.

Morgan looked in on her at ten o'clock. "Jada, why don't you come to bed? You must be exhausted and it's late."

She peered over the textbook. "I have a lot of schoolwork to make up. I've missed so much. I'll only be a little longer."

Jack kissed her forehead. "Okay, but don't stay up too late. You need your rest."

An hour later Jada was still pouring over her lessons when a loud pounding on the clinic door shattered the silence. She rushed to the entrance in an effort to prevent the noise from waking Jack. A stranger met her with a high-pitched shriek. "Oh, thank god, you're still awake!"

He nervously shifted from one foot to the other. "Terrible wreck down the block—two carriages crashed. One was going too fast, and slid down the hill through the intersection. It knocked the second one over and landed on top of it. Killed two horses!" He raised his voice to emphasize the enormity of the disaster. "Lots of people hurt—some real bad."

Jada asked quietly, "How many?"

"I don't know. Maybe ten, maybe more! Gawks showed up at the wreck pretty fast. They're bringing the injured here."

Curious citizens began to congregate at the door, and some were already carrying mangled victims into the clinic. Jada directed a man in the crowd to the rear of the mansion. "Run back to the gardener's house and tell Simon and Rebecca to get here, now!" He sprinted off.

Scanning the crowd at the entrance, she spotted Amanda Armstrong's father. "Mr. Armstrong, please run upstairs and wake up Doctor Morgan. Tell him to come right away."

13

The Apprentice in Action

WITH THE CRISIS EXPANDING by the minute, Jada took charge in Jack's absence. She was everywhere at once, triaging the injured and comforting relatives of the victims. When Simon and Rebecca rushed in, Jada shouted over the hubbub, "Rebecca, set up the two folding beds, one in my office and one in Doctor Morgan's. Then get me as many pillowcases as you can find, and heat some water. Have Simon bring it down when it boils."

As she collected medical instruments on a tray, she called to Simon who was gathering bandages from a cabinet. "Fetch the long tables from the foyer and the kitchen, and put them in the storeroom for treatment benches—ask some men in the crowd to lend a hand. After that, go upstairs and send Rebecca down here. Keep bringing hot water to me until we're done."

Jada tossed the pillowcases to a woman standing outside the entrance. "Find some others to help and fill these about half full with snow." She watched as several women scurried to load the linen cases.

She turned to walk away when an undersized man with a scruffy haircut shouted from the crowd, "Ma'am, can you use an extra pair of hands? I was a hospital orderly in Washington during the war."

"You bet. Get in here!" Jada grabbed the man's arm and pulled him through the doorway.

He introduced himself. "My name's Shorty Hoskins."

Only minutes after she brought Shorty inside, the women returned with the snow-filled pillowcases. Jada and Hoskins seized the loaded bags. "Great, thank you ladies," she said as they hurried toward the patients.

"Mr. Hoskins, two kids with broken limbs are in the back room. Put these cold compresses around the breaks, and stay with them unless Doctor Morgan or I call you. Thanks for your assistance."

Shorty nodded, "Yes ma'am." He dashed off with three ice packs.

Before he reached the back room, Jada was in Jack's office with two snow-loaded pillowslips. She put one under the neck of an unconscious man with a head injury and the other over his forehead.

Jada then went to a teenage girl with massive facial injuries. She stifled a grimace as she checked the girl's mangled face. "I'm going to inject you with some morphine to stop the pain. I'll be right here while I take care of this lady. You'll be fine."

Jada turned her attention to Dora Thomas, an expectant mother in labor on a cot beside the teenager. "You've injured your ribs. We'll tape them for support when you push." She poured several drops of liquid on a cloth. "I'll put you to sleep now with a bit of chloroform. You'll have a new little one when you wake up."

"How safe is that? I mean for my baby," the woman asked.

Jada patted Mrs. Thomas' hand. "It's definitely safe. Even Queen Victoria used chloroform for the birth of her last child." Dora was soon unconscious.

"Rebecca, stay with Mrs. Thomas and tell me if she starts to wake up. I want to keep her under until the baby comes."

"I helped birth dozens of little ones. This lady will be all right." Rebecca shook her head. "Where was this chloroform stuff when I was making babies?"

As soon as Jack stepped into the clinic, Jada began giving him details without his asking. "Nine are alive. I've put a female covered in blood in your treatment room. She has a sucking chest wound, single entry. I sealed the puncture with a piece of rubber sheet until you got here. Don't know who she is—her face is covered with blood."

She motioned to the unconscious man on a folding cot. "That's Lawrence Thomas, the lawyer. He has a depressed fracture in his hairline over the right eye. His pupils are uneven—most likely bleeding around his brain. You may need to trephine him."

Jada nodded toward the man sitting in Jack's office. "That's Goins, the Thomas family coachman. Mr. Goins has a compound fracture—his femur. He'll need surgery."

"The large fellow on the floor is the other driver. Dead—no pulse and no fog on the mirror. I wanted you to check before I had him carried to the closet behind the storeroom."

Jada glanced down the hall. "A young boy, age twelve, and a girl about nine are in the back room. The lad has a broken forearm and the nine-year-old, a fractured tibia above her ankle. Her knee is also swollen, but I think that's just a bad sprain. I can handle those two." Jack smiled to himself as he listened to Jada give her self-assured, professional assessment.

"A teenage girl and a pregnant woman are in my treatment room. The expectant mother is Dora Thomas, Mr. Thomas' wife. The wreck sent her into labor. She's about 8 months, maybe a bit more. The problem is a couple of broken ribs. She's in a great deal of pain—as much from the breaks as from the contractions. I've put her under with chloroform. Rebecca is sitting with her."

"Good decision, but keep an eye on her," instructed Jack.

Jada continued with her evaluations, "The teenager. Oh god!" She went silent for a second. "That's my friend, Susan Gatewood. I couldn't tell—her face is so damaged. The woman with the chest wound must be her mother—Shit!" Jada slipped into the trooper-taught profanity from her childhood days at Fort Craig.

Jack put a comforting hand on her arm. "You've got them well sorted. Don't let Susan distract you. We need to fix them all, so let's get busy."

Jada rushed back and checked Susan. The morphine was taking effect, and she was groggy but awake. Jada gave her friend's hand a quick squeeze to reassure her. "We'll give it a little more time. You'll feel better before long."

She left Susan and she hurried to the two youngsters in the back room. "How are my children doing?" she asked in a calm voice as she entered. "Goodness gracious, Freddy Gatewood! I didn't recognize you. Is Mr. Hoskins taking care of you?"

"He's a good story teller, but my arm hurts real bad." Freddy hugged the cold bag of snow tighter against his injury.

Jada patted his cheek. "Freddy I'm afraid your arm's broken, but we can fix it." She gave a comforting smile. "I'll push the bone together and then we'll put on a cast to hold everything in place."

She poured small doses of laudanum into two glasses for Freddy and the girl. "Fixing it will hurt a little, but I know you are brave a boy. Here, drink this so it won't hurt much."

With the matter of his bravery on the line, Freddy replied, "I guess." Tears rolled down his face as Jada carefully set the bones, but he remained quiet.

"Shorty, how are you with the casting business?"

The former army medic responded, "Well, I've put about a thousand casts on during the war. This is as easy as it gets." He threw a hand up in a nonchalant gesture.

"You'll find some gutter splints over on those shelves. Bring one for Freddy. Then get one of the full leg metal casts for our little lady's knee and ankle.

As Hoskins retrieved the splints and began putting one on the boy's arm, Jada went to the girl. "You're not flirting with my friend, Freddy, are you?"

The tearful youngster whimpered, "No."

Jada sat beside the young lass. "Do you have a name?"

The child blubbered, "Missy Thomas."

"Well Missy, I'm going to fix you up like I did Freddy. You'll have a little pain too, but you'll get a special shiny cast, much prettier than his."

When Jada started to align the girl's broken bone, the child screeched and pulled away, prompting Hoskins to hold her leg steady while Jada worked.

When Jada finished, she said, "Okay kids, the bad stuff is over. Mr. Hoskins will take care of you." She gave Shorty a nod and said, "Stay with them but get me if you have any problems. Thanks again." She looked over her shoulder as she left the room. "Children, be still until he finishes with those casts. It won't hurt."

Susan was pain free when Jada returned to her, but was frantic with worry about her face. "Oh, Jada, how bad is it? Everybody will call me scar-face. Just kill me. I can't go through life looking like a freak."

"Hush that you silly thing." Jada moved around Susan assessing each of her wounds. "You know I'm the best seamstress in our group." Susan tried to smile, or Jada thought she did, but she was so disfigured, Jada couldn't tell.

"We'll work on the top of your head first." A sharp edge had struck Susan at the hairline and ripped a large patch of her scalp rearward to the middle of her head. A hairy flap was folded back to expose the skull from ear to ear. Jada felt a cold chill as she lifted the flap and looked at Susan's bare skull. A memory of her dead father being scalped six years earlier flashed through her mind. She froze in place. Her eyes moistened and she fell silent.

Susan immediately misinterpreted her reaction. "Jada, are you all right? Say something! It must be horrible. Am I going to die?"

Her friend's panic snapped Jada out of her dolor. "Oh Susan, you'll be fine. It isn't so awful. Your scalp is torn a trifle but that's easy to repair. You'll still be beautiful."

Before Jada began stitching, she glanced at Rebecca who was sitting beside Dora Thomas. "How are things going with her?"

"She's doin' okay. That sleeping medicine is working good."

"Can you come here for a minute or two?" Jada nodded toward Susan.

"Yes ma'am. This lady is doing all the work, I'm just watching."

"Grab Susan's hair at the back of her head and pull the scalp forward to loosen it enough for me to close the wound."

Susan fretted as Rebecca pulled and Jada stitched. "Will the scars be hideous?" Susan's voice was doleful.

"I don't know, honey. I'm making the stitches tiny and sewing from the inside so the damage won't show much." Jada thought honesty would be best. "Your hair will cover the biggest scar. It won't show. The other scars are likely to be more visible, but I'm trying to keep them small." Jada took a deep breath, puffed her cheeks, and concentrated on her sewing.

After finishing the scalp, Jada focused on the serious gash above Susan's mouth. Her friend's upper lip hung by a single strip of flesh, exposing her gums and teeth.

Jada reattached the dangling piece, and closed the last cut along her cheek. She knew when Susan healed, her face wouldn't be the same.

At last, all her patients were resting and Jack had done what he could for the others. After Jada offered to stay the night with the patients, he went back to bed. She went to her office, depressed and crying. All the blood, wounds and moans rekindled memories of the slaughter in the New Mexico mountains when she was eleven. She put her head on her desk and contined to weep.

14

Harry and Jada

JADA WAS SURPRISED when she realized they had worked all night. Mrs. Thomas delivered a healthy baby girl before noon, and the two children were taken home by relatives. Shorty Hoskins vanished back into the crowd without a word and an undertaker had come for Ian McGregor's corpse. Mr. and Mrs. Thomas, Susan Gatewood and her mother remained in the clinic for continued treatment. Everyone else was gone.

Harry came by for his usual late afternoon visit and found Jada sitting beside Susan holding her hand. "Jada, looks like you've been busy. Hello Susan." Harry didn't mention Susan's appearance. He was accustomed to the sight of cut and puffy faces from his boxing matches.

Jada patted Susan on the shoulder. "I'll come by again before I turn in. Doctor Morgan will be here tonight."

She and Harry walked to her office where she wiped her forehead with a small towel and felt the energy drain from her body. "It's been a long night."

"Jada, you look exhausted. You must have had a rough go." He reached out and gently stroked her cheek, but caught himself mid-stroke and pulled back.

She smiled at his shyness. "I'm glad you didn't make a big fuss over Susan's injuries. She's worried she'll be disfigured for life." She sighed and touched her upper lip without thinking.

"Will she? Is she hurt that bad?"

"It's serious. She'll recover but she won't look the same." Jada moved to Harry, and hugged him tightly. He returned the hug and kissed her on the cheek. Surprised, Jada quickly turned her face to receive more.

"Whoa." Harry pulled back. "You've got a speck of blood in your ear." He reached in his pocket for a handkerchief and began to dab at the spot. Must've been a nightmare!"

"You should have been here before I washed up. I was covered." She moved closer again. Darn, she thought. We've been seeing each other long enough to at least share a kiss when we're alone. A bit of romance would be nice.

"I'd better leave." He took a small step back, once more putting a space between them. "You're tired and I have to study."

"Oh, Harry don't go." She pointed toward the four patients in the recovery rooms. "Not much left to do now except check on them. Please stay a while. All this brought back some bad memories. I need the company and we could study together." She hoped that if he remained, his brief kiss on her cheek would lead to more, but Harry didn't cooperate.

When Jack returned to the clinic two hours later, he found Harry reading beside Jada's desk and Jada asleep across from him, her head resting on her arms.

"She okay, Harry?"

"Yes sir, she's been checking the patients about every fifteen minutes but she's worn out. After the last time, she finally collapsed. I went around once after that and everyone seems okay. They're all asleep."

Jack beamed with pride. "Harry, she was splendid last evening—saved a couple of lives." He gently shook Jada awake.

"Time for bed, young lady. Go get some sleep." She stood with drowsy-eyes as Jack gave her a hug. "Harry, see her upstairs. It's my turn to stay with the patients."

Harry walked Jada up to her bedroom. At the door they stopped and faced each other. She eased nearer and embraced him. The warmth of his muscular body against hers and the scent of sandalwood cologne sent shivers through her. When he bent down and tenderly kissed her lips, her heart pounded and chills raced up her spine. She pulled him closer and kissed him harder.

Flustered, Harry maneuvered free from her hug. "Good night, Jada. Now go get some sleep." He retreated swiftly down the stairs.

Two days later, Jada still had Harry's kiss on her mind when a correspondent from the *Philadelphia Inquirer* showed up at the Morgan Clinic. He spoke at length with Jack and relatives visiting the injured. Jada noticed those being interviewed glancing at her or nodding in her direction. After interviewing the others, the writer asked Jada to pose with Jack for a hasty portrait. When she started to leave, he intercepted her. "Miss Morgan, may we speak a moment?" Before she could answer, Susan cried out from across the hall.

"Not now. She needs my attention." Jada pointed to Susan's room and rushed off. After examining her friend, she leaned from the door and told the journalist, "This is going to take a while."

The newsman waited for a few minutes but soon became restless. He closed his notepad and left.

The next day the *Philadelphia Inquirer* carried a front page article featuring the photograph of Jack and Jada:

One Killed in Carriage Collision

A serious carriage wreck occurred in North Philadelphia late Monday evening. Ian McGregor, driver of one of the carriages died of a crushed skull. Six others received injuries. Mr. Frederick Gatewood, the well-known banker was the only uninjured passenger. Lawrence Thomas, a prominent attorney, suffered a grievous head wound and remains in serious condition. Mrs. Thomas, eight months pregnant, was injured and sent into labor by the accident. She gave birth to a healthy girl on Tuesday. Two children involved had broken limbs, as did Tom Goins, the Gatewood family driver. One young woman received severe facial cuts. All the casualties were treated at the Morgan clinic.

Patients and onlookers alike commented on the quick actions of Dr. Morgan's adopted daughter and apprentice, Jada. Observers who were there during the episode cited the young aide for brilliant and speedy acts that saved at least two lives.

The 17-year-old trainee triaged the victims before the doctor arrived, recruited and organized volunteers from onlookers to assist, set bones, stitched wounds, delivered a baby, and comforted the injured. Dr. Morgan is quoted as saying "Jada's medical skill is unquestioned. She was remarkable."

Although her friends made much to do about the article, Jada brushed off their comments. "I didn't do anything special. It's what you do in a clinic. There was just a lot of it."

By the end of the week most the patients were released to be seen by Jack on home visits. Only Lawrence Thomas, whose head injury required continued treatment, remained.

Hours of convincing by Jada finally persuaded Susan to return to school after her girlfriends assured her she was still beautiful. Bangs hid the large scar along her forehead but the damage to her upper lip was obvious. It forced Susan's mouth into a little pout which her boyfriend, Albert Amos, pronounced to be most seductive.

Two weeks after publication of the news article, Jada and her friends returned from school to find a larger sign had replaced the placard that formerly stood in the Morgan mansion's front lawn:

The Morgan Clinic
Jack Morgan, MD
Physician and Surgeon
Jada P. Morgan
Physician

The girls congratulated Jada with hugs and kudos. She thanked them and hurried inside to find Jack. "Father! The new clinic sign says I'm a physician." She glowed with excitement.

"I wanted to surprise you. I presented an application for you to the Philadelphia College of Physicians and Surgeons. After they read the comments from our patients, and hearing my description of your work, there was an immediate agreement that you should be licensed as a member. When that article appeared in the Inquirer, the vote was unanimous. Accepting a woman in that group is rare, especially one who is only seventeen-years-old."

"So now I can practice on my own?"

"Yes indeed, but I still want you to get a degree from the Women's Medical College."

Jada beamed at the news. "I can't wait to tell Harry."

Harry arrived for his evening visit as Jack was leaving the mansion. "The new sign sir—does Jada have her doctor's license now?"

"She certainly does and she's busting with pride." Jack pulled on his overcoat and gloves.

"Wonderful! This is important to her," Harry said. He shook Jack's hand and glanced around for Jada.

"Wish I had time to say more, but I need to run. I'm late for a meeting about the proposed hospital for the medical school. Simon's driving me and Rebecca is off for the day. Jada's in her room. She's anxious to give you the news so just go in and shout for her."

Jada responded to Harry's call in a cheerful voice. "I'm upstairs, Harry. Come on up. I have something to tell you."

She was standing in the doorway of her bedroom, bright eyed and bubbling with excitement. "I just received my medical license." She threw her arms around him and bussed him soundly on the lips.

"Come in," she said as she pulled him inside, closed and locked the door, then gave him another passionate kiss. This time, Harry responded.

She held her mouth to his while she pressed him against the bedroom wall and began to unbutton her blouse and skirt. She stepped back and the clothes fell around her ankles. She had occasionally continued the traditional Apache practice of wearing no undergarments. This was one of those occasions.

Stark naked, she extended her arms and faced Harry. "Well?"

In that instant Harry kissed his shyness goodbye, and focused on kissing Jada.

He reached out, cupped her awe-inspiring breasts, embraced her, and gave her a deep, passionate kiss. "What now?" he asked.

"Take your clothes off and let's find out."

They kissed again, and moved to Jada's bed with their nude bodies pressed together. "We can talk about my medical license later."

15

Marriage Proposal Declined

JADA AND HARRY GREW ever closer as the months passed. They spent time together almost daily—studied with each other nightly, attended the entertainment attractions around town, sat for hours in the Morgan's garden, and made love at every opportunity. Harry became a fixture in the Morgan mansion, often taking his meals with the family and on occasion slept—or at least Jack thought he did—in the guest room.

During this period, Pierpont visited the Philadelphia Morgans frequently and developed an interest in Harry and his endeavors in the ring. He was impressed with the young man's good manners and his obvious devotion to Jada. When he learned Harry was studying law, he announced his firm would soon need some additional lawyers.

"Harry I'll pay for your last two years of school, if you'll take a job with me after you graduate. You can start right away as a part time clerk for my lawyer here in Philadelphia and can still finish your education."

Pierpont patted his enormous belly with both hands and added, "My only condition is for you to quit fighting. Your athletics won't give you enough time for school and work." He smiled and added, "Besides, I don't want any punch-drunk lawyers on my staff."

Harry and Jada were flabbergasted, and later she asked, "Are you going to take his offer?"

"I'll miss the fighting but I'd be crazy if I didn't.

Jada entered the Women's Medical College of Pennsylvania in the fall of 1873. Admission was easy for young Dr. Morgan. She possessed the most important requisite for admittance—she came from a wealthy family who could afford the tuition fees.

With her clinical experience and Miss Mather's heavy emphasis on scientific subjects, medical school was not difficult. Her course of study took three years followed by a six month practicum. Classes met in the morning, so Jada was able to continue her work in the Morgan Clinic in the afternoons and still have time for Harry in the evenings.

As soon as Harry graduated from law school in 1874, Pierpont requested that he move to the big city. Several important legal battles loomed and J.P. wanted Harry on the New York team.

The day after learning of the need to relocate, Harry went with Jada for an evening stroll in the Morgan's garden. "Jada, I'd like to ask your father if he would allow me to marry you and take you to New York with me. I think our life would be exciting." He kissed her softly.

Jada pulled away with a troubled look. "Harry, I love you very much, but I have another year of classes, then a six months practicum at the Blockley Almshouse." She wiped moistness from her eyes. "I'd need to quit my education. I'm sorry. I can't do that." She gave him a sad smile.

"I thought you said you loved me?"

"You know I do, but I'm not willing to give up medicine to be a housewife." It was clear she had no intention of changing her mind.

Stung by her reply, Harry stepped back. She realized her rejection hurt him, and made an effort to soften the blow. "New York and Philadelphia aren't so far by rail. We can visit on your days off. Let me complete school while you get settled up there. Then we'll talk."

For a time after Harry left for the big city, he wrote Jada often and visited her on most weekends, but after several months his letters and the trips became less frequent. At first, Jada felt depressed, and although she didn't want to lose Harry, she knew she needed her freedom. She was sure she wasn't ready for marriage.

On June 17, 1876, Jada completed her practicum at the Blockley Almshouse caring for Philadelphia's indigent, and graduated with her MD degree on June 24. Two weeks later, Jada received a letter from Pierpont:

July 8, 1876

My Dearest Niece:

Congratulations on your recent commencement from the Women's Medical College. I suppose I should now address you as Dr. Jada P. Morgan, MD! As a graduation gift, I've added $200,000 to an account your mother established for you in her will and which I managed since her death. The balance now stands at $800,000 and continues to grow. Mary requested I wait until you graduated from medical school to inform you of the funds.

As an additional reward for completing college, and as a favor to me, I request your company at a formal dinner party in Washington. Fanny is steaming her way to Europe again. Consequently, I find myself in need of an attractive and brilliant companion. The occasion includes some interesting people whom I think you will enjoy meeting. The party is scheduled for the evening of July 23. We can leave that morning by rail from Philadelphia and be there well ahead of time.

I expect to return to Philadelphia on the 25th.

With admiration and affection,

Uncle Pierpont

Jada and J.P. arrived in Washington in the early afternoon of the 23rd. Pierpont hired a carriage from the Baltimore and Potomac Railroad Station to the posh Willard Hotel down the block from the White House.

At seven o'clock that evening, a shiny coach with gold filigree trim pulled up to the front door of the inn. J.P. wore white tie and tails. Jada chose a long sleeved, tight fitting yellow dress of silk brocade which exposed a bit of cleavage and accentuated her exquisite figure.

Pierpont gave her an appraising look and said, "Oh my, Jada, you're going to knock 'em dead tonight."

The carriage carrying the Morgans eased its way along Pennsylvania Avenue, by Lafayette Park, and came to a stop in front of the executive mansion.

"Uncle Pierpont, this is the White House. Why are we stopping here?" Jada asked J.P.

"Doctor Jada, our party is right in there." He pointed to the main entrance between the columns.

Jada gasped. "With the president?"

"With the president, a few cabinet members, a general, and most of their wives. I told you we'd be dining with some exciting people." Pierpont chuckled as Jada stared open-mouth at the presidential mansion.

16

Washington, DC

LUCY HAYES, the President's wife, greeted Jada and Pierpont as they entered the White House. She introduced them to three unescorted women; the Secretary of War's wife, Amanda McCrary; General Sherman's better half, Ellen; and Margarethe Shurz, the Secretary of the Interior's spouse.

Mrs. Hayes, who prided herself on her sartorial insight, wore a white hoop-skirt trimmed in red and blue with a lace-lined bodice revealing a generous glimpse of cleavage. A small American flag was attached beneath her bosom. She had worn the same outfit for the 4th of July celebration nineteen days before.

As soon as Pierpont and Jada entered, a butler offered them lemonade in crystal glasses. Jada smiled, thanked the server, and gave Pierpont a puzzled look. "Lemonade?"

"The First Lady is a supporter of the temperance movement." Pierpont took a swallow and swirled his drink in appreciation.

"She's convinced the president to ban alcoholic beverages in the White House. They call her Lemonade Lucy."

While Jada and J.P. discussed the merits of Lucy's alcohol-free potion, President Hayes entered the room with an entourage of five officials. "Sorry for our tardiness," he said. "A serious situation is developing around the country. Gentlemen, I believe everyone knows each other except for Mr. J.P. Morgan and Dr. Jada Morgan. Dr. Morgan and J.P, this is Secretary of War George McCrary, General William Sherman, commanding the army, and Carl Shurz, Secretary of the Interior. Last but not least, these two gentlemen are Ezra Hayt, the Commissioner of Indian Affairs and his son, Edward."

Hayt's son was short and sported a pencil-thin mustache. His oily black hair was slicked down and parted down the middle. Aside from his condescending arrogance, Jada found his incessant fixation on her breasts to be irksome and it made her uncomfortable. She didn't like the feeling, and she didn't like Edward Hayt.

Jada cordially greeted all the dignitaries except for Hayt and Edward. She ignored Edward and gave the commissioner a frosty acknowledgment. "Commissioner Hayt." She declined to extend her hand. Instant animosity flared between the two.

"You appear to be Indian, Miss Morgan," the annoying bureaucrat said with an irritating smirk, and ignoring her correct title.

"A very astute observation, Mr. Commissioner. I am so pleased you noticed," Jada replied.

Hayt's face rumpled into a scowl, but before he could respond, Jada turned and started chatting with the women.

After a few minutes the conversation among the group began to dwindle, and Lucy Hayes announced, "Dinner's ready. Shall we eat?"

The seating arrangements placed Jada beside Pierpont and across the table from Commissioner Hayt and Edward. Jada couldn't watch either of them as they ate. The Indian Office Commissioner stuffed his mouth and talked with it full. Edward continued to be more interested in her chest than his sirloin.

Halfway thorough the meal, the president brought up the issue troubling him. "The national economy is on the verge of collapse. Over 18,000 businesses have gone bankrupt." His expression emphasized his concern. "The trade deficit is increasing and speculators on Wall Street are going broke. Jobs are almost nonexistent. People are blaming the government and the railroad owners." He paused and the room fell silent. Not a sound was heard except Ezra Hayt smacking his lips.

The president continued, "The public is furious. Secretary McCrary can catch us up on the latest."

"Railroad strikes and riots are beginning to erupt everywhere. Strikers all over the country are preventing trains from leaving stations."

McCrary studied a paper beside his plate, then motioned to Pierpont. "Thinking of it Mr. Morgan, I suggest you and your niece stay here in Washington, or take the stagecoach back to Philadelphia. I don't think the railroads will be running for a while."

The president thanked McCrary and took up the conversation. "Mr. Morgan, as you know, the government is in serious financial distress." He clucked his tongue and continued, "The Secretary of Treasury should be here, but he's down with a case of pneumonia. He believes you may be the one person in the country with the financial wherewithal to help. He suggests if you are willing, the treasury could issue guaranteed bonds up to fifty million dollars which would be available only for you to purchase."

"Can you afford that?" Jada whispered with an expression of disbelief.

Pierpont patted her hand. "I think we can swing it—with the proper interest."

The president took a swallow of lemonade and added, "It may not be necessary, but I would need your assurance that you would be willing, if it becomes unavoidable."

"Then, sir, you have my promise that I'll come to the aid of my country if needed—at three percent interest of course. Pierpont leaned back, blew a cloud of cigar smoke, and smiled.

President Hayes sipped his lemonade then changed the subject. "The other item which we must discuss is our effort to control government spending. I want to review the expenses for every department." He looked around the table. "Cuts are imperative. Commissioner Hayt, I understand you have a proposal for savings in the Indian Bureau?"

Hayt glimpsed at Jada. "I don't believe it's appropriate to have an Indian woman present while we discuss such a serious Indian Service matter."

Pierpont's face flushed and was about to offer an angry response when Jada raised her hand, "May I ask Mr. Hayt a question?"

"Of course, doctor, ask away." President Hayes seemed amused.

Hayt's face clouded as Jada leaned toward him. "Mr. Hayt, as I understand it you want me to leave the room while you discuss the Indian Office budget because I'm an Indian woman. I wonder which part you find offensive—the woman, or the Indian?" She waited for a moment as Hayt weighed the repercussions of his answer. When she got no reply, she said, "If it's because I'm a female, I suggest feminists throughout the country will have you in their sights as soon as the word gets out. And you can bet this will get out." Jada took a sip of lemonade and smiled.

She continued, "If you find the Indian part bothersome, one might think President Hayes should reconsider his selection of you as the primary trustee for the country's Native Americans. So which is it?"

All the men, except Hayt and Edward, chuckled while the women covered their mouths at such a brazen response, but Hayes' eyes brightened with amusement.

Hayt had continued stuffing his mouth throughout the episode, and when he started to answer, a piece of steak lodged in his windpipe. He gagged, tried to cough it up, and began a series of grunts as he clutched at his throat. Bill Crook, the chief executive's bodyguard, rushed from his place behind the president to aid the stricken commissioner. He pounded on Hayt's back to no avail. Jada jumped up and dashed around the table, knocking over her chair in the process. She gave directions to Crook in a surprisingly calm voice as she rushed to the gagging official. "Grab his arms from behind and stand him up."

Once Jada reached the blue-skinned Commissioner, she told Crook, "Now hold tight." Standing in front of Hayt, she balled her fist and swung hard, hitting Hayt in his sizable paunch.

Hayt continued to gag and only managed a panicked "Ugh!"

Crook moved to interrupt an apparent attack on the Commissioner, but he was too slow. Jada pulled her arm back and struck Hayt with a fierce blow just as she had been taught by Harry Trenchcott. The uppercut landed below the Hayt's breadbasket. This time a large chunk of half-chewed steak flew from the bureaucrat's mouth with a "Plewheeee." The morsel shot across the table, over the mashed potatoes and embedded in Lemonade Lucy's ample cleavage, just above the Old Glory on her bodice. The little flag fluttered with the impact.

A sucking sound resonated as Hayt inhaled and wiped his mouth. "Damn! I couldn't breathe." He continued to cough briefly, but didn't bother to thank Jada for saving his life.

General Sherman stood and gave Jada a theatrical bow, "Perfect boxing form, Doctor Morgan. You resembled John L. Sullivan throwing that punch! Where did you learn to do that?"

Embarrassed, Jada answered in a hushed voice, "A friend taught me. He was a professional boxer and wrestler."

"You learned well. What might his name be?" asked Sherman.

The dignitaries strained to hear Jada's soft-spoken reply. "Harry Trenchcott. He fought John L. Sullivan once. Sullivan broke his nose."

The president gave a hearty laugh and pointed his fork at Jada. "So you trained with Trenchcott the Terrible? No wonder."

After she returned to her seat, Pierpont leaned over and whispered, "Did you have to hit him twice?"

Jada bit her lip in thought. "Yes." She puffed her cheeks. "I missed the first one on purpose. That was for me. The second one under his diaphragm was to unplug his pipes."

17

Roger Bullard Meets Jada

PIERPONT AND JADA rode alone on the Washington to Philadelphia stage-coach. Pierpont had paid for all the seats so they could travel in private. After settling in, they rehashed the previous night's events.

"Thank you, Uncle Pierpont. I enjoyed everything. The White House is magnificent and the guests were delightful—well, except for the Hayts."

Pierpont chuckled. "I think you left quite an impression—especially when you saved Commissioner Hayt from an embarrassing death. Whamming that pompous twit a couple of good ones proved to be the best part of the evening."

Jada stared from the window without speaking for a moment, then said, "You know if Ezra Hayt remains the Commissioner, all the tribes in this country are in trouble. His plans will be catastrophic."

"You may be right Jada, but Secretary Schurz likes Hayt's policies. I'm afraid the Indians are stuck with him."

On reaching Philadelphia, Jada stood on tiptoes, hugged Pierpont and kissed his cheek. "Thank you again. I had such a wonderful time." Pierpont hired a city-carriage to take her home, and continued his trip to New York alone.

When Jada walked in the front door of the Morgan house she found an envelope from Harry on the table in the foyer. Unlike his earlier letters, this one was a single sheet. Harry included a tintype of himself standing with a spindly blonde woman.

Jada slowly unfolded the solitary page and read:

Dear Jada,

I would prefer to tell you all of this in person but I'm unable to leave work at this time. I feel I must let you know I've asked Amity Denise DeVoe, the lady in the picture, to marry me and she has agreed. She aspires to be nothing but my wife and a mother to our children. I believe we are right for each other.

Jada, I loved you for a long time and I still do, but we want such different things in life. I'm so sorry.

Yours truly,
Harry

Jada walked to the veranda, read the message again, and studied the tintype for several minutes. Hmmm, at least six feet tall. She'd be pretty except for her crooked nose. Jada smiled as she thought of a kiss between the two. It would be impossible without a collision of their noses and appeared only doable because the woman's prominent proboscis and Harry's broken sniffer tilted in opposite directions.

She sat in a porch rocker and reread the letter for the third time. In a low voice, she said to herself, "Harry, you have been my only love, but we wanted such different lives. I've expected this for a while. We were good together, but it would have never lasted."

That night Jada sat at her desk in the clinic and penned a short reply.

Dear Harry,

Thank you for the kind letter informing me of your good fortune and intentions. I imagine Amity will make a perfect wife for you. I pray you two will have many children and be the happiest.

Sincerely, Jada

A good letter, she thought, but she had to rewrite it—teardrops streaked the ink.

The breakup with Harry left Jada feeling her life was crumbling. Her old school friends seldom saw each other, their get-togethers became less frequent, Mary was gone, and Harry was no longer on the scene. After her split with Harry, Jada focused on her work in the clinic, but she needed something different.

In mid-December of 1876, an invitation from Judy Lawson to her family's New Year's Eve party launched a series of life-changing events for Jada. She found a handwritten note on the back of the embossed card:

Jada, it would be wonderful if you could come. I'm off work for the holidays and almost everyone plans to be here. It will be like old times.

The Lawson's yearly bash had become a tradition in those parts of Philadelphia. Party goers agreed the decorations were outstanding, and gas lights imparted the perfect ambiance. Music from a string octet wafted over tables piled high with food.

All of Jada's friends attended except Joanne Tomley whose absence provided for much supposition about her fate. The group was catching up on their recent lives, but the gossip stopped when they caught sight of Patsy Fike working her way toward them.

"Oh darn." Judy warned her friends. "Everybody hang on. Here comes Miss Fike."

Patsy oiled up to the group. "I just came over, Judy, to tell you your family's annual social is the perfect way to start the year, and the holiday trimming is splendid. I'm here with Reggie Allsap. He's an accountant with the J.P. Morgan firm. He says he knows Harry Trenchcott, Jada. You know Harry's getting married to a New York girl. Patsy scrutinized Jada for a reaction. Disappointment showed on her face.

"Old news, Patsy," Jada said with a ho-hum tone. "I gave Harry and Amity my blessing some time ago." She looked over at Patsy's consort and changed the subject. "Reggie is an attractive fellow. Lucky catch, Patsy."

"Oh, he isn't reeled in yet, but I'm working on it."

"Well, the best of luck. You two make a charming couple."

"Thank you, Jada. Before I go, I'd like to invite you to visit the Philadelphia Ladies Archery Club. I'm the president. With your background, I'm sure you would enjoy it."

"I appreciate the offer, Patsy. I may take you up on that, but I haven't held a bow since I came to Philadelphia."

"I'll help you." Patsy gave a wicked grin and hurried back to Reggie who appeared to be enjoying another young woman's company a bit too much.

"Jada, don't you dare go to her club!" Judy wagged her finger for emphasis. "She's some kind of archery champion, and only wants to show off and beat you at something."

"It doesn't matter and it would be fun to shoot again. My Indian father spent a lot of time teaching me after my brother died, but everybody in our village was a better shot than I."

As the evening passed, Jada danced with a series of boring young men. After one mind-numbing partner, Jada retreated to her group and shook her head. "That's all for me. Poor pickings tonight."

The clutch of friends was discussing the paltry selection of interesting males in Philadelphia when they noticed Jada stiffen slightly. Her eyes widened, and her eyebrows rose. She almost always kept her emotions from public view, but on this occasion, she had spotted something extraordinary. Susan turned to find the source of Jada's interest.

"Oh, Jada, that's Roger Bullard. He attended West Point after his family moved from Philly. He's been stationed in Washington since he graduated. You can see why he's popular with the ladies."

As soon as Second Lieutenant Bullard stepped into the ballroom, several women surrounded him, all contending for his attention. Tall, about six feet, and clean shaven with a shock of blond hair, Roger, in his natty dress uniform, looked to be the epitome of a dashing cavalry officer. He obviously enjoyed the adulation.

Judy gave Jada a wink. "He's unattached and he's very adept at entertaining women. You might just find him amusing."

Bullard had greeted the Lawsons on his arrival, but became so ensnared by his phalanx of admirers he failed to notice the group of women standing with Judy off to the side. Jada feigned disinterest in Bullard as she bantered with her friends, but they had to smile as they watched her steal quick glances at the lieutenant.

Lieutenant Bullard was having an uproarious time. He laughed often as he dispensed a constant flow of drollery which left the throng of coquettes giggling, twittering, and sometimes blushing. He took frequent pauses to grace one or the other with a dance.

During his animated oration about army life in Washington, Bullard caught sight of Jada. He dropped his arms to his sides, stopped his monologue mid-sentence, and gave her an appraising look. He turned to his following, raised his hands palms up in a gesture of resigned appeasement, and moved through the crowd toward Judy's friends.

Without taking his eyes from Jada, Bullard greeted the women. "It's nice to see you ladies again." He smiled at Jada. "I don't believe we've met."

18

New Love

ROGER LOOKED AT JADA. "Doctor Morgan, do you dance?"

"Please call me Jada," she nodded and added, "Yes, I do."

"Then would you honor a klutzy-footed trooper with this waltz?"

"It might be fun to sally forth with a ham-footed soldier." Jada grinned and offered Roger her hand.

The waltz was a popular favorite, and several couples entered the dance floor. Jada and Roger started carefully, but soon went into beautiful swirling movements.

She stood in Roger's arms; back arched; and her head turned to the side as they glided across the floor. The duo moved with such grace the other dancers paused to watch as the army officer and the petite young woman triple timed it around the boards.

This is nice, Jada thought. He's an amazing dancer and so handsome. Unfortunately, all the girls say he's a womanizer.

On the sideline Jada's friend, Judy, couldn't contain herself. "Look at them—her eyes are closed and that smile. I think we're witnesses to an actual love-at-first-sight event."

When the music ended, the room burst into applause. Roger and Jada remained motionless and stared into each others' eyes. "You're a superb dancer," Jada said. "Roger, I've never enjoyed a dance more." She found herself taking rapid shallow breaths.

"Likewise. Perhaps we could find a place to talk where there isn't so much commotion?"

"I'd like that." Jada realized she had not released Roger's hand.

They found a refuge for partygoers in an anteroom and selected a table. "Tell me about yourself, Jada. I suspect you are not originally from here."

Jada demurred but reached across and touched his hand. "I want to know about you first." They began an intense talk about their lives and interests.

An hour passed before Judy came into the room and interrupted their conversation which had become increasingly personal. "I've searched all over for you two. I hate to break this up, Jada, but our guests are asking to visit with you. And Roger, that throng who welcomed you is upset over your absence."

As Judy led her away, Jada cast a glance at Roger and slid her hand softly across his.

When she returned to her friends, Jada was besieged with questions. "All right, doctor, what's the diagnosis?" Susan giggled as they clustered around Jada.

"Yes, Jada, don't hold back—tell us everything," Judy said.

"Well, Roger is a charmer. We have a lot in common. He's most interesting and was the perfect gentleman."

Worldly-wise Amanda raised an eyebrow. "Careful there, Jada. All gentlemen can be interesting when they are looking to bed a lady."

"I know, Amanda, but bedding isn't in my foreseeable plans." Jada stood on her tiptoes, straining to find Roger in the crowd. The lieutenant was nowhere to be seen.

The following day, Roger rolled up to the Morgan mansion in a hired carriage. Almost as soon as Simon Stokes answered the door, Jada appeared at the top of the staircase.

A broad smile lit her face as she descended the stairs to the front hall. "I'm glad you came. When you disappeared last night, I thought you had been dallying with me."

"I assure you that wasn't the case," he said. "I was under pressure from that horde of jezebels who surrounded me. If I went back to them, you might think the worst of me, and if I ignored them in favor of you, they would have flooded the room with gossip. It was better to leave the party."

"You're so thoughtful. I regret you left early, but I'm glad you came today." Is it possible he's more handsome than last night?

"I'm afraid I can't stay long. I'm due in Washington tomorrow morning." He hadn't taken his eyes off her since he arrived.

"That's a shame. Will you be coming back anytime soon?" she asked.

"Is next weekend too soon?"

"That's perfect. The clinic will be closed."

"Then it's a date. I'll be here Saturday. I'm assigned to General Sherman's office. I think he'll issue me a pass."

"General Sherman! Please give him my regards, and tell him if he doesn't let you off, I will speak to his wife."

Roger paled. "You know the general?"

"I spent an evening with him and Ellen in the White House about five months ago. They are such nice people."

A half hour later as Roger entered his hired carriage, Jada thought, This could turn into something interesting.

The next week Jada received several thick letters from Roger filled with flowery prose. One note read in part: I had occasion to mention your name to the general, who has fond memories of you. He raved about his visit with you at the White House. He says you saved the Commissioner's of Indian Affairs life. He also warned me not to box with you. What does he mean?

Roger Bullard was a man-about-town. He had achieved legendary levels of philandering in Philadelphia's best social circles before meeting Jada. One wag suggested it was easier to find a socialite Roger had seduced than one he had not.

In the months following their first meeting, Roger remained stationed in Washington, but he came to visit Jada almost every weekend. When Jack learned of the lieutenant's notoriety, he shared his concerns about Roger with Jada. "You're an adult, Jada, but your new friend has a terrible reputation. Surely you can do better."

She sighed and rallied to Roger's defense. "Daddy, after Harry Trenchcott, I'm careful with my feelings about men, but in all honesty, I like Roger, and he's shown complete respect for me."

Jada was aware of Roger's renown as an accomplished rake but once she assured herself he was a changed man, she dropped her doubts about him.

He in turn, frequently declared his undying love and concentrated on courting her in a style befitting a proper lady. The two were inseparable on those weekends he traveled to Philadelphia. He invariably found fascinating things to do and interesting places to visit. They dined in Philadelphia's best restaurants, and attended the most popular stage plays and musical concerts.

One Wednesday, Jada came into Jack's office holding a telegram. "Father, Roger can't come this weekend. There's a big convention in town and all the hotel rooms are taken. Can he stay here with us—please?"

Jack's opinion of Roger had changed over time as he watched the couple's fondness for each other grow. He hadn't heard of any new tales of the young fellow's indiscretions, and his devotion to Jada convinced Jack of his sincerity, but he remained cautious.

"Okay Jada, but I'll be keeping a careful eye on you two."

"Thank you, thank you, daddy. I'm sure there'll be no problems. I'd better run and get a telegram off."

On Friday afternoon, Jada showed Roger to the second floor guest room, just down the hall from hers. Jack's bedroom was between the two—a formidable bastion against an assault on Jada's chastity.

The following day, Roger took Jada on a picnic and walk along the wooded pathways of South Park. The huge forested preserve was just a short carriage ride from the city center. "Roger, you have such a knack. I think this place is a magical escape from the city." Standing on her tiptoes, she kissed him on the cheek. He turned and gave her a kiss on her lips. "Again," she said with her eyes closed. He kissed her once more.

The couple returned to the Morgan's house in the late afternoon. Before they left the carriage, Roger took Jada's hand. "Jada, it's been a wonderful day."

Jada smiled. "For me too," she sighed. "Almost perfect."

That evening, as they sat in the Morgan garden Roger moved closer to Jada. "I know we've only been together a few months and this is much too soon, but the general has told me I'll be transferred out west soon. I want to ask your father for your hand in marriage before my orders come down—if you agree."

"I do love you, Roger, and a wedding sounds wonderful, but you're right. This is awfully quick. Marriage would change so much for me." She was silent for a moment and puffed her cheeks as she considered what to say next. "I'd be giving up my medical practice here and starting over again. Give me a little time to work things out."

"Yes, of course." He gave her a quick playful kiss. "In the meantime, I'll notify General Sherman of our intentions. This may affect where the army assigns me."

The family sat up later than usual that evening. It was after eleven before they adjourned for the night. Lying sleepless in her bed, Jada heard Jack's door opened at midnight and again about one o'clock. That's probably the last time he'll check. Father was tired this evening. I doubt he'll stay awake much longer. She moved quietly from the bed, put her white silk duster on over her see-through chemise, and silently tiptoed across the room. With painstaking care, she opened and closed her door, and walked softly to Roger's room, careful not to step on the creaky floorboard in the hall, and slipped inside. Roger was sound asleep. She inched to the edge of his bed, removed her duster and nightgown, and slid under the covers.

Roger awakened and turned toward her. They embraced, kissed, and explored each other's bodies until dawn. He's so gentle—unlike Harry's awkward lovemaking.

Afterwards, she lay beside him, her head on his chest, and whispered, "Now, it's been a perfect day. Roger, I want this to last forever."

"I love you, Jada. I promise we'll always be together." Roger pulled her closer.

In the next room, Jack awoke when he thought he heard a noise. He moved quietly to the bedroom door, peeked out, and listened for a long moment—nothing but silence. He went back to the bed.

19

Bows and Guns

OCCASIONALLY, ROGER'S MILITARY DUTIES REQUIRED HIM to remain in the capitol city. During one such weekend, Jada called Patsy Fike and asked if it was convenient to visit the Ladies' Archery Club. Patsy replied she would be delighted to meet Jada there the following day.

Jada told Patsy when they met at the club, "I'm sorry; I don't have my own bow. I'll watch."

"Don't worry, I'll find one for you." Patsy left and soon returned. "Here, try this one." She handed Jada an English long bow.

Jada took the bow and drew the string. "This one is too tall for me and the pull feels weak. Do you think you could find a shorter one with a heavier draw?"

Patsy located one of the recently popularized recurved bows and a quiver of arrows for Jada. "Perhaps this one will do. It's the newest thing but most women don't fancy this style."

Jada tried the shorter bow. "This is better for me—more like what I'm accustomed to."

"Here, let me show you how." With slow deliberation, Patsy shot five arrows at a target twenty yards out. All five hit the bull's eye.

"Impressive, Patsy," said Jada as she stepped up, loaded an arrow and held the shaft between her thumb and forefinger.

"No, no Jada," Patsy said with a patronizing air. "Use your first three fingers. Let me show you." Patsy loosed another perfect shot.

"I learned to do it differently. I'll try it like I was taught."

"If you insist but it's not as accurate."

Jada ignored her and raised the bow, holding an additional four arrows along the stave. She quickly fired her five arrows into the target's center.

Patsy's jaw dropped and her face flushed. Her plan to embarrass Jada wasn't working out as she expected. *We'll see how good she is from further back.* "Let's back up to 50 yards."

At the longer distance, Patsy hit the outermost ring on her first shot but scored bull's eyes with her other arrows. Jada repeated her earlier performance; five arrows fired in rapid succession—all five dead-center.

Thwarted, Patsy had one last trick. "Have you ever shot moving targets?" Jada shrugged but said nothing.

The club had a target sitting on a small cart which club members would pull back and forth across the firing range by long cords. Patsy was an expert at this exercise. This time she hit four bull's eyes and put one in the outer ring.

Jada shook her head. "That's some shooting, Patsy. Let me try with a different target."

"Of course, what do you have in mind?"

"Would someone toss the lid of that little barrel over there into the air?" Jada pointed to a water cask on the sidelines. Patsy nervously chewed her lip as she watched.

The crowd fetched the small wooden barrel top. "You mean this?" asked a woman.

"That's it," said Jada.

Down range, a husband of one of the women archers sent the target spinning skyward. As if by reflex, Jada fired her arrows. "Whoops, a little slow with the last arrow," she said with a smile as the crowd applauded. Four had gone into the barrelhead and one struck the ground in front of where the target fell.

She looked around but Patsy had disappeared, so Jada spent the afternoon chatting and punching targets with the other women. She joined the Ladies Archery Society that day and continued to hone her skills when she found herself without Roger.

Despite a heavy workload in General Sherman's office, Roger managed an appearance on Jada's doorstep two or three weekends each month. On one of his visits, Jack invited Jada's friend, Susan Gatewood and her family to join them for supper. In the course of the conversation, Mr. Gatewood mentioned his gun collection. "I've recently acquired the latest Winchester lever action rifle, and one of the new double action Colt revolvers," he announced with unabashed gusto. "Would any of you like to join me at the gun range tomorrow after church to test them out?"

"You bet!—er, at least I would," blurted Roger, then looked sheepish. "What do you think, Jada?" Roger was raring to try the newfangled technology but wanted to make sure Jada was on board with the project.

Jada had never held a firearm, much less fired one, but she had a morbid fascination for them ever since her family was massacred. She thought with a marriage proposal pending and Roger's interest in weapons, target shooting was something they could do together.

"Of course, Roger. I'd like to learn how to shoot—I'd be most interested in guns I would find out West. Who knows? I might end up out there someday." Jada gave Roger a knowing look.

"In that case," Mr. Gatewood said, "I'll also bring along an army Springfield rifle and a single action Colt. You'll find plenty of those on the frontier."

Roger whispered to Jada, "Be sure to take some cotton."

"Cotton?"

"For your ears. Those large caliber guns are loud if you aren't used to them."

"Good idea, Roger. Thank you." Her thoughts flashed back eleven years to the summer of 1866 when she heard the thunder of Mexican rifles raining fire down on her hapless village. I'll never forget that sound. Tears welled up but she wiped them away before anyone noticed.

On the following day at the police shooting range, the men took turns with the weapons, then showed Susan and Jada how to load, aim, and shoot.

Jada tried the army Springfield first. With her feet together, she leaned back and put her elbow against her rib cage to support the heavy rifle. When she pulled the trigger, the gun belched a cloud of black-powder smoke, kicked, and sent her crashing onto her bottom.

Roger laughed as he helped her stand. "Spread your feet for support," he advised.

Amidst much laughter, she managed to remain standing as she loaded and fired several rounds. At last she handed the weapon to Mr. Gatewood. "That one's too heavy for me and kicks too hard."

Later, after Jada had tried the Winchester repeater, she balanced the rifle in one hand. "This one is better and much lighter."

Next Gatewood brought out two Colt pistols.

Jada shot the single action Colt revolver with ease. "Oh, this is more fun."

Then Susan's father handed a double action Colt to Jada. "All you do with this one is aim and pull the trigger," he said. "You don't have to cock the hammer after each shot."

Jada fired six shots, reloaded once and emptied the cylinder for a second time. "This double-action is much faster, but both pistols are easy to shoot."

Roger was delighted to find a common interest with Jada, and he began taking her for target practice twice each month. She developed into a skilled shootist with the Winchester and the handguns.

As Jada's skills grew with the weapons, Roger's admiration and affection for Jada rose to new heights. But General Sherman was on a tour of Arizona and unavailable to meet Roger to approve a marriage between the lieutenant and Jada for several weeks. The couple waited impatiently for his return.

20

Broken Engagement

WHEN GENERAL SHERMAN WAS FINALLY AVAILABLE to meet, Roger's knees went weak at the general's response to his request for permission to marry Jada. "Lieutenant Bullard, you know my opinion of Doctor Morgan. You would be a fortunate man to have her for a wife. However, if you get married, I suggest you resign from the army and remain in the East for your own good and hers. I'll approve your resignation immediately, if that's what you want."

"Leave the army, sir? There's no way."

"Then here are the orders you've been asking for. You're being assigned to Fort Bowie, Arizona for the duration. The Chiricahua Apaches are unhappy about the Indian Office plans to move them from New Mexico to the San Carlos reservation. If they bolt, the troops at Bowie would help contain them before they reach the Mexican border."

"Sir, wouldn't Doctor Morgan be an asset? She speaks Chiricahua, understands the culture, and could be an immense benefit dealing with them."

"Son, you don't understand. Everyone in the southwest loathes the Chirica-huas, civilized or not."

"Sir, I can't believe Jada being an Indian is a problem. She's educated, well-man-nered, and wealthy. Her medical skills would be invaluable."

"Lieutenant, in Arizona she'd be viewed as a subhuman spy and ostracized. You'd be blacklisted by your fellow officers and the women of the post would avoid her like the plague." Sherman expelled a cloud of cigar smoke. "You can do anything you want, but you'll probably never be considered for a promotion if you marry her."

"Damn sir, I've always wanted to be a soldier, and I love her very much. What should I do?"

"Your decision, Lieutenant." Sherman exhaled another gust of smoke and turned his attention to the papers on his desk.

Jada received a telegram the next morning. Jada: Plans changed. Must talk. Will come Saturday and return here same day. Leave for Arizona in five days. Roger.

On the following Saturday, Jada sat deep in thought on the veranda of the Morgan mansion as she awaited Roger's arrival. What does he mean by the 'plans changed?' I have an awful feeling about this. Our marriage won't happen anytime soon if he's leaving next week.

She remained expressionless as Roger's hired carriage pulled up to the mansion, and the lieutenant stepped out wearing a depressed expression.

This isn't good. I think it's over. Her hands trembled as she waited stoically for him to reach the front porch.

Roger forced a smile and nervously blurted out what was on his mind. "Sweetheart, I'm sorry to be in such a rush. I need to be on the next train back to Washington, but I wanted to tell you this in person." Jada stared at him, bit her lower lip, and remained silent.

He continued, "I've planned my whole life around being a soldier. Now I'm in a horrible dilemma. I love you so much, but I can't marry you. The army has an unwritten rule declaring officers should not marry Indians—especially Chiricahuas." He stared at the floor as he spoke. "We would be mistreated on the social scene and I'm told I'd never be promoted again."

Jada was more angry than hurt. "So this is the end of it. I'm a loveable redskin who's nifty in bed but not fit to marry because my race would hinder your career."

"I don't mean that. You're wonderful, but a marriage ruins everything for both of us." He raised his hands in a gesture of conciliation.

Jada stood up and called to Rebecca, "Would you summon a carriage for the lieutenant."

Roger came toward her intending to give her a hug.

She pushed him away and walked to the door.

"Jada, please..."

"Please, what?" she snapped.

"Don't leave like this."

"Goodbye, Roger." She left the porch without looking at him and went straight upstairs.

As soon as the carriage rolled away, Rebecca rushed to Jada's room and found her staring out the large back window. Her cheeks were streaked with tears. "Jada, honey, are you all right?"

"No, not just now. I need to be alone."

"Okay, just tell me if I can do anything."

"Thank you Rebecca. I've some decisions to make, but for now, I want to think about things." She turned back to the window.

For the next two days, Jada attended her patients, read medical journals, and remained unusually quiet. On the third day while having an afternoon tea with Jack in the parlor, she announced her plans. "Father, I'd like to open a practice in New Mexico, maybe on the reservation with my tribe."

Jack gave her a long, intense look. They had talked about the possibility of Jada leaving someday, but this was unexpected. "Oh, sweetheart, I'd miss you so. Are you sure?" asked Jack. He rubbed his forehead with an open hand as he spoke.

"I'm positive. If it doesn't work out, I'll come home. Either way, I want to try." Her eyes flashed with resolve.

"You understand there'll be problems with the Indian Office if you try to establish a clinic on the reservation without their approval.

"I've plenty of my own money. I'll open a treatment center off the reserve but near the tribe. The government wouldn't be involved."

Jack thought about her idea briefly and said, "That's a good plan, Jada. A medical practice in Canada Alamosa would work. The town's near Fort McRae—almost entirely Mexican, but a few Americans live there too. You'll need to learn Spanish."

"How close is town to the Indians?" she asked.

"It sits about ten miles from the reservation—two hours by carriage. Your patients would be Apaches, Mexicans, and Americans." A concerned look flitted across Jack's face. "But it's a dangerous place, Jada. There's lots of violence around Canada Alamosa."

"It's something I want to do for my people," replied Jada. "I'll take my chances."

"You're twenty-two years old now—old enough to know what you want." Jack gave her a paternal smile. "Just remember you're always welcome here."

21

Return to New Mexico

JADA SPENT THE FOLLOWING WEEK packing a large travel trunk with clothing suitable for the dusty west. Recalling when Mollie Shepard saved the Morgan family with her tiny derringer, Jada purchased a similar four-barrel Sharps .22 caliber palm pistol. She also bought two Spanish language textbooks to prepare for life in Canada Alamosa.

Jack wired Pierpont about Jada's impending trip:

Jada leaving for New Mexico next week by rail. Establishing practice near her tribe. Sends love. Promises to write. Jack

A response came from Pierpont the same afternoon:

Jada to travel via my private railroad car. Dispatching today. See my man Riggs on train for letters of introduction. Stay safe. Write often. Will mail separate letter for rail company employees. Much love.
Uncle Pierpont

Two days later the postal service delivered Pierpont's note for Jada's use with the train staff:

To Whom It May Concern:
The young lady bearing this is Dr. Jada P. Morgan, my adopted niece. She owns a sizable number of shares in this railroad. I hold most of the balance. She is to have whatever she wants that the line can provide.
J.P. Morgan.

Jack, Simon, and Rebecca went to the depot to give their farewells to Jada. Amid smiles, well wishes, and a few tears from Rebecca, Jada boarded the train.

When she tried to enter Morgan's' private car she found a conductor standing legs apart and holding his hand up. "Girl you can't go in there. That's Mr. J.P. Morgan's personal coach." Jada pulled an envelope from her purse, and handed it to the man.

Once he read Pierpont's memo, the contrite official returned the note to Jada.

"Oh, yes ma'am. Sorry, I didn't know. Here, let me hold the door for you. I'll tell the others on the crew."

She was astonished by the size and opulence of the accommodations. The rail car was ninety feet long with a spacious observation area and several lesser compartments for visitors and staff. Pierpont's stateroom was large and included an oversized four-poster bed and a bath with polished silver fixtures. As Pierpont's man-servant, Royce Riggs toured Jada through the car, she held one hand to her cheek in awe.

"Holy Moses, Mr. Riggs. This is so lavish!".

"Indeed, Doctor Morgan. Mr. Morgan has a taste for fine things," Riggs said with a smile.

Pierpont didn't want Jada to travel alone in the huge car so he had sent along Riggs, and a French chef, known only as Yves.

When the train moved out of the city, Jada smiled and waved from the window, but her eyes watered as she replayed memories of her eleven years in Philadelphia. A few miles out of town, her ruminations were interrupted by the sound of lighthearted music. She asked Riggs to find the source.

Riggs returned and reported, "All the racket's coming from a troupe of Mexican entertainers in the next car. They call themselves Miss Florissa Forbes and Her Mexican Orchestra," Riggs said in a disdainful tone. "I'll have the conductor make them stop, if they're bothering you."

"Oh, no Mr. Riggs, I'll go myself," Jada said as she started toward the door connecting the cars.

In the next car, Jada met Miss Forbes, an attractive, elegant woman. Six musicians with toothy smiles stood behind her.

"Hello. Are we disturbing you?" asked Florissa in a pleasant voice.

"No, not a bit," said Jada. "In fact, I came to listen, if you don't mind," Jada replied as she looked around the crowded car.

"Of course you can. Please stay. May I ask, are you Spanish or Mexican?" Florissa asked, eyeing Jada's long black hair and golden complexion. "Many Americans don't care for our melodies."

"No, I'm American Indian. I haven't heard this style of music since I was a child. By the way, I'm Jada Morgan, Doctor Jada Morgan."

"Good to meet you, Doctor Morgan. My name is Florissa Forbes. Please call me Flo. I'm a singer by profession. We are doing a nationwide tour."

Flo then introduced the six-member orchestra who were dressed in flamboyant brocaded outfits, complete with sombreros which Flo explained were "good for publicity" when the troupe was on the road.

Jada commented she was surprised the band could play such lively music in the confined space of the crowded car.

Florissa admitted, "Some of the other passengers are complaining about the music."

Jada waved her hand toward Pierpont's coach. "My observation car is more spacious and there are only three of us. If you would like, you can use the lounge to practice. You'll have more room and I'd enjoy your company and the music."

"That's most kind of you. There's sitting room?" asked Florissa in a dubious tone. "May I take a peek before we move our instruments?"

"Of course, all of you come. The car is unique, but there's one thing. My uncle is allowing me to use it for my trip west. Please be careful and don't disturb anything."

Riggs looked dismayed as Flo's troupe poured through the door. Jada pulled him to the side. Standing on her tiptoes whispered in his ear, "Riggs, I invited Miss Forbes and her orchestra to come and provide a little music for our trip. Five or six days alone in this car will get tedious for me."

Riggs hesitated. "I suppose there's no problem. Sometimes Mr. Morgan has small ensembles entertain his guests on longer trips. But these people are Mexicans. You don't think they'll steal anything, do you?"

"I doubt it. Miss Forbes is quite sophisticated, and the musicians seem well-mannered and respectful. Nevertheless, I've warned them not to disturb things."

"I'll keep an eye out anyhow." The unconvinced butler raised one eyebrow.

During the group's tour through the car, Flo spotted the two books Jada purchased before she left Philadelphia; A Spanish Primer, and Learning Spoken Spanish. She thumbed through one. "You're studying Spanish?"

"I'm just starting. I suspect I'll need to speak the language where I'm going in New Mexico," replied Jada.

"You are absolutely right. If you would like, I'll help you while we're traveling. I think we are six days out from Santa Fe—plenty of time for you to pick up the basics. I can also teach you a few Spanish songs. I live in Mexico now but I'm originally from Spain and speak the Castilian dialect. The New Mexicans will understand you perfectly. They'll just think you're from España."

After taking Jada as a student, Flo insisted she converse only in Spanish and directed her orchestra to talk in their native tongue with their new friend. For the following week Jada was immersed in the language day and night. By the trip's end, she was having simple conversations.

Flo also introduced Jada to some of her stage songs as a method of instruction and had Jada sing along with her as the group practiced for their next performance.

As their train approached Santa Fe, Jada took the singer's hand and told her, "The trip has been so pleasant and I've a good start on my Spanish. Thanks so much."

22

The Little Mexican Girl

AFTER JADA WAVED GOODBYE to her Mexican friends, she walked to the stagecoach station and bought a ticket to Fort McRae. Two men wearing dark suits ignored her as they boarded the stage. She listened in silence as they introduced themselves. The thin, frail fellow was Henry Yazser, clerk for the Southern Apache agency near Canada Alamosa. He liked the Apaches and often went to their defense. The second man was William Vandever, a churlish Indian Office inspector from Washington. He announced he would be going to the San Carlos reservation in Arizona to audit the Indian agency's accounts. He declared he despised leaving the big city for isolated out-backs, and loathed with equal vitriol the Indians and the Mexicans he found there. After hearing Vandever's outburst, it occurred to Jada she might learn about the local non-Indian attitudes toward her people if she pretended to only understand Spanish while she listened.

Yazser, the more pleasant of the two, attempted to strike up a conversation with her. "Hello young lady. My name is Henry, Henry Yazser. I work at the Indian agency in Canada Alamosa."

She kept her eyes downward and responded in Spanish. "Yo no hablo Inglés."

Yazser sat straighter and took the opportunity to demonstrate his mastery of the lingo, "Hablo un poco de espanol. Quiero saber si me pueden ayudar."

"Gracias."

"What's that gibberish all about?" Vandever cast an irritated glare at Jada.

"She says she doesn't speak English. I told her I know some Spanish and if she needed any help to ask."

"Why bother? Those damned Mexicans are just as bad as the stinking savages out here. The government should round them all up on a reservation and let them exterminate each other."

"Mighty harsh talk for someone from the Indian Office sworn to care for our native people," Yazser said, his sarcasm oozing.

"See here, I was a general in the war, but now I'm an auditor. I check the agents' accounts, and report to the commissioner. I'm not required to like these backwashes or those Apache bastards."

"So if they sent you to Arizona, what are you doing in New Mexico?" Yazser asked.

"The Agent at San Carlos, John Clum, came to arrest Geronimo and his gang a year ago. Clum decided to force all the Indians on the reservation here to go back with him. As soon as he returned to San Carlos, the bummer resigned from office, abandoned that hellhole, and moved to Tombstone." Vandever took a handkerchief from his pocket, snorted into it, and continued, "When he quit, the only people left to manage the agency were two drunkards. Since I have administrative experience and was coming this way for an audit, guess who they appointed acting agent?"

"Sounds like it would be a feather in your hat," said Henry.

"There's no glory in the San Carlos job. That place is hotter than hell and the Apaches are the most devilish Indians on earth. From my perspective, the whole situation stinks."

"You didn't say why you're in these parts," Yazser said.

"Well after six months those damned redskins with Loco decided to leave San Carlos and run back to Canada Alamosa. I'm here to organize their return to Arizona."

Jada grimaced as she listened to Vandever's rant but said nothing. Henry Yazser took a moment to think about Vandever's comments and said, "Sounds like they should be left alone."

"The hell you say." Red blotches sprouted on Vandever's face. "These ignorant savages need to understand they'll live wherever the government tells them to."

"The boys in Washington could start a war with thinking like that. Victorio won't put up with it. He'll fight."

"In that case, the army will chase him down and kill him." Vandever gave Yazser a smug sneer.

As Jada listened, she dug her fingernails into her palms. Ezra Hyat's policies again. This is insane.

Changing the subject, Vandever asked, "What brings you up to Santa Fe from the agency, Mr. Yazser?"

Yazser replied, "The Indian Commissioner wired the agent to expect a Chiricahua Indian on the train, a fellow named J.P. Morgan—not the tycoon, but a fellow with ties to the family. Seems he was adopted by a Morgan relative and educated as a medical doctor, or so I was told." Yazser glanced at Jada again and added, "Major Cantrell, the commanding officer at Ft. McRae received a similar telegram from General Sherman in the War Department. The man is to receive special attention. It was decided I should meet the doctor and escort him to the agency."

Yazser nodded toward Jada. "He didn't show up today. That little Mexican girl is the only one who got off in Santa Fe,"

Jada covered her mouth to stifle a laugh and stared from the window.

"You couldn't find him because Chiricahua Apache medical doctors don't exist," Vandever snickered. "None of them can even read."

Jada glared silently at Vandever. Good grief that bigot shouldn't be allowed around Indians.

Vandever sensed her hostility. "You sure that little senorita doesn't talk American?"

"Says she doesn't." Yaszer smiled at Jada as he spoke.

They passed through Soccoro, Fort Craig, and into Fort McRae where the stage pulled up in front of the headquarters building. As soon as it stopped, Vandever jumped out. Yazser followed but helped Jada down, then joined Vandever. The two men walked rapidly into the adobe office with Jada close behind. Inside a lone sergeant sat at the reception desk. Yazser scanned the empty room. "Where's the major, soldier?"

"He has a serious problem at the infirmary. Captain Wyatt's wife is having a baby, or trying to. Something's gone wrong. We got several men out looking for the doctor. I 'spose Bones is off on one of his toots. I reckon it'll be too late by the time they find him."

Jada pushed between the two men in front of her. "Excuse me, Sergeant. I'm a physician. Where's the hospital?" she asked in English.

Vandever and Yazser shot each other astonished looks. "Be damned Yazser, there's your Chiricahua doctor. Who would have ever thought?"

Yazser felt sick. "She understood everything we said."

Vandever gave Jada a hostile leer. "Hell, I don't give a crap whether she understood us or not. Chiricahuas don't count for much with me." He didn't look back as he hurried off. "I have important government business at the Indian agency. I need to get moving." He left the office annoyed but unconcerned, and climbed aboard a wagon sent to pick him up.

Yazser, on the other hand, paled when he realized the "Mexican girl" was the educated Chiricahua doctor he was supposed to accompany from Santa Fe. "Damn, I'll never hear the end of this," he mumbled and dashed off after Jada.

23

Bigotry at Fort McRae

JADA EASED INTO THE HOSPITAL ROOM where Lydia Wyatt was struggling to deliver her child. Henry Yazser followed close behind.

Major Obadiah Cantrell standing at the foot of the bed turned to face Jada. "Hey girl, you can't be in here. Mrs. Wyatt is trying to deliver a baby. We're waiting for a doctor."

"Your lucky day, Major. I am a doctor," Jada replied.

Cantrell turned to Yazser. "Henry is this that Chiricahua physician you picked up in Santa Fe?"

Before Yazser could speak, Jada said. "I am and Mr. Yazser took excellent care of me on the trip down."

Henry smiled gratefully at Jada and mouthed the words, "Thank you."

Lydia's distraught husband, Captain Alfred Wyatt was seated on one side of the bed holding his wife's hand and whispering encouragement. Rita Gonzales, a Mexican midwife, was across from him, mopping the distressed woman's face. When Jada confirmed she was a Chiricahua Indian, Wyatt recoiled in disgust and released his wife's hand.

Jada stepped towards Mrs. Wyatt. "Captain, could you move so I can see what we have here."

Wyatt gave Jada a vicious stare. "Don't you come one step closer!" His nostrils flared and he balled his fists. "No Chiricahua squaw is going to touch my wife. Doctor Radborne is on his way."

"Captain," Jada ignored the insult. "Your wife is in serious trouble. She needs help."

Perspiration covered Lydia Wyatt's face. "I can stand the pain. I don't want a savage fumbling around. I'll wait for Doctor Radborne," she moaned.

The Wyatts were so disturbed that Rita moved away and stood beside Jada. Although piqued at the insults, Jada remained calm and whispered to Rita, "I'm Doctor Jada Morgan, what's the situation?"

"I'm Rita Gonzales," she said with a thick accent. "I'm a midwife from Canada Alamosa. I've never seen anything like this. The baby is breach, with the cord tangled around its neck. The fetus is too big and jammed in there very tight—I can't budge it. I don't know what to do."

"Stay here. I'll need some help, if I'm allowed."

"Captain Wyatt, Rita has described the problem. Your wife isn't going to deliver normally. She needs a Cesarean section."

"I'm telling you for the last time, no Chiricahua squaw is getting near her." Wyatt looked agitated and menacing.

"Fine, Captain, Rita and I will stand by and watch your wife and baby die."

Wyatt took a step toward Jada. "You heathen bitch..."

A shout from outside interrupted his tirade. "Wagon's coming from Alamosa. They got Bones with them."

Wyatt broke into a 'You-can-leave-now' scowl. "The real doctor, at last."

As the physician entered the hospital, the strains of an Irish drinking song reverberated down the hall. After an endless wait, two soldiers came in struggling to keep Dr. Ridley Radborne upright. His bright red nose and bleary eyes revealed the doctor was sloshed. "We found him like this at Trujillo's hog ranch," said one soldier.

Radborne continued to belt out the refrains of The Night Pat Murphy Died as the troopers tried to stand him in a corner, but he slid down the wall to the floor. There he sat, legs spread wide, crooning and waving his arms as if conducting an orchestra.

Jada asked Captain Wyatt in a quiet voice, "Is it okay if I assisted Doctor Radborne or should I do it myself?"

Wyatt stepped between Jada and his wife. "Just stay away." He remained agitated and visibly shaken—but now uncertain.

Lydia let out a loud moan, and her eyes rolled back into her head.

Finally, Cantrell intervened and pointed to the patient. "Wyatt, are you going to let Lydia die because you don't like Indians?"

"How the hell do we even know if this girl is a doctor?"

Jada reached into her purse and handed Cantrell a letter of introduction to the commandant of Fort McRae.

This letter will introduce Dr. Jada Morgan, M.D., a Chiricahua Indian and my adopted niece. I request she be treated with the utmost respect by you and your men. Dr. Morgan is a graduate from the Pennsylvania Medical College for Women.

She has practiced medicine for the past nine years, and is certified by the Philadelphia College of Surgeons and Physicians. She plans to establish a medical practice in Canada Alamosa but has offered to help at Fort McRae, if needed.

J.P. Morgan

The major read the letter aloud then studied Jada and asked, "Are you still willing to assist here at the fort?"

"I certainly am."

He rubbed his hand over his face before he spoke. "Troopers take this drunk to the guardhouse. Doctor Morgan you are now the surgeon for Fort McRae. Radborne will be relieved of his duties as soon as he is sober enough to understand."

Captain Wyatt stepped forward to block Jada. "Major, can't we wait until Bones sobers up?"

As Lydia's moans turned into screams and violent convulsions. Jada gave the captain a worried look. "If I don't do something soon, she'll die along with your child."

Cantrell stood nose to nose with the red-faced Wyatt. "Captain Wyatt, I'm responsible for every life on this post, civilian or soldier. Considering that, I'm ordering you out of the way and asking our new surgeon to save these two if it isn't too late."

"Yes sir! But if that squaw kills Lydia, you'll also have a dead Indian on your hands," screeched Wyatt as he reluctantly stepped back.

Major Cantrell disregarded the captain. "Doctor Morgan what do you need?"

Jada ignored Wyatt and spoke directly to the major. "Is an orderly near?"

"Outside in the hall."

"Call him in please."

The major turned to the closed door and shouted, "Private Harley. In here now!"

Private Roscoe Harley, eighteen years old and new to the army, rushed into the room. Jada motioned him to her side. "Private, I need a surgical kit, chloroform, iodine, alcohol, and plenty of carbolic acid. Is there a misting atomizer in the hospital?"

Harley nodded but shrugged. "We got a new one with a hand pump—it's still in the box. Doctor Radborne told me all that talk about germs is a bunch of hooey."

"That man is living in the past. Germs cause childbed fever and will kill Mrs. Wyatt quicker than the surgery. Also bring four clean sheets and put a slice in the center so we can wear them like ponchos. Everything has to be hygienic. Go now, hurry."

The young private hurried off. Jada pointed to the door. "You gentlemen should wait outside. Rita and I will handle things here, but Private Harley will need to stay."

Harley soon returned carrying a stack of sheets, several bottles, the misting machine, and a handful of shiny instruments. "Ain't no chloroform, but here's some ether."

"Ether's good—safer than chloroform anyhow."

Jada moved beside Lydia's bed while Rita watched. Lydia cringed and pulled away. The convulsions had subsided, but she was still dazed. "Hello Mrs. Wyatt. I'm Doctor Morgan. You can call me Jada. What's your first name?"

She turned her head on the pillow and whispered, "Lydia." The sweating patient gritted her teeth in pain and said nothing else.

"All right Lydia," Jada said, "I know you don't like me, but we must do something to get the baby out. You need a Cesarean. I'll put you to sleep with some ether and you won't feel a thing."

"Isn't that dangerous?" gasped Lydia.

"No. I've used ether dozens of times. Lydia, I know what I'm doing. I've been working in medicine for nine years and I've delivered almost fifty babies and done a couple of C-sections. I promise to take good care." Lydia nodded.

The three donned their poncho-sheets. "Now, private, pour some of that alcohol over Rita's and my hands, yours too. Then put the instruments in this bowl, cover them with it and fill the misting machine with carbolic acid."

Jada placed a small cloth soaked with ether over Lydia's nose and mouth. "Roscoe, keep pumping the atomizer. The entire surgical area must stay in a mist of carbolic acid to keep things sterile while we work." She nodded to Harley.

At first, the surgery went well. Jada untangled the cord from around the fetus' neck, but Rita was right, the baby was large and wedged tight. Jada cupped the baby's neck and head with one hand and supported the back with the other. She tugged but the fetus would not dislodge. She put her knee on the bed and strained—a little movement. Not enough. She pulled harder, lifting Lydia's unconscious body off the mattress, but the baby remained in place.

"Rita, hold her hips down."

Jada tugged again using her knee for leverage. On her third try, the blue-gray infant was delivered. She handed the newborn to Rita who hurried to clear the child's mouth and nose. As Jada worked to close Lydia's surgery, she heard a loud smack as Rita tried to get the child to breath. Silence. There were two more loud smacks. Still nothing.

"Doctor, I think the baby is dead. I can't make her breathe." She flashed a disturbed look at Jada.

"Rita, can you finish up here?

"I believe so. I've sewn some large cuts before."

"Good. Make small stitches. Roscoe keep the atomizer going."

In seconds, Jada took the newborn girl and whacked its bottom. The infant remained silent. She checked its mouth and nose. Clear. Rita had done a good job. She next put a small mirror to the baby's face and pressed on her chest.

"No fog at all. She's clogged up further down," she said under her breath.

Jada put her lips over the newborn's nose and mouth and sucked. She came up with a glob of bloody mucus. No handy receptacle, and no time to find one, Jada spit the gunk on the floor.

Jada prepared to try another spank on the baby's bottom but before she could, the little girl started yowling. Rita and Jada beamed. Harley mumbled, "Thank you."

24

Major Obadiah Cantrell

RITA WAS CRADLING THE NEWBORN in her arms, and Private Harley was slumped in a bedside chair when Jada left the room and approached the nervous father pacing in the hall. "Captain Wyatt, you may go in and meet your new daughter now. Your wife is still unconscious from the ether, but it would be good if you were there when she wakes up. Put this clean sheet on over your uniform like a poncho."

His only response was an abrupt nod and a spiteful "Harumph," as he donned the sheet and went to Lydia's bedside.

Jada wiped the perspiration from her forehead with her wrist and gave Major Cantrell a resigned look. "Mrs. Wyatt and the baby will be fine."

As Jada turned to go into the room, Cantrell reached out and touched her arm. "Doctor Morgan. If you wish, I've arranged for you to stay in our guest quarters until you find a permanent place. Also you may eat in the mess hall with the officers."

"That's very kind, Major." She vanished back into the delivery room. Umm, he's mighty good-looking and so charming, she thought, but her affair with Roger Bullard quickly came to mind. Jada Morgan don't you dare get involved with another soldier!

Jada attended Lydia daily throughout her recovery. She remained distant and professional during these visits but continued to be amiable. After a week, Lydia reached out, took Jada's hand.

"Doctor Morgan, I want to thank you for what you did. Rita told me all about it. She said you were wonderful." Lydia smiled and continued to rock her baby. "Private Harley also let Alfred know everything. He's thankful too, but he has a hard time with you being Chiricahua. He's had a close friend killed by the Chiricahuas."

"I understand. When I was a child my whole family was murdered by soldiers. Some things are difficult to forgive."

Embarrassed at the disclosure, Lydia had no response.

Word of Jada's heroics during the delivery of Lydia Wyatt's baby and the subsequent treatment of soldiers' complaints spread through the tiny Fort McRae. After several minor operations, troopers raved about her skill and they eyed her with a newfound respect.

Soldiers were not her only admirers. As the word spread of her social grace and medical skill, women at the post made a surprising effort to speak to Jada when they passed, and a few invited her to their quarters for tea or coffee.

Despite the newfound praise and respect, for the first two days after Jada's arrival at Fort McCrae, she sat conspicuously alone in the dining hall as the officers ate and slipped furtive glances her way. Maybe Roger was right about prejudice in the army. At last, Major Cantrell dispelled her concerns. He had no problem breaking bread with the new surgeon and began taking his meals with her.

Sitting across the table from Obadiah, she studied him in an effort to understand her intense attraction for him. He's unmarried, handsome and charming. Once again she caught herself. Hold up lady. Remember what Roger said about the military's policy on Indian and white romances? This isn't going anywhere. Just enjoy his company.

Jada's only problem was she and Obadiah were immediately bewitched with each other. "So what do you think of army life?" Obadiah couldn't take his eyes away from her.

"My earliest experience with white people was after I was adopted. Father was the post surgeon at Fort Craig..." She went on to describe her time at Craig with the Morgans and their move back to Philadelphia.

"Then this is like a homecoming for you."

She thought about that for a minute. "Well, in a way."

Obadiah took a sip of coffee. "Tell me more of your years in Philadelphia."

"I'd be glad to share with you, if you'll return the favor."

"It's a deal," he said. "We'll be able to talk alone at the river if you'd like. I know a beautiful spot where we can watch the sunset. Do you ride, or should I arrange a carriage?"

Jada laughed aloud. "Obadiah, I rode horses before I was five-years old. An outing on horseback would be lovely, but not sidesaddle—either bareback or with a McClellan."

"Perfect, how about supper tomorrow? I'll bring a picnic."

"I'll be ready."

The next evening, the two rode out to a bluff overlooking the Rio Grande to watch the sun set. They soon began taking jaunts several times a week, each time with a picnic basket and a blanket to sit on. The smells, sights and sounds of the desert, and a view of the river stirred memories of Jada's childhood. "I love this place. It's so beautiful," she said with a touch of melancholy in her voice.

The outings and quiet times with Obadiah were special for Jada, and their conversations grew increasingly intimate. As they talked about themselves; their pasts, and hopes for the future, Jada thought, I know this can't work, but it feels so perfect.

At last, she asked, "Won't being seen with an Indian woman be a problem with the army?"

"It's possible. I'll decide what to do if anything comes up. But for now, nobody is complaining and I like your company. I hope this lasts for a long time."

"Well, Obadiah, when I move to Alamosa, perhaps we'll be far enough apart to prevent any wagging tongues."

"I'm told there's almost no gossip about us now. The women on the base are impressed with you, and the men you've treated adore you. He thought for a moment and added, "It would be good if you were closer but the army won't contract for your services. They're only beginning to allow women to nurse soldiers. You might set up an independent practice near the fort."

"Obadiah, I didn't come out here to be an army doctor. All along this has been temporary duty for me. I intend to establish a clinic for the Apaches and the people in Alamosa. The town's ten miles from the military post, so we'll be able to visit and not be too obvious."

Cantrell stared into her eyes, reached out, and took her hand. "You're right, but Jada, I want more time with you, not less. If you're determined, I'll accompany you on your first visit to Alamosa. I can introduce you to Trujillo, the mayor. He's a rum-runner and a sleazy lawyer, but you need to meet him. He controls about everything in town and might help you establish your clinic."

"I'm glad you're going with me." She moved her face close to his. "Obadiah, I really enjoy having you around."

"Jada, I've never met anyone I like being with more than you." He leaned over and gave her a kiss on the lips.

Jada returned the kiss with passion and a warm hug. The major responded and pulled her down to the blanket. He stretched out beside her and propped up on one elbow. His hand cupped her breast and he kissed her harder.

I'm headed for trouble here. We better stop this before we're out of control, she thought. "Whoa there, soldier boy. Let's talk about this."

Obadiah stopped short, blushed, and moved his hand. "Sorry, I guess I'm moving too fast."

"Oh no. I enjoy it, but I'm not sure an affair between us will go anywhere. This happened to me before. A soldier dropped me like a hot rock when he learned the army didn't think an officer should be involved with a Chiricahua woman, much less marry one."

"Then where does this go for us now?" asked Obadiah.

"First, I believe we ought to know each other better. You need to figure out how you want things to develop with your career and with me, and I'll do the same. Then we'll settle on what to do."

"I understand," he said, but his frustration showed.

"Obadiah, you're a handsome, kind, and sensitive man, and to be honest with you I would like nothing better than to give you all my love. But before I ever do that again, I'll be a married woman."

She sat up and playfully tousled his hair to ease the tension. "Are you still interested in taking me to Canada Alamosa, or would you prefer I go alone?"

He grinned and smoothed his locks back in place. "Jada, as far as I'm concerned, nothing is changed for us."

"Okay mister, let's go to Alamosa on the day after tomorrow.

25

Troubles with Mayor Trujillo

AFTER RIDLEY RADBORNE WAS REMOVED as surgeon for Fort McRae, he decided to forego life in the area, sold his belongings, and left for places unknown. Jada helped finance Radborne's travels by purchasing his sturdy one-horse shay for trips from Canada Alamosa to the Indian reservation. She and Obadiah decided to test her new buggy on her first trip to the little village. Their two-wheel chariot breezed along the dusty, rutted road to town in about an hour.

Her heart sank when she saw the tiny settlement. "How many people live here? It looks too small to support a clinic."

Obadiah swept his arm in a wide arc. "I think there are roughly 400 citizens in town and maybe two thousand in the area, plus about 500 Indians down the road. You'll have plenty of patients."

Canada Alamosa was a cluster of one story, flat roof adobe houses that lined three sides of a stark, dusty town square. Trujillo's Saloon and Social Society sat beside the San Ignacio Catholic Church and a large vacant house on the fourth side of the plaza. Obadiah told Jada the most recent residents were killed a month earlier by Indians while traveling.

Trujillo's two-story clapboard pleasure palace was the largest building in town. The business included a combination saloon and gambling parlor on the ground floor and a bordello upstairs which also served as living quarters and a sweatshop for six drug-fueled hookers.

As the buggy drew closer to the village, Jada saw two men arguing in front of the saloon. Upon approaching them, Obadiah pointed to the pair. "The skinny short one is Jose Trujillo, the town's mayor. The heavy-set fellow in the brown robe is the Catholic missionary. The good Father seems to be giving Trujillo what-for."

The rotund rector was shaking his finger in the mayor's face when Jada's shay pulled up. Obadiah interrupted the squabble. "Gentlemen, can you slow the discussion long enough for me to introduce you to someone?" The spat came to an abrupt end and both men smiled as they walked toward the new arrivals.

"This is Doctor Jada Morgan, a physician from Philadelphia. She intends to establish a clinic in Alamosa for your citizens and the Indians on the reservation. Doctor Morgan, meet Mayor Jose Trujillo and Guale Torres. Father Guale to most folks in these parts."

Obadiah and Jada dismounted from the shay, and after pleasantries, Jada asked, "Do you know of a house around here I can buy or rent?"

Mayor Trujillo, with no real estate to offer, lost interest. "I need to get back to my office. I'll leave you two to do business with Father Guale, but it's not a good idea to ride out to the reserve to treat patients. Those Chiricahuas would like to catch a woman traveling alone."

"Why Mr. Mayor, I'm a Chiricahua Apache myself. I believe I'll be fine."

Trujillo's stare turned cold but he said nothing and walked off. Jada shivered as the unlikable funcionario strutted away. "Darn, Obadiah, I don't like that man. I hope he finds another doctor to treat him."

"Why would he need treatment?"

"He'll want one before long. Did you notice that abscess on his lip? It's a syphilitic canker. They can be painful."

Overhearing Jada, Guale pointed skyward with righteous indignation. "The wages of sin." But his moral frost quickly melted into a smile. "Forget the mayor; you need housing. The house by the church is the rectory, but the sanctuary has adequate space in the back for me to live. It's all I need, so I rent the residence to help support the church. The people here are too poor to donate much."

"How much is the rent?"

"I ask twenty dollars a month, but I'll negotiate."

Jada pinched her chin and thought for a moment. "I'll make you a deal, Father—fifty dollars monthly, if you give me Spanish lessons and allow me to practice medicine there. I'd like a place to treat patients and I have to speak Spanish to live here."

"So generous!" The heavyset priest broke into a huge smile as he contemplated the additional revenue. "The town needs a physician, and teaching you the language will be my pleasure."

"Then we have a deal. When may I move in?"

"I'll show it to you now, but I'll want a day or so to have it cleaned before you come."

"Good, and hopefully Major Cantrell will arrange delivery of my travel chests and medical supplies in the next few days." She gave Obadiah an alluring wink.

On the night before she left for her new home, Jada and Obadiah spoke in soft voices at their favorite spot along the river.

"I'll miss seeing you every day," he told Jada.

"You'll be on my mind too. I hope we can see each other at least once a week." She kissed him on the cheek.

"Probably more. Something's afoot among the Indians. Vandever is keeping the tribe stirred up with talk of moving them back to San Carlos." Obadiah frowned with concern. "I should visit the agency every few days to check on the situation. We'll have some time together then."

"Oh, that's perfect. I'll be going between the town and the Indian village. I can meet you at either place."

Life in Canada Alamosa was everything Jada hoped it would be. Her house was one of the more comfortable residences in Alamosa. A large see-through fireplace warmed the living room and a small parlor. One of two bedrooms served as Jada's clinic, and the other as her sleeping quarters.

Father Guale came to teach Spanish every day over countless cups of bitter black coffee. Jada ground the beans by hand and dumped the grounds into a pot of boiling water. She called the result 'cowboy coffee'.

The citizens were delighted with their new physician. The Apaches received Jada as if she was a lost relative returning, and the women in town welcomed her with enthusiasm, especially after word of Lydia Wyatt's delivery spread.

Everything changed after Jose Trujillo stopped in her office for a scheduled appointment. "Doctor, this sore won't heal," He pointed to his lip.

"I see." Jada studied Trujillo's canker briefly as she spoke. "Do you have any others on your body?"

Trujillo appeared uncomfortable and mumbled something Jada couldn't understand. "Like down here?" Jada pointed to her crotch.

Trujillo nodded and blushed.

"You've got a serious problem, Mr. Mayor. Take a seat."

As they sat at her desk across from each other, Jada grimaced and clucked her tongue. "You're suffering from a case of syphilis. The disease is deadly if it's not treated."

Trujillo gave her a worried look and asked, "What's the treatment?"

"Syphilis doesn't have a good cure yet. Toxic mercury or arsenic are the only things recommended. I've some medicinal arsenic I'll dilute for you. You should drink a spoonful in a glass of water once a day for six months." She pointed her finger at him. "Syphilis is extremely contagious. Don't kiss or sleep with your wife or any of your, uh, employees until you finish the treatment."

"How long will I live if I don't take anything? I have about fifty pounds of strychnine powder. Can I use that?"

"No, strychnine doesn't work on syph. With no treatment you might last anywhere from several months or years." When Trujillo gave a little smile, Jada added, "But you'll be miserable. Over time, the rashes and sores will return or get worse. At some point, it could make you insane and kill you."

Trujillo seemed unconvinced.

"Let me mix up a bit of medicine for you. You'll be fine in six months if you take a spoonful every day."

As Jada walked around the desk, Trujillo reached out, grabbed her arm, and tried to pull her to him. "You know I'm very important in these parts. I'll be able to make things easy for you—with a little cooperation."

Jada tugged but Trujillo refused to release his grip. The grinning politician produced a salacious pucker, intending to kiss her.

"Stop! Mr. Mayor! You need to consider something."

He laughed. "Like what?"

"That I'm going to shoot you right between the eyes if you don't release my arm." She pulled the derringer she had purchased in Philadelphia from her lab coat's pocket and pointed it at Trujillo's head. She heard the mayor gasp as she cocked the hammer.

Trujillo quickly freed Jada and retreated. "You win, but remember if I can make things easy for you around here, I can make them difficult as well."

"Just get out of my office, mister, and find yourself another doctor."

Trujillo was quick to follow through on his threat to cause problems. Jada soon noticed although the people in the square continued to greet her, they seldom took the time to chat. The villagers refused to sell her groceries, requiring her to arrange for supplies to be delivered from the fort's trading post. All of her patients from town stopped coming for treatment.

Several days later, Guale wore a dark frown when he arrived for their usual morning coffee. "I'm worried for your safety, my dear."

"How so, Father?"

"Some parishioners tell me Trujillo and Sheriff Montoya have approached everyone in town, and warned them they would be arrested and fined if they were seen coming to your clinic.

Trujillo spread the word he has more bad things planned for you."

"Well, I guess there's nothing to do but be careful. He knows I have a gun."

Although he also knew Jada owned a derringer, when Obadiah learned of Trujillo's threats, he bought a larger six-shot .38 caliber Hopkins and Allen pocket pistol for her. It was an expensive chrome plated, engraved model with a pearl handle. "Thank you, it's beautiful and I imagine it's more effective than my little peashooter. I'll carry both for extra safety." She rose on tiptoes and kissed him.

With her medical practice at a standstill in Alamosa, Jada began spending most of her time on the reservation where her services were welcomed. She returned to her residence in Alamosa several times a week for Spanish lessons and to pick up supplies delivered by army volunteers at the major's request. Obadiah came courting as much as possible but it wasn't enough for either of them.

26

Poison

ONCE, AFTER A VISIT TO THE APACHE VILLAGE, Jada returned to town to find her clinic ransacked. The cabinets were overturned, papers strewn everywhere, and pill bottles emptied over the debris. Picking through the litter, she discovered a large container of opium and a bottle of medicinal arsenic missing.

She strode across the square to Sheriff Montoya's office to file a complaint but he seemed unconcerned. The constable wore a bored expression and tapped his fingers on his desk as she presented her grievance.

"Unfortunately, I am overwhelmed with other problems," he said. "I'll get to this when I can—probably be a while."

Jada looked out at the sleepy village. "I completely understand. There does seem to be a crime wave in progress." She walked out, disgusted.

The next morning over coffee, Jada told Guale about the incident. The priest rubbed his crucifix and frowned. "I would expect that from Montoya. He's Trujillo's flunky. I know the mayor uses opium to keep the girls addicted so they will continue to work for him, but why steal the arsenic? He has plenty of strychnine."

"Strychnine won't help him. Mr. Trujillo is infected with syphilis and arsenic is the only thing I have to treat it. I wouldn't give him any because of how he acted."

She gave the priest a questioning look. "He told me he had fifty pounds of strychnine. What would anyone do with so much rat poison? A half pound could kill every mouse in Alamosa."

"Doctor, sometimes the mayor makes liquor from the corn grown around here, and on occasion he sells decent whiskey imported from back East. But when he runs low, he mixes up a batch of fuddle-soup from anything he has on hand."

"He makes the saloon's grog from scratch? What's in it?" she asked.

"His concoctions are full of dangerous ingredients and usually contain no alcohol." He leaned forward and spoke in a confidential tone. "He starts with plain creek water then adds whatever he can find; turpentine, gunpowder, ammonia, and fusel oil."

"Heavens to Betsy, Padre, the stuff must look like sewage sludge. How could anyone think such a concoction is liquor?"

"In fact, the mix is clear at first. He wrinkled his nose and added, "Then he adds tobacco juice from the saloon's spittoons, and a few chicken guts to give it the color of good whiskey.

She made a face. "That's disgusting Father, but none of those things would deliver a buzz."

"That's where the strychnine comes in. Trujillo achieves the effect with a little strychnine. He doesn't kill rats with his poison—he makes bad booze."

"Father! You must be joking."

"No, it's absolutely true." The padre shrugged and held out his palms.

Jada was silent for a moment, then she pulled a medical book from the clutter on the clinic floor and thumbed through it for the chapter about poisons. Meanwhile, Guale began picking up the scattered pills, putting similar ones together in separate bottles.

After a few minutes, she held out the textbook and said, "In small amounts strychnine stimulates the nervous system and causes a reaction comparable to whisky. A heavy drinker will be left with a major hangover exactly like the real thing—nausea, headache, and weakness."

Glancing up from his seat on the floor, the priest confirmed her research. "Many people are in terrible shape after a night of boozing at the saloon."

Jada added, "The body takes a long time to eliminate it. On a prolonged binge, enough might build up in a man's system to kill him."

Father Guale sighed and shook his head. "I've seen some very sick folks leaving the barroom. In fact, when I first met you, I was warning him about selling his rotgut."

It took longer than Jada imagined to straighten her office, even with the help of Guale and Rita Gonzales, who joined them later. Darkness had set in by the time they finished. As the three sat around the kitchen table drinking coffee and discussing the day's events, someone pounded on her front door.

When she answered, an excited man pointed toward the casino. "Something's wrong in the barroom. Everybody is sick!"

"Sick, how?" asked Jada.

"Several are complaining about stomach cramps, others are throwing up, and say they're dizzy."

"I better go." She grabbed her doctor's bag.

Rushing through the saloon's swinging doors, she stumbled over a petite young woman, lying on her side with her spine and neck hideously arched. A curious smile played across her lips. Father Guale attempted to roll her on her back, but she was so curved and rigid only her soles and the top of her head touched the floor. He tried to push her flat but she was frozen into a pathological camber.

Jada felt for a pulse. "Who is she? She's dead."

Rita brushed the girl's hair away from her face. "That's Fola Mae, one of Trujillo's girls."

"Well, Trujillo's sauce killed her. I think the mayor added too much fire to his firewater this time." Jada pointed at the dead prostitute. "When you die from strychnine poisoning, your back arches much the same as Fola Mae's, and you leave with a little smile like you see here. Small as she is, it wouldn't take much to finish her."

One of the barflies, overhearing Jada's diagnosis, shouted across the room, "Fola Mae's dead. Trujillo's whiskey killed Fast Fola." Fola Mae was called Fast Fola because of the speed with which she dispatched her gentlemen customers. A roar of anger arose from the crowd.

"Father, find the blacksmith and tell him to bring as much charcoal dust as he can collect. Does the town have a harness maker?"

"Sure does. He makes saddles too." The priest was already moving toward the door.

"Get him to fetch a bucket of tannic acid. Hurry!"

"Rita, get as many women as you can find to bring plenty of clean water and some soap."

Jada shouted above the commotion, "Everybody listen. I want you to vomit. Don't waste time finding a container—just throw up. We must get the poison out of your stomach immediately. Stick a finger down your throat like this."

She grabbed a semiconscious man sitting with his head down on the bar, pulled him erect by his hair, and stuck her fingers down his gullet. A gusher splashed across the counter. Everyone in the tavern began gagging themselves and hurling.

Just then Trujillo and Montoya burst into the saloon. "What the hell is going on?" shouted Trujillo. The response was three simultaneous gunshots from half-sick customers. All missed. The sheriff and the mayor made a rapid retreat.

After the shooting stopped, Rita appeared with ten housewives carrying buckets of water and bars of lye soap.

Guale came behind with the blacksmith who brought a gunnysack of charcoal dust, and the harness maker toting a pail of tannic acid.

Jada nodded toward the women. "Ladies, keep half the water clean and wash your hands with the rest using plenty of soap. Make sure the water is sudsy when you finish." She quickly scanned the room. "Then make everyone drink a glass of soapy water. They will upchuck so stand aside." The women began scrubbing their hands, filling the containers with the soapsuds. "When you're done, stir in a spoonful of charcoal and some tannic acid in a glass of clean water. Make all of them drink the whole glass. Tannic acid and charcoal are the best antidotes for strychnine." The women went to work.

After everyone drank the antidote, Jada shouted across the room. "All right folks, we've done everything we can for you. If you are still alive, you'll probably survive."

Jada turned to face the female volunteers. "Ladies, we're finished here. Go home, burn your clothes, and take a good bath. Thanks for the help."

Heated by the New Mexico sun, a putrid stench from the cantina hung over the town square the next day. A clean-up was essential, but no one volunteered.

In secret, Trujillo threatened to withhold narcotics from the surviving prostitutes if they didn't clean the scented saloon.

As the days passed, the town's hostility for Trujillo grew, but even with the drinkery scrubbed and open for business, Trujillo remained in seclusion. He knew he must act soon. Meanwhile he needed to think of a plan. He did.

27

Payback

IN THE DESERT, a mile outside of Canada Alamosa, the night was a blind man's holiday—no moon and few stars. Three men plodded their way across the sand; two on horses and one astride a mule leading the procession with a kerosene lantern.

The riders came to a sudden stop and the figure with the lamp got down from his mule and began to walk as if leading the others over rough ground. After his first few steps, a single shot rang out and he pitched forward into the dirt. The gunman dismounted, righted the lantern, and jabbed a long stick into the dead man on the ground. He remounted and rode off, back toward town with his companion and the mule.

When the glow from the kerosene lamp vanished into the blackness, a silhouette rose from the desert floor about fifty yards from the scene and eased up to the body. Without a sound, the mysterious man squatted down, checked the carcass, felt the rod sticking from his back, and determined he was a goner. The silent witness stood and slipped away into the night.

For days after the strychnine affair, Trujillo remained in seclusion to avoid the town's rancor. He finally raised enough courage to finalize his plan to clear himself of blame.

As he walked from the mayor's office to the hog ranch, a crowd gathered behind him shouting insults. In front of the saloon, he turned to face his accusers. "I know everyone thinks I ruined the liquor but it was Double O."

Double O was Omar Ortez, the village dimwit who sat for hours outside the saloon's doors and did errands for Trujillo in return for an occasional drink.

"He hasn't been around for a few days. I'll bet he dumped rat poison into my best whiskey by mistake and ran off when he realized what he had done." Trujillo's assertion threw some doubt into the crowd. Perhaps the mayor was innocent. Omar was stupid enough to make a big blunder in the mixing room.

Just as it seemed Trujillo might escape the wrath of Alamosa's citizens, a line of Apache warriors appeared on a ridge west of town. Panic struck the townsfolk when they realized the Indians were bristling with weapons.

They soon calmed as a lone rider left the war party and walked his horse toward the citizens. Jada recognized Victorio, Loco's warlike cousin. When he reached the gathering, everyone spotted a dead man lying across his saddle with an arrow jutting from his back.

"Yo, Victorio." Jada spoke in Chiricahua as she walked toward him. "Who do you have there? What's going on?"

"This is the dummy who sat in front of the saloon every day. White men tried to give the impression my Indians killed him. Some of my men bought whiskey at the backdoor here the other night. One died in our camp, and the rest are still sick. Someone is trying to make it seem like we shot the witless one in revenge."

Jada translated for the crowd.

Trujillo pointed to Jada, his hand shaking. "That woman is a Chiricahua and she's trying to take the blame off the Apaches. It's obvious Double O was running away and that arrow in his back proves they killed him."

Jada interpreted for Victorio who shook his head. "My son, Washington, saw the whole thing. White men shot him, then stuck the arrow in the bullet hole."

Trujillo paled when Jada recounted Victorio's story indicating someone had witnessed the crime. "You can't believe an Apache. They all lie."

Jada translated as Victorio rolled the corpse off his horse. The dead Omar flopped face down in the dust. "I brought my warriors in case these people try to arrest me, but I spoke the truth. We picked up this man's body early today."

"No fight is necessary, Victorio. I think I can prove he wasn't killed by the arrow." Jada kneeled down and examined Omar's wound. "The bullet didn't go all the way through."

The chief nodded but the mayor continued to protest. "That Indian woman is covering for those lying Apaches."

Jada ignored Trujillo. "Gentlemen, if you'll take poor Omar into my office, we can find out."

With Double O on the examining table, Trujillo, Victorio, and a few men looked on as Jada removed the wooden shaft and dug into the wound. She extracted a .32 caliber slug, and held it up between her fingers to show the group.

A man in the crowd shouted, "There's only one gun that size in town. Don't the sheriff carry a .32 Smith and Wesson? Never seen no Indians 'round here totin' a .32." He pointed across the square where Sheriff Montoya was mounting his horse for a quick departure.

Victorio nodded to Jada and without another word galloped out of town. All the Apaches on the ridge turned and vanished.

With Montoya on the run and no proof Trujillo was directly involved in the killing, the mob scattered. Omar was not worth a fuss with the funcionario anyhow. The mayor returned to his office, a smile of satisfaction on his face.

That night Trujillo opened the saloon and served up only his best grain whiskey. Business thrived, but a little before midnight, the building shook from a loud explosion. A panicked reveler screamed, "Fire!—big blaze in the back room." Trujillo dashed around the tavern to his private 'mixing parlor' where he found flames raging inside. Fusil oil and kerosene barrels had been tipped over and ignited. The blaze had touched off a small keg of gunpowder causing the explosion.

Trujillo ran into the inferno with a bucket of water, but slipped in a puddle of flaming kerosene, soaking his clothes. He staggered from the honky-tonk immersed in flames and lurched into the church next door. The old wooden sanctuary burst into flame, and was fully engulfed in minutes. The crowd retreated across the square to escape the heat and stood by helplessly as the two largest buildings in Canada Alamosa burned to the ground.

Outside, beyond the glow of the flames, Victorio and six Apaches watched as Trujillo's flaming figure stumbled from the burning casino. When the hog ranch collapsed sending a shower of glowing embers skyward, the warriors mounted their ponies and rode in silence toward the reservation. Their dead and sick friends had been avenged. Trujillo's charred bones were later found in the cinders. Sheriff Montoya was never seen again.

The following morning, a dispirited Father Guale sat in Jada's kitchen holding a cup of steaming coffee with both hands. "I'm afraid our church is gone. We don't have enough people worshiping here for Rome to give us money to rebuild, and our poor congregation has little to donate. They will help reconstruct the sanctuary, but there are no funds to buy the materials."

"How much do you need, Father?" asked Jada.

"Five hundred, maybe a bit more. I don't know. I'm not a builder."

"Excuse me a minute." Jada walked back to her bedroom. When she returned, she handed Guale a bank draft for one thousand dollars.

"Doctor Morgan! Can you afford this? Are you sure you have this much?"

"Father, believe me, I have it. Besides you've given me a nice place to stay, introduced me to everyone in town, and I think I'm speaking pretty good Spanish."

"You are talking like a Spaniard, and you are heaven sent. Thank you and God bless you."

"One other thing, Father. I'm going to move to the Indian village and return your house. You need somewhere to stay while you rebuild the church. The Apaches will give me a place.

28

Forced to Arizona

IN LATE SEPTEMBER 1878, a month after Jada moved to Loco's village, William Vandever called a meeting of the reservation leaders. Two government employees attended; Dr Walter Whitney, the acting Indian agent, and Vandever, the Inspector from Washington.

When the headmen assembled in front of the Indian offices, they became aware no other agency workers were to be seen. "Seems strange, Dah-zhonne. Where are all the white people?" asked Loco.

"I don't know, Uncle, I'll ask Doctor Whitney," said Jada.

Whitney served as the acting agent before Vandever arrived. Jada liked him and he respected her as well. "Where's the staff?" she asked.

"They've closed the agency. Vandever's going to tell the tribe today they must move soon. It's a serious mistake, I think." He made a helpless gesture. "I tried to talk him out of it and even wrote my brother in Washington to inquire on the Indians behalf—got nowhere."

"Damn Commissioner Hayt. He's behind this." Jada's voice was bitter as her anger rose. "I should've let him choke when I had a chance. Is this travesty supposed to happen soon?"

Whitney hitched his thumb toward the Washington-man. "Don't know. Vandever might let them know today."

Jada interpreted what Whitney said for Loco. The old chief stared ahead in mute disappointment.

Vandever stood on a crate and held up his hands for quiet. "This will be a short meeting. There isn't much to say." Jada translated for the Indians.

"Today, I've come to tell you the tribe is to be returned to the San Carlos reservation sometime in the next month." He pointed his finger at the assembly. "The army can help you transfer, or they will chase you down and attack you if you run away. That's all I have to say."

When Jada finished the translation, angry chatter rippled through the crowd. The noise quieted as Loco stood. "I'll be brief too. This place has been our homeland forever and we've been peaceful. There is no reason for this, but I won't fight. I don't want my children killed on the warpath. I'll go for their sake."

Once again Jada translated as she fought back tears. Loco's people nodded, but Victorio's following shook their heads. She sat down with Loco and waited for his reaction. His face was an unreadable mask as he patted her hand.

Loco's cousin, Victorio, jumped up and angrily shouted over the crowd's rumbling. Jada stood beside him to interpret. "Victorio says he is opposed to going but since he can't change the Great Father's decision, he'll leave with Loco." Jada cast a disbelieving glance at Victorio and continued to translate. "He asks that the army escort his people to Arizona in safety."

Jada sat down close to Loco. "I can't believe he agreed to leave without an argument."

Loco leaned over and whispered to Jada. "Victorio's not going to San Carlos with us. He'll leave."

Vandever hopped from his perch and swaggered into the agency office, confident he had set those damn Apaches straight. Whitney made eye contact with Jada, shook his head and followed the inspector.

Immediately after the meeting, Jada packed her things, requested Loco give her medical supplies to Dr. Whitney, and dashed to Fort McRae.

Obadiah saw Jada's shay race onto the base and make a beeline to the Western Union office.

At the telegrapher's she dictated two cablegrams; the first to government officials and the second to her family.

Identical telegrams to: President Rutherford B. Hayes; Carl Shurz, Secretary of Interior; Ezra Hyat, Commissioner of Indian Affairs; Trinadad Romero, Hiram S. Stevens, Territorial Representatives for New Mexico and Arizona.

September 24, 1878

Insist you halt planned move of Apaches from Hot Springs reservation. Indians' homeland since time immemorial. Relocation will cause widespread bloodshed. Leave for DC next two days. Request meetings with all parties.

Jada P. Morgan M.D.

Identical telegrams to: Jack Morgan; J.P Morgan

September 24, 1878

Will leave for Washington immediately. Must try to stop removal of New Mexico Apaches to Arizona. Need help. Will come to Philadelphia afterwards.

Affection, Jada

Obadiah found Jada seated in the telegraph office holding her head in her hands. "Jada, are you all right?"

"No." Her voice quivered with anger. "It's all turning to shit. You better get your boys ready for a helluva chase and a damned bloody fight."

The telegraph clerk flinched at Jada's profanity but said nothing after he saw her expression.

"Jada, what's going on?" asked Obadiah. "I've never seen you so angry—or heard you cuss like that."

"Vandever just told Loco and Victorio's people they must move to San Carlos." She shook her head. "Loco says he won't cause any trouble, but Victorio is furious and he has a hundred warriors with him. They're going to kill lots of people."

A frown crossed Obadiah's face. "The Indian Office keeps causing these problems and leaving them for the army to clean up."

"I'm leaving for Washington to fight this as soon as I can arrange a ride to catch the train in Santa Fe." she said.

"You don't need to go that far now. The railroad has put a spur down to Albuquerque."

She gave Obadiah a pleading look. "Could you spare a man to drive me there, then bring the shay back to the post and sell it?"

"Corporal Israel is on limited duty. He will enjoy a trip to the big city."

"That sounds good. When can I leave?"

"I'll make arrangements for in the morning. It'll give us time to talk this evening."

That afternoon, Obadiah and Jada rode out to their favorite place by the river. They settled on an army blanket and gazed at the sunset over the Rio Grande. After a few moments, Jada pulled away. "You understand if the government makes this move, I won't come back to Alamosa." She pursed her lips, thought for a moment. "If the tribe stays at San Carlos, I may set up a practice there."

"I figured something like that after we talked today. I'll be stationed here at Fort McRae for at least four years. McRae and San Carlos are a long way apart." His voice trailed off. "About 250 miles. We can write, but no more evening rides."

"I've been here almost a year now." Her eyes filled and she took his hand. "I've gotten accustomed to the place, and I like having you around. This is so hard." She kissed him gently on the lips.

Jada and Corporal Icabod Israel left the next morning for Albuquerque, with Icabod at the reins of the shay. Jada was too depressed to drive.

29

Jada's Failed Intervention

WHEN JADA ARRIVED IN WASHINGTON, she registered in the Willard Hotel and hired a carriage to take her to the Interior Department. The Secretary of Interior's clerk greeted her in the outer office.

"Secretary Shurz is expecting you and requests I tell you he'll be able to meet with you at three-thirty Friday afternoon," He looked bored and his tone was indifferent.

"That's four days from now. This is an emergency."

He appeared unconcerned. "Yes ma'am, but as a convenience to you, the secretary has arranged a meeting regarding your concerns with all those listed in your telegram."

"Friday then." Jada spun on her heels and left the office cursing under her breath.

On Friday afternoon at 3:30 Jada was greeted by the same clerk. "Doctor Morgan, please take a seat. The Secretary will see you shortly. He's in a conference right now." He smirked over his reading spectacles and returned to his paperwork.

Jada took a chair beside the meeting room where she overheard small-talk and laughter inside. Annoyed at the delay, she impatiently tapped her foot as an hour ticked past.

Finally at five o'clock, another clerk rushed into the office and handed a telegram to the bored receptionist. He took the paper and walked briskly past Jada into the conference room. Several minutes later the clerk stepped out and summoned her. "You may come in, Doctor."

"Welcome, Doctor Morgan." Secretary of Interior, Carl Shurz gave Jada a politician's smile. "Please have a seat."

Jada was angry because of the unreasonable wait, but she said nothing. Shurz introduced her to the two territorial representatives, then looked at the Commissioner of Indian Affairs. "I believe you know Commissioner Hayt."

"I certainly do." Jada could not mask her hostility. "He's about to force the Apaches into a war with the United States. The government is stealing their homeland."

"My dear, do you understand the government moved the tribe from Canada

Alamosa to San Carlos a year ago?" Shurz gave his collar an uncomfortable tug. "A month later, President Hayes issued an order restoring the vacant reservation to public domain and ordered it sold. The Indians escaped from San Carlos after that and ran back to their old spot near Alamosa. They've been living there illegally for the past year."

Jada's jaw dropped, stunned at the news. "No, I never heard that. I thought the president was a friend of the Indians."

Trinadad Romero, the representative from New Mexico spoke up. "The president only made the decision after Agent Clum assured him the tribe was delighted with their new location."

Jada felt her face redden. Her fist hit the table. "Mr. Clum is a liar. The tribe went because they were forced to go by the cavalry." Jada knew she sounded screechy and tried to calm herself. "I wasn't around then, but I can tell you the Chiricahuas loathe that place, dislike the Indians there, and the San Carlos Indians hate the Chiricahuas as well."

Ezra Hayt sneered and laid the just-delivered telegram on the table in front of him. "Doctor Morgan, I realize from your wire why you are here, so I'll save us all some time, and read this cable. It just arrived for Secretary Shurz, dated today from a Captain Bennett."

He adjusted his spectacles, lifted the yellow paper, and cleared his throat.

Left the Warm Springs agency this day with units of Ninth Calvary accompanying 169 Apaches under Chief Loco. Others including Victorio, Nana, Naiche managed to escape with a few followers. Believed headed for Mexico. Troops sent to stop them were unsuccessful.

Hayt gave the paper a slight shake, then continued to read. Loco reluctant to leave. Implored tribe be left at Ojo Caliente or moved any place but San Carlos. Has agreed to go peacefully. Captain Frank Bennett, 9th U.S. Cavalry.

Jada pushed her chair away from the table. "My god," she gasped. "Do you fools understand what you've done? Victorio, Nana and Naiche are the Chiricahuas' best war leaders. And if my count is correct, those 'few followers' who the captain mentions add up to over one hundred of the tribe's toughest warriors. Hundreds of innocent people will die because of this."

"Now, now, my dear." Shurz said in a condescending tone. "It's not as bad as you say. And besides, they weren't doing anything with the land."

"You are right," said Jada, her voice rising. "They were just living on it." She pounded the table again with her fist for emphasis. "And sir, this is worse than you can imagine. Those with Victorio will fight to the death."

Her face flushed and she pointed her finger at Shurz and Hayt. "You kept me waiting for four days and had me sit in your outer office until word came that the removal was in progress. You cowards delayed so I couldn't ask the president to stop the removal!" She stood and glared at the group. "It's obvious graft and corruption are behind this."

The four political appointees erupted with denials, but Jada ignored their protests and walked out of the room, slamming the door behind her.

Ezra Hayt smiled. That went better than I thought. We've muzzled the little rabble-rouser for good.

When Jada left the Interior Department, she walked outside and crumpled onto a public bench. Tears streamed down her cheeks. She knew a visit to the president or General Sheridan would be a waste of time. Instead she sent them notes by courier cancelling their meetings.

On the train to Philadelphia, she spoke to no one and stared in silence at the passing scenery. Jada's mood brightened as the locomotive chugged into the Philadelphia depot and she spied Jack waiting on the platform. He greeted her with hugs and smiles.

It was good to be back home, but after her efforts to stop the Apache removal had failed, she continued to agonize over the government's mistreatment of the Chiricahuas. Her spirits plunged further when she received no letters from Obadiah although she had written him every day.

Even in her doldrums, she enjoyed long talks with Jack comparing their Western experiences and how living in Philadelphia had changed her life.

Their long cozy conversations inevitably led Jack to ask, "Have you found that special man? There're lots of unattached fellows out West."

"Well, I thought I had, but I've written him every day since I left New Mexico, and I haven't received a single letter. Now I suspect I've been played a fool."

Hoping she would stay home, he asked, "Do you think you might want to come back to Philadelphia?"

"I miss you, father—and Rebecca and Simon, but I believe I belong with my tribe." She bit her lip as she waited for a reaction.

Jack smiled and nodded. "You know I want you here, but I understand how you feel. Just remember you're always welcome."

"I'm sure of that, daddy."

Jada soon relaxed but her discontent with city life increased by the day. The family medical practice now seemed tedious. She spent most of her time reassuring the worried well and treating trifles. After her adventures in New Mexico, life in Philadelphia was mind-numbing dull.

She tried to reconnect with her old friends, but they were scattered. She managed to get in touch with Judy Lawson and found her in the midst of preparations for the annual New Year's Eve party. When Jada told her she was moving to Arizona soon, Judy insisted she come to the festivities before she left.

"The old gang won't be there but I'll introduce you to some fresh faces."

This time when she arrived at the Lawson's party, Jada thought the ballroom trimmings were gaudy—extravagant and pretentious. A faux snow covered the dance floor. The mirror ball sent irritating slivers of light glistening off the fake snow. Hundreds of paper snowflakes dangled from the ceiling. Judy greeted Jada dressed in a white gown with a sequin-covered bodice designed to coordinate with the ballroom's motif.

It was good to see Judy again but as predicted, none of their old friends attended the party. Nevertheless, the two delighted in each other's company and Jada relished Judy's news of their former schoolmates. The chat prompted Jada to ask about the absence of Joanne Tomley.

"She's still missing and hasn't communicated with any family or friends," said Judy.

"No word at all?"

"None."

"I wonder where she is?" asked Jada.

"Some think she's dead." Other partygoers distracted Judy before she could say more.

Circulating around the room, Judy introduced Jada to dozens of her acquaintances. Judy's friends were nice enough but Jada found their conversation to be trivial. The men blathered on sports or their work, and the ladies prattled about fashions or places to shop. By party's end, Jada was clear she needed to return to where her heart told her she should be—with her people out West.

Three days after the party, a thin wrinkled envelope covered in dirty smudges arrived at the Morgan manor. Jada recognized Obadiah's handwriting and her thoughts flashed back to Harry Trenchcott's last epistle. Now, a slender letter from Obadiah after all this time must mean the end of it. Her hands trembled as she opened the envelope.

She found Obadiah's note inside, begrimed with dirt and written in pencil on a small tear of rumpled brown paper. The message wasn't what she expected.

Dearest Jada,

Please accept my apologies for not writing. I've thought about you every day since you left and wanted to write. You were correct. After you returned East, Victorio and his followers ran away and are killing hundreds around the territory. We've been in the field chasing him all this time and I've had no chance to write.

I miss you terribly. Please consider returning to the West as soon as possible. I received two letters from you before I left McCrae. I hope more are waiting when I return.

I pray we can continue our discussion about marriage.

I must go. I'm sending a scout back to the fort with a report. He'll mail this letter.

With great affection, Obadiah.

Relief flowed through her body as she clutched the ragged brown paper to her heart. She decided to leave for San Carlos as soon as possible. At least she and Obadiah would be closer.

She spent the following days packing her travel trunks and arranging to ship several crates of medical supplies to Arizona.

She planned to take the southern route through New Orleans to Tucson. Pierpont again offered his personal rail coach but Jada, not wishing to inconvenience him declined. Instead she would take a first class Pullman sleeper. She asked Jack to arrange for someone from San Carlos to meet her in Tucson with a wagon to haul her travel trunks.

30

Arrival at San Carlos

THREE APACHES AND A WHITE MAN riding along the dusty road from Globe to Tucson had been assigned to accompany the new doctor to the San Carlos agency. The fair-haired rider was Albert Sterling, Chief of Police for the reservation. With him were his Indian deputy, Sogotal, and two tribal policemen. Sterling and Sogotal trotted ahead of the buckboard shooting the breeze and watching for trouble. The other men rode in the buck-wagon, their horses tethered behind.

The four men reached the outskirts of Tucson two hours after the train had arrived and departed. Sterling sent Sogotal ahead to advise the physician his reception party would be there soon.

After riding to the station, Sogotal returned and shook his head. "Ain't no doctor at the depot—jest a little Mexican gal."

"Shit, Sogotal, I hope we didn't come all this way to find the doctor changed his mind." Sterling removed his hat and wiped his forehead. "Guess we better go see if he's in town wetting his whistle."

Jada sat erect on a travel trunk, waiting unconcerned, as the men approached. Sterling rode over to her and asked, "You speak English?"

"I do indeed."

"Did anyone get off the train with you?"

"Two men—cowboys, I think. Some others brought horses for them and they rode off together."

"Well, damn—uh darn. Sorry, ma'am. We're supposed to pick up a medical man here and take him to the reservation. Did anybody seem like a sawbones? You know, a doctor carrying a little black bag?

"Like this." She held up her medical bag. "Are you looking for Doctor Morgan?"

"I sure as heck am. You must have seen him."

"I am Doctor Morgan, sir. I suppose you're the ones escorting me to San Carlos?"

"I'll be hornswoggled; a girl doctor, Sogotal."

Sogotal frowned at Jada. "You Indian or Mexican?"

"Yes," was her only answer.

The three Apaches began rattling on in Apache. "She must be a Mex. Never seen no Apache that pretty," said one.

"If she's a real doctor, I'm gonna get sick. She can take care of me anytime."

Jada smiled and asked in English, "We still have plenty of sunlight. Do you want to start back or should I pay for rooms in the hotel?"

"We better be moseying on. Hotels around here don't take Indians, Apaches in particular." Sterling shook his head.

Jada winced. "Well, let's get moving. I suppose we'll have to camp for the night. I should be safe sleeping with four brave men." She chuckled at her play on words.

The scouts all started to chatter at once. "She's a Mexican. Apache girls wouldn't say that!"

"Okay men, get her baggage loaded and let's move out." Sterling dismounted his horse and climbed aboard the wagon. "The doctor can ride with me."

The route to and from Tucson wended through a desert valley for ten miles along the base of the Santa Catarina Mountains. Sterling scanned the area, watching for an ambush. "This is the most dangerous part of the ride." He slapped the reins against the horses to speed the pace. When Jada asked why, he nodded toward the mountains. "Don't want to worry you ma'am, but with Victorio raging about, we can't dally around here. This stretch is a good place for an attack."

Just as Sterling's words left his mouth, ten Apache warriors galloped from the rocks a half mile ahead, blocking the way. Turning and running would be useless so Sterling pulled the wagon beside a pile of boulders and prepared for a fight to the end. "We will try to stop them doc, but we're in a bad spot. Here, take one of my pistols and save the last bullet for yourself. They're hard on womenfolk."

Jada pulled her .38 Hopkins and Allen pistol from her doctor's bag as the Indians cautiously walked their horses toward the buckboard. "I've got my own gun." Sterling and Sogotal exchanged surprised glances.

A look of recognition came over Jada as she watched the war party move closer. "Don't any of you shoot unless I do. I'll handle this."

As the men stared in disbelief, Jada ripped out the silver hairclip holding her bun in place, shook her head, let her straight black hair fall to her shoulders and stood up on the wagon bed. One of the scouts shouted "Get down! You're a crazy woman." A single shot splattered through the wagon's sideboard missing Jada by inches. The leader of the Indians raised his hand to stop further shooting.

Jada spread her feet, put her hands on her hips, and shouted in Chiricahua, "Victorio, what are you doing? I'm Dah-zhonne, the medicine woman who fixed your son's broken arm at Canada Alamosa. Leave us alone. These men are taking me to your cousin Loco's people at San Carlos. I'll be their doctor."

"We could kill you all," Victorio shouted back. "You must be stupid to stand up like that. You're an Apache. You know better."

"I won't talk to a great chief while I'm hiding behind a rock. What would killing us get you? Nothing but some dresses for your women. Go find some richer targets."

There was a brief conference as the raiders discussed the surprising turn of events. Then, without another word, Victorio and his men turned and rode back into the hills.

"I guess it's settled. She's an Apache," Sterling grinned at his Indian companions. "Hope you men kept your lingo clean while you were talking Indian in front of her." Sogotal and the scouts blushed and stared at the ground.

After riding three more hours, the group made camp on the banks of the Arivapa River. As they prepared their pallets for bedtime, Sterling surveyed the area. "Who wants to stand guard first?"

"There's no need. We won't be disturbed." Jada arranged her blanket for the night.

"Just what makes you so confident, Missy?" asked Sterling in a patronizing tone.

"Two of them are following us right now. I've been watching them for an hour. Victorio is making sure no one bothers us."

The three scouts and Sterling spun around searching for Victorio's men. They were invisible.

"There's nobody out there," said Sogotal.

"You've been on the reservation too long." She whistled a peculiar bird call. Two rifle shots crashed through the trees above them. Still no one could be seen.

"See." Jada smiled, pulled up her blanket, and fell asleep.

31

Old Philadelphia Friend

THE SAN CARLOS INDIAN AGENCY sat on a gravel-covered flat surrounded by barren desert. The agency proper was a drab collection of tents and adobe buildings scattered over a bleak expanse of sand and gravel. The government office, the hospital, and a few small houses were the only frame buildings.

As Jada surveyed the depressing panorama she glanced at Sterling, "Such an abysmal spot for people to live. What do you do for enjoyment in a place like this?" Al smiled at the thought of his fiancée.

"I'm engaged to one of the teachers. Her name's Jo," replied Al. "There's a lot for us to do."

"Aren't you lucky? I hope I get to meet her."

"I'm sure you will. We all live close together at the agency. I'm in the employees' quarters, but Jo shares a house with the other teacher."

"Where does Jo come from?" asked Jada.

"It's strange, she won't say." He wiped his sleeve across his forehead. "All she'll tell me is she's from back east—never told me where."

Jada glanced at Al. "That's odd." Must be a woman in trouble, she thought.

As Al ushered Jada into the agency building, Joseph Tiffany's office door flew open and a sleazy character barged out. "Tiffany, you're a fool," shouted Edward Knapp over his shoulder. "The commissioner will support me on this. You're delaying the inevitable, and delays cost me money."

Agent Tiffany responded in a loud voice. "You're stealing from the Indians again, and this is nothing but a land grab. The commissioner won't be the only one who hears about what you're up to."

The man spun around and bumped into Jada. She recognized him immediately, remembering his oily black hair and the beady eyes that stared at her chest throughout her visit to the White House.

"Why, Mr. Hayt, what are you doing out here in the wilds?"

The sinister reprobate cast quick glances at Tiffany to confirm he hadn't heard. "You're mistaken woman. My name is Knapp. Now, if you'll get out of my way, I have business to attend." Knapp quick-stepped from the room. Jada stared after him as he slammed the outer door.

Agent Tiffany was still fuming when Al and Jada came into his office. Al spoke first, "Mr. Tiffany, this is Doctor Jada Morgan. She's a woman doctor, sir."

"Damn, Al I can see that," said Tiffany as he stood and offered Jada his hand. "Please take a seat, Doctor Morgan. I hope you realize what you are getting into." He sat down in his worn chair. "San Carlos is under siege by Edward Knapp and his hooligan friends. The man cheats on his contracts; gives the Apaches wormy flour, sick cattle, and inferior clothing." He took a long pull on the stub of a cigar. "Now he wants the government to withdraw a large section of the land from the reservation so he can buy it for himself and his rat pack. Coal deposits have been discovered in that area."

Tiffany leaned back in his chair and exhaled. "Forgive the rant, doctor. I've requested a survey to guarantee the Indians' land is safe but Commissioner Hayt is no help. He won't give his approval. In fact, he has rejected every complaint I've filed regarding Knapp."

"Tell me, Mr. Tiffany, do you know anything about Mr. Knapp?" asked Jada, pursing her lips.

"Not much. He showed up here from Washington a while back with a letter from the commissioner directing me to establish contracts with him for supplies. But everything he delivers is inferior or deficient. He's stealing from the Indians with the commissioner's blessing." Tiffany stubbed out his cigar in disgust.

"I believe I get the picture," said Jada appearing concerned. "I don't want to be presumptuous, but I might be able to help."

"Perhaps you can. You come recommended by some mighty high-ranking bigwigs. Maybe you could use your connections to end this travesty. What's your plan?"

"No plan. But I understand the problem, and something should be done. Could one of your policemen deliver some letters to Tucson in the morning so they can be trained to Washington?"

"Sogotal can go," said Al who was standing behind Jada. "He's our best man."

"Then have him ready first thing. Now, is there a place for me to stay? I've a few letters to write."

Tiffany pointed through the office window at a small white-washed house, "I've asked our schoolteachers to put you up for a little while until your apartment in the hospital is ready. They'll be delighted to have your company."

"I'm looking forward to meeting them. I'm sure we'll have a nice time together."

When Snow Anderson answered Jada's knock, her doe-like eyes blinked wide in alarm. "Yes, may I help you?" she asked as she half-closed the door.

"I hope so," replied Jada. "I'm Doctor Morgan. Mr. Tiffany said you would let me stay with you until my apartment in the hospital is finished."

"Oh, you're the lady doctor staying with us. I was surprised you are an Ind … aah, so young. Please come in. I'm Snow Anderson. Please call me Snow." She turned her head and shouted into the house. "Hey, Jo, the doctor is here. Come meet her."

Turning to Jada she added, "This will be a nice interlude for us. We seldom get to entertain visitors."

Just as Snow finished her sentence, Joanne Tomley walked into the room. Jada dropped her bag and squealed, "Joanne! So this is where you've been."

Snow looked confused. "You two know each other?"

As Snow spoke, Joanne's eyes rolled back and she crashed to the floor.

Snow panicked and rushed to her unconscious housemate, bawling, alternately covering her mouth and flapping her hands. "Oh, what can we do?" Tears streamed down her suntanned cheeks as she yelled, "We need a doctor. Help!"

Jada kneeled beside Jo and spoke in a calm voice. "Snow, I am a doctor. Now, let's get her into bed. She'll be all right."

Snow continued to blubber, shaking her head until her long blond hair fell around her shoulders. At last, Jada took her hand and said, "Snow hush! She just fainted."

Jada pulled a bottle of smelling salts from her doctor's bag and wafted it under Joanne's nose. Her eyes blinked open and she started crying, covering her face with both hands. Her sobbing set Snow off again.

Two teary women were too much for Jada. "Snow, go into the other room and settle yourself." Snow retreated to the parlor.

"Jada, how did you find me? I never wanted anyone to know where I was."

"Well, to be honest, Joanne—or is it Jo, I wasn't looking for you. Everyone back home thinks you're in California or dead."

"I'm Jo now. If they think I'm a goner, that's what I want."

"Why for heaven's sake? They're all so worried."

"I can't talk about what happened, Jada. It's so terrible." She covered her face and rocked back and forth.

"Jo, we've been friends forever. It's all right." Jada offered Jo a sympathetic look. "Okay lady, what's the story."

Jo looked to make sure Snow was out of hearing. At last she said, "This is so hard to discuss but my father made me have sex with him. Not only once but several times a week for a couple of months. I couldn't make him stop and mother refused to believe it. So I ran away and haven't contacted anyone in Philly since. Father told me if I left, he would track me down. I was afraid to tell anybody where I am for fear the word might leak out and he would come for me."

Jada hugged Jo and patted her friend's back. "I'm so sorry. I hate that for you. I promise no one will ever find out from me."

"Let's not mention this from now on, all right?"

"You bet but I'll be here for you if you need me." Jada wiped away the tears streaking down Jo's cheeks.

"We better go and console Snow," said Jo. "She's a sweet sensitive girl and very young. I don't know how she ended up at San Carlos of all places. She is afraid of everything, especially Indians."

"I gathered that. I think she almost passed out when she opened the door and saw me."

32

Corruption Exposed

IT WAS MIDNIGHT before Snow calmed down and fell asleep. Alone, Jada and Jo began to rehash old times in Philadelphia until two in the morning. At last, Jada yawned and went to the front room. "We have a long time to finish this conversation, Jo. You're tired and I need to write some letters before first light."

After Jo said good night, Jada wrote identical messages to President Rutherford Hayes, Secretary of War George McCrary, and Interior Secretary Carl Shurz.

Dear President Hayes:

There is a situation here on the San Carlos Apache Reservation in Arizona so rank your immediate attention is required.

Despite what appears to be an adequate rationing program for the Apaches, the supplies received are much less than the government contract specifies, and are of the poorest quality. Their rations are inedible. The Indians will not tolerate this for long.

Right now, efforts are being made by white men led by Edward Knapp to annex a portion of the reservation on which coal deposits have been found. Mr. Knapp is also the contractor for most of the inadequate and inferior provisions issued to the Chiricahuas. I overheard him declare to Agent Joseph Tiffany that he is assured of the Commissioner's approval on this matter and all other things contractual.

Unknown to anyone here except me, Edward Knapp is in fact Edwin Knapp Hayt, son of Ezra Hyat, the present Commissioner of Indian Affairs. This is a clear case of nepotism and egregious corruption at its worst.

I request you send an Indian Inspector to San Carlos as soon as possible to confirm my observations and respond appropriately. Thank you in advance for your help with stopping this flagrant fraud.

Sincerely,

Jada P. Morgan, MD

Jada finished her letters just as the sun peeked over the eastern horizon. When she looked from the window, Sogotal was sitting on the front step, waiting to take her missives to the postmaster in Tucson. Giving him her dispatches, she shook his hand. "Thanks, Sogotal, these are important."

In response to Jada's letter, Indian Inspector John Hammond was soon dispatched from Washington. Within six weeks of his arrival in San Carlos, he uncovered widespread fraud and corruption involving Edward Knapp, a few friends, and Knapp's father, the Commissioner of Indian Affairs. Hammond confirmed the Commissioner had knowingly approved his son's illegal activities.

Hammond wired his findings to the Secretary of the Interior, Carl Shurz. Shurz was so outraged he stormed into Commissioner Hayt's office, fired him on the spot, and gave him one hour to leave the building. He then wired Agent Tiffany to cancel all of Knapp's arrangements at once and to void any actions taken on Knapp's behalf regarding the coal deposits on the reservation.

Afterwards Tiffany told Jada, "I don't know what you did, Doctor Morgan, but you probably stopped an outbreak."

Jada thanked him, shook his hand, and left for the hospital, satisfied she had struck a blow for fair treatment of her people.

Two weeks after Tiffany voided Knapp's contracts, four men in dark suits slithered into the Snake Hole Saloon on the outskirts of Globe, fifteen miles from the Indian agency. Entering the sleazy grog shop, Knapp scowled in disgust as he viewed the kerosene-lit taproom that stank of sweat, cigar smoke, and stale booze.

The four found a table in a dark corner and ordered a bottle of ninety-proof popskull. While they waited, they shooed off four repulsive prostitutes, so ugly Knapp swore their faces were responsible for the large crack that cleaved diagonally across the mirror behind the bar.

The Snake Hole was notorious for diseased women, diluted hooch, and unsanitary conditions. The tables were sticky and the glasses smudged. While there were spittoons, nobody took careful aim, and dark stains colored the sawdust around the spit-buckets. The saloon, however, was the one place in Globe where the foursome was guaranteed they would not meet the swells in town with whom they did business.

After the drinks were delivered, Knapp opened the meeting. "That damned Indian bitch wrecked our coal deal and ruined my contracting career. We need to do something about her."

"Yeah, but what? They say she has connections in Washington," said Punky Dorkus. "As long as she's around, we don't dare dip into the government's money bag."

A tall man with a waxed handlebar mustache, known only as Roach, hunched over the table, and drew the others in. "The best thing to do is kill her and make it seem like Mexicans did it."

Knapp agreed. "Hell, that would be easy. I've kept an eye on her. I'm familiar with her routine."

Willie Rotter interjected from behind a thick beard, "I'll bet you did, Knapp. She's a looker." The group laughed.

"Quit joking around. This is serious," admonished Knapp.

"Damn Knapp, she's just a squaw. No jury will convict a white man for killing an Indian. What are you afraid of?" Dorkus raised an eyebrow and grinned.

"Nothing. But this one's got clout. Now listen. Like I told you, I've watched her for a while. Two days a week on Tuesdays and Thursdays she takes her little chaise up to those Indian camps in the mountains."

The men agreed they knew the route. "That road isn't traveled much and there's nothing along the way. We could kill and scalp her. If we left a bloody serape behind everybody would think Greasers from Mexico did it."

"Then we'll meet here Thursday morning before sunrise." Knapp proposed a toast to good hunting and they raised their glasses in anticipation of better times.

33

Ambushed

JADA MOVED INTO HER HOSPITAL APARTMENT and established a comfortable routine; checking her in-house patients in the morning and seeing walk-ins throughout the rest of the day. On Tuesdays and Thursdays, she drove her new shay to remote Indian camps to treat outpatients and convince the Apaches to use the hospital when they were sick.

On occasion, Jada took Joanne and Snow to the outlying villages so they could meet the parents of their students. Jada enjoyed their company on the lonely rides to the Indian villages and this gave her a chance to introduce her friends to the Indians. Joanne and Snow were even learning to speak a little Chiricahua.

On the Thursday after Knapp's Snake Hole meeting, Jada invited the two teachers to come along to visit Gordo's camp. At the last minute, Joanne developed a headache. So Jada hitched up her shay and left early with Snow for Chief Gordo's village, twelve miles away.

Seven miles out, Knapp and the wannabe assassins smoked cigars and drank coffee as they waited in dandified Mexican outfits and sombreros. The gang assumed if they were seen, the blame for Jada's death would fall on scalp hunters from south of the border.

They took turns climbing a nearby knoll to lookout for the doctor's approach. Midway through Knapp's shift, he came running down the hill. "Damn boys, we got problems. The Injun doctor has a blonde woman with her. What we gonna do?"

"That's easy, Knapp. We kill 'em both." Roach smiled and downed a swig of bad coffee.

Willie Rotter worried about the change of plans. "Ain't nobody going to believe Mexicans killed and scalped a white woman. They couldn't sell her hair for nothing. They only pay for Apache scalps."

"Well we can't just bump off the Indian and let the other one go, can we?" asked Punky Dorkus.

Roach chipped in. "We shoot them both and dump the blonde in a hole. Once they find the doc, they'll think the Mexicans took the blonde to sell as a prostitute in Mexico."

"Then one of you shoot the white gal," said Knapp. "I want to do the doctor myself. She ruined me and my family." He checked his pistol. Besides, he thought, killing an Indian ain't like killing a real person.

The weather was warm and the desert flowers were in bloom. Jada and her young friend were enjoying the ride when Jada slowed the shay, tilted her head, and sniffed. "Somebody's close," she told Snow.

"How can you tell?"

"I smell cigar smoke and coffee." Sensing trouble, Jada opened her doctor's bag on the seat between them. Just as she did, four men blocked the road to their front.

"Snow, get down! Bandits," Jada shouted as she reached into her bag and gripped her pistol.

As Snow crouched, Roach fired his Colt. The bullet hit her under the armpit, passed through her body, and came out beneath her breast. She screamed and fell from the shay, unconscious.

Jada raised her six-shot and jerked off a round at the shooter. Roach dropped his pistol, grabbed his chest, and tumbled from his horse. He was squirming the dust as Knapp pulled his pistol and aimed at Jada. She snapped off another shot. A stunned expression blanketed Knapp's face. He dropped his revolver, his eyes crossed and looked up as if to examine the bullet hole in his forehead. He jerked to rigid attention in his stirrups and crashed to the ground.

With no time to fire again, Jada tried to dive behind the shay's front panel, but her blouse snagged on the metal folding arms of the leather canopy. She closed her eyes and waited for a fatal shot from one of the other two. Instead she heard loud shouts. When she looked again, Dorkus and Rotter lay dead in the dirt beside Knapp and Roach, each pierced by a half dozen arrows.

Chief Gordo accompanied by six warriors galloped from behind the hill, bows in hand. He stopped his horse and gave Jada a worried look.

"I'm not hurt but my friend is shot." Jada rushed to the wounded Snow. She was still alive but bleeding and needed to be taken to the hospital. She bandaged the wounds and enlisted Gordo's warriors to lift Snow back into the shay and tie her in the seat.

"Gordo, you and your men are the best. I must hurry to get this girl back to the agency, but before I go, we have a problem. No matter what I say, everyone will think your band is on the warpath when they find these dead white men."

"They aren't Mexicans?" The chief eyed the dead men with renewed interest.

"They are well-known white men. They disguised themselves...Wait, I have an idea," said Jada in Chiricahua. "Is there a place we can hide the bodies?"

"Be better to strip them and leave them on Bear Mountain. Wild cats, coyotes, bears, and buzzards will make them vanish, and scatter their bones. There won't be nothing to find in a few days," Gordo lifted his hands, palms up, indicating the problem was solved.

"Good. Leave a sombrero here in the dirt and burn the rest of their clothes. Now, I need to go, but here's what I want you to do…"

Late that night, two mounted Apache warriors silently led four horses with empty saddles into the Tucson city limits. They tied the animals to a hitching post by the railroad depot, and returned to the reservation unseen.

The next afternoon, Sheriff James Calhoun noticed the horses had been unattended for too long. After searching the saddlebags, he determined they belonged to Edward Knapp and his friends. He assumed from the headlines in *The Tombstone Epitaph* the men had left town on the midnight train to avoid prosecution in the big corruption scandal at San Carlos. He confiscated the mounts and sold them at the next public auction.

34

Treating Wounded Friends

AL STERLING AND AGENT TIFFANY were standing in front of Tiffany's office when Jada sped onto the agency grounds with Snow tied unconscious in the seat of the chaise. Her limp arm dangled over the side of the buggy and flopped back and forth as Jada skidded to a stop. She hastened to tell the men about the incident—that robbers in Mexican outfits had attacked her and Snow, but Gordo and his warriors routed the outlaws. Afterwards, she galloped the rig to the infirmary entrance and called for Stanley Pangburn, the agency doctor, to help carry the young woman into the infirmary.

Snow remained unconscious until she was bathed and semi-reclined in a hospital bed. Jada had just finished wrapping her wounds with compression bandages when she awoke.

"Oh, Jada, I feel like I've been stabbed with a hot poker."

"I know sweetheart. I have some medicine for the pain right here. I'm so sorry this happened. Now, take this pill and go to sleep." She set an opium tablet on Snow's tongue, gave her a little water, and put her hand over Snow's until her patient passed out.

After Jada reported the attack, Sterling rode to the scene of the ambush with six policemen. He found bloodstains on the road which he assumed were Snow's and a sombrero. He told Agent Tiffany that Chief Gordo and his men saved the women and were heroes.

Fifty miles from where Jada tended Snow, near the edge of the Black Mountains, Colonel Busby Dogg and Major Obadiah Cantrell led a column of twenty-five cavalrymen. They were accompanied by Lieutenant Zebulon Troy commanding ten Apache scouts. Busby Dogg was known as "Mad Dogg" because he was wont to charge toward any gunfire, damning all caution, and cursing anyone who lagged behind.

Word had reached the army that Victorio's son, Washington, was headed for San Carlos with a band of warriors to retrieve relatives living with Loco. Dogg's troopers had tracked the renegades' for days when scouts leading the procession pulled to a halt where the trail entered a deep canyon.

The Chief of Scouts, Jinx, rode up to the officers, and said, "Good place for an ambush."

"What do you think we should do, Jinx?" asked Dogg.

"Safest to wait here. They won't stay around for long. We can get them when they come out."

Dogg patted his horse's neck and studied the boulder-studded walls. Nothing moved. He glanced at the scout. "If they aren't there, we'll be sitting here while they put distance between us and them."

The Apache cast a wary eye at Dogg, shrugged his shoulders, and remained silent. He knew what Dogg would do.

The colonel pointed down the path. "Let's get a move on. Be ready for a scrap."

The column was halfway through the gulch when Colonel Dogg, three soldiers, and three scouts fell in a blistering crossfire from high on both sides of the canyon. Jinx yelled over the din to Obadiah, "Good idea to run now!"

Obadiah agreed. "Men get the hell out of here the best way you can!" The troopers and scouts turned their horses and raced for cover. Obadiah followed the last man. Just before he reached safety at the canyon's entrance, a bullet grazed him above his temple. He clung to his saddle horn long enough to escape the hailstorm of bullets before he tumbled to the rocky ground.

Unsteady from the wound and the fall, he called out, "Lieutenant Troy, over here."

Troy scurried to Obadiah's side as the major leaned against a boulder. "Lieutenant, take charge. Divide the men and clear the ridges." He winced as he dabbed the blood running down his face. "After it's safe, recover the injured and dead. Send the medical orderly over here—now!"

The soldiers found no Indians. The ambushers had vanished into the desert. At the 'all clear' signal, ten troopers sprinted to the prostrate casualties. Busby Dogg, two enlisted men, and a scout were dead. Two scouts and a cavalryman were injured. The Indians had minor wounds, but the soldier had a nasty hole in his shoulder. They were all taken to where Obadiah sat. The Major gave his orders while the medic bandaged the wounded men. "We are about two days from the San Carlos hospital. We'll go there."

The dead men were tied over their horses and the column headed for the reservation. The wounded sat in their saddles without help. Lieutenant Troy rode beside Obadiah.

"Sir we could make it to Fort Apache—isn't that much further."

"We'll save some time by going to the Indian hospital. The best doctor in Arizona Territory works at San Carlos."

Obadiah felt like hell, but the idea of seeing Jada took his mind off the splitting headache that nagged him after the skirmish.

Jada was standing next to Snow's bed, her stethoscope pressed against the young woman's chest when Dr. Pangburn knocked at the door.

Jada pulled the sheet over Snow. "It's clear. Come."

Pangburn peeked in. "Sorry to interrupt, Doctor Morgan. May I talk with you for a moment?"

"Certainly. I'll be right there."

In the hall, Pangburn told Jada, "Two scouts just came in from an army patrol. The troopers were attacked fifty miles out and they're bringing four wounded here."

"Why aren't they taking them to Fort Apache?"

Pangburn shrugged. "Tiffany asked the scouts that. The commanding officer insisted on coming to San Carlos. He told them the best doctors are here. They should be here by early tomorrow."

At dawn the following morning, Jada checked on Snow, looked in on several other patients, then retreated to her apartment to await the patrol's arrival.

Two hours later, as she watched from her window, she saw a lieutenant leading a line of troops toward the agency. Jada immediately spotted Obadiah with a white bandage around his head being held upright in the saddle by a corporal riding double behind him.

She gasped. Oh god, Obadiah's hurt. She rushed to the front of the hospital and fidgeted with her stethoscope while she waited for the patrol to arrive. Pangburn came outside and stood beside her as the troops dismounted.

Jada had a desperate need to be with Obadiah—to care for him—fix him. She caught Pangburn's attention and shrewdly justified taking Cantrell as her patient. "You're the agency doctor. Take the scouts. I'll treat the soldiers."

Jada stood by as a corporal and a scout helped Obadiah from his saddle. "Lay him down and keep him flat." The trooper hurried to spread a blanket in the dirt while the Apache eased Obadiah down.

Jada pointed to the trooper, "You stay with him. I'll get a stretcher." She ran inside, her haste driven by worry.

She returned with a litter, and directed the two men to put Obadiah on it. "Bring him along." They lifted the stretcher and went with Jada while Pangburn ordered several soldiers and scouts to help the other wounded inside.

By the time Jada reached the room, Obadiah had gone from groggy to unconscious. She nervously checked to make certain he was still breathing.

She turned to the soldier. "You have a name, Corporal?"

"Heathrow Higgins," replied the middle age orderly.

"Who's your friend?" Jada nodded at the scout.

"That's Jinx, Chief Scout."

Jada switched into Apache. "How many more are hurt?"

Jinx was flabbergasted; a doctor speaking Apache without an accent. "Three more—one bad."

Jada smiled at his reaction. "Jinx, can you stay and help Corporal Higgins?" Jinx nodded.

Jada gave Obadiah a speedy but careful exam. He looked gray and in bad shape. "Higgins, I suppose you're the unit's medic. Are you the one who first took care of the major?"

"Yes, Ma'am"

"What happened?"

"He got a small graze here, above his ear." He ran his finger along his temple. "Weren't bad but it dizzied him and he fell off his horse. He was knocked out when he hit the ground, but he woke up pretty quick and seemed okay for the ride back here 'til a little while ago."

"Then what happened?" She wiped her face with one hand in a useless effort to erase her concerns.

"Well ma'am, he started complaining 'bout a real bad headache and he throwed up once. I think he might be bleeding inside his skull."

"You must have been around for a while, Corporal."

"Been in the medical department for ten years. Got my second stripe not long ago." Higgins turned and raised his arm to display his new rank.

As Jada and the medic spoke, she checked Obadiah more thoroughly. He was unconscious. She lifted his eyelids gently with her thumbs. Her heart sank. "Shit!" she exclaimed to herself in a soft voice.

"What's the problem, ma'am?"

"You're right, Higgins. I think he's got a hematoma. His pupils are different sizes."

"I seen him fall, ma'am—he didn't bang his dome bad enough to do any damage, and he seemed all right until this morning."

"If you hit just right, you don't have to bump your head very hard. Sometimes there's a delayed reaction." Her voice wavered as she continued to check Obadiah.

"Go find the other doctor and tell him I have an urgent situation and need his help as soon as possible. Then strip the major out of his dirty clothes and clean him up. There's soap in the bathroom. When you're done, shave his head and scrub it thoroughly with carbolic acid. The carbolic and a misting pump are in the storeroom across the hall. Be sure to wash your hands with the antiseptic also."

"Yes, Ma'am."

"I'll get some clean bed clothes for him. Let me know when he's shaved and ready. Don't waste any time. This is urgent."

While she waited for Dr. Pangburn to arrive, Higgins bathed Obadiah and shaved his cranium. Jada went the few steps to her apartment, closed the door, sat down on her bed, and wept. There was a good chance she would kill Obadiah with the upcoming operation, and even if he survived, he might end up a different man.

35

Brain Surgery

DR. PANGBURN RUSHED INTO THE ROOM where Jada was sponging Obadiah's head with a damp towel. "What's the emergency Doctor Morgan?"

"Our officer here has a subdural hematoma. He needs a craniotomy at once," Jada said with a professional tone, hiding her anxiety.

Pangburn made a face.

"Did you ever do one before?" asked Jada with hopes that he had.

"Well, I tried on a dog once." The old veterinarian's voice was hesitant as he spoke. Pangburn's only medical experience was as a veterinarian before being appointed to be the doctor for the San Carlos Indians. Although he wasn't a trained physician, he was the sole applicant for the position so the Indian Office hired him.

"How did it go?"

"The dog died. Have you done very many?"

"Just one—on a cadaver in medical school. Didn't help him."

"Uh oh," said Pangburn. "I guess our fellow here is done for."

"Maybe not." She searched for the confidence to operate. "But you could help if you would take the soldier with the shoulder wound. Higgins can assist me. He's watched a craniotomy before." She felt unsure about everything.

Higgins vigorously pumped the atomizer sending a fine cloud of carbolic acid floating over the surgical area as Jada made a large C-shaped incision in Obadiah's scalp. She peeled the flap back to expose his skull, then pressed a trephining tool against the bone and drilled a hole through his cranium.

Blood spurted from the opening. "Looks like we found the right place, Higgins. Hand me the Hey saw." Jada started to cleave a two by three inch rectangular section from Obadiah's head. After tediously sawing for what seemed like forever, she cut through the last fraction of bone and levered out the piece. Then she suctioned a lingering pool of blood and removed a large black clot. "He may die from the surgery, Higgins, but he'd be dead for sure if we didn't operate." Jada sutured the scalp back over the exposed brain leaving a soft spot in Obadiah's belfry.

"Okay Corporal, your job now is to keep everything sterilized."

Jada gave her patient a worried glance, said a silent prayer, and went to wash up.

Obadiah was still in a coma the following week when Jada found Jinx, the scout, lounging on the hospital steps. "Is there anyone on the reservation who does silverwork?" she asked in Chiricahua.

"Old man Yazzie is real good—makes fancy stuff. He's a Navajo married to one of our women."

"Go ask Yazzie to make a thin square out of silver like this." She drew a picture to show the size, shape, and curvature of the piece on a small tablet she carried. "About this thick." Jada pinched her forefinger and thumb close together to indicate the thickness. "I want tiny holes here." She put six dots on the drawing. Jinx studied her sketch for a minute, nodded, and tore the page out.

"Let him know I'll need it in two weeks. He should polish it so smooth he can see his face in it."

"Maybe Yazzie's got no money to buy silver."

"The trader keeps a supply of silver for reservation craftsmen. Buy all he has. Tell him I'll pay him the next time I go by the store. Some of it will be wire. Save a piece this long for me." She held up her hands to indicate about twelve inches. Jinx nodded again.

"Tell Yazzie I'll pay him well if his work is good." Jinx smiled at that and headed for the trading post and Yazzie's camp.

Unlike Obadiah, Snow was remarkably improved, at least physically, but on her rounds one morning, Jada found her friend in a dismal depression. She sat on Snow's bed. "Okay Snow, let's talk. What's the matter?"

At first, Snow denied any problems, but the truth finally came out. "Jada, my father's making me leave San Carlos as soon as I can travel. I sent him a letter about all of this, and let him know I was doing well. But he wrote back and said it's too primitive out here and he's coming to take me home."

"Going home might be a good thing for you," Jada began to remove Snow's dressing. "Joanne and I will miss you, but your health is the first concern right now." She patted Snow's hand, and then removed the last bandage from her chest. "You need to rest for another month before you'll be strong enough to travel. Write your father you can't be released until you're hale and hardy again."

Two weeks after Snow returned to her agency house, an army officer and a man wearing a gaudy plaid jacket came to the hospital in search of Snow's doctor.

When she went to her office, the two men were waiting. The civilian rudely stepped in front of the soldier and greeted her with a loutish stare. "I'm looking for the doctor who is taking care of Snow Anderson."

Jada stood in her white lab coat with a stethoscope around her neck. Appears he missed the obvious, she thought and gave the man questioning look. "I'm Snow's physician."

"My god, you're an Indian woman!"

"That's correct, sir—last time I checked." The officer coughed and covered his mouth to conceal a grin.

The visitor was not amused. "I'm Byron Anderson, Snow's father. You don't understand. I want to talk with the real doctor."

"Nice to meet you Mr. Anderson. I am the real doctor. I've been treating Snow since the day of her injury."

"No wonder she's not better. Surrounded by savages in this backwater, and treated by a savage—a woman savage no less. I'm taking her home."

"Sir, I suspect Snow didn't tell you the whole story." Jada let her irritation show. "She was unconscious when several Indian savages saved both of us from the white savages who were trying to kill us. I'm the savage woman who nursed her back to health from near death in this hinterland hospital. And you should know she isn't strong enough for a long journey."

"Well, I believe she is. We're leaving tomorrow morning."

"Sir! Your daughter requires another month of rest before she travels that far."

"I don't think so. She needs to get back East where she'll receive some civilized care."

"You understand that such a trip may well kill her?"

"What I know is she'll die if she remains in this godforsaken hellhole."

"In that case, I'll say goodbye tonight, and tell her how to care for herself during the travel."

"I'm quite capable of attending my daughter." Anderson scowled as he responded.

"Oh, then you're a physician?"

Byron Anderson stood a little taller and stared down his nose at Jada. "Hardly. I'm top salesman for the Maryland Sock Company."

Jada scowled and her eyes flashed. "Excellent training for treating a young woman gunshot through the lungs."

Anderson replied with a loud "Harrumph," spun around, and left the room. Jada turned to the middle-aged General. "And you are?"

"Doctor Morgan, I'm General Eugene Carr, the commander at Fort Apache, and I'm delighted to meet you. Your reputation has spread around the region." He shook her hand and smiled. "You were a lot more courteous to Mr. Anderson than I would have been."

"Well, I'm worried about his daughter. She's too weak to travel. So how can I help you, sir?"

"I'm here to check on three soldiers: Major Cantrell with the head injury, Private Jones with the shoulder wound, and Corporal Higgins, the medical orderly."

"They're all down the hall. Would you care to visit them now?" Jada ushered Carr into the corridor.

"Yes Ma'am. That's why I came. On the way you can tell me about the major's problem. I'm told he's in serious shape."

Jada briefed Carr on Obadiah's condition while they walked to see the unconscious officer. "He's not coming around as fast as I hoped. This could be a long recovery."

Higgins came to attention as soon as General Carr entered the room. "At ease trooper," instructed Carr.

Jada moved to Obadiah's side and touched his cheek. "It'll be some time before our major can return to duty."

The general studied Obadiah in an effort to gauge his condition. "Should I transfer him to the military hospital at Fort Apache?"

"You can do that, but I'd like to finish his treatment here, and it will take some pressure off your staff over there. I hope Corporal Higgins can stay too. He's been a godsend for the major, and for me. He handles most of the day-to-day care."

Jada looked down at Obadiah and took his hand. "You realize even if he wakes today, it might be weeks before he's ready for duty, but your other man, Private Jones, may return with you today."

"When do you think Major Cantrell can be transferred?"

"I can't tell, General. Comas are unpredictable and heaven forbid, often permanent. I still need to cover the opening in his skull. Come here and feel." She motioned him closer.

The General went to Obadiah's side. "Careful now," said Jada. She allowed Carr to gently touch the soft spot in Obadiah's head. "You can feel the size of the piece I removed."

"That's huge," exclaimed Carr. "With a hole that big in his head, he should be dead. Why so large?"

"With the kind of injury the major has, the brain bleeds and swells. Either one can kill him. The opening allowed the blood to drain and gave room for expansion."

"So what's next?"

"When the swelling goes down, I'll replace the missing bone with a silver plate."

"I would like to be here to watch." Carr was fascinated by the whole process.

"No problem, sir. I'll send Higgins to inform you when we're ready."

She gently patted Obadiah then escorted General Carr from the hospital. She said goodbye and told him, "After I insert the plate, we'll know more."

36

Finding Obadiah's Memory

A WEEK AFTER SNOW AND HER FATHER LEFT for the trip east, Yazzie, the Navajo silversmith, arrived at the agency asking for Jada.

Jada smiled as she approached the old man standing by a paint pony. He was the most peculiar Indian she had ever seen. The diminutive Jada could see over the top of Yazzie's head which showcased a tangle of snow-white hair, held in place by an argyle sock that served for a headband. He was taller once, but he had spent a lifetime astride horses and now stood on wretchedly bowed legs which lowered his height by inches.

She greeted him in Apache. "Yaa-daa-gin-di, Yazzie."

He didn't respond, but handed Jada a small pouch, and smiled a toothless smile. She emptied the contents into her hand. The silver rectangle appeared to be exactly as Jada ordered. She started to pay Yazzie ten dollars but then she turned the disk over and discovered he had etched an intricate floral design on the convex side.

"No charge for picture." Yazzie sounded most magnanimous.

Jada thought to return the piece and ask Yazzie to buff out the etching when it struck her as funny. After her initial surprise, she began to laugh. "A flower for Obadiah."

He didn't understand her amusement. "You like okay?"

"Yazzie, you did a good job and your art's beautiful." She handed him a ten dollar gold piece.

"This is good work, Yazzie. You earned this."

Yazzie gummed another smile, threw his bowed legs around his horse, and rode away.

Jada returned to her quarters, sat by a window, and concentrated on the small silver rectangle. She studied the piece for an hour and decided Yazzie was good at what he did. She found no flaws in the skull patch—except for the decorative flower. She reasoned the design would be just under his scalp and shouldn't hurt a thing.

Several days later, Jada stayed late in Obadiah's room. She sponged his face with cool water and had a running one-way conversation with her comatose major.

She leaned forward and whispered in his ear, "Try Obadiah, please try. Come back to me."

She left his side once to check another patient. When she returned, she found him with his eyes open, staring at her. Disregarding her medical etiquette, she started to cry, went to him and kissed him on the lips.

"Oh, you're back. You're back," she kept repeating as she kissed him again.

Obadiah's eyes grew wide as he weakly struggled to hold her off. "Where am I? And who are you?"

Surprised, she now realized he may have some brain damage, and restored her professional demeanor. "You're in the San Carlos hospital. I'm your doctor."

"Do you treat all your patients with such affection?"

"Only my favorite ones." She managed a restrained laugh.

"What's your name?"

"Jada Morgan."

"Do I know you?" he asked.

Oh Obadiah, we were talking about marriage. Try to remember, she thought. "We were very close friends before you got hurt. The question is can you recall who you are?" She bit her lip waiting for his answer which might show the degree of his memory loss.

"If we were good friends, why don't you know?"

"I do. I'm only checking to find out if you did. You took a pretty stout knock to your head."

Obadiah's reflected for a moment. "I'm Major Obadiah Cantrell of the U.S. Cavalry, commanding Fort McRae."

"Excellent, Major. Do you remember how you were injured?"

"I got a slight nick on the side of the head. I don't recollect anything after that."

Higgins peeked in. "Your other patient is asking for you again, Doctor."

Jada nodded. "Major, I need to run an errand but stay in bed. You have a long way to go before you're well."

"I feel fine," said Obadiah.

To show him he wasn't as fit as he thought, she guided his hand carefully across the craniotomy. His expression changed to dismay.

"I removed a piece of skull to save you. That dent is where I took out the bone. You're touching your brain under the skin," she said. "Even a modest tap on that spot could be devastating. I sewed your scalp back over the opening until I can cap it."

"Cap the opening?"

"We'll put a silver cover over that place soon. I'll keep you awake for most of the operation but you won't feel any pain."

"Okay, so I can't go after Indians and I should stay in bed."

"You'll be wobbly for a while, Major. The safest place for you now is where you are. After I operate, you'll need a little time to get strong enough to move about safely, so stay there while I look in on another patient. I'll be right back and then we'll talk."

When she returned she was relieved to find he had remained in bed and was still awake. "Still with us Major, I see."

"Yes, and I'm ready to be moving again. How long was I out?"

"Tomorrow will be almost six weeks." Jada didn't tell him she had held his hand and had lonely soliloquies with him for much of that time. "Did you notice it was hard for you to reach up to your head?"

"Yeah, my shoulder and elbow were stiff."

"You've been inactive so long that your joints are becoming rigid. You'll need about a month to get things moving properly—maybe longer for your memory."

"I should be back on duty." Obadiah frowned.

"Not if you can't walk or mount a horse. Be patient. You can't hurry this. Besides, we need to find out how much memory you've lost."

"So what happens now?"

"General Carr has arranged an extended sick leave for you and has transferred you to Fort Apache so I can continue treating you here. Meanwhile, in the morning, we'll go hunting."

"Hunting for what?" The major gave Jada a perplexed look.

"Your memory." She smiled but at the same time she worried Obadiah did not remember her at all.

37

A Flower for Obadiah

JADA ARRIVED IN OBADIAH'S ROOM early the next morning. "Okay, Major, let's find out how much you remember. You took quite a bump when you fell."

"So you think I've lost some of my memory?"

"If you don't remember me, mister, something is gone." She hid her sadness behind a smile.

He frowned, concerned. "Were we friends or what?"

"We were very good friends—maybe a bit more." Obadiah grinned for the first time.

He stared at her for a long moment, searching for a recognizable feature, and expelled a breath in frustration.

"And you don't know me?" she asked.

"I can't recollect ever seeing you before."

"Too bad. We had some pleasant times together. Your recall might come back, but we need to find out what's left."

"Okay. So what do I do?" he asked.

"I know a gentleman should not stare at a lady but right now I want you to look me over. Check it all; hair, face, eyes, mouth, everything. Tell me if you can conjure up anything."

Obadiah sat up in bed as Jada moved to where she could give him a full view. He stared her up and down; her long black hair, her face, and her well-formed body.

She watched, hoping for the best, and searching for any signs of recognition. Remember, Obadiah, think!

"You're beautiful, doctor, but I don't believe I know you."

"Let's try something else. Wait a minute." Jada left the room and returned with a packet of letters and a tin-type. She handed him the photograph.

"Here, look at this picture. Remember, a photographer came by Fort McRae and took it of us together." Her thoughts went back to a day when they had talked about marriage.

Obadiah took the ferrotype. He stared at himself standing beside Jada who was seated in a chair. His hand rested on her shoulder. Fort McRae was in the background.

He studied the picture for several minutes and shook his head. "I recognize the buildings, but I don't remember you or us like that." Jada's shoulders slumped slightly as she struggled not to let her feelings show.

"All right, try this." She handed him the letters he had written to her. "Read these and see if you remember what you were thinking when you wrote them. I'll be back in a few minutes."

When Jada returned, she found Obadiah sitting in his bed with the envelopes scattered around him, the epitome of dejection. His only comment was "Nothing—but I must have admired you." She blinked away tears and once again concealed her disappointment.

"Well then, forget about me," she said and laughed. "I guess you already have. Let's concentrate on other parts of your life and find out what's left in there."

For the next several weeks, Jada and Obadiah talked about his personal history from his childhood to the firefight in which he was wounded. He remembered most things, but could not remember her or anyone in Canada Alamosa. He did better with the men in his command at Fort McRae, but he couldn't recall Jada's presence at Lydia Wyatt's delivery.

After a month, Jada decided the time had come to set Yazzie's silver plate in place. She sent word to General Carr at Fort Apache to come and observe if he wanted.

When Carr arrived to view the operation, Obadiah confronted him. "General, I'm fine. I don't understand why I was relieved of command at McRae and assigned over here."

"According to Doctor Morgan, and Doctor McCreery at the fort, you'll need a while before you are ready for duty. After that, we'll have to wait and hope your memory recovers. Doctor Morgan thinks it will take some time before your strength returns. She won't hazard a guess about how long before your mind is clear."

Obadiah settled for a glum "Yes Sir." He put his head down, closed his eyes and mumbled, "Damn." The laudanum Jada had given to relax him was taking effect.

She carefully sanitized the silver piece with iodine and carbolic acid then explained what she was doing. "I'll inject a numbing agent in the surgical area. You'll feel me working but there won't be any pain."

As Jada injected morphine, she thought, I wish I had done this on a live one before. She blew a puff of air, held her hands out to assure they were steady, and signaled Higgins to begin pumping the atomizer. She paused for a moment, and began cutting a second U-shaped flap around the craniotomy.

Using a hand drill, Jada carefully bored six tiny openings through Obadiah's skull and aligned them with holes in the silver piece. She and Higgins had earlier stretched the wire Jinx saved for her into flexible thread-thin lengths which she used to hold the shiny rectangle over the opening. Yazzie's etching was blatantly obvious, prompting Carr to ask, "Is that flower supposed to be there?"

"What flower?" asked Obadiah.

"The man who made your silver plate etched a blossom on the outside of it," explained Jada. "He thought a little decoration would add a nice touch," she said. "So you can say you left the hospital with a flower from an admiring doctor. The etching won't show and can't hurt anything." Obadiah rolled his eyes. General Carr chuckled.

After careful examination of her work, Jada pulled the scalp into place and closed the cut. "Now you're fixed and beautiful again—well, you will be when your hair grows back."

She gave Obadiah a stronger dose of laudanum to allow him to sleep. Carr shook her hand. "Excellent work, Doctor Morgan. Thanks for fixing our major. He's fortunate to have you for a doctor."

"Thank you, sir. I hope we'll see more of each other as he progresses. I'll keep Doctor McCreery informed." She returned to Obadiah's bedside just to be with him, and prayed all this would turn out.

38

Incident at Cibecue

JADA BEGAN TAKING OBADIAH ON SHORT THERAPY STROLLS, walking a little further each day until they reached the banks of the nearby Gila River. Standing by the cool clear water, she asked, "Do you remember our rides to the Rio Grande—our picnics there? It was our favorite thing to do." She brushed a tuft of windblown hair from her face.

Obadiah picked up a pebble, and tossed it into the water. "Don't believe I do."

Jada smiled to hide her disappointment. "Keep trying. I think things will get better for you soon." But doubts stalked her mind.

"Anything you say." Obadiah had become increasingly depressed over the past month. This wasn't the same man she knew at Fort McRae; he was sullen and was often given to spells of irritability.

Back in his room, she placed her hands on her hips and said, "Major, I'm sure your memory loss is frustrating but this depression isn't helping your recovery." She took his hand and asked, "Tell me what would get you out of this gloom?" She hoped a life with her would be included in his response.

He stared through the dusty hospital window for a moment, before he spoke. "It's not my memory. I need to get out of here. I want to go back on duty. This Apache problem will be over before I can get into the fray."

Jada held back tears. The memory of Roger Bullard dumping her for the army still tormented her and Obadiah was doing the same.

She finally caved in. "All right mister. I'll talk to General Carr and Doctor McCreery at Fort Apache but I'll warn them you aren't your old self yet. Then you and the military can work it out."

Obadiah beamed at the possibility. "At least I'll be doing something worthwhile."

The following day, Jada found Carr and McCreery in Carr's office at Fort Apache. The general greeted her, "To what do we owe this honor, Doctor Morgan?"

"I want to discuss Major Cantrell with you. I'm glad you're here Doctor Mc-Creery." She walked over and shook the general's hand and nodded to the doctor. "The major is regressing and depressed because he's not with his troops, but I don't believe he's up to it yet. He still has serious memory problems."

Carr looked at Jada. "Can he handle his army duties?"

"Maybe. He's strong enough, but I'm not sure he's thinking straight. He's had a personality change." Jada shook her head and appeared uncertain. "Now he's often impulsive and agitated. He was never like that before."

"What do you think, McCreery?" Carr asked.

"He'll do fine as your aide-de-camp. I'll pick up where Doctor Morgan leaves off. I'm sure he'll be okay here, but I would keep him behind a desk and out of the field until we have a better handle on this."

"All right Doctor Morgan, tell Major Cantrell to report for duty next Monday. We can use him. We're short one officer. I'll have orders cut and sent over by messenger tomorrow."

"Thank you gentlemen," she said as she turned to go, but she thought, Darn, it isn't going to work.

Obadiah was elated when he received his orders from the general. While he energetically packed his few belongings, Jada leaned against the wall in his room with her arms crossed brooding over her decision to release him.

The major sat tall in the saddle as he and Corporal Higgins trotted out of the San Carlos Agency on the road to Fort Apache. An uneasiness engulfed Jada as her eyes followed the riders. The thought that he might be gone from her life forever sent a shiver through her.

Things were frenetic when Obadiah and Higgins arrived at the military base. Troopers hustled to ready their equipment for the field and officers scurried about shouting orders.

"What's going on sir?" Obadiah inquired as he walked into Carr's office and saluted.

"I've been ordered to capture or kill a White Mountain medicine man, Noch-ay-del-klinne, who's been stirring up the Indians. We'll make our move in a day or two. Here's the file on him. Bone up on the situation. I'll take you along if you're up to it." McCreery gave General Carr a concerned look, but Carr ignored him and lit a cigar.

"So, why such a stir for one Indian?" Obadiah asked.

"Mr. Klinne claims to be some kind of prophet. He's had a little Christian schooling and believes in the resurrection. He's convinced almost a thousand Apaches he can revive their long-dead war chiefs, and he guarantees they will lead the Indians in a campaign to rid the country of white people."

"The Apaches know better don't they?"

"You would think so, but Klinne charges for his services and he's doing a booming business. They must believe he's on the right track," Carr said.

"It'll be a scaly job to extract him from a crowd of irritable Apaches—worse if you kill him," Obadiah said.

"That's why we're taking so many men."

No matter the risk, Obadiah was ready to go. He'd grown tired of being cooped up in the hospital with Higgins and that clingy Indian doctor.

On August 29, 1881, General Carr mounted his expedition to capture Noch-ay-del-klinne. Carr with Obadiah as aide-de-camp led a procession of 117 men out of Fort Apache toward the wayward spiritualist's dance grounds.

The next day, when the troops reached the edge of Noch-ay-del-klinne's camp they were met by a horde of surly Apaches casting malevolent stares.

In a low voice, Carr told Obadiah, "Take Sergeant MacDonald with five men and go pull the son-of-a-bitch out of that crowd." Dr. McCreery started to remind the general about Cantrell's condition but changed his mind.

The seven soldiers strode straight to Klinne's shelter. At Obadiah's command, two of the troopers took him by the arms and walked him back to Carr's position. Angry murmurs rippled through the crowd as they led the medicine man away.

"MacDonald, you and Private Foran guard him. If he tries to escape, shoot him," ordered Obadiah.

While General Carr contemplated his next move, a gunshot rang out. Foran slumped forward with a mortal wound. Klinne started running toward the throng of Indians. As instructed, MacDonald shot Klinne dead.

Instantly, a drumfire of bullets thudded into the soldier's ranks. The outnumbered troopers retreated to a small hill intending to establish a defensive perimeter, but the Apaches were already upon them.

At the height of the bedlam, Major Cantrell drew his pistol, picked up the dead Foran's sidearm and mounted his horse.

Whooping at the top of his lungs, he charged headlong into the prophet's combative congregation, pumping lead from both six-shooters. Shocked, the Indians paused and turned their attention to the major.

Several soldiers claimed they saw four bullets strike Obadiah as he plunged into the crush of insurgents and disappeared from sight. Everyone agreed Cantrell died a hero, diverting the assault long enough for the troop to form a defense and repulse the attackers.

Word of the fight and Obadiah's death reached Jada by telegraph at San Carlos. Upon receiving the news, she burst into tears, ran to the stables, mounted a horse bareback and raced to Fort Apache. She crashed into General Carr's office, tears streaming down her cheeks. "It is true?" she wailed.

Carr nodded. "He saved the day. He's a hero."

The officer rose to console her but she pushed him away. "Dead heroes don't offer much except a chance to mourn." Tears continued to pour down her face. "I want to see him. Has his body been recovered?"

"We think so but we aren't sure."

Jada wiped her wet cheeks with the back of her hand and blinked at Carr. "What do you mean, you aren't sure?"

"We found a man's body stripped naked and burned to a crisp—unrecognizable, but after the attack, the Apaches also killed several white citizens around the area. The remains might be one of the settlers. The deceased was about Major Cantrell's size, and was found where the major would have fallen after he rushed the Indians."

The color drained from her face. "I want to do a postmortem to be positive. He has that silver plate in his head." She felt numb. The thought of performing an autopsy on Obadiah's charred body sickened her, but she had to know for certain.

Carr coughed. "That's part of the problem. They cut off the man's head and carried it away. It's missing," he said.

Jada moaned, "Oh god, no." She reeled across the room and retched in the office trash can. Sobs continued to wrack her body as she kneeled by the general's wastebasket, holding her head in horror and despair.

39

Geronimo Abducts Jada's People

THE NEXT MORNING JADA WEPT quietly as the casualties from the Cibecue fight were buried in the post cemetery. Afterwards, General Carr arranged for a sergeant to drive her back to San Carlos in an army wagon.

Throughout the following week, she often broke into spells of crying and refused to leave her apartment. Her close friend, Joanne Tomley, visited daily and offered consolation, but Jada was inconsolable.

"I'm so sorry about Obadiah," Jo said as she moved to the sofa and sat beside Jada. "I don't know what I'd do if something happened to Al. His work is so risky and things are going crazy all over the reservation."

Only a week later, Jo appeared at Jada's door, fists clenched and bawling. In a role-reversal, Jada put her arm around her and walked her over to the couch. Oh god, Albert's been killed, she thought.

After Jo caught her breath, she blurted out, "Snow's dead. She was my best friend in this miserable place. I can't stand it." She started weeping again.

Jada hugged her for a moment and asked, "What happened? Are you sure? How do you know?"

"Agent Tiffany just received a telegram from the station master in El Paso." Jo read the message she had copied on a crumpled sheet of paper:

To Agent Joseph Tiffany; Former employee of San Carlos Indian Agency, Miss Snow Anderson, died on train two weeks ago. Complications from recent wound to her chest. Anderson accompanied by her father. Sorry for delay reporting. Telegraph lines were down. No action required.

"Mr. Tiffany thought I should know since Snow and I had been housemates and were such good friends." Jo covered her face with both hands and continued to sob. "Everything is bad here. I'm trying to convince Al to quit his job and leave the reservation with me."

Angry at the news, Jada said, "Damn, Snow's father is responsible. He made her travel before she was well enough." The loss of Snow coupled with Obadiah's death was more than Jada could handle. She began to think of returning to Philadelphia.

In the meantime, Jada started seeing a few patients again; all the while thinking of leaving San Carlos, but Pangburn soon noticed her uncharacteristic lack of enthusiasm for her work. He shared his observations with Agent Tiffany.

Tiffany invited Jada to his office. "Doctor Pangburn tells me you're depressed over the deaths of Major Cantrell and Miss Anderson, and are considering leaving."

"That's true. This place is a curse for me—losing my friends is too much. I just need to get away."

"Well, you have to do what's best for you." He flicked the ash from his cigar. "I can tell you this. No one here wants you to go. The Apaches consider you special—an important tribal member. The agency staff thinks you are exceptional, and says their health care is the best in the territory. Even some of the people at Fort Apache have high praise..."

Jada was encouraged by Tiffany's talk. She smiled more and was livelier at work. The pain subsided slowly and she became her old self again, but the death her two friends continued to haunt her and thoughts of returning to Philadelphia lingered.

During one visit to Jada's apartment, Jo told her, "After that terrible mess at Cibecue, the military is pouring troops into the area. It's making the Indians nervous. Al is at his wit's end trying to keep them calm. It's so dangerous for him."

Rumors that the army planned to exterminate the tribe spooked Geronimo. He and several other Chiricahua leaders decided to run. They left their families with Loco for safekeeping, and bolted for Mexico. With the firebrands gone, the atmosphere on the reservation settled into an uncomfortable normalcy.

Jo Tomley's 27th birthday fell on April 17, 1882. Jada invited Albert Sterling and most of the agency staff to a party in her hospital apartment.

She gave Jo a pair of moccasins and a green two-piece Apache outfit with a flower pattern. "You can wear these when we go to the big dance tomorrow evening. You'll fit right in," she said as she handed Jo the dress.

"Oh, it's perfect, Jada, but I hope folks won't laugh at me for wearing a native outfit."

"They'll be pleased you wore it. You'll be fine."

Al Sterling brought the best present. He presented Jo with a small box containing a diamond ring. As he slipped the band on her finger, he announced, "I told Agent Tiffany that we're planning to get married soon and I'll be resigning on May first."

Jo squealed with delight. She jumped up and gave Al a hug. "This is my best birthday present ever!" Al blushed and smiled.

The following evening, Jo and Jada arrived at the dance grounds in their Apache outfits. Earlier that day, Al learned a few outlaw Apaches were seen south of the reservation. He apologized to Jo, and left with a dozen policemen to search for the fugitives. He had spent the day looking for the Indians and by the time he returned to the agency empty-handed, he was too tired to attend the festivities.

Al was sure the marauders were the same crowd that ran off with Geronimo. After the fugitives reached the safety of Mexico, their leaders decided to revisit Arizona, recover their families, and force Chief Loco's bunch to accompany them on the return trip to Mexico. The outlaws reached the banks of the Gila River during the night of the dance, hid in the underbrush, and watched the merrymaking with bad intentions.

Just before dawn the next day, Jada and Jo were awakened by horsemen galloping through the campsite, pulling over wickiups with lassoes and shouting, "Get up! Get up! Don't run! Stay where you are."

After they threw on their clothes, Jada fashioned a scarf to cover Jo's brown hair. "They might ignore you if they think you're an Apache."

By the time the two women were dressed and out of their brush shelter, Geronimo's warriors had surrounded the dance ground. Loco and thirty-two men were cordoned away from the womenfolk who were ordered at gunpoint to sit on one side of the camp. Jada pulled Jo to the center of the crowd where she would be less conspicuous. Jo trembled, her eyes wide with fear. "They are going to rape and murder us."

"Hush that, Jo," Jada looked annoyed. "If they planned to kill us we would already be dead, and Apache men on a raid don't molest women captives. It's bad luck." Jada doubted the attackers wanted to dispatch anyone. Many of those attending the dance were relatives and most were friends. Rape was unlikely.

Jada told Jo, "If they fire a single shot, the law will be down here in a heartbeat."

"You're right, Jada." Jo's spirits brightened at Jada's reassurance. "Al will bring the agency police and deal with these brutes. He knows we're here. He won't let anything happen to us."

Across the camp from the women, Loco refused to order his band to follow Geronimo in a grueling run for the border. He told the renegade leader, "Kill me. We won't go. If you shoot anybody, the agency police will be here as soon as they hear a shot. You won't get away alive."

Geronimo turned, pointed to the womenfolk seated in a large circle surrounded by guards, and issued orders to the raiders who picked up pieces of firewood.

Without warning, his men began wading into the crowd of women, beating them with the sticks of wood. One young warrior reached Jada and Jo and raised a heavy chunk of wood, intent on striking Jo. Jada wheeled atop her friend and the blow bounced off her shoulder. Angered by Jada's intrusion, the man swung again and whacked her solidly above her eye. She collapsed unconscious and fell over Jo, protecting her from a further beating. The wood-wielding warrior moved on, bashing others as he went.

On the other side of the camp, Geronimo told Loco, "We'll keep this up until you agree to leave."

At last, the old one-eyed chief yielded. "Stop it! We'll go. You're crazy. We'll never get to Mexico with all these women and children." He waved his arm over the scene. "The army will chase us down."

Geronimo's eyes narrowed and he grinned over Loco's compliance. He shouted for the assailants to stop the beatings.

"Now go and set up the ambush," he said.

As soon as the men turned away, Jo rolled Jada to her back. She rubbed her arms, shook her, and called her name. "Jada, Jada, wake up. Please open your eyes." After several minutes, Jada stirred, opened her eyes, and sat up. Everything was spinning and blood from a cut on her forehead ran into her eye and down her face.

"Speak to me Jada. Say something! Oh please."

Jada looked around slowly in an effort to take away the fog. She had a terrible headache. "I'm so dizzy. I'll be okay in a minute." She sat up and took a deep breath to clear her confusion.

When Jo pulled her up to her feet, Jada thought she saw ten or twelve men jogging toward the agency. She shook her head and squeezed her eyes shut to stop the flashes in her vision. When she opened them, the warriors were gone.

40

Forced to Mexico

JADA WAS STILL TRYING TO CLEAR HER VISION, when the renegades began to press the captives south toward Mexico. Geronimo stood to the side of the unhappy procession shouting, "Keep 'em moving! Shoot anyone who refuses!"

As the crowd shuffled forward, Jada grabbed her medical bag and two wool blankets. She tossed one to Jo. "It gets cold at night."

A few of Loco's band were able to hang on to family horses and were riding, but most were on foot. Jada's pony had been taken by the outlaws, so she walked holding Jo's arm for support.

The raiders had kept the affair unusually quiet to avoid attracting attention from the nearby Indian Agency. Therefore it was a surprise when one of the desperados fired his pistol into the air.

"Oh, thank goodness. Al will come with the police now," Jo said.

Sterling and Sogotal were talking on the agency porch, when the shot echoed across the desert. Al heard the discharge but when no shots followed, he told his deputy, "That's probably a drunk still celebrating, but we better check it out. I want to see Jo in her Apache outfit anyway."

Riding toward the Indian camp, Sogotal caught sight of a large dust cloud near the village. "Something's wrong." He signaled Sterling and stopped his horse but Al continued along the narrow pathway.

The minute Sogotal halted, Joanne spotted the two men. "Oh, god no. There's only one policeman with Al." She jumped up and down, waved her arms, and screamed to warn him, "Al, go back, go back!"

Her warning came too late. Twelve renegades, who seemed to vanish after Jada first saw them, sprung from hiding and emptied their rifles into the two policemen. When they fell to the ground, Jo let out a mournful shriek and jerked Jada down with her. The tumble sent spikes of pain and flashes of light through Jada's head.

Distraught, Jo pounded the ground with her fists, wailing, "Not Al. Please not Al."

Jada was struggling to calm Joanne when Bittersweet, a teenager Jada met in Loco's camp four years earlier, stopped her pony beside them. "You two better get up or they'll kill you," she shouted over the pandemonium.

Looking at Jada, Bittersweet jumped from her horse and asked, "How bad are you hurt? There's blood all over your face."

"I don't know. One of them hit me in the head. I'm not so good. My eyes won't focus and I'm awfully shaky."

"Ride with me if you can't walk."

"I think I'll be okay," Jada said through a haze. "But my friend here needs some help."

"What's wrong with her?" Bittersweet searched to see Jo's injury.

"They just shot her man," Jada said. "She's not hurt but she's acting crazy."

"She can ride with me. Help me get her on my horse." The two women lifted Jo onto the pony and Bittersweet mounted behind her.

Even after being seated and held in front of Bittersweet, Jo continued to flail her arms, and wail over Al's death. At last, Jada reached up and slapped her on the thigh. "Get hold of yourself." Startled, Jo stopped her histrionics but continued to whimper.

"Jo, I understand how you feel, but these men won't tolerate a weepy white woman. Right now, you need to control yourself or they'll kill you."

"I don't care. I might as well be dead."

"Stop it, Jo." Blistering pain shot through Jada's head when she raised her voice. "We're in a bad situation and crying won't help. You'll have plenty of time to grieve. For now, try to hold things together."

Jada's words quieted Jo, but she continued to whine, "Why would they shoot Al?"

The raiders herded their captives toward an open plain called Dewey Flats that stretched for ten miles to the Gila Mountains. As they entered the flatland, the warriors noticed three heavily-loaded prairie schooners headed for the agency.

Geronimo thought the vehicles were carrying rations for the reservation. "Here comes food for our trip." He left the younger men to keep the prisoners moving toward the mountains, and motioned for the others to follow.

Howard Gilson, owner of the transports, caught sight of the Apaches galloping after his convoy. He yelled to his two teamsters, "Oh hell, run boys. Indians!" The three jumped from their wagons and scampered for their lives. They were spared when the raiders glanced inside the Conestogas and brought their horses to an abrupt halt.

Gilson's wagons were big slow movers designed for hauling large quantities of supplies. On this day, the wagons carried twenty-five crates of Mason jars, several bundles of burlap sacks, and fifteen thirty-gallon casks of whisky—450 gallons of commercial grade skullbender.

When Geronimo spotted the liquor barrels, he halted his pursuit, broke open a case of Mason's jars, and tapped the kegs. It presented a rare opportunity for the Indians to choreograph a splendid binge unhindered by their federal minders.

Despite knowing the army and Indian police were in hot pursuit, Geronimo's bandits stopped to guzzle jars of the ninety-proof dust-cutter. Even being gloriously drunk, they realized an escape run was prudent. They loaded their saddlebags and burlap sacks with jars of firewater, and raced to catch up with their cohorts and the column of captives.

Meanwhile, the prisoners from San Carlos inched their way along a twelve-mile stretch of road that ran beside the Gila River and onto sun-baked Dewey Flats. Jada and Bittersweet broke leafy branches from saplings growing on the riverbank and braided garlands for protection from the blazing sun. Jada made one of the wreaths for Jo who had slipped into a stupor.

"Joanne Tomley, you've got to come out of it or you won't get out of this alive." Jada handed her a wreath. "Here put this on and talk to me." Suddenly without warning, Jada staggered and grabbed Bittersweet's leg for balance.

"Dah-zhonne!" shouted Bittersweet.

"Sorry, I had a dizzy spell. I'll be all right in a minute," Jada shook her head to clear the fog.

Bittersweet motioned to another young woman on a brown pony. "Put Dah-zhonne on with you. One of those men hit her in the head. She's not right yet. Dah-zhonne, this is my cousin, Bly."

"Thank both of you. I wasn't sure I could make it walking."

Things had been so rushed earlier that day, many captives did not bring canteens, and Dewey Flats was dry as a bucket of dust. Jada's medical bag contained a small bottle of distilled water which she shared with the other three women—a tiny sip for each, but nothing after that. By mid-afternoon everyone was suffering. Bittersweet's cousin, Bly, rode up to a young mother walking with two children and said something in Chiricahua. The woman nodded, picked up four smooth pebbles, and handed them to her. Bly plopped one in her mouth and gave the others to her companions.

"Jo, put this stone under your tongue," said Bittersweet. "It will make your saliva flow."

The column continued to travel throughout the evening but stopped briefly to rest when they reached Eagle Creek. They had slogged for seventy miles in eighteen hours. When they reached a small stream, Jada held Jo back from leaping into the water. "It'll be freezing by morning. You don't want wet clothes then. Just splash some on your cheeks."

Jo nodded, lay down on the creek bank, and stuck her face into water, cooling and drinking at the same time. With her thirst satisfied and her sunburn cooled, she seemed to settle down.

Geronimo's raiders were drunk as lords when they rejoined the larger group. They happily shared their jars of hooch with their cronies who had remained behind to control the prisoners, and continued to gulp Gilson's gut warmer into the night.

41

Jada's Friend Escapes

AFTER THEIR REST AT EAGLE CREEK, the procession continued to travel for another two hours in pitch black darkness. They rendezvoused with eight men Geronimo had sent to raid the nearby Steven's ranch. The rustlers waited with fifty of George Steven's sheep corralled in a rope fence.

The hungry crowd made camp, immediately butchered the herd and ate a late-night meal of roast mutton. The raiders had continued to toss down fiery swallows of Gilson's coffin varnish nonstop since the Dewey Flats drinking binge. By midnight Geronimo's men were asleep in alcoholic oblivion. Their captives had to settle for creek water and remained sober as Baptist deacons.

Jada was sitting beside Jo when Chief Loco appeared at their small campfire. "Bittersweet told me you have the white teacher with you."

"That's right." Jada pointed at Joanne sleeping by the fire. "She came to the dance, and she couldn't get back to the agency after Geronimo showed up. I don't think he's seen her yet."

"I was told he knows about her but intends to leave her alone until they get to Mexico," said Loco. "He wants to sell her to the Mexicans."

Jada imagined how hard life would be for Joanne as a Mexican slave and made a face. "Is there anything we can do?" Jada asked.

"I came to tell you my oldest wife, Burning Wood, is leading some folks out tonight. She's taking them to Chief Marianna's village on the Navajo Reservation. Marianna's married to her cousin. He lives near Fort Wingate. You better send your white friend with the group. The army at Wingate will take care of her when she gets there."

"I'll tell her. She'll be relieved."

"You should go too."

"I don't think so. My legs are wobbly. I couldn't keep up. I'm riding double with Bly now."

"Suit yourself." Loco waved as he walked back into the darkness.

Joanne was exhausted and sound asleep when Jada shook her. "Jo, wake up and pay attention." Her friend sat up but still had her eyes closed.

"Let me alone. I need to sleep," she mumbled.

Jada slapped her leg for the second time. Joanne's eyes snapped wide open. "What?" she barked.

Jada cast a quick glance around to see if any of Geronimo's men stirred. She put her finger across her lips and whispered, "Chief Loco's wife is running away tonight and she's taking some people with her. Loco wants you to go with them."

Jo's eyes opened wide at the possibility of escaping. "What about you?"

"I'm not going. You will have to go it alone," Jada said. "You must do exactly what she tells you. Her name is Burning Wood. These men will beat you if you're caught, so pay close attention to what she says."

"This scares me, Jada." Her voice quivered in the darkness. "Can't you come with me?"

"You won't have horses. They'll be walking all the way and my legs aren't up to it, but here's what you should do." Jada explained why it was important for Joanne to make the trip. "You understand enough of the language to get along and they'll need a white person to explain everything to the authorities once you reach Wingate."

Jada took Joanne's hands and made a request, "I want you to telegraph my father and J.P. Morgan in New York about what's happened. Let them know I'm all right, but I'm in a dangerous situation and need help."

"Oh, Jada, I can't do that." Jo shot Jada a panicked look. "My father will find out and he'll come after me."

Upset at Jo's reluctance, Jada vented her concerns, "Jo, if our friendship means anything to you, you'll send a telegram. Doctor Morgan won't say a word if you ask him not to. But you must do it."

"I don't know." Jo nervously bit her lip. "The idea of father catching me..." Her voice trailed off.

"Just send the cable, Jo, you can travel someplace else before he gets out here. There's plenty of Indians in the Dakota territories. He won't find you out there."

Before Jo responded, Burning Wood came over and asked Jada in Apache, "Is the white girl ready to go?"

"She's right here." Jada spoke rapidly in Apache so Jo wouldn't understand. "I've told her to mind every thing you say. She understands a little Apache. Her name is Jo. She isn't strong or brave and Geronimo's people killed her man yesterday." Jada put her arm around Jo's shoulder. "She's still upset, so be strict with her."

The woman nodded, took Jo's hand, smiled, and pulled her toward the others who were ready to move out.

"Let's go, girl," she said slowly in Apache.

Jada watched her friend leave the light cast by their campfire. I wonder if she'll be strong enough to reach Marianna's, and if she does, will she wire Jack?

An hour passed before Burning Wood's runaways reached safety. Once out of the renegades' hearing, the old woman released Jo from her grip and indicated she must keep up. She motioned for everyone to pick up the pace. The tempo was brutal for Jo who had never traveled any distance by foot. She strained to stay with the group as they hurried toward the Navajo reservation.

As soon as Geronimo waked the following morning, he discovered the missing captives. He found two semi-sober men who were not as hung over as the other drinkers, and ordered them to catch and return the runaways. "Track them down, but don't hurt the white girl. She'll fetch a good price in Mexico." He pointed north. "You shouldn't have much trouble. They're all women and children except two men, and one of them is almost dead with the lung disease."

The two warriors clambered aboard ponies, let out yells, and galloped off, following the tracks of the twenty-nine escaping Indians and Joanne.

42

Bushwhacked by Burning Wood

TWENTY MILES NORTH OF THE APACHES' CAMP, Burning Wood looked back at her followers. Everyone kept the pace except Jo and Asttewahlah who straggled a distance behind the others. Burning Wood stopped the group and shouted, "Hey you two, keep up. Geronimo's men will be after us."

"I'm done for. I can't take another step," Jo said. She bent over with her hands on her knees panting.

Asttewalah, kneeled on all fours and spit a wad of bloody mucus. He was in the last stages of tuberculosis. "I'm finished too." He gasped as he tried to catch a decent lungful of air. The sickness has me." He coughed again. "I'll stay here so the rest of you can escape."

Burning Wood silently considered the circumstances. Even if we leave Asttewalah, the white girl will still slow us down, she thought.

Cicero, the other man who escaped with the group, came running up as she pondered her dilemma. Cicero was a Navajo married to a Chiricahua woman.

He had walked a mile behind the others, watching for threats approaching from the rear. He breathed heavily from his dash to catch the group and pointed back down their trail. "Two men on horses are trailing us. They're riding hard. We can't out run them."

Fast action was needed. Burning Wood motioned for everyone to come closer. "Hurry, Hurry! Here's what we'll do..."

Following her instructions, the women scattered and hid in the tall deer grass surrounding Jo and Burning Wood. Cicero and Asttewalah went in opposite directions, each with a bow.

Geronimo's two pursuers followed the runaway's tracks until they spotted an old woman and Jo sitting alone on a large rock. The men stopped their horses several hundred yards from the two women. One pulled a pair of stolen opera glasses from his saddlebags.

"See anybody with them?" asked his crony.

"No, just an old woman and the white girl. They seem worn out. I guess they fell behind."

"This is too easy. Wonder where the rest of them are?"

"They probably went on and left those two behind. We can take them back and forget about the others. Better for us and that should satisfy Geronimo." The man continued to scan the terrain around the two women with the spy glass.

"Check again. Make sure there isn't anyone else,"

The older warrior surveyed the landscape once more. "I can't spot anybody. I reckon they're gone."

"There is lots of tall grass. They could be hiding," said the younger man."

"Doesn't seem like it. It won't be a problem anyhow. They're all women and they don't have any guns." He handed the small binoculars to his cohort. "You look."

"Maybe you're right. Let's go get them."

The pursuers galloped up to the two left-behinds. "Where are the others?" demanded the older man.

The Loco's old wife answered, "They left us. We couldn't keep up."

"Bad luck for you." He smirked and started to raise his rifle.

She affected a resigned appearance. "I'm old. Just don't hurt the young one."

"Don't worry. Geronimo has plans for her."

Burning Wood took out a white cloth and wiped Jo's forehead. It was the signal for action.

Without warning, the outlaw dropped his gun and crashed to the ground, Cicero's arrow protruding from his side. There was no time for his partner to react. A second arrow from Asttewalah sent him tumbling from his horse. The women hiding in the brush rose from concealment as the two writhed in pain, and hurled apple-sized stones at them. Most of the rocks found their mark and reduced the overconfident assassins to carrion for coyotes.

After making sure the outlaws were dead, Burning Wood announced, "Asttewalah and the girl should take their horses—anyone else who needs to can ride double with them."

The escapees reached Marianna's camp after fifteen days of walking. Unfortunately, the post blacksmith noticed them when they passed Fort Wingate and the army detained them. The crush of prisoners were gathered on the fort's parade ground when soldiers caught sight of a white woman in their midst. Joanne soon found herself in Colonel Luther Bradley's office.

The military sent the Chiricahua women to Fort Union near the Texas border to be held as hostages until their relatives headed for Mexico surrendered. Asttewalah died of tuberculosis on the day after they arrived at Wingate. The army released Cicero and his wives to rejoin relatives on the Navajo reservation.

From the time of her escape, Joanne struggled with the predicament posed by

Jada's request to contact Jack and J.P. She loved Jada but the thought of going back into that sordid life with father was intolerable. As she reflected on her quandary, Colonel Bradley forced the issue. "Who do I contact to come for you?"

Joanne was silent for a long minute as competing thoughts grappled in her mind. At last she replied, "Doctor Jack Morgan in Philadelphia or Mr. J.P. Morgan in New York."

Bradley raised an eyebrow. "The J.P. Morgan?"

"Yes sir, Doctor Morgan is the father of a friend who is still Geronimo's prisoner, and Mr. J.P is her uncle."

"What's your amigo's name?"

"Doctor Jada P. Morgan. We're very close."

"Oh yeah. The word about her got around when she was at Fort McRae. Chiricahua Apache isn't she?"

"Yes, her Chiricahua family was killed, and she was adopted by the Morgans in Philadelphia. She's a college-educated physician," Joanne explained.

Bradley shook his head. "If she's Apache, educated or not, I don't think even the famous J.P. Morgan can help her. The government won't spend a penny to rescue a Chiricahua woman living with her own people—kidnapped or not."

Jo stared silently through the window at the women seated on the parade ground. Then she asked, "May I at least wire Doctor Morgan?"

"Of course.

Telegram to Dr. Jack Morgan, Philadelphia

Dr. Morgan: Jada and I captured by Geronimo's outlaws at San Carlos. Forced from reservation. I escaped with Loco's wife. Jada still held. Being taken to Mexico. Ask JP for help. Situation dangerous. Beg you not to tell my family where I am. Joanne Tomley.

When Joanne returned to Bradley's office, she gave him a pitiful look and requested, "Colonel, I need to borrow enough money for a stage to Gallup and then a train back east. I'm sure Doctor Morgan will repay you."

"Isn't someone coming for you?"

"Probably, sir, but I don't want to have anything to do with him." She blanched at the idea of meeting her father again.

Not my business. I'm not getting involved in that, Bradley thought. Must be an abusive husband.

"I think there's enough in the petty cash fund for a loan," he said. "A wagon's headed to Gallup tomorrow for supplies. You can get a ride with the crew." Jo left the following day after sending her cablegram to Jack. She told Colonel Bradley she was going "back east" to throw off anyone searching for her.

Despite Joanne's request, word that Jack had received a telegram from her leaked to her father. In a gab session, Rebecca Stokes unintentionally revealed Jo's whereabouts to the Tomley's maid who reported the intelligence to the family.

Mr. Tomley left for Arizona immediately, but he was unable to find any word about his "darling daughter" in Wingate, Gallup, or San Carlos. He returned to Philadelphia unaware Joanne was the new teacher on the Pine Ridge Sioux reservation in South Dakota.

Geronimo was waiting for the return of the recaptured women when sentinels he dispatched earlier reported, "Lots of soldiers are moving this way."

He was immediately more interested in escaping than in recovering the escapees and decided to resume his run for Mexico. He reverted to an old Apache scheme for eluding pursuers.

"Split up and we'll meet at Black Point Mountain. It's not far from the border." The Indians divided into dozens of small groups and scurried away on different routes toward the meeting place.

The next morning Jada and Bittersweet were traveling with a splinter group of ten women and four Chiricahua escorts. To avoid the military, they kept to the high mountains as they angled toward their rendezvous point. The cool air invigorated Jada and gradually eased the effects of the blow to her head.

"I'm feeling much better now," she told Bittersweet. "I can walk if you prefer."

"That's not necessary. My pony is doing fine and it'll be easier to talk if we ride double."

"Aside from being prisoners and the army chasing us, it's a pleasant trip." Jada said sarcastically.

43

Bittersweet and Gillee

ON THE SECOND DAY after they left Eagle Creek, Jada's group heard shots fired in the distance. One of their Chiricahua escorts, Gillee, rode up beside Jada and Bittersweet. "The older men say a bunch of our people went through Doubtful Canyon after we split up. The army must have caught them."

He blatantly ogled Bittersweet, spellbound by her beauty. Leaning from his horse with a salacious smile he reassured her, "Don't worry. We'll get you safely to Mexico." He couldn't take his eyes from Jada's stunning partner.

Gillee was the youngest of the four warriors escorting the group and was about the same age as Bittersweet. Jada grinned at her young friend when Gillee rode away. "You realize he likes you."

"I couldn't miss it. He keeps staring at me and telling me how many horses he has. He's trying to impress me and to be honest, I like him."

Gillee's amorous interest in the young woman grew increasingly audacious as their journey continued and it was apparent to Jada that Bittersweet was more than a little interested in him. When he walked his horse beside her, the couple often exchanged scorching glances. He would stop by their campfire every evening, always with a roughish grin and suggestive quips. She entertained him with come-hither looks and brazen flirtations.

Late one night when Bittersweet left their campsite for a personal moment, Gillee started to follow her. Jada sat upright and wagged her finger. "Stop right there, Gillee. Until that girl is with her parents again, treat me like I'm her mother." She gave Gillee a smile and drew her hand across her neck, "Come back here and sit down or I'll cut your throat." He was unsure if she was serious, but he offered a sheepish smile in return and plopped down on a log.

Jada rested on her elbow and gazed into the flames as she thought about her comment to Gillee. Her life in Philadelphia was slipping away—the genteel manners, polite conversations, family visits with Uncle Pierpont, chats with Jack, the Lawson's annual New Year's bash—everything was gone. She was changing as she returned to the hardscrabble Apache life.

As days wore on, the two women spent hours in conversations evaluating their situation and the possibility of escape.

"I wonder how those folks who left with Burning Wood are doing," Jada said. "I hope Joanne made it to Wingate and wired my father. Otherwise we're stuck with these thugs for a long time."

"They didn't come back. Maybe they got away," Bittersweet wanted to put a positive spin on the episode for Jada.

"I trust you are right—I just wish I knew what happened to Jo."

Jada and Bittersweet also enjoyed happier chats about the new fellow in Bittersweet's life.

"How are you feeling about Gillee?" Jada asked.

"I think he's a good man. He's handsome and nice too. I think he'll make a fine husband."

Jada frowned. "Too bad he's mixed in with these ruffians."

"I still like him, but that is a worry."

"You better be careful. You've lived your entire life with peaceful folks on the reservation," Jada said. "Living in the wild like Gillee is difficult and dangerous. His people are a violent bunch. They fight all the time with everybody." Jada shook her head. "Life would be so hard for you. I don't think you'd be happy."

"If I marry him, I hope we live near my parents at San Carlos."

Jada's splinter group was among the first to arrive at Black Point Mountain. She and Bittersweet watched as small clusters of people approached from all directions.

Chief of Scouts Al Sieber, Tom Horn, and a Navajo scout, Smiley Begay, also viewed the gathering crowd from the nearby Animas Mountains. Their position overlooked the Janos Plain, Cloverdale, and the Apaches' hilltop rendezvous.

"I 'spect there's five hundred of 'em," Sieber said as he stared through his spyglass.

"What we gonna do, Al?" Horn asked.

"Damn Tom, ain't nothing to do but eyeball 'em. They're pulling out for Mexico now anyways. My guess is they're headed for Enmedio Mountain. They camp there sometimes."

44

Tillius Tupper's Surprise

BY THE MID-AFTERNOON OF APRIL 26, most of Loco's four-hundred Apaches, accompanied by Geronimo's sixty warriors, left Black Point Mountain, hurried across the Mexican border, and traveled seventeen miles down the length of the Janos Plain to the base of the Sierra Enmedio range.

The Plain is an elongated expanse of desert extending from the international boundary to a sandy basin about the size of five Philadelphia city blocks. A high ridge to the south separates the open tract from the mountains behind. Two circular boulder-covered knolls dominated the center of the otherwise level field. A bold spring flowed below the two hills creating a gully along the length of the basin.

The exhausted crowd relaxed after they straggled onto the sandy plain. "Well at least we're safe from the Americans," Jada said. "It's illegal for them to cross the border."

Geronimo decided a victory dance was in order and shouted to the crowd, "Gather some wood for a fire and we'll celebrate our escape."

As night settled over the encampment, scores of small campfires flickered across the flat. Merrymaking began as soon as inky darkness cloaked the camp. A huge bonfire illuminated the dance area.

Bittersweet was anxious to join the celebration but Jada told her she wasn't interested in the festivities. "I'm not in the mood for dancing," she said.

Stretching out on her ragged blanket, Jada rose on one elbow and cautioned Bittersweet. "Stay around the bonfire and don't wander off in the dark with Gillee." She lay down again, put her medical bag under her head for a pillow, and fell asleep.

Back in Cloverdale, New Mexico, supper was still hot when Al Sieber, Smiley Begay, and Tom Horn stumbled into Captain Tillius Tupper's camp bustling with two companies of Sixth Cavalry and fifty Indian scouts. Tupper planned to continue the hunt for Geronimo after dark so the Indians wouldn't spot the tell-tale dust cloud that followed the cavalry's every move.

Sieber conferred with Tupper while his soldiers served up field rations for the three new arrivals. "Mights well go back to Fort Bowie," Sieber said as he chewed a bite of salt pork. "The Indians are already in Mexico." He gestured toward Horn and Begay. "We saw 'em cross the border."

"Have any idea where they're headed?" Tupper asked.

"Sometimes they camp near Enmedio Mountain—about seventeen miles south of the line."

"Can you find the place?" Tupper seemed to have a plan.

"Yes sir, I've camped there a few times myself."

Captain Tupper scratched his beard. "I'm confused, Seiber. Enmedio Mountain is due east from here isn't it?"

Sieber started to correct him but realized Tupper was laying the groundwork for an excuse to cross into Mexico. He pointed south and told Tupper. "Reckon you're right, Captain. You could find them if you headed thataway."

"Well Sieber, let's go. I want a chance to get a hold of that gang. Take five scouts and run ahead. Send word back when you locate them. We'll be a mile behind you."

Two hours later, Sieber's trackers spotted the Apaches' campfires in the distance. He sent a scout to inform Tupper.

"Bring the captain here but tell him to dismount the company and walk when he sees the fires."

As soon as Tupper caught up with Sieber's scouts, he laid out his plans for the attack and deployed his troops. "I'll charge from this direction with Company M," he said.

He motioned to Lieutenant Timothy Touey. "You take Company B and set up on that hill to the southwest. Stop 'em if they try to escape in that direction."

He then quietly waved Lieutenants Darr and Mills over to him. "Move your scouts behind the Indians and form a firing line along the crest of that ridge." He indicated the rise on the opposite side of the campground. "We'll wait until you are in position before we attack."

By four o'clock in the morning, Touey's men were in place, and Tupper's company M waited beside their horses, watching the dancers step and sway around the large fire. The scouts were inching into their positions overlooking the Apaches' camp.

"We'll hit them from all sides. Be ready to charge when the scouts fire the first shot." They had about two hours to wait. The scouts had the farthest to go and had to slip silently on foot past the Indian camp.

Bittersweet heeded Jada's admonition to stay near the bonfire for most of the evening, but as she talked with Gillee, Yst-sohu, a girl Bittersweet's age, approached the couple. "I'm roasting a load of mescal up on the ridge. Would you and Gillee help bring it down here? You'll save me an extra trip."

Bittersweet said without thinking, "We'll assist," and grabbed Gillee's hand. The three headed to the dark ridge line. Jada's sound asleep. She'll never know, and this is my chance be alone with Gillee, Bittersweet thought.

Loco's son, Little Loco, joined the threesome as they ambled toward Yst-sohu's fire pit. He was sweet on Yst-sohu and this was an opportunity to spend time with her.

"I heard you're cooking a lot of mescal up there. I'll help you bring it down." Little Loco pointed to the ridge, took the girl's hand, and walked toward the smoking agave pit. Bittersweet and Gillee deliberately lagged behind for privacy.

As the four climbed toward the smell of mescal, they headed straight for Tupper's scouts concealed among the boulders. Bittersweet's thoughts were on Gillee. Gillee was fixated on Bittersweet, and Little Loco's mind was on Yst-sohu. Yst-sohu fretted she had overcooked the mescal. No one was expecting trouble.

45

Long Day at Sierra Enmedio

CURLEY AND BA-COON, two of Tupper's Indian scouts, stared in disbelief as the four young people ambled up the dark slope.

"They're going to walk right over us," said Curley.

"Suits me! I'm gonna kill 'em," replied Ba-coon.

"Ba-coon, the men at the other end of the ridge are supposed to fire first. They aren't in place yet. Shoot now and it'll warn everybody down below before our fellows are ready." He pointed his weapon at the dancers in the basin.

"If we don't, those kids will give us away anyhow." Ba-coon shouldered his rifle. "That bunch killed Sogotal when they left San Carlos. He was my brother and somebody's gotta pay."

Ba-coon's first shot sent a bullet through Little Loco's heart. When the scout's single-shot Springfield roared, a dozen other shots followed instantly, honeycombing Yst-sohu and knocking her lifeless to the ground. Gillee and Bittersweet were far enough behind to avoid the fusillade. As soon as Gillee heard the initial shot, he dived behind a boulder and pulled Bittersweet with him.

The couple lay still until the scouts turned their attention to the partygoers at the bottom of the ridge. They then crawled back to the dance ground, while those in the basin extinguished their campfires and dashed for protection on the larger of the two knolls.

Jada was sound asleep when the barrage shattered the night. She bolted upright, but quickly rolled flat on her stomach. She inched over to her low-burning campfire, smothered the glowing coals with sand, then ran with the crowd as they rushed for the closer of the two hills. When she came to the remains of the bonfire, she found four women's bodies crumpled beside the ashes where they died extinguishing the flames.

Jada crawled on her hands and knees to each of the corpses, searching for Bittersweet. Her companion wasn't among the dead.

After she scampered to safety, she snaked her way around the boulders, and found Gillee. "Are you hurt?" she hollered over the hullabaloo.

"No, I'm okay," he yelled.

"Where's Bittersweet?" Her eyes darted back and forth searching for her friend.

It was almost impossible to hear above the commotion, but he bellowed to her, "She wasn't hurt when we got separated, but I don't know where she is now. We walked up the ridge with some others. Scouts were on top of us before we knew it. They killed Little Loco and Yst-sohu. Bittersweet and I were lucky."

Worry filled Jada as she scanned the boulder piles around her. "If you come across her, tell her to stay in a safe place. I'll find her. Right now, I need to help some of these injured people."

Tupper's men were a thousand yards out and unprepared to attack when Bacoon fired the first bullet. The captain ordered his company to mount and charge, but sunrise was still an hour away. The onslaught proceeded at a walk because darkness concealed desert hazards which would break a horse's leg.

The Indians found natural parapets among the boulders as the troops rode carefully toward the fight. By the time the cavalry arrived at the hill, Apache riflemen sat in protected firing positions high in the rocks. Tupper was forced to reign up and take cover in the gully 200 feet below the entrenched Apaches.

Pandemonium prevailed as the sounds of gunfire from Geronimo's sixty men and Tupper's troops exploded in the morning air. People leaped behind boulders, built small rock breastworks to lie behind, and ran from one massive stone pile to another seeking better shelter. Bullets spattered against the stones and flung shards of rock and deadly lead fragments down around the star-crossed Indians. People clamoring to find relatives filled the air with shouts. Screams and moans of the wounded echoed over the hill. As Jada inched upward through the tumult, her ears rang, dust clogged her nose, and obscured her vision. No place was safe.

Jada came upon Chief Loco leaning against a large slab as she neared the crest. She looked on as he shouted to the scouts on the ridge. "Stop shooting. We don't have any guns. Geronimo's men forced us to leave the reser..." A shower of lead peppered the rocks near him before he finished his argument. One bullet hit the chief in the leg sending him to the ground beside Jada.

She kneeled next to him. "Hold still; let me see how bad you're hurt." She found a furrow across Loco's thigh.

"Do you have something to bandage this?"

Before he could answer, Old Lady Toklanni jumped atop a nearby boulder and shouted, "Rogers, stop this. You know who we are!"

Rogers Toklanni, the woman's son, had enlisted as a scout, but he wasn't with those on the ridge as she thought. A bullet ripped through her and she thudded into a limp heap beside Jada and Loco. Jada felt for a pulse. She was dead. Jada pulled her knife, and cut a dozen strips from the cadaver's skirt for bandages.

She motioned for Chief Loco to hold still. "Let's put a wrap on that." She pointed to Loco's thigh and bandaged his wound with a strip cut from the dress. He smiled and patted her arm in appreciation.

"Keep it clean," she shouted, and left the old man sitting behind a rock while she continued her search for more wounded. She turned when she reached the top of the hill and started making her way back down, treating victims as she went.

Gunfire stopped by the time she arrived at the base of the dome. The army's ammunition was running low and Captain Tupper had ordered a withdrawal around midday. The retreat took hours but most of the soldiers escaped unharmed except two privates, Goodrich and Miller.

Jada came across Gillee again at the bottom of the knoll. He was glaring at the two soldiers splayed on the open flat between the Indians and the troopers. Goodrich was dead on the spot. Miller was making clumsy attempts to crawl back to safety with a shattered hip. Gillee watched the struggle, tense and poised for action.

She went to him and asked, "Gillee, what do you think you're doing?"

"I lost my rifle on the ridge but I'm gonna kill that soldier." He pointed a large hunting knife at the struggling trooper.

"For Pete's sake, Gillee, borrow a gun and shoot him from here."

"I want to cut his throat," He raised his blade and nodded toward Miller.

"Think Gillee! You'll be a perfect target." She motioned to the dead trooper. "Look at what happened to him."

Jada grabbed his arm, but Gillee jerked away and ran for the wounded Miller. She shouted after him, "Gillee, don't..." Too late, he was on his way. Just as he got to the injured Miller, he crumpled to the ground. Jada shook her head.

The sun was setting before the retreating soldiers were out of sight and the Apaches felt safe enough to leave their sanctuary. Bittersweet appeared as if by magic from behind a pile of boulders. She and Jada rushed to find out if Gillee was alive. He was in critical shape and his breath came in short pants. Bittersweet stood back, wringing her hands as another woman, Jose-ee, a traditional medicine practitioner, hurried over to see if she could help.

Gillee's leg was broken. A massive exit wound left the bone jutting through the skin. He was unconscious and the injury to his thigh continued to pour blood onto a large bloodstained patch of sand beneath his leg. As Jada started to tie a tourniquet above the bloody leak, Jose-ee stopped her. "Here let me put some of this in the wound first."

"What is it" asked Jada. She examined the powder carefully. She respected Apache medicine but only to a point.

"It makes wounds stop bleeding and keeps the pus away." She held out a small, round tobacco tin of gray granules for Jada's inspection.

"Like styptic powder." Jada dampened her finger, touched the talc, and put it to her tongue. "Good." She spit out the bitter taste.

"You're the one who knows white medicine aren't you?" Jose-ee sprinkled the dust into the wound.

Jada nodded. "I am. Call me Dah-zhonne." She gave her Apache name.

"I'm Jose-ee. Lots of hurt people here. Maybe we can help them together," suggested Jose-ee.

"Good idea," said Jada as she tightened the strip of cloth around Gillee's thigh.

"I don't think there's any need to set the bone right now. He's not going to make it." Jada held her finger against Gillee's neck to check his pulse. "He's lost too much blood."

"Can't you help him?" pleaded Bittersweet. She hovered over the boy with tears pouring down her cheeks.

"Nothing we can do," said Jose-ee. "We can't put his blood back."

Jada and Jose-ee glanced helplessly at each other, shaking their heads while Bittersweet kneeled and stroked Gillee's face. The two healers backed away and joined several women gathering reeds around the spring to weave makeshift stretchers for the worst of the wounded.

"We'll need one over there." Jose-ee pointed at Gillee.

Jada, Jose-ee, and Bittersweet lifted Gillee onto a stretcher, and found three volunteers to help Bittersweet carry him. With the army lurking just miles behind them, everyone knew they faced another sleepless night.

46

Apaches Rush for Safety

AFTER THE APACHES LEFT EAGLE CREEK, they had traveled for a week with only brief rests. Jada had slept for a few hours before Tupper's attack, but not enough to recover from seven sleepless nights. While the Indians nervously watched for a return of the army, Jada and Jose-ee spent their time treating the injured.

"I'm worn-out," Jada told Jose-ee as she wiped the perspiration from her forehead, leaving a smear of blood and black powder.

"Me too. I could use a drink and a long nap." As they talked, a dozen men galloped in with fifty of the group's horses which had scattered during the battle—half the number they rode into the basin with on the day before. Bittersweet's pony was missing, so Jada and she would be walking.

The refugees and Geronimo's warriors left Sierra Enmedio when darkness closed in and began the all-night trudge toward the Hauchinera Mountains. Four sweat-soaked young women, Bittersweet, Tzon, Hahles, and Nahno, labored to carry Gillee. Hahles and Tzon were about Jada's age, in their late twenties. Nahno was an older woman in her early thirties, and Bittersweet was nineteen.

None of the women spoke as they lugged Gillee's litter along the dusty trail. They were too tired for conversation. Her cheeks wet with tears, Bittersweet stared straight ahead in silence as she helped carry the comatose Gillee.

Before she left the battlefield, Jada retrieved the .38 caliber pistol Obadiah had given her from her medical bag, then tossed the bag to the side of the trail. She tucked the revolver into a leather belt she found earlier, and without thinking, felt for her derringer in the folds of her moccasins.

Just at first light, Jada and Jose-ee approached two matriarchs kneeling beside Gillee's unmoving body. Three of his stretcher bearers huddled nearby whispering to each other while Bittersweet stood alone, her tears flowing. She watched as the old women combed out the dead man's long hair, retied his headband, and painted his face with red ochre. Jada and Jose-ee stopped when they saw the activity around Gillee.

"He's dead," said one of the old grannys. "We're fixing him to bury."

Jada pressed a finger against the artery in Gillee's neck. Lost too much blood, she thought. Didn't have a chance. She shook her head. Poor Bittersweet.

Jada rejoined Jose-ee. "He's done for," she whispered. Jada pointed her chin toward the tearful Bittersweet and said, "She planned to marry him."

Bittersweet was beside herself and her sobs grew louder. "Why would he run out like that?"

To be helpful, Jose-ee remarked, "They've fixed him nice for burial. He looks so dignified in those beaded moccasins." Jose-ee's words were no consolation.

Suddenly, someone at the back of the column shouted, "The army's behind us!" They had spotted a whorl of dust and thought the cavalry was approaching. It turned out to be a large 'dust devil' but the crowd panicked and rushed forward, leaving Gillee's corpse laid out on the stretcher.

Meanwhile fifteen miles back, Tupper's dog-tired soldiers were in their bed-rolls when Colonel George Forsyth trotted into their camp leading 450 cavalrymen. He wanted to continue the pursuit, but Tupper declined. "We haven't slept or eaten for twenty-four hours," he said as he saluted and shook Forsyth's hand. "We've spent twelve hours in a tough fight with those Indians. The men need some sleep but we'll be ready in the morning." Forsyth decided to wait with Tupper before resuming the chase.

The next day over five-hundred soldiers and scouts lumbered after the Apaches. They stopped only long enough to bury Private Goodrich and count seventeen dead Indians left on the Enmedio battlefield. Forsyth ordered a travois for Miller and sent a squad of men to accompany him back to Fort Bowie.

Forsyth and Tupper's combined command easily followed the panicked Apaches. The Indians made no effort to conceal their trail as they raced for the rugged Hauchineras. Some miles out, the column came across Gillee's abandoned body decked out for a funeral. Ba-coon caught sight of the boy's corpse, and screamed, "Yieee, those are Sogotol's moccasins." Gillee had stolen the moccasins from Ba-coon's dead brother at San Carlos.

Raging with anger, Ba-coon leaped from his horse, snatched the beaded foot-wear and stripped Gillee, wielding a large hunting knife to cut his clothes away. Then with the help of the other scouts, he dumped the naked body into a hole and kicked sand atop the corpse. Untroubled by Gillee's inelegant last rites, Colonel Forsythe waved the column forward and shouted, "Let's move it out."

As dawn broke the following morning, the Apaches slogged onto a sandy flat running alongside Alisos Creek. They could see the safety of the Hauchinera Moun-tains five miles ahead. Everyone was sleep-deprived and used up. When they entered the level plain, Jose-ee lifted her head and sniffed. "I smell coffee."

"Me too," said Jada. "Maybe we should stop and hear what the scouts find." Fifteen men ahead of the Apache crowd served as a vanguard to watch for trouble.

Jose-ee said hopefully, "The scouts will warn us if there are any problems. I'm too bushed to worry about it. Some of Juh's people probably came to meet us."

Tired and in a rush to escape their pursuers, the advance guards failed to notice signs of a company of hidden Mexican soldiers behind an elongated low dune. Colonel Lorenzo Garcia, commanding the troops, concealed his men only yards from the creek bank and the Indians' path. Garcia, the same officer whose men killed Jada's family sixteen years earlier, had received a warning telegram from the Americans indicating the Apaches were making a run for Mexico. Anticipating Geronimo's return route, he rushed to organize an ambush with two hundred riflemen and fifty Tarahumare Indian scouts.

His chief scout, Lizard, reported. "There's a big bunch of 'em coming toward us." He then looked south. "Headed for those hills, I 'spose."

As soon as the colonel received Lizard's report, he swung into action. "Smother the fires," he pumped his arm to indicate the need to hurry. "Apaches on the way. Conceal yourselves along this ridge," he shouted. "Let the first ones pass. I want to hit the main body. Nobody shoots until I do."

47

Captured At Alisos Creek

AN EERIE QUIETNESS ENVELOPED THE BANKS of Alisos Creek as dawn broke over the weary Apaches. Plodding along with the column, Jose-ee and Jada walked past a young mother carrying her sleeping toddler. She staggered, so exhausted she could hardly walk.

As they passed, Jada asked, "Are you all right? Can we help?"

"I can't go much further. My legs are giving out, but if I stop, they will kill us." Her eyes were moist with frustration as she clutched the toddler.

"You look completely used up." Jada glanced at the child. "How far have you carried her?"

"All the way from Enmedio. She's been sick."

"That's almost thirty miles! No wonder you're worn out. Here let me take her for a while." Just as Jada reached for the youngster, two hundred rifles belched thick clouds of smoke and lead.

A bullet swished past Jada and she jerked back as the slug cleaved the tot's head and tore into her mother's chest. Blood splattered over Jose-ee and Jada as mother and infant were cut down.

Jada instantly grabbed Jose-ee's hand and joined the panicked throng as they dashed helter-skelter for protection in the sunken creek bed. Before they reached safety, Jada watched as a man, his wife, and two children fell into a pile, riddled with Mexican bullets.

Jose-ee yelled to Jada, "Maybe one of them is alive. Let's see if we can help!" She started to change directions.

"You're crazy, woman. We'd be shot to pieces. Stay with me." Jada pulled Jose-ee into a small dip.

Thirty-two men were among the Indians with Loco who were forced from San Carlos. None had guns but a few carried bows. The other four-hundred people were women armed with knives. The only firearms among the fleeing column of Indians were in the hands of a van leading the procession a mile ahead, and the rearguard two miles behind. Jada had her two pistols.

When no gunfire was returned after their first volley, the Mexicans rushed the Apaches in a fanatical bayonet charge. Loco's men moved forward to thwart the attack with bows and arrows. It was a heroic but useless effort. The troops plunged into the creek bed as the women tried to protect themselves with sheath knives but they were no match for the army's rifles and saber-like bayonets.

Alisos Creek was almost dry when the ambush began. Along its length, deep crater-like washouts pot-marked the river bottom. With the temperature rising into the nineties, puddles of water in these hollows provided thirst-quenching relief. They soon turned red with blood, but the parched Indians drank it anyway.

Jada and Jose-ee felt safer after they leaped into one of the deeper sinkholes, but minutes later a soldier peered over the edge with his rifle at the ready. When he pointed the gun at Jose-ee, Jada snatched Obadiah's pistol from her belt and snapped off a shot. Her bullet hit the soldier under his jaw and shattered his skull. He dropped his weapon and fell back dead.

Soldiers continued to rampage among the throng, shooting and impaling the helpless women and children with bayonets. The victims fought back with anything they could find. Jada saw a young girl throw a handful of sand into a soldier's face. When he reached to clear dirt from his eyes, the youngster jumped from her protected position and stabbed him in the throat. The teenager never spotted the other soldier who shot her in the back before she could return to cover.

Through the smoky mayhem and carnage, Jada caught sight of a small child about three-years-old crying beside his dead parents. Jada abandoned her caution. "Jose-ee, stay here. I'm going for that baby!"

But before she left the safety of her pit, a soldier jammed his bayonet into the tyke.

"Monster," Jada shouted as she pumped three shots into the man.

Jose-ee reached out and put her hand over the revolver before she could empty the cylinder. "Better save your bullets."

Jada nodded agreement. "Yeah, only two left."

The struggle raged until Geronimo and his men arrived from the rear of the procession. Armed with sixteen shot repeaters, they drove the Mexicans back to the ridge and ended the wholesale slaughter.

Around noon, Captain Antonio Rama led a second charge. Despite intense fire from Geronimo's Apaches, dozens of troops made it to the Indian's line. They leaped into the creek bed behind Rama brandishing his sword skyward and shouting encouragement.

When Jada saw him with the raised blade, she held her pistol with both hands, took careful aim, and shot him in the chest. Rama dropped his saber, clutched at the wound, and collapsed.

The soldiers immediately turned their attention to Jada and Jose-ee. Several troopers, screaming curses, rushed toward the two. Jada slowed their attack with her last bullet then hurled her pistol at another attacker without much effect.

Soldiers jumped into the foxhole in an effort to capture the women alive. Jada and Jose-ee fought like trapped cats, biting and kicking. One soldier grabbed Jada by her long hair, but she sent him to the ground writhing in pain when she stuck her finger into his eye. As the trooper floundered in the dirt, Jada pulled her four-shot muff pistol from the folds of her moccasins, killed two more assailants with it, and wounded a third. She did not get her last shot off. A trooper clubbed her from behind.

She awoke the next morning with her head in Jose-ee's lap. A dozen Mexican guards stood in a circle around them and a gaggle of captured women and children.

"What happened?" Jada asked as her eyes blinked open.

"A soldier hit you in the head with his rifle butt. You've been out cold all night. We're prisoners."

While Jada was unconscious, Geronimo's men set fire to the reeds and high grass beside the creek allowing the survivors to escape into the inky night behind a curtain of thick smoke. They left thirty women and kids captured, and almost half of Loco's people dead in the shambles at Alisos Creek.

48

Jada Requests American Help

FORSYTH'S CAVALRY RODE HARD the next day to catch the Indians but the only Apaches they came across were cast-off corpses of the wounded who died along the trail.

At dusk, Tupper suggested to Forsyth, "Let's hang it up, colonel. My boys are bushed from the fight yesterday."

"Damn Tupper, those Indians can't be too far ahead."

"Yeah, but it would be suicide to follow them after dark. I reckon they're expecting our company. Let's make camp and get some rest tonight. We can catch 'em tomorrow." Forsyth grudgingly agreed.

After a mile ride the following morning the Americans reached the ghostly-silent Alisos battlefield. Tupper, shocked at the gory scene, leaned toward Forsyth. "I saw some appalling sights in the war, but this beats all."

Forsyth studied the bodies strewn along the creek. "Appears that most of the dead are women."

As the two officers examined the butchery, Colonel Garcia rode up. "What, may I inquire, is the American army doing in Mexico?" He spoke arrogantly in accented English.

"We're chasing some of your Apache friends who left their reservation in Arizona last week. They've been killing settlers all the way down to the border." Forsyth pointed north. "We followed them from there."

"Well, colonel if your sole intention is to punish these Indians, and you aren't invading our sacred soil, it's obvious we've done the job for you."

"May we inspect the battleground?" Forsyth gave Garcia a scornful stare.

"I'd be delighted to give you a tour myself." Garcia bowed from the saddle and held his arm out ushering the Americans over to admire his work. "After you tour the field, I must insist you leave our country."

Wandering the battlefield, Forsyth shook his head at the carnage, but feigned interest as Garcia bragged about his brilliant victory. During the gruesome walkabout, Tupper spotted a cluster of women and children surrounded by a dozen guards. One of the prisoners silently motioned for him to come to her.

"These are Loco's people." She spoke in flawless English with a sophisticated accent. "Geronimo forced us to leave the reservation and walked us into this slaughter."

"Who are you?" asked Tupper.

"I'm Jada Morgan. I'm a doctor and was with these people when they were taken."

"I've heard of you," said Tupper. "Aren't you the Chiricahua woman who J.P. Morgan took in?"

"No, his cousin, Jack Morgan, adopted me. He was an army doctor sometime back."

"Jack! I knew him. We were in the Civil War together."

"Please Captain, I beg you, try to secure our release. It'll be terrible if these brutes keep us. They'll sell us for slaves and prostitutes."

"I'll try." Tupper turned and walked over to Garcia.

"Colonel, your prisoners are United States Indians. How about releasing them to us for return to their reservation?"

"That's impossible. We're at war with the Apaches. It's a matter of national pride for us to keep them—but I might consider giving them to you for a small consideration." Garcia rubbed his thumb and forefinger together.

"How much would that be, Colonel?" Tupper asked in a sarcastic tone.

"Considering my losses and expenditures, three hundred pesos apiece is fair. I can sell them on the slave market for a good deal more," he lied.

"You know a soldier doesn't carry money in the field. How about a promissory note?"

"Cash on the barrel, as you Americans say."

After more negotiations, Tupper walked back to Jada. "I'm sorry, Doctor Morgan. Colonel Garcia won't agree. If we tried to take you from him, it would create an international incident and probably a shootout."

Jada's shoulders slumped. "Then please notify my father and my uncle as soon as possible. Uncle Pierpont may have some influence with these barbarians."

"I promise I'll wire them from the first telegraph office we reach on the way back." He scribbled the addresses on a small tablet he carried in his shirt pocket.

Tupper then went to Forsyth. The colonel bent down, patted his horse's neck, and whispered, "Garcia wants us to leave Mexico at once. If we don't, he says he's ready to fight." He shook his head and spit. "He's bluffing. He asked for ammunition only minutes ago, but we better take off anyhow. We don't need to rankle the state department over a few Indians."

Tupper returned to Jada and shook her hand. "Good luck, Doctor Morgan. I'll get those telegraphs off as soon as I can. I'm sure the government will do everything they can to obtain your release." He turned and galloped away with Forsyth's column.

When the last American trooper was out of sight, Colonel Garcia went to the prisoners. He stood in front of the women, struck a match on his belt buckle, and kindled an outsized cigar sending a cloud of blue smoke toward the captives.

At first, Jada did not recognize Garcia, but as soon as the cheroot's distinctive stench stung her nostrils, memories of her dead family flashed through her mind. The huge corona, his thick black mustache, and yellow teeth came back to her in an instant. The man standing before them was responsible for the murders of her relatives and friends. Her eyes narrowed. She clinched her jaw as she scrutinized the killer and remembered her pledge for revenge. Give me just one chance at him, she thought.

Garcia turned to his men who sat gawking at the women. "Company A, go bury our dead. Company B, retrieve the dropped weapons, and Company C, harvest the scalps from the bodies. Give them to Sergeant Rodriguez. Rodriguez, I want a count when they're all collected."

The troops set about their grim work as Garcia chewed his cigar and swaggered around the cluster of women appraising his catch. He strutted by Bittersweet, Tzon, Hahles, and Nahno, Gillee's young stretcher bearers and pointed. "Pull those four out for me to take back to my hacienda. I require a little extra help with chores at the ranch."

His officers laughed as they grabbed the four and jerked them away from the larger group. "Now you need three more, sir—one for every day of the week," said one officer.

"Two will do. I rest on Sundays." The men hooted.

Jose-ee frowned and touched Jada's arm. "Do you understand that jabber? Why are they laughing?"

"They're joking about their commander taking some of us as servants but I believe he's picking out girls he wants for sex."

"Pig." Jose-ee's inquisitive frown became a scowl.

Garcia continued to strut around the group, chewing his stogie, and evaluating each woman for sale or as a conquest in his bed. He came to Jose-ee and Jada holding each other. Black powder smudges smeared across Jada's face. Both were covered with blood spatter and dirt. Garcia poked the air with his cigar. "Put those two with the other four. They ought to clean up nicely."

Thick leather chokers, especially designed for the purpose, were strapped around Jada and Jose-ee's necks and linked by a rope to similar neckwear on the other women Garcia had selected to keep for himself.

"Dog collars." Jada fingered the neckpiece with disgust.

As the soldiers were forming up to leave the scene, Sergeant Rodriguez rode up to Garcia. "Nice haul sir. Eighty-one topknots."

Garcia fingered his Havana, calculated for a minute, and smiled. "With the bounty for scalps going for a hundred fifty pesos each, that's about twelve thousand. We can sell the other twenty-seven prisoners I don't save for myself for at least fifteen thousand more. A good day's work."

49

Captives' Fate

FROM WHAT JADA HEARD of Garcia's banter with his men, the colonel intended to meet his commanding officer, General Benardo Reyes, at army headquarters in Bavispe to report the battle.

As the troops lined up for their trip to the military base, the six women Garcia had selected for himself were compelled to lead the column. The procession took five long days of labored plodding to reach the army post.

Upon their arrival, soldiers herded the captives into two fenced pens. They forced Jada, Jose-ee, and the four special prisoners into a smaller enclosure adjacent to one holding twenty-seven women and several children.

Colonel Garcia walked into Reyes' office, gave a natty salute, and announced, "General, I've a great victory to report."

Reyes stood up, returned the salute, and offered his hand to Garcia with enthusiasm. "So I understand Lorenzo. Several travelers from Janos stopped by with the news of your success. You'll be a national hero when the word gets out."

Garcia responded with a nonchalant shrug. "Sorry you weren't leading the fight, Bernardo. There would be more dead Apaches if you'd been in charge."

"Thank you for that, colonel. Still, it is an impressive triumph," Reyes said with feigned modesty.

"The Indians had those damned repeaters. Our single shot Remingtons couldn't match them. Even so, the boys did a lot of good work with their bayonets." Garcia pulled out two cigars and offered one to the general.

"What's your plan now?" Reyes asked as he lit up.

"I want to give you the children we captured. We're holding twelve of them ranging from babies to ten-year-olds. I think if you distribute them among the citizens who need an extra peon, it should boost your popularity with the local folks."

"Gracias, Lorenzo. The children will be most appreciated by my friends.

"I hope so, but right now I would like to ask a favor, sir."

"Yes." Reyes sent a gigantic cloud of smoke toward the ceiling.

"I want to requisition three wagons—two large freighters to take twenty-seven prisoners to the slave auction in Guaymas, and a small one to haul six of them to my hacienda in Hermosillo." He offered a wry smile. "I need a little extra household help.

Both are long trips, and hauling the girls chained in wagons will remove any chance for an escape."

"No problem for Mexico's latest hero, and I understand the benefits of more helpers at the ranch." Reyes winked and gave Garcia a grin as he waggled the large stogie between his fingers. "I'll send a dozen officers' wives out to collect the kids. I suspect you'll meet some resistance when you take them."

Garcia shook his head confidently. "My troops will keep things under control. There won't be any problems."

"Good luck. Don't overwork the new housekeepers."

"Gracias." Garcia chuckled, offered a salute, and left the room.

In the corral, the prisoners waited in silence, staring into space, or attending their children. Jada, Jose-ee, Bittersweet, Tzon, Hahles, and Nahno sat in a small circle discussing their dilemma when a bevy of Mexican women and a squad of soldiers walked toward the corral.

"This isn't good," Jose-ee said as the group moved to the larger enclosure.

"What are they up to?" Jada asked.

"You'll see in a minute." Hahles shifted her position for a better view. "They've come for the children. They'll give them away to Mexican families for slaves."

Shock spread over Jada's face as she watched the soldiers and officers' wives approach. "These people are pure evil. That's horrid."

"Yes, maybe as bad as what's going to happen to us," said Bittersweet.

They looked on as three troopers went to each woman with a child. While two held the mother, the third man pulled the screaming youngster away and presented the moppet to one of the waiting Mexican women. Unforced, one Apache woman with a nursing baby, walked over to the Mexican housewives, holding the newborn out to be taken.

The "foster mother" smiled and took the baby from the Apache woman, but suddenly she rolled her eyes aghast, dropped the infant to the ground, and screamed, "Oh god! The baby's dead. This child is dead!"

The Apache mother had smothered her bantling. She fixed an icy stare on the shaken señora and said in broken Spanish, "Better to kill her than to know she would be a Mexican slave!" She turned and walked back to the huddled prisoners.

Jada viewed each exchange with increasing frustration and anger. She was educated, wealthy, experienced in three cultures with powerful friends in high places, and yet she felt helpless to stop the heinous proceeding. When the woman dropped the dead child, Jada's face flushed and her chest heaved with shallow breaths. She screamed at the top of her voice, "You dirty bastards." She shook her fist and kicked a pile of sand at the soldiers and the women. Jose-ee and Bittersweet rushed to calm her before her captors could retaliate.

Supervising the operation from the sidelines, Garcia turned to his lieutenant and said, "She'll be a lively one in bed." They both chuckled.

After the children were taken away, three wagons rolled up to the corrals. The twenty-seven women in chains were taken from the larger corral and loaded into two freighters at bayonet point. They left as soon as the women boarded. The cart holding Jada and the other five young women pulled out about an hour later, accompanied by Colonel Garcia with fifteen cavalrymen.

With his six personal prisoners traveling in a wagon, Garcia reached his hacienda in four days. A ten-foot outer wall enclosed the entire compound to protect against unwanted outsiders, or in this case, to prevent escapes. The ranch was enormous, consisting of the main house, barracks for a few troops, small bungalows for employees, blacksmith and carpentry shops, a bakery, stables, and a variety of other buildings. Jada's attention went to one well-kept building with a sign above the door, "Clinica Médica," the hacienda's medical clinic. She couldn't imagine a ranch large enough to support an infirmary.

Five soldiers removed their restraints and roughly shoved the six women into a large adobe building. Their lockup included nothing more than one oversized room with a dirt floor. Two barred windows provided the only light. The thick wooden double doors were bolted shut.

Their prison reeked from the piles of horse manure that dotted the dirt floor. As soon as Jada's eye's adjusted, she told the others, "Our jail seems to be an indoor riding rink."

50

Inside Help

GARCIA KEPT JADA AND THE OTHERS in the foul-smelling lockup for a week. An open tin bucket which served as a toilet intensified the feculent stench that filled the chamber. A barrel of stagnant drinking water sat beside the smelly pail.

Once a day a stout woman and a young girl brought food. The older server toted a large kettle of soup. The girl carried a tray of stale corn bread and table scraps from the ranch hands' dining hall. When Jada caught her staring, the matronly woman quickly averted her eyes and went about her business.

After their servers departed and slammed the heavy door shut, Nahno stirred the brew with a wooden paddle protruding from the kettle. A calf's head complete with eyeballs and fur swirled to the top. Nahno turned away and made a face. At first the prisoners ignored the nasty concoction but scarfed down the crusts and leftovers.

Jada stared into the container for a moment, and thought, Disgusting, but at least it's boiling hot and probably has a little nutrition. "We need to keep our strength up if we're going to get away from here." She began filling tin cups their jailors left. "Everyone should drink a little." The women were ravenous so it took only a word from Jada for them to down the soup.

The following day, the matron returned carrying the same vessel with the day-old calf's head still bobbing in the swill. She remained silent as she set the steaming gumbo down.

I recognize something about that woman, Jada thought. I've seen her before. As the attendant turned to leave, Jada remembered. She called out in Chiricahua, "Francisca, I know you. You were with Chief Colleto when they killed everybody."

The woman's head jerked around. She answered in Chiricahua, "The Mexicans call me Celina now. I remember you too. You're Dah-zhonne, Nitis and Alope's daughter. I'm surprised you're alive. I saw your parents fall in the attack." She stepped back for a full view of Jada. "You're all grown up."

The prisoners were astonished to find an Apache in Lorenzo Garcia's hacienda and crowded around her. Jada asked, "Why are you working for that maggot? We thought you were a Mexican."

"I'm one of his slaves. The colonel's scouts captured me after their attack on our village and I've been held here ever since—sixteen years. What happened to you?"

"The Americans found me alive after the assault. A doctor adopted me and took me East. They call me Jada." Jada didn't mention she was a physician or could speak Spanish. After the years Francisca spent with the Garcia family, her allegiance could be a problem.

"You fared better than I did," Francisca said. "This is a horrible life. I've tried to escape, but they caught me." She cringed at the memory. "When they brought me back, the colonel beat me with a whip." A disturbed murmur passed through the six prisoners when she raised her blouse to show a crisscross of scars covering her back

"I can't do this," Nahno said. "We've got to get away."

Francisca shook her head. "I want to run away also but I've almost given up. The guards are everywhere at night. The wall is too high and covered with spikes and broken glass on top." She remained silent for a minute then added, "Things will improve for you. Garcia is trying to break your spirit now. Later, he'll let you stay in a cleaner place, bathe, and you'll get better food—if you do everything he says."

"Exactly what would that be?" Tzon asked.

Francisca hesitated. "It's the worst part. You'll be taken to a doctor in the hacienda's clinic. The colonel wants to make sure he won't catch a disease when he makes you sleep with him." She hugged herself and shivered a little.

"I'll fight like a bear." Hahles shook her fist.

"I thought so too, but if you give him any trouble, he'll beat you and sell you to a man who owns a whorehouse." She made a face as if she had bitten a lemon and shook her head. "The man who buys you will force you to have sex with dozens of men each day, and you'll die from a terrible disease—unless some drunkard kills you first."

"So what should we do?" Bittersweet asked.

"Pretend the colonel is a very attractive man and you enjoy whatever he does. He is so dumb. He always believes those things. If he likes you, he'll keep you to work for him here at the hacienda. If he doesn't, he'll sell you."

Francisca gave the soup a stir, then nervously looked around at her teenage keeper and left the wooden paddle in the broth. "I must go. I've stayed too long, but I'll be with you to translate when you go to the doctor." She grinned as she thought of the physician. "He doesn't speak Chiricahua."

She smiled at the Mexican girl. "She's Rosita Garcia, one of the colonel's relatives. Lucky for me, she doesn't know our language either. Her job is to follow me around and report on what I do."

Jada began to form a plan for escape as Francisca described their upcoming medical examination. "Will you help us if we try to get away?"

"Perhaps, if I think it's safe, I'll go with you. What are you planning?" Francisca was obviously interested.

"Nothing yet. Just thinking," Jada stared at the courtyard's front gate through the bars in the window, still uncertain if Francisca could be trusted.

Dr. Pedro Padilla operated an efficient and professional infirmary for the Garcia family and hacienda employees. A man in his late forties with an insipid personality, Padilla was a good doctor, educated in Spain. The colonel hired him as the hacienda's physician at twice the salary of most Mexican doctors because he was unmarried and showed no interest in females. Garcia was certain the doctor preferred men and would not be doodling with his captives.

After a bath in the river, the six women were left naked while the guards tossed their ragged clothes into a fire built for that purpose. Afterwards, Jada and the five other prisoners were marched buff-bare to the clinic and forced to sit au naturel on a wooden bench in the waiting room. Mortified, they sat looking at their feet, one arm crossed over their breasts and a hand in their laps to cover their nudity.

"And these people call us savages." Bittersweet growled through clenched teeth.

Jada was not so much embarrassed as angry but she remained silent. Francisca sat across the small reception room and tried to comfort the women. "This is another way the colonel tries to shame his captives. Be strong."

After a short wait, Padilla peeked from the clinic door. "Bring in the first one."

Francisca took Hahles' hand and walked with her into the examining room. She sat in one corner, her eyes down, translating for Padilla.

Hahles returned in twenty minutes, sobbing as she came from the room. "That crazy man touched me all over my body." She trembled, horror stricken. "He put his head on my chest." She pointed to the area between her breasts. "He even spread my privates and looked inside!"

"All doctors do those things," Jada explained. "He needed to listen to your heart and make sure you don't have any sores inside," Jada's explanation didn't placate Hahles or the others.

Jada was last to go in for the examination. Familiar with physical exams, she remained stoic throughout. He's doing a reasonable job and following correct medical procedure. Garcia must make him keep us naked to further shame us. The doctor knows better.

About halfway though Jada's exam, the doctor excused himself. "I'll be back in a minute," he told Francisca.

When he hurried from the room, Francisca tiptoed over to Jada and whispered, "Something is wrong with him. He needs to pee often."

Prostrate, thought Jada.

While they waited for the doctor's return, Jada hurried to the clinic's large medicine cabinet and examined dozens of bottles arranged on the shelves. Reading the labels, she picked out a small rectangular one and handed it to Francisca. "He has several of these. He won't notice."

Francisca slipped the flat brown-glass bottle into the pocket of her dress. "What is it," she asked.

"It will help us later. Be sure to keep the cork tight." Jada did not reveal the contents.

After their checkups, Francisca called Garcia's teenage relative who brought nondescript peon skirts and blouses for the prisoners. "They burned your old things but you can keep your moccasins for now. Mexican shoes will come soon," she said.

Once dressed, Jada retrieved the bottle from Francisca and slipped it into a pocket.

"They are all healthy, Colonel Garcia," announced Padilla. "You can enjoy your fun in safety."

"Excellent. Sadly, I'm busy until tomorrow evening."

51

Seduction

WHEN FRANCISCA BROUGHT THE WOMEN'S FOOD the next afternoon, she told Jada, "The colonel ordered me to take one of you to him tomorrow night."

"Then that's when we'll escape, but I'll need some assistance."

The older woman's face clouded with concern. "What kind of help? If Garcia catches you, he'll whip you while you're tied naked to a stake. If he finds out I helped, he'll torture me to death."

Jada took the woman's hands into hers. "I hope you'll go with us, Francisca but it's all right if you are afraid to try. I won't ask you to do anything that puts you in danger."

"What then?" Francisca was dubious.

"You should take me to the colonel first. I think Nahno and I may be the only ones who have been with a man." Jada glanced sideways at the group of women. "Better me than one of them, but I'm not planning to let things get out of hand."

"The colonel's very strong. How will you stop him?"

"That's where our medicine from the clinic comes in. You said one of your duties was to make Garcia's bed every day. When you do that, can you slip the bottle under his mattress?"

"It would be easy," Francisca's voice grew more confident. "Rosita pays no attention when I arrange the covers."

Jada handed the little receptacle to her. "While you're cleaning his room tomorrow, stick this under the mattress on the right side with a handkerchief and a needle and thread—a little way from the head of the bed." Jada held her hands two feet apart. "Not too far in—I'll need to find these things quickly. Otherwise, I'll have to finish him."

"Aren't you going to kill him anyhow?" Francisca sounded disappointed.

Jada gave a shrug.

"Why not?" asked Francisca. "How will we get away?"

"I'm planning something else for him. He'll be unconscious during our escape." Jada smiled sarcastically and added, "I'll tell the others to be ready to leave when we return from my romantic encounter."

At seven the following evening, Francisca entered Garcia's hacienda holding Jada by the elbow as if controlling her. When they turned a corner into a long hallway, the older woman stopped and frowned. "Ut-oh, two guards tonight. There's usually only one," she said in Chiricahua. "Will that ruin your plan?"

"I don't think so, but I'm not sure." Jada studied the sentries, appraising their size and positions.

"Those two will take you into his sleeping quarters. I'm supposed to wait down the hall for you to come out and then escort you back to your cell. After the colonel has finished his business with a girl, the guard always returns to his barracks."

"It may take a while, but when I peek out and ask one bodyguard to come into the room, be ready," Jada whispered as she eyed the two soldiers.

Upon reaching the soldiers seated on each side of Garcia's bedroom door, Francisca joked with the older man, "Sergeant Enrico, are you getting so old you need younger help?"

Enrico gestured toward Jada. "I could handle that little one with one hand." He introduced his companion, "This is Salvador. He was a hero in the Alosis fight. He killed many Apaches and as a bonus for his bravery, the colonel is training him to be one of his personal bodyguards."

Jada said nothing but sent a piercing stare through the skinny young man. *I'll present you with an additional bonus later.*

"Give her here. Is she a problem?" asked the sergeant.

"Not at all. She seems resigned to her fate." Francisca flicked her eyes at Jada.

"I'm sure she'll leave a happy woman after tonight." Enrico said as he gawked at Jada with a lascivious grin.

Francisca gently shoved Jada toward the two soldiers. They grabbed her by each arm, took her into the room, and came to attention, still holding her. She appeared tiny and pitiful between Garcia's troopers, but her plan to escape was coming together. *You're pretty tough now, boys. Just you wait.*

Seated in an overstuffed chair, Lorenzo Garcia wore a black bathrobe and held an oversized cigar. "Damn, except for those tits, she could be a child. Good thing. I like 'em young. Is she resisting?"

"No sir. She hasn't struggled at all. You'll enjoy tonight, sir," said Enrico.

At that point, Jada stood erect and said in flawless Castilian, "If you make these bullies let me go, you might have an even better time."

Thinking they were manhandling a Spanish noblewoman, the shocked soldiers released her without orders from Garcia.

Stunned, the colonel dropped his cigar. "You speak like an elegant Spanish lady," he said. "Where did you learn?" he asked while he retrieved his stogie from the floor.

"As a child." Jada spoke with a bravado she didn't feel.

"You men can go—nobody enters until I call." Garcia waved the guards away with a dismissive salute, sending the soldiers to their stations outside the door.

"Now my dear, I've never had a sophisticated lady in these circumstances," he said sarcastically. "Mind you, I don't care—Apache, Mexican, or Spanish nobility are all the same. We'll have an evening of passion and sex."

"That's fine with me colonel. I'll do some things for you that will satisfy me immensely and which you'll never forget." She gave him a sensuous smile. Garcia was agog at her enthusiasm.

You fool, she thought. No woman in her right mind would ever agree to touch you unless she was forced.

"But for me to satisfy you completely, we should take our time. I want to learn about you first." She fluttered her eyes seductively. "That way I can treat you properly." She smiled, but prayed silently she wouldn't need to follow through on anything she promised.

"I've never had someone so willing in here before. How did you get mixed up with these savages?"

"I was a captive—let's leave it there. I don't like to talk about it." I must keep this discussion away from my background.

"This is an interesting room," she said to change the subject. "These are fascinating displays on your walls. Tell me about them."

"I'd be delighted." He stood, took her arm, and proudly led her around the room. "My assortment of baskets and pottery is on these shelves. I picked up most of them in different Indian villages I defeated."

He walked her across the bedchamber to a wall featuring dozens of guns, knives, war clubs, and bows with quivers of arrows. "This is my arms collection. I captured all these weapons in battles with the Apaches."

Perfect! My war chest displayed for the taking. "It's an amazing assortment." She pretended to be fascinated as she sized up the killing instruments which the women might need later.

He pointed to a large jumble of hardware in the corner. "Those are weapons we seized in the big fight where you were captured. I haven't put the best ones on display yet." Jada immediately spotted her chrome plated pistol and derringer in the pile.

She feigned interest in each piece of the collection and awed Garcia with her knowledge of firearms. I can't believe he doesn't see through this. His mind is on one thing.

"You're quite a woman," he said with genuine admiration. "What is your Spanish name?"

"I was known as Julena Caballero," Jada lied.

"Well Julena, let me pour you a drink." Out of the blue he grabbed her and kissed her fiercely, forcing his tongue deep into her mouth. She almost gagged. Yuck! I wonder if he ever cleans his teeth. This is disgusting, but it's our best chance to escape.

"Not so fast big boy." She smiled and deftly slipped from his grasp. "Let's take a drink first to loosen up. Then we can get naked and I'll give you my special massage. You'll never receive another one like it."

With his arm around her shoulders, they walked to the bar near the colonel's bed. "What would you like, my dear?"

"I haven't tasted scotch in a long time." She thought a strong drink would serve as a cleansing mouthwash for her and tone down the disgusting taste in Garcia's mouth.

"I keep a Gringo brand, Johnny Walker. I think you will appreciate it."

"I'm sure I will, but it's been a while—just give me a small swallow. I need to be in top form for our love-making."

"Indeed, indeed. This promises to be an excellent night."

"I guarantee you'll remember tonight for as long as you live," Jada replied with a wicked gleam in her eyes.

He kissed her again—the scotch didn't help. "Are you ready?" he asked.

"I was set to go when I first came in the room," she announced with a flirtatious wink. "What do we have here?" She untied the sash holding his bathrobe. He was naked underneath, and aroused.

Standing back with a hand on one cheek, she gave him an admiring look and announced, "Oh my, very impressive, sir. Worthy of a general." Garcia beamed.

Jada undressed, teasing him as she slowly removed her clothing. Once naked, she held out her arms. "Approve?" She smiled, but inwardly detested the way his eyes played over every inch of her body.

"Magnifico!" was Garcia's only comment as he gaped at her. He tried to hug her but she slipped away again. She didn't want any face-to-face contact while they were undressed for fear Garcia was so aroused she couldn't fend off his advances.

"A little longer. I want give you my special massage first. It will increase our pleasure." She pushed him playfully toward the bed. "Go lay on your stomach so I can work my magic. You'll remember this forever."

Garcia chuckled, removed his bathrobe, and complied. Jada grimaced at the sight as he lay face down. His backside was covered in thick black hair. Jada climbed into bed and straddled him. She began massaging his muscles, moving up his spine to his shoulders.

Garcia moaned as Jada worked her way up his back. She leaned forward so her breasts nestled in the colonel's fur hoping she wouldn't throw up before she could pull this off. His body tensed and he gasped. "Oh, soooo good."

She slipped her arm under his throat as if to give him an embrace and at the same time, nuzzled her cheek tightly against his. "Are you about ready?" she whispered in his ear.

52

Surgical Revenge

STRETCHED OUT ON THE COLONEL'S BACK, Jada whispered romantic promises in Garcia's ear as she worked her right arm into position across his throat. Without warning, she grabbed the crook of her left elbow and pulled her arm into a garrote-like choke. Jada knew stopping Garcia's blood supply to his head would render her aspiring rapist unconscious in about ten seconds—holding it longer would leave the colonel brain damaged or dead. She didn't much care if that happened, but for now she wanted him out cold.

Her chokehold wasn't tight enough at first and Garcia struggled to his feet and tried to shake and spin Jada off as she rode him piggyback. She tightened her grip on his neck and locked her legs tightly around his waist until he staggered and collapsed on the bed.

Jada managed to roll the unconscious officer to his back and quickly ran her hand under the mattress to retrieve the flask Francisca had secreted there with a handkerchief. Jada soaked the hanky with chloroform from the bottle and hastily draped the cloth over Garcia's nose and mouth.

She watched his body relax then hurried to fetch a small pot from Garcia's assortment of pottery displayed on the shelves across the room. She placed the damp handkerchief in the container and positioned it next to Garcia's nose with a pillow. He could breathe, but would continue to inhale enough chloroform to keep him unconscious throughout the night. She took a bandanna hanging with Garcia's clothes and tied it around her face to avoid inhaling the anesthetic. The kerchief smelled of cigar smoke.

Jada threw on her skirt and blouse and hurried over to the colonel's weapon collection. After rummaging through the arsenal, she found a small razor-sharp knife along with her Hopkins and Allen pistol, and the Sharps derringer. She also picked up two bows with full quivers, and four Colt revolvers. Garcia's Colt hung on the bedstead in its holster. She added that to the other weapons.

Piling the ordnance near the door, Jada went back to Garcia's bedside and poured more chloroform into the small pot.

She again searched under the mattress until her fingers located the needle and thread left there by Francisca. Jada placed the sewing items on the corner of the bed and spread Garcia's legs wide. She paused for a moment and recalled the Oath of

Maimonides she took during her graduation from medical school: The eternal providence has appointed me to watch over the life and health of Thy creatures...

Well God, she thought, I'm watching over the lives of the future women victims of this monster. This is certainly no violation of the oath. She smiled when she considered the last line in the pledge. Today he can discover his errors of yesterday...

No time for white ethics, she thought, this man is responsible for the deaths of my mother, father, and dozens of other innocent members of my tribe. The Apache culture of her childhood demanded payback for the murder of a loved one, and this was sweet revenge. The Maimonides Oath was irrelevant.

Jada stood at the foot of the bed and contemplated the task before her as she thumbed the edge of the scalpel-sharp blade. "This is for my family, and big man, you have raped your last woman," she said aloud as she set to work.

Afterwards, Jada wrapped Garcia's medical waste in a towel and used the pitcher of water on the bedroom washstand to clean blood from her arms and hands. She then returned to the colonel's weapons collection to retrieve a war club she had seen earlier. Holding the bludgeon behind her, she went to the door and peeked out. "The colonel wants to reward the hero of Alisos. Salvador, he asks you to come in." She looked distraught and deflated. "Sergeant, he says you should keep guard. No one is to enter for any reason."

"Salvador, you lucky dog. He let me join in once. Enjoy it, kid." The prospects were so arousing that neither was concerned that Jada was fully dressed.

"Here, take my gun." Salvador laughed and handed his rifle to Enrico. "My personal weapon will suffice for this job."

Salvador closed the door and threw a smart salute. When there was no response, he moved toward the bed. The colonel remained unmoving, silent, and hidden under the covers.

Meanwhile Jada clutched the heavy war club in the folds of her dress. It was a three pound round stone attached to one end of a foot-long shaft by a leather sheath—a deadly weapon.

When the soldier stepped closer to the colonel's bed, he walked in front of Jada. She took aim at the young man's head and swung the weapon with all her strength, smashing it into the boy's temple—a deathblow that caved in his skull. Afterward, she dragged his twitching body behind the bed where it couldn't be seen from the doorway.

Jada glared down at the dead soldier and murmured in a low voice, "A last reward for the hero of Alisos." She was already planning a way to dispose of the sergeant sitting outside.

When she eased the door open to invite Enrico in for the party, she found him slumped in a chair, appearing to be asleep. With the entry opened wider, Jada came face to face with Francisca leaning against the wall with her arms crossed. As Jada stepped out of the room, she saw a splotch of blood on the soldier's tunic and a kitchen knife planted deeply between Enrico's ribs.

Jada nodded toward the cadaver, and said, "Good! That makes things easier. Quick, let's drag him inside." They each grabbed a foot and pulled Enrico's corpse next to the dead private.

"The colonel is very still. Did you kill him?" Francisca asked as she looked at Garcia.

"No, but when he wakes up, he'll wish he was dead." Jada drew the covers back to display her handiwork.

Stunned for a moment, Francisca covered her mouth and stared at Garcia's surgery. "He's going to kill us if he catches us. We need to get going—fast."

"He'll be unconscious for a long time, but you're right." Jada emptied the remaining half-full bottle of chloroform into the pot next to Garcia's face. "Here, help me carry these weapons." She began picking up their arsenal.

Francisca eyed the colonel's shiny chrome-plated revolver with its belt and holster. "Can I take this one?"

Jada nodded and heavy-set Francisca strapped on the gun without making any adjustments to the length.

"You're the same size as the colonel." Jada laughed as she cut a second belt from Garcia's wardrobe and tightened it around her tiny midriff. They each jammed two Colt pistols in their belts. Jada added her Hopkins and Allen. She slipped her derringer into the folds of her moccasins.

Francisca pulled her large butcher knife from the sergeant's chest, cleaned the blade in the washbasin by the bed, and stuck it into the holster with the Garcia's Colt. They each picked up a bow and a quiver of arrows.

"Let's get out of here," Jada said after they filled the pockets of their skirts with handfuls of bullets they found in Garcia's cabinets. She even discovered four loose cartridges for her little derringer.

As they left the room, Jada picked up the war club. "This might be useful." As an afterthought, she also scooped up the towel containing the excised part of Colonel Garcia.

Back in the hall, Francisca returned the guards' chairs to their usual places by the door. "With the sentries gone, everyone will think all went well for lover-boy and he's sleeping late," she said.

53

The Getaway

AFTER LEAVING GARCIA'S RESIDENCE, Jada and Francisca crept along carefully, staying in the shadows until they reached the lockup. Francisca warned Jada what to expect. "In addition to the guards at your jail, two others are stationed beside the hacienda's outer gate. I think we can handle the jailhouse guards—our return won't be a surprise. The guards at the front entrance are a different matter," she said shaking her head. "No one is supposed to be out at night, and we have to cross an open area before we reach them. They'll spot us and know something is wrong. If we shoot them, everyone in the hacienda will come running."

"How are you with a bow?" asked Jada.

"I never was very good and I haven't shot one in over sixteen years. We'll have to get close for me to have a chance."

"Maybe one of the others can do it," Jada said.

When they arrived at the prisoners' cellblock, two guards were slouched in wooden chairs on each side of the door with their rifles propped against the wall beside them. A hanging kerosene lantern cast a circle of light around the men.

Francisca whispered, "Leave that nasty towel and the bows here. We'll get them on the way out." She put one hand on Jada's elbow again to appear she was controlling the prisoner. Jada walked with her head bowed, looking traumatized from her visit with Garcia.

"They'll think I'm bringing you back," Francisca whispered under her breath. "When we reach them, the one on the left will stand up and unlock the door—he always does. I'll take care of him. The one on the right is yours."

Holding the club concealed behind her, Jada gripped the handle tighter, her hand slippery with sweat. Almost as soon as they stepped into the light, the guard closest to Francisca stood without speaking and started to unlock the keep. The other man cast a salacious grin at Jada but his expression abruptly changed. "Pistolas, Antonio! They have pistolas!" he yelped as he reached for his rifle.

Jada swung the war club from below her waist in a wide arc toward the man's head, but he shifted his body. The heavy stone struck him on the tip of his shoulder, shattering the joint. He yelped in pain, but when Jada tried to deliver another blow, he seized her neck with his good hand and shook her until the club slipped from her palm. She struggled to free herself, but his grip tightened, squeezing her wind pipe.

Gasping for air, she tried to knee him or scratch his eyes. She was unable to loosen his grasp. As she was about to pass out, her attacker went limp, released his hold, and fell to the floor. Jada drew in a breath, coughed, and saw Francisca with her foot on the soldier's neck, pulling her butcher knife from his back. The other guard lay behind Francisca with blood gurgling from a slit across his throat.

"Oooh, that was close." Jada sputtered.

"I always thought this was the best knife in the kitchen," Francisca wiped her blade on the soldier's tunic. "Here, let's prop them up in their chairs. From a distance, no one can tell they're dead. They sleep most of the time anyway." Francisa took the first soldier's arm and indicated Jada should help lift him.

The women in the building heard the scuffle outside and gave a cheer of relief when Jada and Francisca came into the room. "Shush now. Move fast girls, but be very quiet," Francisca said. "We need to get as close to the front gate as we can without attracting any attention."

"Have any of you ever shot a pistol?" Jada asked. Jose-ee, Hahles, and Nahno, raised their hands. Tzon said, "My uncle let me dry-fire his revolver once. I only clicked the empty gun."

"How about a bow and arrow? Is anyone competent with a bow?" Jada asked.

"I'm pretty good," Hahles said. "My brother taught me, and we hunted rabbits and jumping rats with them."

"We have two bows outside. I'll keep one and you get the other. We'll use them on the guards at the front gate," Jada said. "Now, everyone gets a pistol except Bittersweet. I'll hang on to my .38 and my peashooter. Francisca has Colonel Garcia's Colt." Bittersweet wanted a weapon and pouted a little but acted indifferent.

Jada and Francisca parceled out the bullets they found in Garcia's room. "I don't need any," Francisca said. "The colonel's gun was loaded when I took it."

Jada nodded and carried on with her instructions. "Be careful. These are the new Colts. You only have to pull the trigger, and if one goes off by accident, we'll be goners." She clicked one of the empty Colts to demonstrate. "We don't want to rouse anyone inside the compound."

"We'll pick up the bows on the way out. Everyone stay behind me, and no talking." Francisca motioned them forward.

As they were leaving, Bittersweet spotted the shiny solid brass handle of a bayonet protruding from a dead guard's tunic. She took the scabbard holding the long blade and tied the sword-like weapon around her waist with the trooper's belt. She could conceal it under her skirt if necessary.

The seven women walked in silence toward the gate, and as they passed the hacienda's pig sty. The group watched in the moonlight as Jada unwrapped the medical leftover from Garcia's surgery and tossed it to the fattest hog.

Subdued chuckles and whispers followed when the escapees realized what Jada had lobbed to the porker. "That should add an interesting flavor to the colonel's bacon," Jose-ee said with a giggle. The others continued to chortle and agreed the Apaches were wise not to eat pork because of the oinkers' disgusting dietary habits.

"Shhhhh. Let's keep the talking down," Jada said. "I didn't want Doctor Padilla sewing that thing back on." With a satisfied look, Jada washed her hands in the pigs' water trough. "Let's go."

The buildings in the courtyard were dark as the women moved through the compound. After they came to the large open space leading to the hacienda's gate, the seven huddled behind a small tool shed. Two sentries could be seen twenty yards away alone in the dim moonlight.

Jada held out her bow and motioned Hahles up beside her. "You take the one on the right. I'll get the other one," she whispered. "Shoot together when I count three." They loaded their arrows at the same time and drew the strings.

Jada's shaft pierced the guard's chest and shattered his heart. He collapsed, dead before he hit the dirt.

Hahles' shot was low. Her arrow lodged in the second sentry's hip, passing through his pelvis with its point protruding from his buttock. Both she and Jada quickly re-loaded their bows.

The wounded guard gave out a startled scream when the arrow hit. He dropped his rifle, and hobbled off shrieking, "Indians, Indian attack..." His warning was cut short when he was struck again by two arrows. Hahle's second try struck him in the center of his back. In her hurry, Jada aimed high and her shot pierced the soldier's neck. He was silenced instantly.

The seven women remained behind the shed and waited to see if the guard's shouts attracted any attention. A light flickered on in a nearby house. Everyone held their breath as a man came to a window, but after a moment he closed the curtains, satisfied it had been nothing. Seconds later, the house went dark and there was no further movement.

Francisca signaled the others and ran to the gate. Not wasting a second, the women braced the two dead troopers against the wall. "Why don't we take their rifles?" asked Bittersweet hoping to arm herself.

"We can't hide them when we walk and they would slow us down. Our bows will look like walking sticks when we unstring them." Jada thought a moment about the weapons in the women's waistbands, and added, "Pull out your blouses over the pistols. That will cover them if we meet any one during the day." She added, "Bitter-sweet put that bayonet inside your skirt."

They crowded at the hacienda's entrance as Francisca unlatched the huge wooden door, shoved it open enough to slip through, and pushed it shut after they were outside. There was a satisfying click as the latch fell back into place.

"No one will notice anything unusual until the morning," Francisca said. "They change the guards just after daybreak."

"Let's go toward those mountains," Jada said pointing northeast.

Francisca agreed. "That's the way home and it will make it harder to track us once we reach higher ground, but we need to move fast. They'll be after us as soon as they find the colonel and the dead soldiers."

54

Morgan Family Plans Rescue

TRUE TO HIS WORD, Tillius Tupper, the officer who spoke with Jada after the Alisos battle, sent cables as soon as he returned to Fort Bowie notifying Jada's father and Pierpont of her captivity.

Fort Bowie, Arizona Territory
May 5, 1882
IDENTICAL TELEGRAMS TO:
Dr. Jack Morgan, Philadelphia:
Mr. J.P. Morgan, New York
Regret to inform you that your daughter/niece Dr. Jada Morgan taken April 19 by renegade Apaches from San Carlos reservation. Captured on April 29 with others by Mexican forces under Colonel Lorenzo Garcia. Spoke to her briefly. Urgently desires help.
Captain Tillius C. Tupper, 6th Cavalry

Jack and Pierpont were distraught over the news of Jada's capture and imprisonment. Tupper's telegram unleashed a storm of telegraphic and written exchanges between Jack, Pierpont, President Arthur and an assortment of federal executives.

The day after Tupper's communiqué arrived, Pierpont fired off the first of a series of cablegrams to big wigs in Washington.

New York City
May 7, 1882
IDENTICAL TELEGRAMS TO: President Chester A. Arthur; General Sherman, Commanding the Army; General Crook, Commanding the Department of Arizona; Secretary Interior Teller; Secretary State Frelinghuysen; Commissioner of Indian Affairs Tufts
My adopted niece Jada Morgan kidnapped from San Carlos reservation by renegade Apache Indians last month. Working there as physician. Subsequently taken prisoner by Mexican forces commanded by Colonel Lorenzo Garcia. Demand that government exert all efforts to secure her release. Treatment of women prisoners by Mexicans known to be brutal. Urgent action required.
J. Pierpont Morgan

There was little else either of the two Morgans could do, except to commiserate with each other and wait for responses from Capitol City officials. Jack cancelled his appointments and placed a handwritten sign on the clinic door, "Closed for the duration." He wrote countless letters seeking help from old friends in the army out West, and to members of Congress.

Pierpont sent letters and telegrams daily to politicians and military leaders demanding the government, especially the War Department, to take action on Jada's behalf.

The wait for a response to their correspondence seemed interminable, but two weeks after Pierpont sent his initial telegram to the President and others, a reply finally came.

White House,
Washington, DC
May 16, 1882

> To: J. Pierpont Morgan
> At present negotiations are underway by State Department to return all en-slaved Apaches including your niece to this country from Mexico. I will contact you when we receive more specific information.
> Chester A. Arthur
> President of the United States

Pierpont and Jack met after the letter came. Pierpont was frustrated and furious. "Damned little help that is. We may have stirred things up in Washington, but I doubt if anything will happen soon enough to help Jada."

"I'm worried sick about Jada," Jack told J.P. "No Apache captives ever returned from Mexico while I was in the army unless they escaped on their own."

Pierpont said nothing, shook his head and blew a cloud of cigar smoke. Both men were aware of lurid tales about the fate of women held in Mexico and pictured "their girl" as an abused slave or prostitute. "I can't shake the image of her in those circumstances," Pierpont said.

Stress and anxiety wore heavily on Jack and a few gray hairs began to show but three months after Jada's capture, a letter from President Arthur raised his hopes.

White House
August 11, 1882

Dear Messers Morgan:

This is in reference to my May 16 telegram concerning the imprisonment of Dr. Jada Morgan by Mexican authorities. An informant in Sonora, Mexico has notified the War Department that Dr. Morgan recently escaped from the hacienda of Colonel Lorenzo Garcia after wounding the colonel and killing six guards. The extent of Garcia's injuries is unknown as he has not left his villa since the attack on him. The informant believes several Apache women escaped with Dr. Morgan. Our man assumes they are on foot, headed through the mountains for the U.S. border. This information must be kept confidential so as not to endanger ongoing negotiations for the release of all Apache prisoners still held in Mexico.

I continue to pray for the safe return of your daughter/niece.

Sincerely,

Chester A. Arthur

President of the United States

Inside the Morgan mansion, Pierpont and Jack discussed the news as they sipped glasses of brandy. "It's difficult to tell how accurate this is," said Pierpont. "It's hopeful if true. It takes Jada's fate out of the hands of State Department negotiators but gives us a chance to find her without all the government rigmarole." J.P. stubbed out his stogie. "We've waited long enough on those useless baby-kissers in D.C. When I return to New York, I'll cable the President that I'm sending one of my attorneys to Arizona to recruit a few mercenaries and Indian scouts to search for Jada. There are no restrictions to keep civilians and Indians from crossing the border."

"Brilliant idea, Pierpont. Tell your man to put a rush on. Jada is traveling through some mighty rough mountains and those damn Mexicans will be after her like coyotes chasing a rabbit."

Prompted by Pierpont's notes to Washington officials, the mail brought more promising news from General Sherman a week later.

War Department

August 18, 1882

Dear Messers. J.P. Morgan and J. Morgan

I've received your letters and government reports of Dr. Jada Morgan's plight and her subsequent escape from Mexican hands. I'm sure you will be encouraged to know the State Department has consummated an agreement with the Mexican government allowing our troops unimpeded border crossing if they are in hot pursuit of Indians.

Therefore, I've ordered two American units to cross the Mexican border in "hot pursuit" of my friend, Jada, and her companions in order to return them to this country.

We assume the women are traveling north through the Sierra Madre since it would be the safest route if they are pursued. In consequence, I'm dispatching a force of Indian scouts from Fort Apache to search the mountains from the border to the Garcia ranch in Hermosillo. I'll also send a small squad of soldiers from Fort Bowie. Both detachments will be led by officers who are acquainted with Jada.

My understanding from the president is the Morgan family has employed a civilian to facilitate Jada's return. I recommend your employee join our two army units in Tombstone, Arizona. It would be desirable for him to meet my officers at the Bird Cage Theatre and Saloon in Tombstone on August 25. The Bird Cage on Allen Street is open twenty-four hours, seven days a week.

Sincerely,

William Sherman, Commanding General, U.S. Army

Jack and Pierpont were buoyed by Sherman's message and shared small glasses of sherry to celebrate. But a somber silence fell over their celebration when Pierpont said, "This isn't over, Jack. We need to get our show on the road. Jada's still out there."

55

Garcia Discovers Escape

THE MORNING AFTER THE WOMEN ESCAPED, Rosita, Francisca's teenage keeper, arrived late at Colonel Garcia's bedroom door. Assuming Francisca would already be cleaning the room, she walked in without knocking.

Where is that slave-woman? she thought. She'll be in big trouble when Uncle Lorenzo finds out she's tardy. As she scanned the chamber for Francisca, Rosita noticed Garcia stretched out in bed. He appeared to be sound asleep.

He told me he has a meeting this morning. He must have overslept. Phewee, something stinks. She wrinkled her nose at the strong odor of chloroform, walked over to the bed, and touched Garcia's arm, but got no reaction. When she shook him, she noticed a large blood spot on his bedspread.

"Heaven help us," she squealed and ran for Dr. Padilla in the clinic.

"Doctor, something's wrong with Uncle Lorenzo. I can't wake him, and there's blood on his covers."

Padilla grabbed his medical bag and scurried past Rosita who bolted after him. He burst through the door to Garcia's bedroom, got a whiff of chloroform, and immediately recognized the anesthesia arrangement Jada had left to prolong the colonel's medicated slumber.

He handed the pottery containing the chloroform to the girl. "Open the windows—right away girl—and throw this outside."

As Rosita turned from tossing out the pot, she stumbled over the dead guards beside the bed. "Oooh no, doctor! Two soldiers over here are hurt bad."

Padilla hurried to examine the bodies. "These men are beyond help, Rosita. You should leave now. You've seen too much already, but don't you dare talk to anyone about this. Go directly to the sergeant of the guard and tell him to come right now. Guards must remain outside the door day and night." He shook his finger at the girl for emphasis, "No one is to enter this room until the colonel or I say so."

After Rosita left, Padilla threw back the covers and examined Garcia's surgery. Oh! Madre de Dios. There'll be hell to pay for this," he thought.

Appalled, he searched for the missing part. Gone—nowhere to be found. All I can do now is give him something to relieve his suffering.

While he waited, Padilla examined the surgical site. The colonel dallied with the wrong woman this time. She removed everything. The sutures are well placed and she left the urinary track open. She knew exactly how to do this.

Garcia gave a loud moan as he began to wake from the anesthesia. Padilla covered the semiconscious man and waited beside the bed with a concerned expression.

"Ow, ow. What happened?" The woozy Garcia tried to move but the pain in his groin forced him to remain on his back. "My crotch is killing me." He spoke between clinched teeth. "What's going on? Why are you here, Padilla?"

"The woman you were with last evening drugged you, and cut you up, colonel. I found an empty chloroform bottle from the clinic. She probably stole it during her physical exam."

Garcia's eyes opened wide as he put the facts together: Padilla's presence; ache in his crotch; chloroform; and 'cut me up'. He jerked away the covers and stared, horrified at what he saw. His lips quivered as he asked, "What the hell has she done to me?" He glared in desperation at Dr. Padilla for an answer. "Nothing's down there."

"It appears she amputated your entire manhood, colonel—the whole thing. I could understand if an Apache attacked you but this required great skill by a trained surgeon. I thought she was an Apache. She spoke like one during her physical exam." Padilla looked chagrined.

"The little slut tricked you. She was from Spain. She talked with a Castilian accent—must have had a medical education..." His sentence was cut short by a burning spasm in his private area.

"This is horrible. Damn her time. Don't let the men know," Garcia mumbled as his eyes flicked around the room checking for unwanted observers.

Padilla's tone was sympathetic, "I told no one anything, but Rosita came to get me when she couldn't wake you and saw blood on your covers. She hasn't set eyes on the surgery. Right now, I'm the only one who knows."

"Can you sew it back on?" Garcia asked. His hands trembled out of control.

"I would try, if I could find it. I searched, but she must have taken the leftover parts with her."

He changed the subject hoping to calm Garcia. "Here, drink this, colonel. It's a heavy dose of opium. It'll ease the pain and put you to sleep."

"Where's that tramp now? Bring her to me. She'll suffer a slow death." He hissed the edict between clinched teeth.

"The staff reported this morning that she and six others escaped during the night."

"The damned guards. Where were my damn bodyguards?" Garcia's words began to slur.

"They're all dead including the ones who were outside your door. Their bodies are beside the bed. I've instructed Rosita to tell the sergeant of the guard to replace them right away and notify everyone to stay out of here unless you or I invite them in."

Garcia gave Padilla one final command before he succumbed to the opium, "Instruct Lieutenant Torres and the ranch foreman to find and kill those women except the one who did this. Make sure she's unharmed. I'll crucify her myself." Garcia moaned as he shifted uncomfortably.

When the colonel drifted off, Padilla dragged the two dead soldiers into the hallway and waited for their replacements. The sergeant arrived first. "These are your problem." Padilla pointed to the cadavers lying at his feet. "Take them for burial and stand by for orders. The colonel may have some instructions for you when he awakens. He's sedated now."

"That makes six men those women killed. How bad is the colonel hurt?" the trooper asked.

Padilla concealed the nature of Garcia's wound. "He's been stabbed—very serious. No one is to enter his room except me. Put guards on the door to make sure."

"Rosita told me," said the sergeant. "A couple of men will be here in a moment."

By the time the sun rose, Jada and the six others were twenty-five miles from the hacienda. The women were exhausted. They had been walking for seven hours, but Francisca insisted they continue.

"If he catches us, there is no telling how long the colonel will torture me before he kills me, and he'll save the worst for you," she told Jada. "You won't die for days."

"I know," said Jada. "I'm scared too, but the others and I haven't eaten properly for over a month and none of us slept last night. We are weak and worn out. We need to rest a while or we won't be able to keep on."

Finally, Francisca agreed. "You're right, we'll move faster after a nap, and since the colonel was kind enough to dress you like Mexican peasants, we'll be able travel on the road without attracting any attention."

As Francisca and Jada were speaking, a farmer hauling a wagonload of apricots passed by and offered the women a ride. "Want a lift? I'm headed for the festival in Ures and would welcome some company."

The other women who spoke no Spanish looked panicked until Francisca motioned them into the back of the large, rickety cart. Jada and Francisca took seats beside the apricot rancher.

"Now we can rest and ride. We'll make better time too," Jada whispered as they climbed aboard the carryall.

They chatted with the old man as the wagon rolled toward town. "Mighty hot again today." He looked up at the cloudless sky. "If you walked all the way to the festival in this heat, you'd be too tired to celebrate."

"You're so kind to give us a ride. We're already worn-out. We'll need to rest a while in Ures before the celebration," Jada replied.

"Headed for the big Corpus Christi festival, eh?" the man said as he wiped his brow with a sweat-soaked handkerchief. "I'll get you there by mid-afternoon—plenty of time to relax before the party begins."

"I hope so. We want to be fresh when we reach town," Francisca said.

Jada hesitated for a moment then asked, "I wonder if we might sample your apricots? They look delicious and we missed breakfast this morning."

"Of course, help yourselves. I have plenty. My produce is always a big seller at the festival so I bring extra."

Francisca reached back, selected a large apricot, and took a bite to show the others it would be all right. "These are delicious."

"They're the best in Mexico," replied the farmer with a smile.

After attending Garcia throughout the day, Padilla called Lieutenant Orlando Torres and Desi Gutierrez, the ranch foreman, to the hacienda office in the early evening. "Colonel Garcia is badly wounded and under heavy sedation now, but he ordered me to tell you to organize a search party to find the prisoners who escaped." Torres and Gutierrez gave Padilla disbelieving glances. The thought of finding seven Indians in such an enormous area was daunting.

Padilla decided to sweeten the pot. "You can do what you want with the women when you capture them but kill them all after you've had your fun, except the small pretty one. Return her undamaged. The colonel wants to execute her himself." He added, "If you catch the runaways, every man will receive a reward of fifty pesos. Torres, you and Gutierrez will get one hundred."

"Our garrison is small," said Torres, "and we just lost six men. Who'll protect the hacienda?"

"Good point," Padilla nodded his agreement. "Just take a half dozen men and any Indian scouts who'll go." Turning to Gutierrez, he added, "Gutierrez, you round up as many gauchos as you can spare and still keep the place running. Comb the mountains from here to the border. The women will probably go that way."

"We better get started first thing in the morning." Gutierrez stood. He was anxious to start. "It'll take a little time, the vaqueros are scattered all over the rancho." He and Torres hurried out to round up their posse.

"When we catch those women, the men will have a lot of fun before we kill them," Lieutenant Torres said as they left Padilla.

56

On the Run

TO AVOID GOING into the center of Ures, Jada asked the farmer to leave the group near the outskirts. "We have some friends in this part of town," she explained. "We'll attend the celebration with them."

An hour after the old man waved goodbye, the seven women sat concealed in a mesquite grove overlooking the village. Exhausted, they rested throughout the afternoon, and waited for the cover of darkness. Mariachi music played in the distance and the smell of spicy dishes wafting from the plaza sent hunger pangs through the women. After days of table scraps and Garcia's cow's head soup, they were famished for decent food.

As darkness set in, families doused their household lanterns; and went to join the merrymakers in the town square; leaving the neighborhood dark and vacant.

Jada studied the darkened residences for a moment. "Francisca, we need food and supplies to make it back to San Carlos. Let's pay a quick visit to those empty houses and pick up some supplies."

"That's what I was thinking. The mountains are cold so everyone needs a blanket," Francisca said. "During this season, the blankets will probably be stored in a chest or closet. Only take one each so they won't be noticed right away."

"Also pick up anything else that will help us while we're on the move—only little things the people won't miss," Jada said and held her hands apart to indicate small items that would be easy to carry. She got to her feet. "If the people find they've been robbed, word will get back to Garcia. Then his men will start looking for our tracks around this area." She motioned toward the dark street. "Let's get started."

Francisca added one last caution. "Spread out. Don't go to houses next to each other and don't be greedy. If you find any food, only take a little."

As they left Jada said, "We'll meet back here."

Most of the homes were poor and had little food to steal but each woman found a thick blanket. Jada was in a bedroom of one of the larger houses when the front door opened and someone entered. A woman said, "I'll be just minute. I need to get my scarf."

Jada had rolled up the items she intended to take in a blanket. When she heard the intruders, Jada grabbed her bundle, and squirmed under the bed. A second woman came into the room with a lantern. "A little light will help."

Jada watched as two pairs of feet scurried around the bedroom. They stood for a moment with their shoes inches from her head, giggling about a boy they had seen at the festival.

After what seemed to be a never-ending wait, the front door closed. She lay still and listened until she was certain she was alone, then crawled from her hiding place, and eased through an open window into the dark night.

When Jada returned to the mesquite grove, Tzon hugged her and said, "We thought they caught you."

"Almost," Jada explained. "Some women came into the house and nearly found me. I had to wait until they left." She shook her head and pushed a strand of hair from her face. "I couldn't get any food but I did pick up a bottle of iodine, some thread, and a package of needles."

Everyone chortled at her tale as they unloaded their spoils on one of the blankets. All the women, except Jada, brought back a few tortillas. Bittersweet found a pocket knife and three oranges. Hahles returned with several pieces of jerky and an old knapsack she found in an outbuilding. Tzon made off with a pair of binoculars she snitched from a closet, and Nahno scrounged a box of matches and a cold baked potato.

In addition to her blanket and some beef jerky, Francisca returned with a canteen she had filled from a water bucket in the house. She patted the heavy canvas-covered flask. "We'll need water until we reach the mountains."

Jose-ee smiled and handed Jada four cartridges. "Maybe you'll save me again with your fancy pistol. I think these will fit." She paused and added, "I didn't take but four because the box of bullets was almost empty."

"Thanks," replied Jada as she studied the cartridges in her palm. "They are thirty-eight caliber. Good pick, Jose-ee. They're just right."

Francisca chipped in, "When we grabbed the bullets from Garcia's cabinet, we were in a hurry to get away."

Jada continued, "In the rush, we ended up with just two thirty-eights. All the others were forty-fives for the Colts. These will work fine. I have a full cylinder now."

In the starlight, Francisca looked to assure the group was ready. "Everyone, give the small things you picked up to Hahles. She can carry them in this backpack. We better move." Francisca held the canvas haversack open to collect the stolen items.

"I know everyone is tired, but we must keep going. It'll be horrible if Garcia's men catch us," said Francisca as she helped Hahles slip on the rucksack. "We'll rest at dawn."

With the stars to guide them, the exhausted women began their off-road trudge into the blackness between Ures and the nearby Sierra Madres.

Tzon asked, "How long before we reach the mountains?"

"At this pace, maybe three days. We need to travel in the dark while we're down on this low land," Francisca said. "We can be seen from miles away while we're down here. We'll go faster when we reach the trees on higher ground."

Despite the countless hand-rolled cigarettes Desi Gutierrez chain-smoked, and a stream of profanities from Lieutenant Torres, the search for the escapees was off to a sluggish start. Torres alerted six soldiers to be ready to travel when called, but the Indian scouts had returned to their village and refused to leave for another pursuit of Apaches.

After some negotiations, Torres convinced five Tarahumare men to volunteer, but not before he gave their families two cows. Lizard was once again named as chief scout.

Gutierrez's ranch hands had been working odd jobs in scattered locations around Garcia's six thousand acre ranch. It took hours to round them up. In the evening of the third day after the women escaped, the pursuers were finally assembled. Torrez and Gutierrez decided to wait until the next morning to launch their chase. At daybreak, the searchers galloped off, headed for the mountains, over fifty miles behind the runaways. The Indian trackers raced ahead of the posse looking for seven sets of footprints.

After inching along for two nights, the runaways reached the higher elevations where trees and bushes were thick enough to allow the women to speed their pace safely during the day. Soon the seven came to a stream with a bed of moss along its banks, and the bone-weary women dropped to the soft green cushion and slept throughout the night.

The next morning Jada awoke to find Francisca shielding her eyes, looking to the northeast. She pointed to a large mountain with a flat top rising straight up from the desert floor. "I know where we are. That's Wet Rock Mesa. My band camped on top often. Water flows from the rocks around the campsite."

Jada took Tzon's binoculars and studied the huge monolith. "How do you get up there? The sides go straight up," she asked.

Francisca nodded toward the mountain. "A narrow animal trail goes all the way to the top. It takes several hours to reach the summit. You can fall off either side if you aren't careful. We'll have to climb up in a single file."

Staring at the enormous mesa through the binoculars Jada asked, "Are you sure there's a trail? It looks like its vertical on all sides."

"You'll see. She raised her hand to a forty-five degree angle pointing upward. "I've gone up there many times to escape when we were being followed, but it's very difficult to climb. Usually, the Mexicans won't even try to make it. That's our safest and fastest way home. Let's get started." Francisca hurried the group toward the gigantic mountain.

"I'm so tired. Can't we go around?" asked Bittersweet.

"Not a good idea," said Francisca. "We want to be on top if Garcia's men catch up and it's the shortest way to Fort Bowie. We'd have to walk three days to make it around the mountain. With Garcia's bunch after us, that would be suicide. Right now let's get to the top of the mesa. We still have a way to go."

57

Wet Rock Mesa

REFRESHED BY A NIGHT'S SLEEP and the cooler high-desert air, the fugitives kept a fast pace after leaving their stream-side camp. Still, it took the entire morning to reach the soaring stone monolith known as Wet Rock Mesa. Everyone was panting and damp with perspiration when they arrived at the foot of the mountain. Dog-tired, they collapsed to the ground beside a tiny spring flowing from a mound of rocks at the base of the gigantic rock formation.

Jada gasped as she leaned back to view the upper reaches of the tallest mesa she had ever seen. The vertical 1400-foot rocky walls towered above the surrounding desert. "How do we get up there?" she asked.

Francisca pointed to an obscure trail stretching along the crag's wall to the summit. "We have to be careful."

"I went to the top once when I was younger," Josee-ee added as she arched back to study the towering column. "It was dangerous and scary."

"A good thing," Francisca said. "Garcia's men might decide we aren't worth the trouble."

"What happens if we see them after we reach the summit?" asked Hahles. "Is it difficult to get down the back side?"

"There's a gentle slope, but right now let's get to the top. I'll show you when we're on the crest."

While preparing to leave, Jada spotted hoof marks in the damp ground around the spring. "Deer tracks—if we're lucky, maybe we'll have some venison."

A few feet away, Jose-ee shouted as she stared at the ground, "Over here!" The group hurried to her and gathered around an oversized paw print. Jose-ee measured the track with her hand. "Cougar—a big one. We better be careful."

"Don't worry about critters. Concern yourselves with Garcia's cutthroats," said Francisca as she refilled the canteen. "We should keep moving." The seven weary women began the arduous climb up the precipitous trail.

The footpath to the mountaintop was an animal path running along a thread-thin ridge that zigzagged up the mesa. As she scaled the dangerous trace, Jada thought, Jose-ee was wrong. This isn't scary. It's terrifying.

One misstep after the first hour would send a climber into a free fall of several hundred feet. After three hours of sweat-soaked legwork, the group reached a rocky shelf about two hundred feet from the top and a thousand feet above the canyon floor. The ledge extended for ten yards on both sides of the trail.

The women crawled onto the stone mantle and studied the breathtaking view. Jada stared into the distance. "We'll spot anybody following us miles before they get here."

"That's what we want—gives us time to escape," Francisca said.

After climbing for another hour, the women arrived at two gigantic boulders teetering on the rim of the shear drop. The massive stones created a narrow tunnel leading to the flat mountaintop. One at a time, they stooped and squeezed through a body-hugging passage.

When Jada reached the level ground at the crest, she looked over the terrain. Piles of stones had been stacked to form a low wall for ten yards on both sides of the entrance.

Francisca saw Jada studying the rock bulwark and told her, "The old people built this long ago for protection, I think."

She shrugged her shoulders indicating she didn't really know. "It was before my time." Jada decided the barrier might add an additional shield from marksmen below.

Near the center of the summit, a grove of windblown ponderosa pines grew next to a wellspring that gurgled from beneath a massive stone pile and formed a small pool. Countless animal tracks covered the soil beside the pond. Seventy-five feet from the trees, another large mound of massive boulders formed a deep cave-like recess.

Nahno lagged behind for a drink of the clear water as Francisca led the group across the open flat toward the sloping route down the rear of the butte. Without warning, a bloodcurdling scream came from behind them. They spun around in time to see an enormous mountain lion pounce from the rocks surrounding the little pond and land on Nahno's back, pinning her face-down. The other women drew their revolvers, but couldn't shoot without hitting Nahno.

The cougar's powerful claws plunged deep into Nahno's arm as he sank his teeth into her opposite shoulder. In a brutal frenzy to control its prey, the cat's rear paw shredded Nahno's buttock and the back of her thigh. The would-be rescuers dashed for the screaming woman seeking a clear shot at the panther.

Francisca shouted as they ran, "Don't hit Nahno."

As they raced to help Nahno, another hair-raising shriek pierced the air behind them. Before anyone could fire their pistol, Bittersweet plunged through the clutch of women, wide-eyed and screeching at the top of her voice. Holding the bayonet she took from the dead Mexican soldier above her head with both hands, she leaped high and straddled the lion as if mounting a horse. She plunged the long blade into the lion's back, piercing his heart. The beast roared once, released Nahno, and turned to give Bittersweet his final swat. Two shots rang out as the cat's claws sliced four gashes across Bittersweet's shoulder and upper body. The beast gave out a roar and collapsed between Nahno and Bittersweet.

"That's the bravest thing I've ever seen," Jada exclaimed.

"Yeah," agreed Francisca, trembling as she holstered her gun.

The women gathered beside the dead mountain lion and their two injured friends. Jada examined Bittersweet's wounds; four deep slices running from the fleshy part of her shoulder to her chest.

"Jose-ee, can you stitch up Bittersweet?" Jada asked.

"For sure," Jose-ee replied. "I usually use sinew to sew cuts, but the thread you took will work."

"Clean the damage and swab the gashes with this." Jada handed Jose-ee the dark brown bottle of iodine.

"Okay, but I'm also making some prickly pear medicine to put over them."

Jada pulled Nahno's blouse from her upper body and lifted her skirt to check her other wounds. The lion's bite left several punctures on one shoulder. Claw-cuts spread across her opposite arm, and the cat had ripped ragged gashes from the center of her buttock to the back of her knee.

"Francisca, bring the canteen over here. Let's clean these two up," said Jada.

Jada pointed at the cactus Jose-ee was carving. "Jose-ee, we don't have enough iodine for all this. Make some of your medicine for Nahno's cuts too." Jada threaded a needle as she prepared to sew Nahno's wounds.

Jose-ee continued to dig the pulp from the cactus but tucked her head and smiled with satisfaction at Jada's confidence in her.

"Let's put both of them in the cave. With the rains this time of the year, it'll be a dry place to stay," Francisca indicated the opening. "We can also build a little fire in there for warmth. If we keep it small, the smoke won't be visible from below."

After several hours, the two wounded women rested on beds of buffalo grass inside the rock chamber. The others gathered outside the cave's opening and quietly talked. "Nahno's going to need a couple of weeks before she can walk," Jada said as she glanced back at wounded women.

Francisca shot a panicked look at Jada. "We can't stay here for an extra day, much less two weeks. Garcia's men will find us for certain. We have to leave those two and save ourselves."

"Do what you want, Francisca." Jada replied. "I'm staying with them. Bittersweet might be able to go now, but she should rest for at least a few days before she tries."

"I'm not waiting around for Garcia's people. I saw him torture a slave to death once just for running away. This is much worse. I can't imagine what he'll do if he catches us. I'm leaving and all of you should go too."

"I believe I could make it," Bittersweet said, "but I'd slow you down. I'll wait with Nahno."

"I'll stay also," Jose-ee told Jada. "You don't know how to make Apache medicine and we're almost out of your magical cure."

Hahles looked at the injured women. "Nahno's our best friend. Tzon and I will stay until we all can leave together."

Francisca shook her head. "Well, I'm not taking any chances. If you change your minds, go that way." She pointed to the northeast. "You'll find a river. Just follow the stream north."

The next morning when the women awoke, Francisca was gone.

58

Old Loves Join Search

TWELVE MILES NORTH OF TOMBSTONE, Colonel Obadiah Cantrell's unit of fifteen scouts from Fort Apache linked up with Lieutenant Roger Bullard and ten cavalrymen from Fort Bowie. Both squads had been dispatched in "hot pursuit" of Dr. Jada Morgan and an unknown number of Apache women.

As they met, Bullard practically shouted, "I can't believe it! Major Cantrell, you're alive and well." He saluted and reached over from his horse to shake the colonel's hand. "Looks like it's Colonel Cantrell now."

"Yeah, I got a brevet promotion after the Cibecue incident."

"I heard the Indians killed you there."

"They tried," Cantrell said.

Bullard shook his head. "The rumors had it you had several holes in you the last time anyone saw you."

"Five to be exact. The one in my leg still gives me trouble when I ride." Cantrell frowned and rubbed his thigh. "Speaking of riding, we better get moving. We're supposed to meet J.P. Morgan's man from New York at a place called the Bird Cage Theater and Saloon in Tombstone today."

"Mighty peculiar to have a bunch of soldiers and Indians ordered to a jug-joint," Bullard said. "If we have to wait for long, these men won't be able to find their horses, much less Doctor Morgan."

Cantrell pondered Bullard's comment for a moment, still rubbing his leg. "I think Sherman believed it would be easy to locate and it's open around the clock. Otherwise, our big city partner might not know how to find us." He looked perturbed as he told Bullard about the Bird Cage. "The damned place has only been in business for a little more than a year and already has a reputation. The New York Times says it's the roughest and bawdiest establishment between Basin Street and the Barbary Coast. We'll bivouac outside of town and order the men to stay in camp."

The two fell quiet as their horses trotted toward Tombstone. Bullard spoke first. "I understand you know Doctor Morgan, the lady we're looking for."

"I do," Cantrell confirmed. "She was my doctor at San Carlos when I was wounded."

"You mean after Cibecue?"

"It was before then. I got nicked in the head at the Maple Peak shootout. I'm told she did some remarkable brain surgery and saved my life." He rubbed his scalp covering the silver plate Jada had implanted. "During my stay in the hospital, she told me we were close friends two years before Cibecue, but I don't remember. She seemed to think we had a romance going when I commanded Fort McRae and she was the doctor at Canada Alamosa." He shook his head. "I had amnesia after the brain operation and totally forgot her—or anything we did together." He stared in silence for a moment, trying to recall his relationship with Jada. "All I remember is she took good care of me once I woke up and she's the prettiest doctor I ever had." He broke into a little smile. "I'm told you were acquainted with Doctor Morgan also."

"Right, in Philadelphia. We were pretty serious for a while but I chose the army instead of a Chiricahua wife. So here I am. Maybe not the best decision I've ever made."

"I imagine I might have had the same problem, if she was telling the truth. I don't know where it stands with her now. Just doctor and former patient, I guess." Cantrell grinned and added, "I got 'killed' at Cibecue and then Geronimo's bunch kidnapped her before I was resurrected. I 'spose she thinks I'm dead. She's probably with an Apache buck by now."

"I understand J.P. Morgan's man from New York also knows her. Wonder what his story is." Bullard was worried and inquisitive.

"Don't know anything about him, but I understand they were acquainted."

The two rode side-by-side without speaking for a while, each with different thoughts of Dr. Jada P. Morgan. Roger's mind went to romance. Probably not a good idea to mention that I'm planning to resign if she'll take me back, he thought.

Obadiah continued his effort to remember Jada as more than his physician, but couldn't. Maybe seeing her again will help pull things together. Hell, at this point I would hardly recognize her. Anyhow, I'm not much interested in leaving the army for an Indian gal, even if she is beautiful.

Cantrell and Bullard ordered their men to camp a mile outside of Tombstone while they went in search of the Bird Cage Theatre and Saloon. Once in town they buttonholed a scraggly cowhand leaning against a hitching post.

"Hey mister, we're looking for a thirst parlor and gambling house," Bullard said to the disheveled stranger who was lighting up a hand-rolled cigarette.

"Well, I 'spect ya'll are in the right place." He blew out a stream of smoke. "There are a hundred and ten saloons in town, fourteen gambling places, and more whorehouses than you can shake your pecker at." The wrangler pointed his cigarette toward the business district. "I reckon two experienced troopers like yourselves could scout out a place if you set yer minds to it. Jest go down Freemont, Allen, or

Tough Nut streets. You'll find rows of 'em." The cowpoke took a long drag and blew another plume.

"We need to find a particular one—have to meet somebody at the Bird Cage Saloon," Bullard explained.

"That's an easy one," the cowboy replied. "The Bird Cage is a threefer; drinks, whores, and gambling, all in one place. There's some real salty stage shows too, if raunchy dancing is your druthers."

Bullard repeated, "We're just meeting someone," the cowhand shrugged and gave directions to the Cage. "It's the only jug-joint on Allen Street with three arched doors." He mounted his pony and added with a grin, "Have fun."

When the two officers walked into the Birdcage, it was apparent the place was everything the cowpuncher implied. Several tarts took the soldiers by their arms and propositioned them as soon as they stepped through the swinging doors. The soldiers gave the strumpets a courteous rebuff and found a table facing the front.

The first floor of the Bird Cage was a large hall filled with a bar, roulette wheels, faro stands, and card tables. A stage for dancing extravaganzas, songbird concerts, and slapstick routines dominated the far end of the honky-tonk. An upright rosewood piano in front of the stage provided a tinny ambience for the surrounding bedlam.

On the second story, fourteen theater boxes, seven on each side, called bird cages, overlooked the raucous activities below. The cages featured upholstered easy chairs and fold away Murphy beds for personal entertainment at the cost of twenty-five dollars per hour. Thick red velvet curtains could be drawn for seclusion. Small intimate rooms in the basement served more discerning customers at a pricey forty bucks an hour.

"See anyone who strikes you as a New Yorker?" asked Cantrell.

"Lotta folks here but none of them seem flashy enough to be from the big city. Any idea what this guy looks like?" inquired Bullard.

"Not a clue. If he's hunting for a couple of army officers, we'll be easy to spot."

Bullard and Cantrell ordered beers and waited. Two warm brews later, a citizen pushed open the swinging doors and shouted, "Stagecoach from Benson just arrived."

As the officers drained their last mugs, an outsized man with broad shoulders and a massive chest walked into the bar obviously looking for someone.

"That's bound to be our greenhorn." Cantrell nodded toward the newcomer. "He's big enough but that outfit is a prizewinner. That boy's gonna complicate things."

The dapper New Yorker appeared to be a cosmopolitan pantywaist. He was dressed in an exquisitely tailored beige three-piece sac suit of the latest cut, and a starched white shirt with mother-of-pearl buttons and a stand-up collar. A paisley ascot highlighted the ensemble. Matching russet spats protected low cut dress shoes, and a tan bowler topped off the natty giant's sartorial splendor. A carpetbag decorated with a floral design complimented the outfit.

The immense clotheshorse stepped into the saloon, and wagged his hand in front of his face in a failed effort to clear the clouds of smoke assailing his skewed nose.

Every head in the room turned to watch the newly-arrived popinjay. A few chuckled. Others lowered their heads and whispered sarcastic comments. The dandy soon spotted Cantrell and Bullard and gave a quick wave. He started toward them when a drunken barfly staggered in front of him, blocking his way.

"My name is Billy Mince. They call me Mincemeat 'cause I can beat any man in here to mincemeat. Fact is mister; I don't like your looks."

"Sorry you have a problem, Mr. Mince." The dandy kept his eyes on the army officers and ignored the sot.

"I reckon you irritate my gizzard, and I'm fixin' it right now." Billy took a wild roundhouse swing at the new arrival.

The fancy dude dropped his carpet bag and leaned back without so much as blinking. The punch swished by the goliath's face causing Billy to wobble off balance. Chuckles rippled around the room. Mincemeat regained his equilibrium, cursed, and launched a furious blizzard of punches. The stranger blocked every one with ease, then threw a straight right to Billy's jaw. The clout sent him tumbling through the swinging cafe doors and splayed unconscious on the boardwalk outside.

Obadiah and Roger's jaws dropped in unison. Cantrell said in admiration, "There's more to that fellow than meets the eye."

The new arrival straightened his fashionable jacket, reset his expensive derby, picked up his carpetbag, and walked over to the two officers with his hand outstretched. "I'm Harry Trenchcott. I assume you're the men leading the search for Jada Morgan. Mr. Morgan, Jada's uncle, sent me to help, if I won't be in the way."

"Sit down, Mr. Trenchcott. Let's talk about saving Jada," the colonel said.

59

Injuries Halt Escape

COLONEL CANTRELL GREETED HARRY with a handshake. "Welcome to Arizona, Mr. Trenchcott. Seems you received a proper reception."

"I suppose so, but isn't this an odd place for a meeting." Harry cast a glance around the large room. "Appears to be full of gamesters, painted professionals, and problem drinkers."

"The Bird Cage is open day and night, and it's near the border," Cantrell said. "Good choice for that."

"Trenchcott," Bullard snapped his fingers trying to remember how he knew the name. "I've heard of you somewhere. Did you ever spend any time in Washington or Philadelphia?"

"I've been in DC a few times, but I'm a Philadelphia boy," replied Harry.

"I was stationed in Washington but I went to Philly often to court Jada. Did we meet there?" inquired Roger.

"That's after my time. Jada and I were an item in college for a while. I graduated and asked her to marry me but she wouldn't quit medicine to be a lawyer's wife." Harry was quiet for a moment recalling Jada's rejection. "So she declined and after I went to New York to work for Mr. Morgan, I proposed to someone else. I haven't seen Jada since, but we were very close for a while."

"I remember now." Roger slapped his knee. "Your name was in Harper's Weekly. You're the famous pugilist, Terrible Trenchcott, who quit the ring to attend law school!"

"Got me." Trenchcott smiled. "Call me Harry."

"No wonder you put Mince out like you did."

"Yeah." Harry gave a dismissive wave of his hand but when he spoke, he looked beneath the saloon's cafe doors. Pedestrians on the boardwalk were stepping around and over Billy Mince's unmoving carcass.

"Wait a minute; let me do a little business." Harry surveyed the selection of soiled doves populating the Bird Cage's game room and motioned to the largest mattress thrasher at the bar.

She responded immediately to the fancy fop. From the way that stud's dressed, he's holding a wad of cash.

"My name's Kate." Her voice was loud and brassy. "What can I do for you boys?" She was full-sized; almost as tall as Harry with muscles a weight lifter would envy.

"I want to rent a cage." Harry pointed to one of the upstairs theatre boxes. Obadiah and Rodger exchanged embarrassed glances.

"Anything you want, honey," Kate winked salaciously. "Never done three at once before. That'll cost you extra."

"I don't mean that." Harry plunked down three one-hundred dollar gold coins on the table. Kate's hand involuntarily covered her mouth. "I want to rent one of the cages upstairs for a day or two and engage your services full time." Obadiah and Roger appeared more worried than ever.

Kate's eyes narrowed with suspicion. "Okay, so what might I be doing for all that gold?"

"You take two hundred for yourself to cover the cage rental and your usual charge, plus a tip. Then you haul the man lying outside up to one of the beds and stay with him until he's up and about. I assume you can hire some cheap help to get him up there."

"I'll handle it myself." The brawny woman flexed her arm. "What's the other hundred for?"

"Find a doctor to check him over. I think I hurt him. You can keep what the doc doesn't charge and if Mince leaves early, keep that too."

"You got a deal mister." Kate smiled at her good luck. "Doctor Ridley Radborne has an office across the street. He's a regular at the Bird Cage." Kate gleefully swept the coins off the table into her other hand. Ridley works for peanuts, she thought. He'll probably treat Billy for drinks. Hell, that idiot is just knocked out. He'll most likely wake up in a little while. I'll make a bundle. Obadiah said nothing but frowned as he remembered firing Radborne for drunkenness at Fort Craig.

The three men watched Kate walk to the unconscious man, throw him over her shoulder, and head for the upstairs accommodations to the cheers and applause of the saloon's customers.

Obadiah reopened the conversation. "Okay Harry, let's get back to the task at hand. Tell us why you're here? Exactly how are you planning to help with the search for Jada?"

"Mr. Morgan instructed me to do anything possible to find and free her."

"You planning to go it on your own? Join our crew? Or what?"

"He gave me money to hire some mercenaries if you need men, or I can pay for any supplies you want. He'll wire additional funds to the Pima County Agency Bank here in Tombstone if necessary. No matter what you decide, I've been instructed to go along with you."

"We don't need any more men. We aren't going there to fight a war," said Obadiah. "Apparently Jada and her friends escaped sometime ago. If she's been recaptured, I hope we can negotiate her release. Bribe money would help with that. If she hasn't been caught, we'll try to find her and escort her back." He tapped a silver dollar on the table as he considered Harry's offer. "We could use a little more grub and a couple of mules to haul it. Do you have enough money to handle all that?"

"Mr. Morgan gave me five thousand cash to bribe the Mexicans if she's still their prisoner, and for anything else we need."

Roger and Obadiah blinked at each other. "How do you get hold of all that money?" asked Cantrell.

Harry patted his carpetbag. "It's right here in my bag."

"Are you crazy?" blurted Bullard. His eyes scanned the room for sleazy characters. It was full of them. "A stickup man would kill you in a heartbeat for much less than that."

"Folks don't tend to bother me and the money is in a hidden compartment. I'm also carrying a two shot derringer just in case."

"Okay Harry, if you agree, Lieutenant Bullard will purchase a horse and saddle for you from the blacksmith, and buy two mules to haul supplies. You do ride, I hope?" Harry nodded.

"I'll pull the vittles together and in the meantime, go buy some comfortable clothes." Then giving Harry the once-over, Obadiah added, "Don't try for style. Canvas is best. Get things for both hot and cold weather, and for Pete's sake, get a real gun."

After leaving Tombstone, Cantrell, Bullard, and Trenchcott rode hard, galloping southward with twenty-five scouts and soldiers in search of Jada Morgan.

South of the seven women, Lieutenant Torres and Desi Gutierrez with fifty-two soldiers, vaqueros, and Tarahumare scouts pounded leather northward, determined to return Jada to the hacienda for Garcia's pleasure and their reward.

Walking north toward the border between the Mexicans and the Americans, Francisca was feeling free for the first time in sixteen years. She had no remorse about leaving the other women.

She told herself, It would be stupid to stay with those wounded girls and get killed.

Meanwhile on Wet Rock Mesa, Jada stood behind the stone rampart at the edge of the chasm searching the landscape below for any sign of pursuit. Since they found themselves stranded on the mountain, the women had taken turns standing watch from dawn to dusk. While she studied the scene below, Jada was distracted by an ear-shattering thunderclap. She looked to the west where gigantic black clouds hurled webs of deadly lightening flashes through the sky.

Another storm. They're coming every day now. Francisca said we're in the season for downpours. This looks like a bad one.

She turned to run to their rocky cave but from the corner of her eye she spotted a glint at the bottom of the abyss. She stopped abruptly, lifted her binoculars, and focused on the figure below. Through her spyglass she saw a Tarahumare Indian looking at her with his telescope. Shivers shot up her spine. Oh god! They've found us.

The storm rolled over the mountain bringing a drenching rain. The torrential downpour came in sheets and inundated the already saturated ground. Lightening flashed and thunder erupted in a maelstrom of electricity and noise. Jada removed her moccasins and dashed barefoot for the cave. She found everyone inside except Tzon and exclaimed with urgency, "I have some bad news..." As she shouted, the deluge of blowing rain turned into bullet-sized hail. The women turned in unison and saw Tzon run into the woods for protection from the hailstones.

As Tzon huddled under the trees, a shaft of lightening exploded down a tree trunk, hissed through the air, and stabbed into her body. The strike lifted her off the ground, left a deep palm-sized burn on her side, and charred the bottoms of her feet where it exited. Jada and the others dashed into the storm to help Tzon. Wisps of smoke curled from the burns on her ribs and feet.

"She's dead." Tears rolled down Hahles' cheeks.

"No, she's unconscious," said Jose-ee as she studied the deep charcoal-like wounds.

"We better get her out of this rain before it starts to hail again," said Jada.

The group gently carried the injured woman to the rocky shelter. Bittersweet limped behind holding her shoulder. Jada breathed a sigh of relief. "Tzon'll live but she might not be right in the head for a while. Jose-ee, does your cactus salve work on burns?"

"I believe it'll help, but I'm not sure—never used it on burns before."

When things calmed down in the cave, Hahles asked, "Jada, you mentioned bad news?"

Jada's mind returned to the Tarahumare scout with the telescope. "Right—the bad news. I spotted one of Garcia's scouts looking up here with a spy glass. I think they're on to us."

The women began to chatter nervously among themselves. Jada leaned against the rock wall and spoke quietly. "I'm staying to take care of Nahno and Tzon." She pointed to their injured friends. "But all of you should go."

Jose-ee declined straightaway. "You don't know how to mix up the cactus salve. I need to be here."

Bittersweet gently rubbed her wounded shoulder. "I'm still weak. I'd be too slow to outrun them. I'll wait until we can all go."

Hahles sat by Tzon holding her hand. "I'll stay too. She's my best friend."

60

The Battle Plan

"SINCE WE'RE STUCK HERE, we need a plan," Jose-ee said.

Hahles tossed a pebble over the cliff and asked, "Like what?"

"They'll have to come through the opening between those boulders one at a time. Each of us has a gun and Jada has two if you count her derringer. We can take turns shooting them when they step out."

Hahles did the numbers. "We have six pistols, but not enough bullets for all of them,"

"Don't forget the two bows," Bittersweet added, "with five arrows for each."

"That should be plenty." Jada noticed Bittersweet holding her bayonet seemingly hoping for a better weapon. "In the meantime, give Tzon's gun to Bittersweet. Tzon's too confused and Bittersweet can shoot with her good hand."

"What now?" asked Jose-ee. Everyone turned to Jada.

"We wait. I believe we're as ready as possible."

Later, taking her turn on watch for the Mexicans' arrival, Jada sat on the rock wall along the edge of the precipice. She re-counted the group's bullets. As they hurried to escape the hacienda, she and Francisca had failed to scoop up sufficient cartridges from Garcia's stock to fill all the pistols. With the addition of the rounds Jose-ee stole in Ures, Jada had a full cylinder of six .38 caliber bullets, and four little ones for her muff pistol. There were only three of the larger shells for each of the four .45 caliber revolvers. Twenty-two shots and ten arrows in all. Perhaps Garcia won't send so many men, but...

Without thinking, Jada kicked a fist-sized rock over the edge. A few seconds later, the stone clattered on the shelf 200 feet below. That's it! Those stones were put there to throw over, she thought. She ran back to the cave to tell the others of her new idea.

"I've come up with something else we can do." The group gathered around the recumbent Nahno and listened to Jada's plan.

"They're likely to retreat to those ledges when we start shooting. We'll drop stones from the wall down on them." Everyone agreed it just might work.

Positioning the women around the opening, Jada pointed to a large square stone the size of a travel trunk situated five steps in front of the entryway. "One of us can hide behind that rock and shoot from there. We'll have clear shots from every direction when they step through the opening."

Hahles stood beside Jada and pointed to the two large boulders forming the entrance to the mountaintop. "Maybe we could push those big rocks over the edge. They would roll down and kill a lot of Mexicans on the trail."

"Good idea, Hahles, but they're too heavy for us to move, even if we all pushed." Jose-ee leaned against one of the boulders and shoved with her back to demonstrate.

Jada considered Hahles' suggestion for a moment. "You know, Hahles, I think a couple of levers might do the trick."

"The big pine that fell when the lightening hit Tzon knocked over some smaller hardwoods." Hahles bubbled with enthusiasm as the group warmed to her suggestion. "We can hack off the branches with Bittersweet's knife and have poles that might work." Hahles picked up the saber-like bayonet and hurried to the trees with Jose-ee. Within a few minutes they returned dragging two long saplings stripped of limbs.

The women wedged the shafts under the entrance boulders and laid them across the box-like stone in front of the entranceway for a fulcrum. After their trap was set, they walked over to the edge to see if the Mexicans had arrived. All was quiet below, giving Jada a chance to check on Nahno and Tzon. Meanwhile, Jose-ee, Hahles, and Bittersweet sat with their backs against the wall talking and checking for any movement below.

With their Apache scouts far in advance, the Americans moved south in search of Jada's location. The rescue party stopped suddenly when Obadiah raised an arm to halt the column, and stood in his stirrups. "Looks like a couple of our scouts are headed back fast."

Obadiah caught sight of a woman riding behind one of the men as they approached. As they reached Obadiah, Jolly, the scout, skidded his horse to a stop in a swirl of dust and called to the colonel, "This is Francisca. She was captured by Garcia a long time ago. She escaped with the other women. Says she knows where they are."

Obadiah, who knew a little Spanish because of his work in Canada Alamosa, asked the woman if she spoke English or Spanish. "Habla Inglès o Español, Francisca?"

She sat a little taller behind Jolly. "No English, but I speak Spanish. They made me talk like them when I was a slave."

"Were you with a woman named Jada Morgan?"

"We call her Dah-zhonne. Yes, she and I escaped from Colonel Garcia's hacienda with five others. They're hiding on Wet Rock Mesa."

"Why didn't they come with you?

"Two were hurt by a wild cat. Dah-zhonne and Jose-ee, a medicine woman, stayed behind to care for them. I think the others decided to remain too."

"Can you take us to them?" asked Obadiah.

Francisca fell silent and bit her lip. "I can't go back. Garcia will torture me to death."

Obadiah understood her concern. "You'll be safe as long as you are with us. Fifteen Apache scouts are out searching for the others now. We'll protect you and your friends if we get to them in time."

Francisca cast a doubtful glance at the ten troopers, but then agreed. "All right, I'll show you. We need to hurry. The Mexicans are searching for them too."

Obadiah gave instructions. "Foghorn, give Jolly's horse a rest—let Francisca ride with you. Jolly, round up the scouts and meet us on this side of Wet Rock."

Foghorn acquired his nickname because he once found an old Spanish bugle left on a long forgotten battlefield and honked it in tuneless blasts whenever he was excited. Francisca mounted behind Foghorn while Jolly raced off to recall the outriders. The rescue party cantered toward Jada with Foghorn and Francisca in the lead.

Back on the mountain, Nahno was still lying prone in pain, waiting for Jose-ee to mix cactus medicine for her and the other injured women. Kneeling beside Tzon, Jada rubbed her arms and legs in an effort to restore her dexterity. Across the flat, Bittersweet and Hahles sat at the edge of the abyss with their backs against the rock wall watching for any pursuers. Hahles spotted the movement first. She gave an excited shout. "They're here!"

As they watched, single wisp of smoke came from below, followed by a bullet ricocheting off the stones beside Hahles. The two women leaped behind the long rock parapet.

After calling Jada and Jose-ee, they gathered and peeked over the stone rampart. Jada silently counted the climbers. "Looks to be over fifty of them."

"It's almost twenty more men than we have bullets and arrows," Bittersweet said.

"Well, if we shoot the first few," Jada said, "the others might leave."

61

Mexican Attack

THE WOMEN TOOK COVER in strategic places on the mountaintop as the first of the Mexican posse struggled past the ledges two-hundred feet below. Hahles crouched behind the trunk-sized rock, holding a bow and five arrows with her pistol jammed in her waistband. Jada stationed herself behind one of the boulders framing the entrance with her .38 in one hand and the heavy war club in the other. Jose-ee stood across the passageway from Jada, her revolver at the ready and a bow dangling from her shoulder. Bittersweet sat concealed in the grove of trees, holding her .45 with both hands on bent knees and pointing it at the entryway. In the cave, Nahno lay on her stomach aiming her six-shooter at her expected target. Jose-ee had pulled a flat rock in front of Nahno for a gun rest. Behind her, Tzon stared vacuously into space.

As the six women waited with their nerves tingling, Jose-ee peeked around the large entrance boulders with the binoculars. "The ugliest Indian I've ever seen is leading the pack. There're a few soldiers behind him, and then a long line of ranch hands."

She handed the glass to Jada who stared through it for several minutes. She was outraged when she lowered the field glasses. "That devil!" She spit the words out.

Jose-ee asked, "What's the matter?"

"That scaly Tarahumare rat scalped my father. They call him Lizard. This doesn't change our plans. I'll finish him first." Her cheeks flushed with anger. "That monster is mine."

Jada then turned and shouted, "They're almost here, but they're moving slow. All the rain has left the trail slick and muddy."

"They look scared too" added Jose-ee. "Some are crawling on their hands and knees."

Lieutenant Orlando Torres and Desi Gutierrez stood at the bottom of the mesa craning their necks as they watched their men climb the narrow, slippery path.

"Damn Torres, the climb is too dangerous. Maybe we should go around to the back side of the mountain."

"That would take a week and by then those Apaches would vanish in the high mountains." Torres shook his head. "We've got them now. Be patient. This is the hard part. Taking them will be a breeze."

"Colonel Garcia warned Doctor Padilla they probably escaped with some guns." Gutierrez's voice was filled with concern. "The colonel had a pile of weapons he captured at Alisos Creek, but he isn't sure if any were taken. Padilla told me Garcia's pistol is missing."

"A man or two might catch a slug, but we'll simply force our way onto the top." Torres pointed to the crest. "Even if they have guns, they can't have much ammo." He was flushed with excitement. "Most of the weapons we captured at Alisos were empty. They're out of luck if that's what they have."

"Lieutenant, your soldiers might charge in the face of fire, but my vaqueros are in this for the money and Lord only knows what those damned Indians are up to." Desi continued to stare up at the thin procession of climbers.

"That's why I put the soldiers at the front," said Torres. "And our best scout, Lizard, is leading the way. The other scouts are at the rear to shore up your fellows. Don't worry. My troops will finish the job. Guierrez was silent but continued to stare as the snake-like line inched up the mountain.

"Get ready girls," shouted Jada. "Take turns. Only one shot for each Mexican and don't shoot until they are close. Remember, the first one is mine. If you can, use the bows to save bullets.

The women held their positions while Jada leaned against the large boulder and waited for the man who scalped her father.

62

Final Fight

LIZARD, THE SCOUT LEADING the assault, reached the entrance and signaled the climbers behind him to stop. He scrutinized the summit for the slightest irregularity that would indicate where his prey might be hiding. He saw no movement, no sounds; nothing to show the women were on the mountain, but he knew his quarry was there. He squeezed through the entranceway, his Winchester at the ready.

Her back pressed against the massive stone at the opening, Jada slid her pistol into her waistband and waited as Lizard's rifle barrel eased out from the narrow entrance. An instant later the scout's hideous face emerged. The image of this man scalping her dead father years earlier exploded through her mind.

With the truncheon she had carried from Hermosillo in one hand, she grabbed the rifle barrel with the other. Screaming, "Die, bastard," she jerked Lizard forward as she swung the club with a force driven by long-suppressed grief and rage. The blow from the club's three-pound leather-covered stone slammed into Lizard's face leaving a concaved bloody ruin. The deathblow knocked the scout back into the soldier behind him. The man tried to stop the Indian's momentum before Lizard tumbled over the drop-off, but failed. The trooper was struggling to regain his own balance when Hahles rose from her concealed position, bow drawn, and sent an arrow slicing into the man's chest. The impact sent him tumbling over the edge after Lizard.

As soon as Hahles launched her arrow, Jose-ee spun from behind the boulder across from Jada, raised her pistol, and fired two quick shots, killing the second and third troopers. Both were dead before they tumbled into the gorge. The next two soldiers turned terror-stricken, waved their arms in panic, and shouted to the line of vaqueros and scouts behind. "A trap. Go back, go back." The Mexicans abandoned all caution, and scrambled helter-skelter down the incline.

Jada, raised Lizard's rifle and using skills she learned on the Philadelphia target range with Roger Bullard, squeezed off two rounds into the two remaining soldiers. One teetered for a moment in an attempt to avoid the lethal fall but soon plunged into the abyss. Jada's second bullet slammed into the last surviving soldier. He grabbed the vaquero behind him and pulled the cowboy over the side with him. The next fourteen panic-stricken climbers scrambled to the ledges, out of the women's line of fire. They pressed against the rear wall of the ledge, out of the shooters' sights, but became unsuspecting targets for a rain of stones soon to drop from above. In their haste to retreat down the path, a dozen other pursuers stumbled, slipped, and plunged from the muddy trace screaming as they fell. The chaos quieted as the last nineteen men in the queue rejoined Torres and Gutierrez at the base of the mesa.

After the women were certain none of the Mexicans were still climbing the ramp, they lined up along the stone wall. "Now start throwing these rocks down on them," instructed Jada.

"You don't have to lift them, just roll them over the edge. That ought to kill a few down there," Jada said, "or at least it'll keep them too busy dodging to charge up here again."

Below, Lieutenant Torres cursed as he analyzed his situation. More than half his force was dead or trapped on the ledges, twelve hundred feet above. All of his professional soldiers and his best scout, Lizard, were done for. The remaining vaqueros and Indians were divided; fourteen on the outcrops high above and nineteen on firm ground at the base.

"Desi, I underestimated those damned women. We need to keep up a sustained fire on them so they'll keep their heads down."

As Torres explained his plan to Gutierrez, they noticed the surviving four Tarahumare scouts huddled a short distance away. Without a word to the lieutenant, they mounted their horses and rode off ignoring the officer's profane shouts to stop.

The gauchos at the bottom also began to whisper among themselves. After a few minutes, Carlos, one of the ranch hands, speaking for the others came over to Torres and Gutierrez. "Most of us want to go back to the hacienda. We aren't climbing up there again." He pointed toward the mountaintop.

The lieutenant was furious and chastised the group as cowards "Are you going to leave your friends trapped up there? They need help."

"We feel bad for them," said Carlos, "But we aren't soldiers and our deaths won't do anything for them."

Twelve of the cowboys refused to make the climb again, but seven reluctantly agreed to try once more. Lieutenant Torres glared at the obstinate ranch hands, furious at the hold outs.

"Okay, I'll lead these brave heroes," he said finally, nodding to the volunteers. "The rest of you chicken-shits stay here and shoot into that barricade on top. You probably won't hit anything, but it'll keep their heads down and stop that rock-dropping business." Torres waved his arm and the group of willing cowhands followed him as he began to climb.

At the top, a stream of bullets whistled overhead and chipped at the rock wall.

"Keep low and move back," shouted Jada. The women crawled away from the edge about ten feet and crowded behind the large stone which had concealed Hahles. Jada realized what the Mexicans were doing. "Girls, it's time to pry those big rocks at the entrance over the side."

Jada and Bittersweet crawled to one of the poles. Jose-ee and Hahles took the other. "Now everybody push down together," yelled Jada. The giant stones didn't budge.

"It's not working!" shrieked Bittersweet.

"Okay, put all your weight on them," shouted Jose-ee over the gunfire. One woman of each pair sat on the end of their respective levers while their partner lay across the pole. Nothing happened at first so they began bouncing as bullets whined above their heads. The long green saplings bent to the verge of snapping.

Finally the boulders moved an inch, then with little more effort, and the two huge stones went over the edge. Instead of rolling down the trace as planned, both stones cascaded straight down, one on each side of the trail. Seconds later, deafening dual crashes reverberated over the mountain. The women looked around in surprise when the ground under them began a violent tremor and a wide crack opened along the length of the wall.

Jada screamed, "Run, run!—get back. The mountain is breaking off."

An ear-shattering roar followed. The ground began to shake in front of the crack and slipped downward several feet at first but gained momentum until it expanded into an immense clamorous avalanche.

When the rumble stopped, the wide-eyed women inched their way to the new cliff face and peered over. The landslide had obliterated the assault ramp and buried Lieutenant Torres and his 'heroes' on the trail under tons of sludge and stones.

Higher up, the ledges holding the other attackers were broken off by the impact of the giant boulders, leaving the occupants interred under the massive pile of muddy debris. Five of the seven men standing with Desi Gutierrez at the foot of the mountain were also entombed by the mudslide. Through the binoculars, Bittersweet spotted two lone survivors walking in the direction of Garcia's hacienda. They left their horses buried under the mud.

Jose-ee looked over the devastation and observed, "I guess they're all dead. No one's moving down there. They can't get to us anyhow. It's a sheer drop to the bottom."

Hahles said, "It was the rain. The ground was soaked and when those big rocks hit the ledge, everything broke away."

Jada sat on a large stone, wiped perspiration from her forehead, and smiled, satisfied the crisis was over. Her heart pounded in satisfaction over the death of the man who scalped her father.

The women congratulated themselves and breathed sighs of relief while Bitter-sweet scanned the surrounding area with the binoculars. All of a sudden, she pointed northward, and shouted, "More riders are coming at a gallop!"

The group dashed to the north side of the mountaintop with their guns and bows, prepared for another assault.

63

Late Arrivals

JOLLY SOON FOUND THE OTHER SCOUTS scouring the mountains and led them to rejoin the soldiers about four miles north of Wet Rock Mesa. When the two groups met, they paused for a smoke as Obadiah, Roger and Harry discussed plans to reach the women.

Unlike the steep, dangerous footpath Garcia's men faced on the south side of the mesa, the route up the northern side was a three-mile long gentle slope. "We'll go straight up to the crest," Obadiah said. "Francisca told me Jada and her friends held the high ground on top. If they're still in control, I want to get them and be on our way before the Mexicans arrive." As he spoke, the sound of gunshots erupted through the hills.

"Mount up men!" shouted Obadiah. "Sounds like they've been discovered. Anybody have something we can use for a white flag? We want to avoid a shootout if possible."

Harry dug out an expensive silk shirt from his saddlebags, and Francisca found a woody rib from a dead Saguaro cactus. He winced when she knotted the sleeves of his pricey blouse to the stick. Francisca mounted behind Foghorn, held the fancy standard high, and waved it back and forth.

As the Americans prepared to make their charge, an ear-splitting crash echoed around the mesa and a fierce vibration shook the ground.

"What the hell?" exclaimed Roger.

"I can't imagine," Harry said. "Earthquake, maybe."

After the tremor abated, Obadiah ordered his men to charge up the incline. From on high, Bittersweet watched through her field glasses as the riders galloped toward the women. "I think they're Americans." She handed the binoculars to Jada.

Jada put the spyglass to her eyes. She spotted Francisca in the lead waving Harry's white shirt as she rode behind a scout who blasted tuneless honks on a brass bugle. Behind them, two army officers and a civilian galloped ahead of a line of soldiers and scouts. As they charged closer, she saw Obadiah. Jada lowered the glasses, turned pale and spoke one word: "Ghost." Then she fainted and crumpled to the ground.

Hahles rushed to her side and wiped the perspiration from Jada's face while Jose-ee rubbed her arms. She soon regained consciousness and stood.

"What happened?" asked Bittersweet.

Jada trembled as she spoke. "One of those riders is dead. I attended his funeral." The women murmured among themselves. Ghosts were considered dreaded specters by the Apaches.

Bittersweet raised the binoculars. "You sure? Which one is the ghost? They all seem alive to me." Jada's companions giggled, but she didn't crack a smile.

She took the field glasses from Hahles and studied the approaching riders again. No doubt about it, one of the horsemen was Obadiah, and he indeed appeared to be living. Crazy thoughts shot through her mind. But he had been killed at Cibecue! General Carr saw him shot. The army held a funeral.

The sight of the other two rescuers, old friends and lovers, Harry Trenchcott and Roger Bullard, also left Jada shaken. Maybe all of them were ghosts! Could the spirits I feared as a child be real? She shook her head and blinked to clear her vision. The three kept coming with the troops.

The charge ended when the four women slowly eased from their rocky redoubt, their weapons in hand. Obadiah ordered the men to dismount and walk the final twenty yards to where the group stood.

As the Americans approached, Jada felt as if her heart would pound out of her chest. It was hard to breathe and she trembled with joy and relief—and then, righteous anger.

Obadiah walked to the women and asked, "Is everyone all right?"

Jada responded, "We're safe. The Mexicans are all gone." She then went over to him with tears streaming down her cheeks and delivered a hard punch to his chest, forcing him back a step. The astonished women covered their mouths, soldiers chuckled, and the Apache scouts grinned.

"What's that for?" Obadiah asked.

"Where the hell were you? I thought the Indians killed you. Why didn't you write or send somebody to tell me you were okay?"

The colonel rubbed the spot she hit. "Doctor Morgan, I didn't know I was supposed to. I don't understand what makes you think I should have kept you posted on my whereabouts."

She instantly thought, Obadiah must still be having memory problems. "You don't remember me—us before San Carlos?"

He studied her carefully. "Sure don't. My first recollection of you is after I woke up in the hospital—sorry."

Jada choked back more tears, but she now realized that anything Obadiah and she had was gone, taken by the trauma to his mind. She calmed herself enough to ask, "Tell me what happened at Cibecue."

Obadiah surveyed the surrounding landscape nervously. "Shouldn't we get out of here before the Mexicans arrive?"

"They're all dead. Don't worry about them." She grinned.

The colonel and Roger exchanged disbelieving glances. Obadiah repeated, "Dead?"

"Yeah, now what happened at Cibecue?" Jada wanted closure to the events surrounding the battle and Obadiah's alleged death.

"I got shot up pretty bad in the fight, but my horse carried me for 20 miles until some homesteaders found me slumped in the saddle." Obadiah shifted his feet; the wounds from the Cibecue battle ached after straddling a pony for five days.

"I was delirious for a while. The settlers nursed me for over seven months before I could contact General Carr at Fort Apache. It took another month to get me back to the base. I couldn't ride. I was too weak." He shifted positions again. "So I had to wait until the army sent an ambulance."

"Go on," urged Jada.

"Not much else. After Cibecue, I was told they found a mutilated body and thought it was mine." He chuckled. "Even had a funeral for me. Sorta glad I didn't attend."

"Well, I attended, mister, and I cried my eyes out over you," Jada's anger flared again. "You should have told me when you got back."

"Even if I'd thought of it, I couldn't. Geronimo had taken you by the time I returned to Fort Apache, and nobody knew where you were until J.P. Morgan received word."

He smiled and asked, "Are we squared away now?"

"I think so." She fought to control her emotions. Obadiah was a different man, not the person she had known during their romance. There would be no chance to ever revive their previous bond. She shook his hand. "Thank you for coming. Sorry about the punch." He nodded, as he continued to rub his chest.

Jada stepped over to Roger but did not extend her hand. "Hello, Roger," she said in a frigid tone with steel-cold eyes. She would never forgive him for his tactless, abrupt breakup with her in Philadelphia. "I suppose I should thank you also. I'm surprised you came considering your opinion of Indian women."

"Orders," he murmured, glancing away. "Jada, I want..." He fell silent before the sentence ended. She was such a sweetheart before but she's changed. She's not interested in what I say. I'd be crazy to leave my career for her.

She sent Roger a scornful glance and turned toward Harry who stood apart from the others. She took several quick steps, raised on her tiptoes and gave him a hug and a kiss on the cheek. "Bless you for coming. It's so good to see you again. How's Amity?"

"I don't know. Haven't spoken to her in quite a while."

"You haven't talked with your wife?" She frowned with a quizzical expression.

"I didn't marry her, Jada. We broke up when I discovered she was interested in marrying me because I'm a lawyer for Mr. Morgan, not because I was good old Harry Trenchcott. The truth is—she wasn't Jada Morgan."

Obadiah interrupted the nostalgic reunion. "Where are all those dead Mexicans?"

"Down below on the other side, under a pile of dirt and rocks." Jada pointed with her chin.

"You buried them?"

"God helped us with that." She pointed to the ragged edge of the mountaintop.

Obadiah, Harry, and Roger walked to the south end of the mountaintop and peeked over the drop-off. Lieutenant Torres' legs with gold stripes along the seams of his trousers jutted skyward from the massive pile of rubble.

"Wonder how those girls managed that?" Roger asked as he leaned forward to peer over the edge.

"Apaches are clever about that sort of thing. I've seen 'em do some wicked stuff when they are on the run," Obadiah said as he turned to walk back to Jada.

"Satisfied?" she asked when he returned.

"We better get out of here. There could be more Mexicans around," Obadiah said.

Jada motioned to the cave and told the colonel, "We need to stay a while." She pointed to Nahno and Tzon. "We can't leave without them, and they can't ride or walk. I'll need to re-stitch their wounds with surgical thread, and put clean bandages over the damage before we move them. I assume you have a medical kit."

Obadiah went to the women and examined the claw-cuts on Nahno's back, then kneeled to inspect the soles of Tzon's charred feet and the deep burn on her side. He stood and nodded toward the two. "You're right, those women can't walk or ride anywhere. The other one with the bum shoulder can sit a horse."

He pointed to Bittersweet. "That girl seems familiar. I must have seen her somewhere."

"That's Bittersweet. You met at a dance in Loco's village near Alamosa when she was fifteen. She had a crush on you in those days. She's nineteen now."

Obadiah gave Bittersweet a second look, grinned, and ordered Roger to fetch the unit's medical kit. Jada and Jose-ee began to re-stitch and bandage the women's wounds.

Obadiah watched as two physicians worked on the injured women, and then gave Roger another order. "Unload the supplies from the mules, distribute them among the men, and rig a couple of travois. Those two gals get a ride home."

64

Garcia's Reward

THE NEXT MORNING, scouts cut four lengthy saplings from the grove of trees and rigged two travois to carry the seriously injured women. They fitted the rigs on the mules and carefully helped Nahno onto one. A young scout carried Tzon over to the second litter and gently laid her on the conveyance. She draped one forearm over her eyes and remained unmoving and silent throughout the trip.

Just as it was at a dance in Alamosa four years earlier, Bittersweet couldn't conceal her fascination for Obadiah. As the other women mounted horses with the scouts, she walked over to him. "I want to ride behind you," she said with unusual boldness.

Obadiah scanned the horizon for trouble. There were no threats. The colonel had an affinity for attractive women and the nineteen year old Bittersweet was beautiful. He leaned down from his saddle and lifted the young woman onto the horse behind him, careful not to hurt her injured shoulder. She held him tightly and snuggled her head against his back.

Francisca climbed on behind Foghorn, and the two laughed and chatted like old friends as they rode along. Hahles hitched a ride from Jolly, and Jose-ee rode with another scout. Jada sat behind Harry.

As Jose-ee and Jada's horses walked along together, Jose-ee joked, "Look at that Bittersweet. She's after that white man."

Riding beside Nahno's travois with Bittersweet holding him close, Obadiah bantered with both women mixing basic English, Spanish, and simple Apache. Jada grinned. "I think Nahno's after him too"

Nahno and Bittersweet were delighted with the colonel's attention, and it appeared he relished their company. Jada had not seen him so cheerful since they were a couple at Fort McRae.

After two days of body-hugging closeness riding behind Harry chatting about good times past, their conversation gradually returned to the relaxed openness they enjoyed ten years earlier.

On the second night out, Harry and Jada sat alone in the glow of their small campfire. After everyone was asleep, Harry took her hand and said, "Nothing has been right since I left you for New York. I thought Amity was the answer but I learned my lesson. I think you and I are meant to be together."

Jada stared into the glowing coals with a soulful expression. "I tried to forget you too, but I thought she was a good woman for you. Over time after you left, I fell for two men, Roger in Philadelphia and later, Obadiah in New Mexico." She pointed with her lips toward the sleeping officers.

"Obadiah forgot me altogether because of his brain injury and Roger preferred the army to me. They both are only distant memories now." Tears welled again as she thought of Cantrell, but she was quick to wipe them away.

Neither spoke for a moment as they stared into the remains of the fire. Then Harry gazed into her eyes. "I love you, Jada. I still think we should get married."

Things went quiet again as Jada looked away into the darkness. She puffed her cheeks, a long-held habit whenever she was deep in thought. "Harry, remember our last conversation in the garden that evening?" He nodded and remained silent.

"I'll always be fond of you, Harry, but things haven't changed. You are a city boy and the desert is my place. I dislike the rush and noise of urban life. I could never live in a town again, and I can't imagine you'd do very well out here."

She tossed a small stick onto the coals. "It just won't work."

"Let's don't give up yet." Harry was still hoping to convince her. "Keep my proposal in mind. I know we'll find a way if we stay in touch."

Jada puffed her cheeks again. After another long pause she said, "Maybe it's worth a try, but with one condition." She studied Harry's face for a reaction as she continued. "If you or I find someone else, we will inform the other one right away."

"Fair enough." His disappointment showed.

They hugged good night and went to sleep in separate bedrolls.

On the road the second day after leaving the mesa, a single scout rode up to Obadiah and spoke to him in a low voice. The colonel abandoned his conversation with his two admirers, helped Bittersweet to the ground, and began issuing orders.

"Dismount the gals and take them to the back of the line. Francisca, give your white flag to the corporal." Then he pointed at the two troopers leading the travois-laden mules. "Pull the travois to the rear. We have some company on the way." The squad of soldiers led the column as the scouts arranged themselves in a protective circle around Jada and her companions.

The procession rode on for less than fifteen minutes when a pillar of dust appeared in the distance. Obadiah ordered the group to continue toward the border as the approaching plume drew closer. A small Mexican patrol of six soldiers and a sergeant soon galloped up to the Americans and blocked their path. None of the Mexicans spoke English. Obadiah twisted in his saddle and shouted, "Doctor Morgan and Francisca, come up front please."

The two women exchanged fearful glances as they walked toward Obadiah and the sergeant, but relaxed when Obadiah explained. "This is a touchy situation and my Spanish isn't good enough to handle it. I need help with the translations." They agreed and introduced Obadiah to the Mexican in Spanish.

The Mexican spoke. "May I ask why an American force is in Mexico?"

"Chasing hostiles," Obadiah responded. "The recent agreement between our two governments gave us the right to follow Apache Indians in hot pursuit. The men we were after escaped, but we're taking their women back to the reservation."

"So you went further south?" asked the sergeant.

"We were about fifty miles below here." Obadiah pointed to the trail behind them.

"Did you happen to meet any men from Colonel Garcia's hacienda?"

Jada's body stiffened at the mention of Garcia. She stammered, unable to speak for a moment. Francisca, who had suffered Garcia's cruel venom for years, was petrified—speechless.

"Well?" asked Obadiah. "What did he say?"

At last Jada translated the Mexican's question.

She calmed down when Obadiah answered. "I think we caught a glimpse of one soldier on the other side of Wet Rock Mesa. He might have been one of Garcia's men, but I didn't see much of him."

The sergeant gave a tired sigh and looked toward Wet Rock. "We'll check around the mesa, but if you meet anyone from Garcia's place, tell them to return to the hacienda. Their mission has been cancelled. Colonel Garcia committed suicide last week."

A smile of satisfaction spread across Jada's face as she interpreted the news. She recalled the vow of revenge she made on the day her parents were murdered and said to herself, "Now colonel, go bask in the flames. Be sure to tell the Devil Dah-zhonne sent you."

65

Five Years Later

THE FIVE YEARS FOLLOWING JADA'S RESCUE were eventful. Roger Bullard died from a broken neck when he fell from his horse one year after the expedition. Obadiah Cantrell resigned from the army within months of the Wet Rock incident. He bought a two hundred acre spread near Snowflake, Arizona, built a spacious ranch house, and raised a few cattle. After he paid a dowry of four ponies, he married Bittersweet and Nahno according to Apache customs. Nahno's family had been killed at Alosis Creek but Bittersweet's folks spoke for her. The three newlyweds moved into the roomy farmhouse and filled it with four healthy children; two girls and two boys.

Francisca married Foghorn and lived at San Carlos in marital bliss, but she refused to let him sound his bugle after their romantic interludes. Hahles wedded Scout Jolly and resided happily in the same village as Francisca and Foghorn. Tzon moved in with relatives and under their care, recovered her health, but the lightening strike left her with an unearthly countenance and an eerie personality. Most people on the reservation believed her appearance and behavior bespoke a macabre link with the spirit world. She was often asked to participate in traditional religious ceremonies.

Chief Loco and his band were resettled near Fort Apache on the White Mountain reservation adjacent to San Carlos after they were rescued by General Crook in a daring campaign into Mexico.

Once settled back at San Carlos, Jada invited Jose-ee to train with her as an apprentice in the agency hospital until she built a treatment center on the White Mountain reservation closer to the Indian village. With her traditional medical background, Jose-ee was a quick study of white medicine and two years later, they hung a shingle in front of their new clinic.

Jada Morgan, MD
Physician and Surgeon
Dr. Jose-ee
Physician and Medicine Woman

The two received government contracts to provide medical services for the White Mountain and San Carlos Indians, and the military at Fort Apache. Settlers from miles around traveled to their offices for treatment.

Jada arranged her schedule to allow occasional trips to see Jack in Philadelphia. He had taken on an Irish nurse, Clare Callihan, to help in the clinic, fell in love, and married her after a year-long courtship. Jada attended their wedding on one visit, and the next year, she went back to help Jack with Clare's delivery of twins; Brianna and Jackson Pierpont—affectionately known as Bree and Little J.P.

On one occasion Harry visited Jada on the reservation, but he missed civilized company and complained of the isolation, heat, dust, and insects. He found no future there for a man of his sophistication. He invited Jada to come live with him in the big city.

She went to New York once to spend time with Harry and to tour his metropolis, but found the cement cityscape laced with noisy, dirty streets and filled with ill-mannered eccentrics.

Upon her return to the reservation, she wrote Harry, I don't believe I will ever go back to city life. I would rather spend my life alone in the desert than in any town I can think of.

Despite their distaste for each other's lifestyles, Jada and Harry continued to write long missives declaring their affection and discussing how to resolve their differences.

A week after she returned to the reservation from her New York trip, Jada attended a tribal social dance along the banks of the Salt River. Sitting on a log in Loco's fire circle and holding a chipped enamel cup of tiswin, she thought, I love all of this. It's like a large family. This place is beautiful and life is good. I never want to leave.

As Jada considered her blessings, a striking man about her age walked over and sat beside her. He was a member of Chief Pedro's Coyotero band. Jada learned his name was Draco Dandy. The chap was an eye-catcher; tall, wiry, with long black hair down to his shoulders. Dressed in jeans with an open leather vest over a plaid shirt, he watched the world through steel-rimmed glasses. A pair of expensive brogans, suitable for the dusty reservation terrain, completed his outfit. Jada was smitten at first sight.

They talked and laughed together for most of the evening, as drum beats continued well into the early morning hours. When he could abide it no longer he said, "I've been waiting all night for an invitation, so I'm going to break tradition and request a dance with you."

She frowned at him. "That's not the Apache way, Draco."

Draco looked down, embarrassed. Jada laughed. "But I could ask if you would dance with me." It had been a long time since she had such an enjoyable evening with a man.

Jada learned Draco had been sent to the Carlisle Indian Boarding School in Pennsylvania at age fourteen for four years. He then attended Dartmouth College in the Native American charity program and graduated with an education degree. Draco had taught small classes of Indian children for several years in a room he wrangled from the army at Fort Apache.

Jada later confided to Jose-ee, "Draco is such a smart man and good looking too. He's incredibly fun to be with."

Jose-ee smiled. "Maybe, you'll marry him someday."

"Maybe so." She and Draco had much in common, and within weeks they were in each other's company most days.

A few months later Jada wrote to Harry in New York. "Dear Harry, I've met a man for whom I have developed very strong feelings."

Author's Note

THE ANNIHILATION OF JADA'S (AKA DAH-ZHONNE) VILLAGE is an example of hundreds of similar incidents endured by the Apache tribe in the 19th Century. Archival documents are rife with accounts of both Mexicans and Americans decimating peaceful villages. The only difference was the inhumane treatment of prisoners captured by the Mexicans.

Adoption of Indian children has been a common practice since first contact between Europeans and Indians. The account of Jada's adoption and early years in Philadelphia roughly corresponds to the experiences of two historically significant American Indians. Dr. Carlos Montezuma was a Yavapai-Apache boy who became a doctor after being adopted by a white photographer and educated in Chicago. Dr. Susan La Flesche Picotte, a Ponca, was the first American Indian woman physician. Both served as the basis for details about Jada's social acceptance, medical education and practice. The therapeutic procedures in the story reflect those used during the late 19th Century.

Jack Morgan, Jada's adopted father, is a fictional character as is his wife, Mary. Jada's romantic interests, Harry Trenchcott, Lieutenant Roger Bullard, Major Obadiah Cantrell, and Drako Dandy are creations of the author's imagination. Rufus Rawls, Dr. Ridley Radborne and Dr. Pedro Padilla are also chimerical.

On the other hand, Mollie Shepard, the prostitute who saved the Morgan family on the stage ride back east was a soiled dove and bordello madam in Prescott, Arizona in the late 1860s and early 1870s.

Edward Thudeau, the physician who treated Mary Morgan's final illness, is recorded in history as a pioneer in tuberculosis research.

Miss Florissa Forbes and her Mexican Orchestra toured the United States in the 1870s and 80s. Chiefs Loco and Chatto attended one of the troupe's performances in Washington on July 22, 1886 with an Apache delegation.

J.P. Morgan, Jada's "uncle," (1837–1913) lived in New York City. Many facts about him in the story are found in Jean Strouse's 1999 biography. American Indians were of special interest to Morgan. He collected Indian art and paid Edward Curtis $75,000 to produce a massive anthology of Indian photographs which remain popular today.

Jose Trujillo is historically documented as mayor of Canada Alamosa, New

Mexico, and probably as malevolent as he is portrayed, but he did not die in a fire. The saloon and church fire, and mass poisoning in that town are imaginary.

Events surrounding the scandal and firing of the Commissioner of Indian Affairs, Ezra Hayt, are accurate except for Jada's involvement. After news of the outrage reached the public, Hayt's son, Edward, fled the Globe, Arizona area and avoided prosecution. He was not shot.

Colonel Lorenzo Garcia, a historical figure, was renowned as a vitriolic Apache hater and slave merchant in Mexico. His role in the Alisos massacre is factual. Jada's mutilation of the colonel and his subsequent suicide are story bound.

As reflected in Jada's yarn, 33 women and youngsters were in fact captured at Alosis by Colonel Garcia and probably sold on the slave block in Guaymas. The children under ten years old were actually given out to Mexican families. The names of Jada's companions who fought off their pursuers on the fictional Wet Rock Mountain were taken from a list of prisoners actually seized in the Alisos Creek fight. Francisca is found in earlier historical accounts as an escapee from Mexican slavery. All the Apaches named in this tale were de facto Indians, except Charlie Talker, Jinx, Jolly, Foghorn, Bittersweet and Lizard who are author-created.

The historical Cibecue skirmish was the pivotal event for the actual Sierra Enmedio and Alisos Creek ambushes. All are based on documented records, but Obadiah's melodramatic heroics at Cibecue are not real.

The 1882 kidnapping of Loco's people and subsequent incidents are accurate but viewed from a participant's personal perspective.

Non-fiction accounts of many of these events in Medicine Woman's Revenge can be found in my book, Chief Loco: Apache Peacemaker.

Readers Guide

1. Jada, our protagonist, eventually lived in four cultures: aboriginal Apache, U.S. military, wealthy Philadelphian, and southwestern Hispanic. What do you think was the most important thing that allowed Jada to move between cultures and which culture most affected her life?

2. Why are the chapters about Jada living at Fort Craig with Jack and Mary Morgan important to the story? Why do you think Jada chose to go East with the Morgans rather than stay with her Indian people in New Mexico?

3. What does Jada's interaction with the prostitute, Mollie Shepard, and the villain, Rufus Rawls, show about the young girl?

4. How do you feel about the effects of Jada's aboriginal upbringing on her anguish over Mary's death?

5. How did Jada's relationship with the young army officer, Roger Bullard, affect Jada's life and the story?

6. What did the social obstacles Jada faced when she returned to Fort Craig from Philadelphia reveal about American-Apache relations in the west? How did she personally overcome them?

7. Jada's hurried trip back to Washington from New Mexico was not successful. What were the reasons for its failure and was there anything else she could have done?

8. After returning to the East from New Mexico, Jack Morgan wanted Jada to stay in Philadelphia but she had several reasons for returning to the West? What were they and do you feel they were well-founded?

9. How was Jada's life affected by her response to the criminal activity she discovered upon her arrival at the San Carlos Indian agency in Arizona?

10. When Jada arrived at the San Carlos reservation she discovered her long-missing friend from Philadelphia, Joanne Tomley. How do you feel about Joanne concealing her whereabouts from her family and friends back East?

11. How did Jada deal with the changes in Obadiah and their relationship after his brain surgery?

12. The day after the fight at Sierra Enmedio, the captive Apaches, including Geronimo's kidnappers, walked into an ambush by Mexican troops at Alisos Creek. Jada and thirty-two other women were captured. What effect did Captain Tillius Tupper's response to Jada's desperate plea for help have on future events in the story?

13. Do you think Jada's surgery on Lorenzo Garcia was an appropriate punishment for the murder of her family and his other crimes?

14. During the 19th Century, over two thousand Apaches were captured in conflicts with the Mexicans and Americans and held as slaves or peons. Many were treated as badly as described in Jada's story. The practice was not clearly eliminated until 1937. Do you believe this has any impact on Apache relations with the U.S. and Mexico today? In what way?

15. The seven women fleeing from Garcia's pursuers halted their getaway to care for three injured members of their little band. How do you feel about Francisca abandoning the group?

16. What do you think about Jada declining to marry Harry? Do you believe she will do any better with the new man she found on the reservation?

www.ingramcontent.com/pod-product-compliance
Lightning Source LLC
Chambersburg PA
CBHW031943010726
47493CB00007B/2055